THE BOY
MUST DIE

To my
Pal Azar (Gabriella)

THE BOY
MUST DIE

JON REDFERN

MISFIT

ECW PRESS

JM Redfern
2003

CANADIAN CATALOGUING IN PUBLICATION DATA

Redfern, Jon, 1946
    The boy must die

"A misfit book."
ISBN 1-55022-453-0

    I. Title.

PS8585.E34218B69 2001   C8131.6   C00-933251-0
PR9199.3.R43B69 2001

Edited by Michael Holmes / a misFit book
Cover and text design by Tania Craan
Cover image by Tony Stone Images
Author photo by Heidi Meek
Layout by Mary Bowness
Printed by Transcontinental

Distributed in Canada by
General Distribution Services,
325 Humber College Blvd.,
Etobicoke, ON, M9W 7C3

Published by ECW PRESS
2120 Queen Street East, Suite 200
Toronto, Ontario, M4E 1E2
ecwpress.com

This book is set in ATSackers and Minion.

PRINTED AND BOUND IN CANADA

The publication of *The Boy Must Die* has been generously supported by the Government of Canada through the Book Publishing Industry Development Program.

Canadä

FOR CY, GLADY, CATHY,
JOAN, JOANNA, AND SUE

ACKNOWLEDGEMENTS

Many friends and first readers contributed to the making of this novel: Geri Dasgupta, Kathy Eberle, Nicole Gnutzman, Allan Hepburn, Toni Laidlaw, Sue and Jennifer Neimann, and Margaret van Dijk. I owe its genesis to Jack David, who always said I should write about that place in Alberta. I cannot say thank you enough to Lyn Hamilton — novelist and fellow music lover — for her sound pointers and encouragement. Many thanks are also due to Tania Craan for her striking cover design, and to Michael Holmes, sensitive, supportive editor extraordinaire. Dean Cooke was generous with his professional knowledge about contracts, and it was much appreciated. The Sharpe siblings, Ann and Kathleen, never hesitated to praise my strengths. My own sisters, Cathy and Joan, were guiding lights: Cathy, you're the best plot carpenter; Joan, I'd be nowhere without your keen eye — you can spot a phony character a mile away! Catherine Gildiner made me laugh, but also taught me about getting a book from computer to bookseller.

Penultimately, I owe much to three fellow writers who inspired me to finish the manuscript: Brian Stein, old pal, and avid reader; Bruce Hunter, spirit-guide, and the best damn poet I know; Andrew Podnieks, title composer, the Dominion's finest sports scribe, and mentor.

Finally, I am grateful to Cecil for telling good stories all those years, and to Gladys for loving mystery and crime (and her first born).

FRIDAY, JUNE 28

The boy was running. On the deserted moonlit sidewalk, he was a dashing shadow, small even for fourteen years. His appearance might have frightened a younger child: the shaved head, the skinny back, the black denim legs ending in scuffed army boots. His bony hands were full. The right clutched a book with a pentacle on its cover, the left a cloth bag and a portable tape player.

Stopping, Darren Riegert pressed against a stucco wall and checked that no one was following him. He knew he could not rest. *Don't stay more than a second.* Then he began running again. He had been planning this ever since Cody had gone. For the last three days, he'd prayed and chanted to work up his courage. He knew how far he had to go. The smell of freshly cooked bread from McGavin's Bakery ten blocks away reminded him of his last bite of food. A Mars bar at lunchtime. *But it don't matter now.* It was late Friday. The quiet streets of the small city lay spread out along the edges of a vast cut of coulees by the Oldman River. To Darren, Lethbridge was a place of malls, a junior high school, and a broken-down bungalow where he lived with his mom and where her boyfriend Woody came over to drink away welfare cheques. Tonight, at least, Darren had escaped Woody's mean temper.

Never again. He was glad to be out in the dark. Nobody cared if he went missing. A car passed. His breath tightened, as if he were in school again, in the hall with Mr. Barnes yelling at him for breaking a window. The same cold fear. The same sadness because Cody was gone. Darren's closest friend had taught him to steal, given him the sacred text, *Thanatopsis*, brought him to Satan House. Only three blocks away now, the old mansion made Darren feel wanted. He liked the room he crashed in. He liked Sheree, too. She always left the back door open because, she said, "You kids are welcome here." One time she'd helped Cody come down from a bad acid trip, though she didn't allow drugs in the house. "This is a clean place," she'd said. "A place to rest your spirits."

Darren hurried on, his thighs aching. The sharp corner of the book dug into his wrist. Crossing Baroness, Darren didn't notice the verandas and the trimmed lawns. Instead, he thought about his mom, her stomach hanging over the tops of her jeans. "Once," Sharon Riegert bragged, "I was good lookin'." Darren wondered when that was. He also thought about his Gran, about the time he spit on her grave. Now, more than ever, he wanted to tell her he was sorry.

The glaring moon brightened the gnarled cottonwoods along Ashmead as Darren paused to take a breath. A cat leapt into a hedge. A city bus turned the corner, headlights forcing Darren to squint. He was in full stride again when a siren whined in the distance. *They'll be comin' for me like that.* Darren glanced at his beloved army boots. *Cody took his off.* He wanted to hold onto his, to have them with him. Panting, he told himself it was okay. *Remember, you promised Cody.* Memories of that night still made him want to cry. *Don't lose it!* He clenched his teeth and blinked his eyes hard.

Get ready now.

Satan House rose out of the shadows, pointed dormers like two giant witches' hats. *Come, come to me.* All its windows were dark. Cody had named it, that night on acid, as he lay on its warped floor and cried "Satan, our master, is among us!" The back door was always open to them; the large rooms and thick walls reminded Darren of the haunted castle ride at the summer fair. *Careful, go easy.* He stopped at the edge of the dirt yard. The old tree stump was weathered as white as bone. He knew now he must go ahead. He did not hesitate though his heart raced. Up the rough gravel of the driveway, he passed the garage's caved-in door, its bank of broken windows like jagged teeth. He scurried through the yard, the elms and weeping willows hiding the door at the top of three wooden steps. There he stood and calmed himself. He looked at the fence hemming in the overgrown garden and laughed.

Is that a voice calling out? There was movement in the garden. A black shape like a cat slouched, then wove its way through the brown grasses. *A sign.* Darren grabbed the doorknob, and like always the old door slid open, welcoming him. *Quiet, quiet.* Cody had always said to sneak in. "They can't hear ya," he'd said, "they're sound asleep upstairs." But Darren wanted to be sure, especially tonight. He found his way to the top of the basement stairwell. His eyes took a moment to adjust to the darkness. He waited and listened. *If Sheree's upstairs in her bedroom, I'll make sure she won't hear me.* He liked Sheree's room, its dark curtains and its candle guarded by a chimney of red glass. *Maybe she's at her boyfriend's place. The professor. It doesn't matter.* Following the rail, Darren soon found himself in the shadowy black of the musty-smelling basement. He set down his book, his boom box, and the cloth bag. He pulled a pack of matches from his pocket. The flare created instant shapes — a broom, a bicycle. Holding up the flame, he gathered his things and walked around the corner.

The tiny room he entered smelled of piss. A rustling noise made him jump back so fast the flame blew out. *Someone there?* He tore off another match. His hand shook, and he had to strike it a second time. Tiny eyes caught the fire and flashed like red pinpoints as grey bodies fled into corners. Dried mouse turds crunched on the pebbled concrete floor. "Something's wrong." The rasp of his own voice alarmed him. *Don't fuck it!* "Cody, help me," he whispered. But then Darren remembered. Cody had always said to trust the power of the sacred text. Sweaty-palmed, he lifted the thick book towards his chest and embraced it. *You've got to believe.* Ahead of him, in the corner stood another small doorway. Moonlight seeped through to make a square on the floor. Another match flared. Darren crept into the second room and saw the dryer, the sink, and the window. For the first time this evening in the silence, he felt truly alone. A shape passed in the garden outside, throwing its shadow into the blue dimness.

"What?"

The shape stopped, turned part of itself towards Darren.

Darren puffed up his chest. In words set far back in his mouth, he quietly uttered "*Mene Mene Tekel.*"

He knew he must hurry, do it right or start again. His pants came off over his boots. His black T-shirt was next and dropped on top of his pants. Naked, he turned three times to his right, three times to his left, chanting the words, sure of the power of the song. When he stopped, he brushed cold sweat from his forehead. *Keep your mind pure, like Cody said.* Out of the cloth bag he slid a long glimmering knife and laid it beside the sacred text, its pages open to the picture of the tongue and the star. He'd memorized the words and repeated them now: "Naked come I, pure and ready for thee." Stroking his bare chest and thighs, he let the sacred words swirl in his mind. Then he stopped. A few feet from where he stood, a noise. Then he heard another. And one more again.

Darren slowly raised his head. His mind warned him: *Hide the knife! The book!* It came closer. Reached the doorway. Darren stepped back, his boot scraping the knife over the concrete. The creak came again and sounded like screaming in Darren's ears. A heavy footstep, a whiff of body odour. A click, then a whirring sound. Darren stumbled. His eyes darted frantically. He cupped his hands over his penis. *Find a corner, grab the knife!* As he opened his lips, panic froze his vocal cords. His knees began to shake as a flash of light exploded into the room.

"Who the fuck's there?" he whispered, the floating red from the flash blinding him to the huge shape lumbering towards him from the dark doorway.

SATURDAY, JUNE 29

Billy Yamamoto shivered in his thin cotton pyjamas though the June air was warm. He was sitting on the steps of his wind-worn back porch waiting for the dawn to brighten the distant butte of Head-Smashed-In Buffalo Jump. Before him stretched open ground covered with wild bergamot and gently waving spear grass. The line of barbed-wire fence to his right ran west into foothills and stone outcroppings. What always came to him at this dark hour of sleeplessness were childhood memories. This morning he was recalling winters in the 1950s skating at the Kinsmen's rink. No wonder you're cold, he thought.

Billy turned east to ponder the gold band along the horizon. The light stirred other memories. Three weeks earlier. His father in the white room, yellow edging the lowered blind. Arthur's cold face a shrunken version of its former self. And then the vista of the Coaldale cemetery surrounded by a green haze of barley standing like blades in the nearby prairie. Billy heard again the Anglican minister intone the final prayer. He stared again at his older half-brother. Toshiro held his arms tightly at his sides, his face bent in solemn obeisance towards Arthur Yamamoto's pine coffin.

The first shafts of daylight were streaking the plain as Billy got up and walked back into the house. Saturday was shaping up to be another long, lonely day. He was tired of reminding himself why he'd taken early retirement, leaving his job of twenty-five years as a detective inspector with the Vancouver city police force. Seven months now since he'd last picked up a day roster for his team and assigned squad duties. He headed into the bedroom, knowing his pounding mind would not let him off easily. He climbed into bed. Should he take Ativan and grab a few hours? *For Christ's sake. Pull yourself together.*

After a while, he flicked open his eyes. He had fallen into a dreamless sleep. The throaty, desperate howling outside the window sounded like a cougar. He sat up. The red letters on the digital clock glowed: 5:47. So it was only for a moment or two. It was like suffering a persistent back ache, this bloody insomnia. He cautioned himself not to blame Arthur's illness for finally prompting him to move back to the Prairies. True, a respectable pension and full medical benefits were nothing to scoff at. Even so, Billy couldn't help conjuring up the face of Harry, his former homicide partner. Billy and Harry Stone had worked side by side for eleven years until the cold, wet April night one year ago when the salt breezes off Juan de Fuca shook the cherry blossoms in backyards from English Bay to Shaughnessy.

Billy grinned at the memory of him and Harry sitting in the unmarked cruiser on East Hastings. They'd been keeping tabs on a Triad that peddled twelve-year-old girls out of the Stanton Hotel. Most of east-end Vancouver was a warren of sad avenues lined with dollar stores, crack houses, and hookers. Harry suggested getting coffee at an all-night greasy spoon; he climbed from the cruiser, and four Triad goons jumped him. In the ensuing scuffle, Harry got shot in the stomach; Billy's left knee took a second bullet, but he was still conscious when the goons tied him with a red bungee cord and shoved him blindfolded into the back seat of a Mercedes. Later, weak with blood loss, he met kingpin Robert Lau, who greeted him like a lost twin, held him for a moment in mock embrace, and then watched as the goons rammed their fists into his stomach and kidneys. "That's only a warning, brother," Lau said. The next day Harry died. In court, Billy testified and sent two of the goons to the pen for killing an officer. But Billy read the signs. Soon after, his apartment windows were regularly smashed. His car was ditched and set ablaze. Doors all over Chinatown were slammed in his face. Lau was into contraband as well as heroin, and he wasn't about to turn friendly with cops he couldn't bribe.

Billy took in a breath. Was memory the only exciting thing he had left? He rubbed the scar on his left knee and was thankful it hadn't pained him lately. He carefully lifted the top sheet, trying not to yank it. Amazing how old habits persist. Cynthia hadn't lain beside him for years, sleeping like a baby, her arm thrown over her eyes. As if the night were not dark enough, he thought. The old pine floor creaked. Billy pulled on a robe and padded quietly around the foot of the four-poster. Sun cut through the space between the curtains and began to outline the shapes of the meagre furniture. Billy made two fists, lay facedown on the dusty floor, and started his push-up routine — one hundred with fists closed, one hundred with splayed palms turned inward. Counting, he held his breath for every five and let his mind feel the burn, then exhaled.

His spirits felt better after his workout. From the bedroom, Billy walked barefoot down the narrow hall into the kitchen. How regular these early mornings had become. Not like Vancouver days, sleeping until eight-thirty, taking a quick coffee before leaving for the office at nine. Billy filled the percolator and made his first pot. He drank a cup, sitting with his legs crossed at the small metal table he used for meals. Around the kitchen were the tools of his early retirement: garden shovel, hoes, drill kit for roof and porch repairs. On every side-table in the front parlour lay the mysteries and biographies he'd started and then sworn to pick up again. Be proud of one project, at least, he thought. The honour garden in memory of Arthur. He'd drawn a good design; he'd researched traditional Japanese dry gardens. The turned sod and pressed sand foundation were only the beginning.

Billy listened to the old wood cracking in the rising warmth. He poured a second cup and thought about the time he first described his grandfather Naughton's ranch to Harry Stone. "A small spread," he said to him, "by Alberta standards. No more'n five hundred and twenty acres of grazing pasture and hayfields." The day he drove east from Vancouver into the Rockies, Billy swore to himself: "I have no intention of raising horses on granpa's ranch. I intend to stay calm in my retirement."

Billy was now pacing the kitchen linoleum. He clicked on the radio. Nothing but classical music and weather at this early hour.

A male coyote was standing five feet from the back steps as Billy opened the screen door and stepped onto the porch.

"You old rascal," Billy whispered. "You keep early hours. What was it you were howling over? Some hawk steal your breakfast?"

The coyote turned its head away. Along its spine and haunches, its coat still carried the thick hair of winter. A skinny male, not young, but not sickly. Granpa Naughton had taught Billy how to tell a mangy rabid specimen from a healthy one.

"Go on, you."

The coyote loped away towards the concession road, a long winding cut of gravel bordered by more barbed wire.

The coffee needed reheating when Billy sauntered back into the kitchen. Crows were cawing on the rooftop of the house. A flock of angry sparrows flew up from a willow outside the sink window and startled him. Billy sighed and looked up. The ceiling plaster sagged near the light. The tin mouldings and borders cried out for fresh paint. To hell with them, he thought. Back in the bedroom, he changed into his gardening sweats. He stared at his five-foot-six frame in the mirror. It was his mother's Scottish ancestry that had shaped his square forehead. He was still holding fast to one hundred and sixty pounds. At fifty-four, his thighs were hard and his stomach flat. When he and Cynthia were married, she always said she loved the hazel of his eyes and the deep rich black of his hair, as thick on his head now as it was the day they divorced.

Billy glanced at the digital clock. It was 6:45, and he decided to pull out his mat. He sat down, crossed his legs yogi style, clearing his mind for the *za-zen* and the wave of calm. After ten minutes, he climbed back into bed.

Later, when a car turned from the concession road and clanged over the Texas gate leading into the ranch house yard, Billy sprang up from the mattress and shook his head. It was 10:05.

"Damn," he said. He rose and went to the window. A trail of dust swirled by the fence posts. Running into the kitchen, he saw a blue-and-white city cruiser pull up to the back steps. The driver honked once and then jumped out of his seat. Billy recognized him and walked out onto the porch.

"Royce. What brings you out here so early?"

"Chief didn't get a hold of you yet, sir?"

"Come in, Royce. I can put a fresh pot on the range."

The young sergeant pulled off his sunglasses and walked into the kitchen behind Billy. He waited by the screen door as Billy filled the percolator with fresh water.

"Don't bother about me, sir."

"You sure?"

"I don't take coffee, sir. Or tea."

"I beg your pardon. You Latter Day Saints?"

"No, sir. I have an allergy to caffeine."

Royce blushed at his own words and shuffled his feet. After he'd ventured a pause, he spoke up.

"Chief said you'd been having trouble with your Pontiac, so he wondered. . . ."

"You came out here just to tell me that?"

Royce took a step back.

"No, sir. Chief said he was going to call you and let you know I was on my way. He said he'd explain the whole matter to you."

"A case, you mean?"

"I'm not sure, sir. You on contract with us?"

"Well, your police board thinks I should be put on per diem stipends if and when I'm called in. But only as a part-time deputy. Not much call for homicide back-up in the city."

Royce nodded and seemed to show interest.

"My last case was that stabbing in April. A couple of rednecks from Montana decided to ass around with Bobby Weasel Woman."

"He got convicted."

"Yes. It wasn't easy."

Royce crossed his arms and stood more at ease. Billy had met him a couple of times with Chief Eddy "Butch" Bochansky. Royce was polite, no more than twenty-five, and curious. He'd asked Billy once about his work in Vancouver. Small talk among policemen, certainly, but Royce had a sincerity about him that Billy had liked from the start.

"Chief is lucky to have you."

Billy stood quiet for a moment. Nothing was worse than the loss of his father. But then to have to spend days grieving in an empty house full of empty hours. Well, he was lucky *he had Butch.*

Billy counted the rings as he headed towards the hallway. The black rotary phone hung in a corner by the kitchen door. Above it was a tarnished wall sconce in the shape of a tulip, made of brass and smoky glass. Billy clicked the switch on the plate of the sconce. Ring seven. No need to guess who this was. He pulled in a breath and grinned. He wondered for a second, his hand poised on the receiver, just how long Butch would let the phone go before hanging up. Billy knew his old friend well enough to figure he'd ring it a hundred times and keep on ringing it until he got an answer. He rubbed his hand through his rumpled black hair, cautioned himself. Ever since February, he and Chief Eddy "Butch" Bochansky had met once a week to drink Colombian, Butch claiming he liked to talk over police business. This kind of call had come many times before, but as he lifted the receiver on ring sixteen, Billy sensed he was not going to spend the rest of his morning on the ranch.

"Get you out of your easy chair, buddy?" Butch's voice sounded tired and edgy.

"I was digging up sod, Butch. Or planning to. You having a slow morning?"

"Is the pope Catholic? I wish! Young Royce make it there?"

"Right on time, Butch."

"I got held up," Butch coughed. "I need a favour."

"Go."

"We had a juvenile case last winter. Just before you moved back. Around Christmas. A fourteen-year-old boy was found hanging in Satan House."

"Satan House?"

"The old Bartlett place on Ashmead. The press got hold of the story, discovered the local kids called the house that, and the nickname stuck. Evidence put the case down as teenage suicide. No foul play. Coroner Hawkes uncovered no proof to the contrary. Now, I know you'd rather be at home staring at the view, but we got us a messy plate of worms this morning. Satan House again. Same basement room. Another male of fourteen. But this one smells like homicide."

"When did you find the body?"

"About an hour and a half ago. The kid was strung up and mutilated. Around Friday midnight we figure."

"How bad?"

"Surface knife wounds. One cut in the shape of a pentacle on the chest area. Also, both wrists scored."

"Anything else?"

"I need your experience, buddy. Sergeant Dodd has asked to be on the case. He and I don't quite see eye to eye. Let's say he's a bit slow on the uptake. You ever met Dodd?"

"Not yet."

"This body we got now is a different barrel of minnows. And I'm not so sure I know where to stick my hand in."

As Billy's excitement grew, doubt and concern cut in to warn him to go easy. He always thought of himself as cautious, and Butch was a man who liked to run things his own way. Billy didn't want to spend his time stepping on toes.

"I've got trees to plant, Butch. Rocks to move."

"Listen. I'll arrange a per diem like last time. You can hedge your bets. If it's simple, you've only wasted a day. I buy you a sandwich at the canteen, give you a tour of our new facilities — you've never seen the new offices, have you? I spot you a couple of coffees, then you're home for supper and a good three hours of gardening before the sun goes down."

"Second body in six months in the same locale?"

"Take a look."

"You sure you need me? Sounds like you've tagged this one. Once you've done the cutup, you'll see if there are parallels to the first. I'd look into what the kid was doing with his peers. A lot grab onto Satanic hocus-pocus through their music." Even as he said the words, Billy sensed he'd lost an opportunity to go to town.

"I thought about all of that. But the site has a couple of problems. Real quirks. If you've got the time, I'd appreciate your take."

"Well, you know I can't refuse canteen food, Butch. But I'm going to have to find some time this weekend to get at the garden before all my plants shrivel up."

"Thanks. I'll count on you to be in my office at what time?"

"How's Dodd going to feel about this?"

Butch's comment about Dodd seemed out of character since Billy had the impression Butch respected his staff. He always spoke of them during their coffee talks as loyal, hard-working people.

"Don't get me wrong. He's a good man, Billy. He *rubs me* the wrong way is all. His manner, I guess. I asked him before I called you if he or any of the other men would feel put out if you came in for a while to look around. He's fine with it. So, it's a yes, then?"

"As soon as I get dressed and put the Pontiac in drive."

"Hell, catch a ride with Royce. That's what I sent him out there for."

"If it's all the same with you, Butch, I like to come and go on my own time and gas."

"Get in here, then."

Billy hung up. He told Royce to head back into town and apologized for taking up his time.

"No problems, sir. You got a fine piece of land out here."

The two men shook hands, and Billy watched as Royce steered the cruiser out of the yard towards the Texas gate. He then walked into the bathroom, where he turned on the water in the shower. He placed his sweats on the new hook he'd screwed into the wooden door, then eased his way under the pelting force of the showerhead, his mind leaping forward, timing how soon he could finish shaving and dressing before he climbed into the Pontiac. The drive into Lethbridge could take thirty minutes, maybe longer if traffic was slow, it being Saturday and the highway crowded with half-tons and mini-vans coming in from towns like Fort Macleod, Monarch, and Kipp. Out of the shower, Billy dried himself, quickly shaved, put on a white shirt and his clean blue suit. Mixed with his anticipation was foreboding: it wasn't like Butch to insist as he had unless things were bad. "Real quirks," Billy said to himself.

In the kitchen, he picked up a couple of Bic pens from the table, checked the stove, and rinsed out the percolator. He then walked onto the porch and decided not to lock the door. He was in the country now. There was nothing to steal from the house. Hearing the screen door slap shut, Billy felt sudden joy. He took in a deep breath. The sun was hanging hot and yellow in a cloudless blue dome of air. He put on his aviators and crossed the yard of wild oat grass, climbed into the Pontiac, and cranked the engine. He backed out and braked. Beside the porch sat two fir trees in their burlap sacking. The honour garden needed water. But he could let it go for one more day. He pushed the gear into drive. The Pontiac moaned, its innards rattling as Billy manoeuvred the car towards the concession road.

Staff Sergeant Richard "Ricky" Dodd opened the door carefully. In his left hand was a tall Styrofoam cup. The coffee was at the rim, and Dodd was trying not to spill it on his wrist.

"Morning, sir."

"Morning, sergeant."

Billy glanced at the clock on the sergeant's desk: 10:48. He'd made the drive and found his way into this office in record time.

"Sorry about all of this."

"Don't worry about it."

"He's got a couple of hysterical people in there with him. The mother is right off her hinge. She's brought along her boyfriend. Chief is trying to calm them down."

"Understandable."

"It was with milk, wasn't it, sir?"

"It was."

"Chief tells me you used to be with the city force in Vancouver. Detective inspector. Headed vice and homicide."

"Homicide. Twelve years. Before that, general investigation, drug squad, some sexual assault."

"That so?" Dodd shook drops of coffee off his left hand. He scanned Billy Yamamoto's face.

"I took early retirement from the Vancouver unit seven months ago."

Dodd did not move but licked his lips. "Chief tells me you lost your dad a while back?"

"Three weeks."

"I'm sorry, sir."

"Thank you, Dodd."

"You retiring to the coast, then? Out where balmy breezes blow?" Dodd grinned, trying to lighten the atmosphere.

"No, I've moved back to an acreage west of here, outside Fort Macleod."

"You like it? You're from around here, right? Originally?"

"Yes. And, yes, I love it."

Billy Yamamoto crossed his legs. He stared down at the beige liquid in the Styrofoam cup. It was the usual hot coloured water, no worse than the brew he'd swallowed for twenty-five years in the offices at 52 Division on Granville Street in Vancouver. Driving into Lethbridge this morning, Billy had been impressed by the new station and understood Butch's pride. The building's red metal canopy faced the 1910 post office clock tower. Two miles east from the parking lot, Billy had seen the city's single giant grain elevator, its eight round silo bins painted a gun-metal grey. Billy recalled the old wooden brewery that once stood where he was now sitting. One summer, at age nineteen, he'd worked stacking bottles and loading beer crates onto CPR boxcars in the basement. He gazed at the clean blue rubber tiles under his shoes and wondered what his father, Arthur, had been like at nineteen, isolated from women, having only brutal field labour to keep him occupied.

Dodd got up and pulled open a drawer. Spoons rattled as he lifted out a box of sugar cubes. "You want any of this?"

"Never touch it, thanks."

A rest should come between us, Billy thought. An old lesson of *Rinzai:* "Let silence speak."

"Chief should be out soon, sir." The sergeant softened his voice, giving it the tone of an apology.

Ricky Dodd topped six-one, had bushy light brown hair, and wasn't bothering to hide his paunch. Billy surmised he was one of those clean-faced young men you meet in most small towns in rural southern Alberta. Men brought up by strict Protestants who worked hard with their dads on a ranch or in a two-room store. Dodd suited this small police station. It had only two patrol teams, two canine units, and a general investigation branch with a revolving roster of three sergeants. Dodd was Staff Sergeant, Criminal Investigations. Chief Eddy "Butch" Bochansky had explained to Billy that most of the crime in the city was property theft. Murder and drugs were occasional, not on the scale of Vancouver by any means. Butch handled the murders himself. He didn't want the cable TV people and the religious radio shows riling up the public against the police for not doing their duty. "Murder scares people," Butch had said. "And scared people like to blame the law for not keeping order and peace."

Dodd sat down at the table across from Billy; behind him the computer screen saver twisted and turned: a wave of palm trees undulating in front of an ocean of stars.

"When did you get the call?" Billy asked.

"Around eight. Dispatch sent over a constable to Satan House, then he called the chief and me around eight twenty-nine. We got to the site at nine."

"A neighbour? Someone in the house?"

"You mean who called in? The tenant. She leases the place. A woman, name of Bird. Sheree Lynn Bird."

"How old was the boy?"

"Fourteen or fifteen. Similar case happened last winter."

"How similar?"

"Juvenile, too. A hanging."

"Butch said it was suicide."

"Yes, sir." Dodd slid a notebook out of his upper right pocket. He flipped it open and read over the scrawled lines on the page. "Miss Bird knew this kid. And the other one. She called this kid's mother and informed her. Bird said she'd been helping him. Talking to him. She's some kind of part-time psychologist. Used to be with family services. Her home was a sort of halfway house for these two boys. Cody Schow and Darren Riegert. The kid's mother sure as shit took it bad. She's been wailing at the chief now for an hour. She says there's no way her little boy should've been in that house."

"Anything unusual at the site?"

Billy found himself automatically falling into the old routine: drinking coffee, grilling the staff sergeant. Dodd didn't seem to mind. He leaned back in his chair.

"I did the walk-around upstairs before I viewed the corpse in the basement. The place was run-down. It's been changing hands for years. I'd always heard it was a flea trap. Chief and Tommy, our medic, were examining the victim's body, strung up on an old steel heating conduit. Blue nylon rope. The kid was naked, with a kind of drawing on his chest — carved with a knife point. Star shape. Crosses on his wrists. Star scrawls on the walls. Chief thought they were done in latex paint. Candles. Some kind of cult thing."

"Cult?"

"I guess. From the looks of the book we found by the body. One of those Satanic jobs. What my dad calls a false bible. And the candles too, in a circle at the kid's feet. The last kid, Cody Schow in December, he had the same book with him. Seems these kids, according to Miss Bird, were buddies at school."

"So, you figure there's a tie-in?"

"Chief won't say for the moment. But I guess that's why you're in on this."

"Well, we'll see, Dodd." Billy's interest piqued. "How do you read Sheree Lynn Bird?"

Dodd looked puzzled for a moment; then he blushed. "She's *real* something, sir."

Billy blinked and on examining Dodd's face understood that his question had embarrassed the young sergeant. "Dodd?"

The sergeant sat up in his chair. "Sorry, sir. I figure she's on the level. Responsible." His voice trailed off.

"Was she upset?"

"Yes. She'd been crying by my reckoning."

"How many boys and girls did she counsel in this halfway house?"

"As far as we know, it was just the two of them."

"And both of them are dead." Billy held Dodd's gaze for a second before he went on. "The knife turn up?"

"No, sir." Dodd seemed uneasy about this and moved his eyes down as he spoke.

"Fingerprints?"

"Johnson is there now."

Billy downed the rest of his coffee and stood.

"You known the chief long?"

"Since high school. We're old buddies." Dodd grinned. He rose and hiked up his trousers.

Billy folded his cup and dropped it in the waste basket.

"I can get you a refill, no problem."

"What I need is a washroom."

"Right through here, sir. It's the chief's private toilet."

Billy waited as Dodd took out a key from the desk, strolled to a door at the back of the room, turned the lock, and switched on the light.

"Yamamoto. That's Chinese, right?"

"Japanese. Canadian born and bred. My mother was Scottish."

"That so?" Dodd nodded, lifting his eyebrows.

"We got some good Vietnamese restaurants here in town now."

"Thanks, Dodd."

As he washed his hands, Billy wondered what Dodd was thinking back in the computer room. Billy knew how territorial sergeants and bureau chiefs could get about their precincts. And their jobs. From what he could tell, Dodd was a man at ease with a retired big-city detective poking his head into a local case. So far so good, but old anxieties were beginning to surface. What did Dodd see when he looked at Billy? *A wiry middle-aged guy with a Jap name? Skin not quite white?*

"Seems the chief is still at it."

Billy had walked through the reception room and joined Dodd in the main hallway of offices. His ear was against Butch's door.

"Chief suggested I show you the mother's statement if he got held up. Looks like we have time if you want to, sir. We got it on tape earlier this morning."

Dodd led Billy along the hall to a staircase. They walked down two flights, through a set of glass doors, along another hall, then into a ten-by-twelve windowless room. Dodd snapped on the overhead fluorescents. There was a cabinet and a television on a table. A VCR sat on a shelf under the TV. There were three metal chairs set out. Dodd opened the cabinet with a key he took from a hook beside the door. He turned the lock. Rows of tapes were lined up vertically. Each tape had a cardboard sleeve and a white label.

"Here she is."

Dodd handed the cassette to Billy.

The label of the cardboard sleeve read JUNE 29, SHARON RIEGERT, FILE NO: 64.

On the screen, the woman looked pale, tired, her acne-scarred face pudgy and ill-fed. Her voice was hoarse from cigarettes. Billy watched her eyes dart as she told Dodd about her last twenty-four hours, what she could remember. The sergeant's voice interrupted her at times, trying to keep her on track. Behind her, the wall was white. Her hands were folded in her lap.

THE BOY MUST DIE

"No, I didn't even see my little boy go out. No way he shoulda been there, no way. She's been stealing him and all those kids from us. She made him die. She killed my baby."

"She was hard to keep on track, sir. She was out of it."

"What else do you know about her?"

"Not much. No driver's licence. On welfare. She and her boyfriend, Woody, spend a lot of time in her rental place, a two-bedroom bungalow. Seems he lives the rest of the time in his own place a few blocks away. Sharon Riegert is divorced. Darren's father left her when the boy was born. No relatives in town. We ran a quick check on her. No arrests. No record."

"Anything on him? On Woody?"

"Not yet. I've only had time to do her."

"Roll it again."

This time Billy took mental notes. The woman said she'd been at home all night. She'd been at home the day before as well, though she couldn't prove it. Only the boyfriend, Woody, was her witness.

"Where's the boyfriend's statement?"

"Uh, we didn't get that far, sir, like I said. He was real upset. Shouting and slamming doors. We had him restrained upstairs while she talked for the camera. He was drunk, I think. Smelled of rye when he came in. Chief said we could do him later. Now he's got the two of them together."

Billy sat still and thought for a moment. He straightened his back.

"Okay. Thanks, Dodd."

They went back upstairs by a different hall and staircase. Dodd pointed out two interview chambers and the records room. There was a computer and three vertical filing cabinets. "We are on-line now with every police station — both civic and RCMP — in the province." Dodd beamed. The window in the door showed a narrow room no bigger than a horse stall. The computer sat against one wall. Maps of the city and the province were tacked up by a filing cabinet. Also, there was a desk the size of a TV table cluttered with paper. At it a woman sat alone staring into the computer screen. "She's the best computer jockey and filing clerk at the station." Billy quickly memorized the room number. As they continued, he decided to get some professional history from Dodd.

"You've done homicide before, Dodd?"

"A couple of cases. But mainly I do commercial crime."

"What were the cases like?"

"The homicides? Husband shot his wife last October, hid the rifle in the basement in the washing machine, then turned himself in. Worst case was the postman. He'd been having an affair with a woman on his route. When wifey found out, she went off the deep end and stabbed the man in his privates." Dodd laughed.

"You think homicide is funny, Dodd?"

Dodd's expression stiffened. "No, sir. I didn't mean any harm."

Billy wondered if the man's awkwardness might be a cover for naïveté or disdain.

Dodd's young face reddened. "I meant no harm," he said again.

Billy nodded. You can let it go for the moment, he thought. They moved on, stopping by reception, where Dodd picked up the mail for Butch. "So," said Billy, "why is this mutilated body promising trouble?"

Dodd stopped. "From what I saw, this was no normal killing."

"What do you mean, normal?"

"The blood, the . . . it was like a lynching, sir. Like someone was crazy or enraged. It sure spooked the chief, I can tell you." Dodd went silent for a second. "It was one of the worst things I ever saw."

"Yes, Dodd. I can imagine."

"What's your take so far?"

"Let me see the site first."

"Even after the body's been removed?"

"All the more reason. A body can be a big distraction. If your site is intact, you'll sometimes find clues."

Dodd raised his eyebrows. "Is that so?"

By this time, they had stepped through the swinging door leading to the main hallway. It was quiet as Dodd and Billy went to knock on

Butch's office door. Billy hardly had time to step out of the way as an overweight blonde wearing a pair of dirty jeans pushed by him, her face reddened from crying. Sharon Riegert. With Darren's mother was a tall thin man hunched in a leather jacket. He sported a short ponytail. He glared at Dodd and Billy in passing. A constable came up the hall and took firm hold of Woody Keeler's elbow and led him and Sharon Riegert down the hall. Billy took note of the hair band around the ponytail: red elastic, the kind Safeway uses to hold together fresh spinach.

Billy gazed at last into Butch's office. Chief Bochansky was a big man, over six feet and built broad and round, a foil to Billy's compact, slender frame. Lorraine, his wife, once described him to Billy as chunky, by which she meant, Billy presumed, overweight and needing a good diet. "No," she said when Billy asked her to explain. "Not at all. Chunky means hunky to me." She then remarked with pride on Butch's huge upper arms, a legacy from his boxing days. Butch's eyes were blue and frequently flashed with sudden temper. He was standing beside his metal desk crumpling up a piece of paper, his face creased by fatigue.

"Billy!"

"Morning, Butch."

"Am I glad to see you."

Dodd pressed his bulky frame into the open doorway.

"What we up against, Chief?"

"Hell, high water, and more hell."

"Johnson's not back yet, Chief. You want me to get a hold of Hawkes?"

"Yes, Dodd, I do. I won't know if it's murder until he's done his autopsy."

"Yes, sir."

Butch drummed his fingers on the desktop, then yanked open the drawer and pulled out a dog-eared blue notebook. He signalled to Billy to step inside the office. "See you later, Dodd."

"Can I get anyone a coffee before I go?"

"No thanks. Just get the door," Butch growled.

Cigarette smoke floated like a wave in the still air of the office. A large computer sat by one wall — screen, keyboard, printer, and above it a bookcase full of pamphlets and official-looking yellow binders.

"That yours?"

Butch turned and nodded at the framed colour photograph of a waterfall hanging over his desk.

"Took a Nikon course last year. Some guy from Toronto on a tour. Pretty good. Finally learned how to use the camera Lorraine gave me for Christmas seven years ago."

Billy sat down in an armchair by the computer. His sensitive nose picked up the smell of Woody Keeler's cheap aftershave. Butch coughed, ran his hands through his thinning red hair.

"You look dapper. That your old outfit from Vancouver days?"

"Felt I should dress up for my official visit to headquarters."

Butch was wearing khaki pants and a green golf shirt open at the neck. Billy wondered if his suit made him look overdressed for this station. In Vancouver, among the Asian community, his blue suit had commanded respect, granted him "face."

Butch went over to a filing cabinet. "How's the bum knee?"

"Behaving itself. Dodd showed me the Sharon Riegert tape."

"Not much on it, was there?"

"What's she been telling you the past hour?"

"How the world turns, according to her. How she's been a victim and couldn't help beating her own son. Claims the ponytail sidekick who came with her was the only real father figure Darren ever knew. Poor bastard."

"They both have alibis?"

"Both at home, drunk, though I'll get Dodd over to their neighbours to verify. Boyfriend Woody says it was Miss Bird who harmed their darling boy. Somehow, Miss Bird had the two of them pretty scared. Must have warned them that child abuse was a no-no and that she might have to take the kid away."

"Riegert's statement leads me to think she's torn."

"Between what?"

"Mourning her son and protecting her boyfriend."

"You think so?"

"We'll definitely need a background check."

Billy sat forward. "Sharon kept claiming Woody was home with her all night. Said it five times by my count. But she also said he went out for a time, then denied it when Dodd tried to pin her down. We need to determine when he went and came back. If she's telling the truth."

"You suspect Woody?"

"There's a history in this family. Torture and abuse go together. You hear about the couple who sexually abused and tortured their three-year-old daughter? Big case, a year ago, down in Arizona."

"Religious couple. Both got life."

"Torture is possible given the nature of this crime. The cult connection. The choice of locale. As if whoever did it wanted it to be well known. The Arizona couple took videos of their handiwork and left the tape in the machine."

"Jesus."

Butch tossed a new notebook over to Billy.

"You'll need one of these. You have a ballpoint?"

Billy grinned. "Ballpoint? How can a ball have a point?"

Both men laughed. They had invented the joke years ago. Posing the question to all the girls one slow afternoon in the study room of Lethbridge Collegiate. "I put a requisition in for your cell phone. You'll need these, too." Butch rummaged in a paper-filled box. He stood up, his face suddenly flushed. He handed Billy a pack of four-by-six lined note cards. "Come in handy for giving witnesses your name and phone number."

Billy put the notebook in the upper left hand pocket of his suit jacket. He peeled off a number of the note cards and slid them into the upper right-hand pocket, leaving the rest on Butch's desk. He noticed his friend was sweating. "You got a cold, Butch? You've been coughing a lot this morning."

"The demon weed. Got back to it a month ago. Lorraine's not too pleased." Butch grinned, then moved his husky body around the end of his desk, where there was a manila envelope marked with a code number. Butch pulled the envelope open and spread out a series of black-and-white and colour photos.

"These are the site pics from the first hanging. In December. Cody Schow."

Billy stood and examined the photos.

"See," Butch said, "the Schow boy is hanging from the heating pipe. Naked. His feet are about six inches clear of the crate he'd stood on. Here, his clothes are folded neatly by the doorway. We found no evidence of foul play. No sexual molestation, no drugs in the bloodstream, no prints on the scene except those of the kid himself. Other than Miss Bird's, of course, since she lives in the house."

Billy picked up each photo. "You can read my statement and the dispatch reports," said Butch, "but like I told you when I phoned, what we have this morning is not exactly like the first hanging."

"You've got a mutilated body."

"Other differences, too. There was no evidence in the room this morning, or anywhere else in the basement, of the crate or box the boy had used, even though the tie-up was similar to the Schow case, the noose flush against the underside of the pipe. There were blood splatters beneath Darren Riegert, which led me to assume he was bleeding as he was hanged. But these were not directly under the body, like you'd expect. And there weren't any drops on the candles either, and they were placed directly below the boots and left arm, both of which were heavy with blood spots."

"Quirk number one. So we can assume something was covering the area under the body that was then taken away."

"I guess."

"Pentacles were drawn in paint on one wall, am I right?"

"Right. Tommy estimated from the temperature and the initial signs of lividity that Darren had been dead from midnight or half past." Butch coughed. "What also doesn't sit right are the clothes."

"Quirk number two."

"Yes. The Schow kid's clothes were folded. I assumed he'd undressed and placed them to the side. Riegert's were not found."

"In my years of dealing with killers, Butch, I was surprised at how many of them took souvenirs of the crime. But Riegert's clothes may be hidden somewhere around the site, maybe buried near the house, since killers of a different ilk will leave a calling card."

"Dodd and Johnson and me, we were flummoxed when we first saw the mess. You know, we don't get this kind of thing around here very often."

"Why the same house, the same basement?"

Butch shrugged. "Seems both boys lived in the place on and off when they wanted to get away from their parents."

"Any signs of a break-in?"

"None. Miss Bird claimed the back door was open, but she admitted she had always left it unlocked — and kept it so, even after Cody Schow's suicide — so that Darren could come and go. I got something else I need you to see."

The two men left the office and went down a long hallway, turned left and then right. The low-ceilinged room they entered seemed all too familiar to Billy. It had tiles on the floor, walls, and ceiling, and there were two stainless steel scrub sinks. Unusual for a small police unit to have the lab and morgue on site, Billy thought. The smell of cold air and disinfectant assaulted his nostrils. Butch pulled two paper masks from a box near the scrub sinks and handed one to Billy. "Now, this isn't normal procedure — not like you're used to in the big city — but come take a gander. Look but don't touch."

Darren Riegert's naked body lay tilted on its right side on the stainless steel surface, uncovered, the faint odour of cold dead skin filtering through the morgue's antiseptic air. Billy unfolded two fresh rubber gloves from the morgue dispensary box and fitted them onto his hands. Butch tied him into a rubber apron that covered his chest and groin, and then Billy laid a ballpoint and his new notebook on a table by the gurney.

"Telltale sign." Butch pointed to the semi-erect penis. "The last boy was at full mast, blue as a grape popsicle."

Billy clicked on the overhead light. The body shone a waxy white. Pooling had already begun. Mauve patches on the lower half of the body. Rigor mortis was evident in the stiff neck, the taut look of the abdomen. Darren's lips had swollen, and his tongue protruded slightly, blue, as if he'd been out in freezing snow. Into Billy's mind rushed the words he'd spoken in warning to his own rookies: "Separate the cadaver from the living person. Don't take the body home with you if you want to sleep at night."

"See, the kid kept his boots on."

Butch shifted, moving his hips from left to right. He kept two feet away and allowed Billy free movement around the gurney. Billy went up to the head, bent close to the neck, pressed a gloved finger gently against the mottled bruise under the chin.

"Was it a nylon or hemp rope?"

"Nylon. Standard blue half-inch."

"Some burn here. More typical of hemp or a rough natural fibre."

"Burn is burn."

"Have your coroner check for hemp particles. Just in case. By the way, when does this Hawkes come to work?"

"He's part-time and has a practice in town. He sees patients in the morning and does rounds at the regional ward after lunch. Crazy old cuss, a Brit with a bow tie. Comes in early evenings, mainly, when I call him. We don't do a big volume here."

Wiping his right hand with a paper towel, Billy picked up his notebook, then reached for the ballpoint. "Male — fourteen, fifteen, pooling, dried blood — dripped, streaked — on chest, pentacle shape cut into chest skin roughly between pectoral muscles. Shape five to six inches wide, five long cuts, shallow. Tongue protrusion, penis semi-erect. . . ." Billy walked down to the end of the gurney, staring at the front side of the body. "Kneecaps blood-spattered, upper left thigh blood-streaked, blood spots on toes and laces of both boots. Boots on, laced, no socks."

"What was Hawkes's final analysis on the Schow case?"

"Asphyxiation from ligature marks on neck, crushed frontal. No evidence of drugs."

"Any sign of a note?"

"Suicide note you mean? No."

"No tips or leads? Nothing suspicious?"

"The counsellor at the junior high said Schow had been in trouble with low grades, acting up in class. His mother was on welfare."

Billy moved around the end of the gurney and began studying the back side of Darren Riegert's body. He still felt odd examining the corpse before the coroner had seen it, but he reminded himself he was no longer with a big-city unit on the coast. Procedure back there was hierarchical, more formal. No detective touched the body until Dr. Janes had examined it with his tech unit. Here in Lethbridge, procedure was evidently more casual. And the morgue was empty except for Darren Riegert.

"Butch, who bagged this kid?"

"Tommy and Johnson. Why?"

"They bagged him facedown, right?"

"As I recall, yes. They had to. . . ."

"Because of his arms."

Butch came up beside Billy. Darren Riegert's arms had been bent back and tied with a piece of rough binder twine.

"Look where the twine is tied," said Billy. "Why would you tie up someone just under the elbows?"

Billy turned his back to Butch. "Hold me, Butch. Grab my wrists and pull them back. Now, look at the way the wrists are crossed on the body. Now press my arms tight, at the elbows."

"Jesus."

"See? I can push you away, no problem. Elbow you away."

"Okay. So why not tie you at the wrists?"

"Exactly. And look at the wrists."

They leaned towards the body. Both wrists were marked with X cuts, dried streams of blood leading down into the palms of the hands. The left wrist lay crisscrossed flat over the right.

"I don't get it."

"This boy was tied up after he'd been cut. No way you could slice your victim with a knife with his wrists tied close or at the angle these are. The victim could elbow his way free in one shove. And see the twine. It's not very tightly knotted. I'm surprised it didn't slide down the kid's arms. When you bagged the body, was the twine like this? Loose?"

"I don't recall thinking the twine looked odd, but you're right. It was too loose, tied more like a bow on a birthday present than a hog tie."

"Look at the right hand. The palm is smudged with blood. But the left palm. . . ."

"Yes. Only a streak or dribble. From the wrist wound."

"This body was bleeding standing up. I'd guess that smudge in the right hand was from holding something bloody."

Billy snapped off his gloves, undid the apron, and switched off the overhead table light. He and Butch unfolded a plastic cover and pulled it over the body. Billy stepped back and gazed at the form under the cover before completely removing his paper mask.

"Ugly things were done, Butch. Could've been a game. A ritual."

"Sure bugs the hell out of me. Where is this coming from?"

"And the tampering is post-mortem from the angle of those arms. Rigor mortis had already started in when they were bent back. Which means the time of death and the time when the arms were tied back were at least three to four hours apart. Rigor mortis starts from the head and goes down to the lower limbs. And with the hanging, the angle of suspension would speed up the process. There is more than ritual here, or a show-off killing. The perp may be playing a game with us, trying to trick us or mislead us. Or we have a real psycho on our hands. . . . Necrophilia, maybe? Hawkes will let us know that with the tissue and fluid analysis."

"Beats me. So you agree a second pair of eyes was a good idea?"

"Sure thing. The question is, where do we separate the killing from the game?"

As they washed their hands at the scrub sinks, Billy recalled a body he'd encountered five years earlier in Vancouver. "A woman hanged in a garage," he said. "Turned out she'd committed suicide. Her son later confessed. The mother had suffered a nervous breakdown and in desperation hanged herself with an extension cord. The son said he was so embarrassed that he went into the garage, tied the feet, and slashed them — post-mortem — with a razor blade and then slipped on the pillowcase so the police would think his mother had been murdered by a sadist."

"Jesus."

"I need to see the murder site, Butch."

"It's pretty well bagged by now."

"I know. But I'd like to do a walk-around."

"Let's grab a bite at Mac's on the way. I'll radio Johnson and have her hold on to Miss Bird."

Justin Moore trained his eyes on the changing traffic light, trying to calm himself. He clutched the steering wheel of his mother's battered Oldsmobile and slowly counted under his breath, aware of a police cruiser idling at the intersection across from him. *Five minutes to go. Five minutes from here to Yianni's store.* It was nearly 11:30 in the morning, the time Yianni said to come by. With payment. A bit of luck and Yianni would say, "Kid, you did good, don't worry, you can pay the rest next time." The light turned green. Justin watched the cruiser turn north before he stepped on the gas. Don't be late, he warned himself, as he thrust his hand into his right pants pocket to make sure all the twenties and fifties he'd gathered were still there.

At five-foot-eleven, with blond hair and blue eyes, Justin Moore looked very much like his late father, a man Justin had both loved deeply and feared. How disappointed his father would have been seeing his only child ruining his life. "You are nineteen, Justin. A college degree ahead of you. All tossed away for a man unworthy to shine your shoes." Tears welled in Justin's eyes. "Dad, what am I going to do?" *You can never tell with Yianni. You should never have gone to him. What did you think would happen? Sure, you needed the* DVD *player. You deserved the laptop, the Cross pens. And the Sony thirty-six-inch stereo surround. There was always cash before Dad died. Lots of it. And guys get loans. But you should have stopped to think. Triple interest? You didn't imagine it could apply to you. And what about the cashmere coats?* Justin hated this blaming ritual. This morning, he had only twelve hundred dollars to pay Yianni, money scraped together from his friends at college and the remains of his savings account. Of course, Yianni always demanded cash. He'd laughed when Justin suggested he pay down his debt with a piece of the Moore family silver. "Go to your bank, kid," Yianni had said. What a joke! Justin knew his bank would refuse. Justin's father had left behind a failing business, and in the year since his death the remaining Moore collateral, the family home on Baroness and Aunt Marion's Ashmead Street mansion, what everyone called Satan House, had financed loans to pay back taxes and creditors' bills. Besides, Yianni could act like a mad dog broken loose from its chain if he sensed someone was trying to cheat him. *Remember the car dealer.* He had borrowed a thousand only, then been late with payment. One night, the loan shark drove the car dealer to Fort Whoop-Up Park, took out a blowtorch, and burned the man's shirt off his chest.

Wiping his mouth, Justin pulled the Olds into a parking space, shut off the engine, and closed his eyes. *Only six thousand left.* It seemed like a million. He climbed from the car, checked his hair and his jeans in the cracked side mirror, and walked across Dawson towards a brick building with the sign "Mountain Man Sports." Yianni put up a good front. Paid his taxes. Kept his store clean. When he dealt dope or handed out small loans, it was always off-hours. Justin paused by the door of the store and patted the wad of dollars in his pocket. *For good luck.* Inside, the clammy, cool air made Justin think of a dungeon. He strolled past the clerk at the counter and went to the white door of Yianni's office. It swung open slowly with a touch of Justin's hand. He saw the desk, the ashtray in the shape of a bull's head, the posters of Greece, the leather couch. Smoke and aftershave filled his nostrils. An exotic mix of cinnamon and lemon and oil.

Yianni Pappas was lying on the couch, his shirt open. A thin gold chain hung around his right ankle. His left hand sported a long pointed nail on its baby finger. "My personal coke spoon," Yianni once joked.

"Justin."

Yianni rolled up. He spoke in a liquid voice. His mouth was small; his larger upper lip jutted over the lower in a permanent pout.

"Coffee?"

"No thanks, Yianni. I can't stay."

"You look tired, my friend."

"Look, Yianni."

"Here. Sit down."

"Look, I know. . . ."

"Sssh. Have a Pepsi?"

Yianni opened a mini-fridge by his desk. The shelves were stacked with cans and bottles of pop.

"No. Thanks anyway. Look, Yianni."

"Justin. You're in a big hurry. Slow down."

"I don't have all your money, Yianni. I'm sorry." Justin reached into his pocket and yanked out the wad of bills he'd brought. "It's all I could pull together, honest. But listen, Yianni. . . ."

"Justin, shut the fuck up. You're upsetting me. Slow down. Have a Coke?"

"Okay, okay." Justin pulled in his stomach to settle the burning panic. "A Coke."

Yianni reached into the fridge, slid out a Coke, opened it, and handed it to Justin.

"Justin, please sit down. Drink your Coke."

Justin sat and watched Yianni stub out his cigarette and start counting the bills. Yianni lit a fresh cigarette, not breaking his count. Justin studied the ceiling wondering if he'd leave this airless room with a broken arm or a burnt face.

"Good kid. This is good."

Justin sat forward.

"Drink your Coke. Relax."

Justin took a short gulp. The sweet fizzy mouthful caught in his throat, and he began to cough. Stepping over to him, Yianni slapped Justin gently between the shoulders.

"There, there, kid. Slow down."

The cough died. The room seemed to brighten a little.

"Justin, this is not what I was hoping for, but it's a start."

"You sure?"

"For a nice clean kid, Justin, you like to spend money, run up bills. I know you. I can help you. You got to trust me. Do you trust me?"

"Sure. Of course, Yianni." Justin stood up. "Look, Yianni, the money. I can still. . . ."

"Sit down. Relax."

Justin sat down. Yianni counted the money slowly one more time. After he finished, he wiped his hands with a blue handkerchief lifted from a drawer in his desk. He then stood up.

"Come out here with me, Justin."

"Where?"

"Relax, Justin. Come out here with me."

"This is your storage room?"

"I put stock in here, yes. Pull on that light chain. I ever show you this?"

Justin began to sweat. Before him stood a long table with a zinc top. Over it hung a particle board studded with hooks. On each hook was a heavy tool: wire clippers, hacksaw, steel hammer. A blue, brass-nozzled portable blowtorch lay on the surface of the table.

"You didn't know I was a handyman, Justin?"

"No."

"You ever use a blowtorch like this one before?"

"No."

"Pick it up, Justin."

"Why?"

"Pick it up. Careful. That's good. Light, isn't it? Fits into your palm."

"Yes. Sure."

"It can burn bark off a tree in six seconds. Did you know that?"

"No."

"Put it down gently, Justin. Good kid."

"Yianni." Justin wanted to run. Wanted to be far away, out of this dark oily room.

"Kid, are you ever jumpy. Let me ask you something."

"Yes, Yianni?"

"You still seeing that girlfriend of yours? You still fucking her? You got to be careful, Justin. You got to play right and play safe with women. You still seeing her?"

"No. We broke up."

"You broke up? I am sorry to hear that. You like to spend money on her? You spent a few dollars on her, didn't you?"

"Yes. A few."

"A bracelet, maybe. Some gold earrings? Am I right?"

"Yes, Yianni."

"Am I right?"

"Yes, Yianni. You're right."

"I like you, Justin. I'm here to help you. You understand?"

"Yes, Yianni."

"You owe me some money. I'm going to say this only one time. I want you to stick around, don't go on any holidays, you understand?"

"Yes."

Yianni suddenly placed his right arm around Justin's waist. He held him close, looking into Justin's eyes. He broke into a soft smile.

"You're a good-looking boy, Justin. I'll tell you what. If you have a little trouble pulling your cash together, and I know six thousand don't seem much, but it's the principle of the thing. If you do have trouble, maybe we can work out a different deal. You have to cooperate with me, Justin."

"What kind of deal?"

"A little more personal. More one on one. You come here after hours, and we spend some quality time together. Just you and me. Bring your bathing suit. We can go have a swim at my apartment. We got a sauna, too. You like a sauna? Good and hot in there. Makes you feel relaxed, gets you in the mood."

"I-I don't know, Yianni. I never. . . ."

Yianni released his arm. The odour of his breath and his aftershave hung heavy in the air by Justin's mouth.

"Come."

Justin followed Yianni into the office, where Yianni sat down at his desk. Watching this short frightening man gather the flattened fifties and twenties into a pile, Justin remembered what one of his college friends had said. "Yianni lives for money, Justin. He gets off on hurting people, too. He'll push any button he can to get his thrills." Each time Yianni flicked one of the bills and folded it into a wad, Justin felt his neck tingle.

"This is the last time you come here without full payment," Yianni then said, folding the wadded money into a green leather wallet. "You understand? I don't want a little loan to get in the way of me liking you."

"Yes. Okay."

"Now, kid. You get to the bank. Or to your rich uncle. Or to a rich sugar-momma you can fuck for a loan. Low interest. You get my six thousand and come back here next Saturday. You bring me the cash, full payment, you have a Coke, I count the bills, we celebrate with a joint. Am I right?"

"Sure. Yes, Yianni."

"Am I right?"

"Yes. You are right."

"Until next Saturday."

Justin turned and reached for the door handle.

"Wait a minute, kid."

Yianni opened a cupboard and lifted out a small Ziploc bag. In it were clusters of green marijuana flakes. One of Yianni's dime bags.

"I don't do this very often, kid. 'Cept for my preferred clients. You are special, Justin. Here. Take it."

"No thanks. It's okay, Yianni. . . ."

"Come on, kid. Don't hurt my feelings. You don't want a gift from an old friend? It's on the house. You can't say I never cut you a deal when you was buying from me. Remember?"

"Yes, Yianni."

"So take it. Give it to your ex-girlfriend. Fuck her and have some fun."

Yianni dropped the bag into Justin's open hand.

"Now get your ass out of here."

Outside on the street, Justin noticed the sky for the first time that morning. Empty. Clear. "A bit of time," he whispered. He began to shake and went to pull up his collar as if he were wearing a heavy coat. *Think, think.* He felt the dime bag in his pocket. It wasn't more than fifty bucks worth, not even to that kid who hung out at Sheree Lynn's. He didn't want to think about the barrier tape, the police cars outside Satan House. *Poor Auntie Marion would've freaked if she knew everyone called it that.* He remembered Cody. Dead in the basement last December. Justin wondered why the police had never questioned him. Thank God. Selling dime bags to the two boys was definitely illegal, but Justin still needed more than a few small dope sales to pay off Yianni. Who could he ask for a real loan? He started to run towards the Oldsmobile. His legs were like rubber. The street gave off waves of heat, and he stopped for a moment. In front of him was Boorman's Men's Store. Justin spotted a red silk tie in the display window. "Why not?" he whispered under his breath. And without hesitating, he walked into the panelled showroom of the store with its neat shelves of folded shirts and racks of suits. A well-dressed older man walked up to him.

"Hi, how much is the red tie in the window?"

Before the man had time to answer, Justin's stomach contorted. It was like a signal, a warning. Justin blinked, broke into a sheepish grin. "No, it's okay," he blurted. Turning, his neck hot with shame, Justin mustered his courage and strolled out purposefully. Once more in the brazen sun, he froze on the sidewalk, his back to the display window. His stomach cut into him again. Oh, yes, his mother had always *said* he was a spendthrift, a compulsive, just like his father. Oh, yes, he knew he couldn't resist buying something he liked no matter what the price. This was the very disease, the blind need to spend, that drove him towards a man like Yianni. Justin had always known it. But today was the first time he really *felt* it, and it was like being hit by a bucket of ice water. "It's all Yianni's fault," Justin said. But he knew that was a lie. At this instant, all he wanted to do was hide. All he felt was an urge to cry. Running blindly off the sidewalk and into the traffic, he dodged a couple of honking cars and sprinted down the streets until he reached the place where he'd parked. Inside, he locked the doors and suddenly broke into huge sobs. "I'm sorry, Dad." And then he leaned his head against the steering wheel, the horn bleating like a frightened animal.

Two blocks north of the parking stall where Justin Moore sat with windows closed against the June sun, Billy Yamamoto quickly glanced at his watch. The spindly green hands read 12:29. He and Butch were now driving up Ashmead Street, and Billy was finishing off a Colombian he'd picked up from Mac's coffeehouse. Through the windshield, he admired the canopy of leafy cottonwoods and the immense vault of the sky. "Glad you're here?" Butch asked. He waited for Billy to answer, and coughed. "This city," Butch went on. "I've been cruising around for almost forty years. Stays the same, but it changes every time I get a chance to look." He nudged Billy with his right elbow. "You okay?"

"Yes." The city *was* different: smaller, cleaner than Billy had remembered it from high school days. What a change from the Pacific coast. No bouncing rain day after day. The air here did not cut through your skin and make you feel you were rotting from the inside out. Passing the clapboard houses along Ashmead, Billy pictured the nights years ago when the two of them as teenagers had gone joy riding up and down this street. One night very long ago, they'd driven to a dance at a dilapidated hangar in the city's old Flying Club, and a couple of rednecks had started pushing Billy around, calling him Chinky and Jap. Butch had stepped in, raising his championship fists to defend his friend.

Butch had been leaner then, shoulders harder from daily workouts, his face framed by tight cropped red hair, his callused knuckles a reminder he was western Canada's junior amateur middleweight boxing champ.

"Fill me in on Sheree," said Billy.

"I've met her only once before. Investigating the Cody Schow hanging. Youth care worker, got downsized, according to her boss at family services. They weren't too keen to give out much more information. She and her boyfriend seemed pretty close. He's a professor at the university."

"How's he connected to the Cody Schow case?"

"He was there with Sheree, in the house, staying over when the first body was found in the basement."

"They were *in* the house?"

Butch nodded.

"Sound sleepers?"

"They both claimed they heard nothing. Sheree Lynn said she always left the back door unlocked. . . ."

"Even after the Schow suicide?"

"Seems so. She says the kids came and went. Half the time she never knew if they were out or in."

"How did she know this Schow boy?"

"Before Sheree left family services, she met Schow and the Riegert kid. Her job was to assist the head psychologist looking into allegations of abuse brought forward by the boys' school. Riegert and Schow followed Sheree to her house one day, what we call Satan House now, Marion Bartlett's old place on Ashmead. According to her, they asked if they could see her and be counselled. We questioned Riegert after the Schow suicide and found that Sheree often let the two of them sleep over. She made them meals once in a while."

"How many times did you talk to the Riegert boy?"

"Just the once."

"And your impressions?"

"Shy, withdrawn, unhappy."

"Suicidal? Any follow-up done on him after the Schow hanging?"

"Not much. We contacted the school counsellor, and he kept close watch on the boy for a month or two but never reported back to us with any matter of concern."

"How about Sheree? Did she report anything? Was there any need for intervention or further counselling?"

"I spoke to her a few times. She claimed Darren had adjusted well. I had doubts. Hell, the cable TV people grabbed hold of the story. They went nuts, calling the house a drug hangout, a nest of Satan worship. The local school boards even put out a bulletin warning parents to keep their kids away from Satan House. I was surprised no one trashed the place. Darren, though, got through the mess, so I let the matter go."

"This morning, did Sheree offer any theory about how or why Darren ended up dead in the same basement as Cody Schow?"

"No. She wasn't too clear on anything. Her boyfriend, Randy, was with her again trying to calm her. She was pretty broken up."

"Who found the body?"

"The boyfriend."

Billy paused.

"I asked Dodd about Sheree Lynn. He blushed."

"I'm not surprised." Butch grinned.

"Surprised?"

"You can judge for yourself, my friend."

Butch steered the Ford cruiser to the curb in front of a tall white mansion covered in peeling paint. Satan House sat east-west on Ashmead Street. Two tree-lined avenues, Baroness and Dufferin, stretched southward from Ashmead. Their old-money homes had three storeys, big fences, and back gardens that butted up against each other. Satan House had a pitched roof with two identical A-frame dormer windows. Stucco and wood slatting decorated the upper half of the once-proud façade, while on the first floor bay windows with cheap curtains bordered the front door. Billy remembered the place as a grand home on a select street. There had always been flowers and a clipped lawn. Stories, too, about the rich eccentric Bartlett spinster who lived alone and refused entry to all visitors. A long pillared porch once skirted the ground storey. All that was left was the line of its former roof running across the slatting like a crusted scar.

As Butch was about to switch off the engine, a compact woman with curly brown hair emerged from the front door of the house. She marched towards them carrying a black briefcase and a 35mm Nikon slung over her right shoulder. Billy noted her powerful stride as she crossed the dirt yard. The fullness of her breasts was evident beneath her uniform jacket. She passed around a small group of people gawking at the fluttering barrier tape. At the passenger window of the cruiser, she peered with blue eyes into the shadowy interior. Butch lowered the window.

"Afternoon, Chief," she said. "We're wrapping up."

"Meet Billy Yamamoto. Constable Gloria Johnson."

Johnson extended her hand and with a firm grip shook Billy's.

"Billy was chief homicide detective with the Vancouver city police force for twelve years," Butch said. "He's agreed to join us on the investigation, if you have no objections. In fact, I want Billy to take charge of what we're doing here since he has offered us his time."

"Fine with me, sir," said Johnson. With quick eyes, she looked Billy up and down.

"What have you found, Johnson?" Billy asked.

"We're done with the dusting and the rest of the photos and the site sketch, sir. I got up and took a look at the overhead pipe. Lots of rust. Tommy — he's our medic — got blood samples from the floor. We also went around the neighbourhood like you suggested, Chief. No one home at one place. But Mrs. Aileen Moore, who lives with her teenage son next door, claimed she saw and heard nothing. The neighbour on the other side is bedridden, and his nurse said she sleeps in the basement and can't hear street noise."

"What did the teenager see?" asked Billy.

"Pardon me?" Johnson replied, her voice rising a little as her lips parted in a sudden smile.

"You said a Mrs. Moore lived next door with her son. Did he see anything? Did you meet him?"

"Actually, no, Inspector. At the time, Mrs. Moore said he probably was still asleep."

"He may have been up in the night though. Or in late. Get their number and have the son come down to the station. Just routine. Get a hold of the nurse again, and the other neighbour, and have them come down, too."

"Sure thing."

Johnson smiled again. Billy liked the way she spoke. He liked the way her face took on colour when she smiled.

"Can you leave behind your kit, Johnson? Billy and me'll need tweezers and Ziplocs."

"And gloves."

"And gloves."

"She's yours, Chief." Constable Gloria Johnson lay the briefcase down on the sidewalk by the cruiser, then took out a couple of large envelopes. "Got the prints here. I'll take 'em over to the lab. And do some cross-checks with the Schow case."

At first glance, Gloria Johnson had seemed older than she was. Billy gazed now at a woman no more than twenty-five, a staff constable with an important job, forensics being only one part of it.

"You may need some more consent-to-search forms, Chief. They're in the kit, too."

"Thanks, Johnson."

"Better go gentle with her, sir. She's still shaky from this morning. And the attack. Her professor boyfriend had to go off for a meeting. I gave him permission to leave. He'll be back as soon as he can since he knows you need to talk to him again."

"What attack?" asked Billy.

"Chief, you want to, or shall I?"

Butch coughed. "Go ahead." Butch pulled out a pack of cigarettes for the first time since he'd been with Billy and lit up. He lowered the

THE BOY MUST DIE

window on his side of the car and blew the smoke into the open air.

"The mother, this morning, when she got here, caused a ruckus. She's a hard one. We were chalking off the scene when she comes screaming down the basement stairs. Right, Chief? She was crying. Tommy and me had to hold her back from tearing the body down. Then Miss Sheree appears. All polite and trying to comfort. The mother goes at her. Spits in her face. Calls her a bitch."

"Thanks, Johnson."

"Did she get near the body?"

"No. She was restrained by Tommy. There was no tampering from her or her male companion. Quite a lad he was, eh, Chief?"

Butch nodded, then thrust open the driver's door.

"Come on."

"Nice meetin' you, sir," Johnson grinned.

"You, too," Billy smiled back.

"You be back after lunch, Johnson?"

"If you need me, Chief."

"On your way back, drive over to Professor Mucklowe's apartment. Check up on his story this morning. Talk to the landlord." Butch turned to Billy. "Mucklowe claims he and Miss Bird were talking to the landlord before they got here. Tap on a few doors around, see if anyone's home for lunch who may have seen them earlier on."

"Done."

Johnson waved and headed off down the sidewalk in the direction of the police station. She turned suddenly.

"Chief? I left the keys to our cruiser on the hall table in there. I can pick up another at the station."

Butch nodded and waved.

As they approached the house, Butch did some explaining. Billy moved beside him, listening and looking around at the dirt yard, the broken tree stump, the general dereliction.

"The spitting this morning was the second time something has happened."

"Oh?"

"Cody Schow's mother shoved Sheree at her son's funeral. Called her a demon."

"What had she done?"

"Nothing except threaten the mother with removal of her kid to a foster home. Cody Schow, like Darren Riegert, was underage — legally. Still classed as a child by Children's Aid. Schow's mother was a drunk. Claimed Miss Bird was putting a cross on her son's coffin. A devil jewel, she called it."

The shadow of the house fell over them as they climbed the steps.

"Here we go," Butch said. He reached for the handle of the broken screen door. Billy looked up at the twin dormers. Only the stucco, stippled with thousands of sharp peaks, had defied time and neglect. The doorbell rang with a muffled jangle. Butch pressed it one more time, as a gesture of courtesy, then entered into the fetid, bare-floored front hall. Billy suddenly imagined a ghostly Marion Bartlett standing there, her sad voice imploring them to leave, the oak staircase behind her rising into mournful shadow.

A door opened. Behind it, there was a room painted orange with furniture draped in madras cloth. A woman appeared holding a lit cigarette in her left hand. She cocked her head. Billy couldn't help but notice her smooth white skin and her almond-shaped green eyes. No wonder Dodd had blushed. She was lithe, like a dancer. Her breasts pressed firmly against the folds of her white muslin gown. Her feet were bare; her neck was decorated with silver and wooden beads. Flowing chestnut hair framed her high cheekbones and small chin. Sheree Lynn Bird was no more than twenty-four. Billy resisted the desire to run his eyes again over her body and face.

"Please come in," she said. "Why have you kept me waiting so long?" Her voice quivered, and Billy caught in it a dark sensual sound. "Your constable has been keeping me company. He complimented me on my new dress." Billy approached her. She followed him with her eyes. A shudder of fear crossed her face.

The attending constable rose. The room harboured an oak dining table-and-chair set, and by the fireplace sat a small television. Butch nodded to the constable to leave as Sheree Lynn Bird settled at the table, a cup of coffee in front of her. She drew an ashtray full of butts up to her right elbow. Through the bay window, Billy noted a sagging wooden garage with leaning doorframes and a row of shattered glass panes. Light from the June afternoon stretched across the floor now. It promised to be a long day of dry heat.

"Miss Bird, please meet Detective Inspector Billy Yamamoto."

"Can you call me Sheree, please? You make it sound like I'm on trial or something."

Billy sat down across from Sheree and pulled out his ballpoint and his new notebook. He laid the notebook flat on the table and wrote the date and time in the top left corner of the first page.

"I don't use this room much, Inspector. I got a deal on this place. The bank leased it to me for next to nothing." Sheree retrieved her cigarette and relit it with a blue plastic lighter. "Mainly I stayed upstairs. The boys used this room. To chill as they would. . . ."

Sheree Lynn Bird bent her head forward and covered her eyes with her left hand. Billy reached into his pocket. But he'd forgotten to put tissues there this morning. In the old days in Vancouver, he always put tissues in his pocket. Sheree lifted her cigarette to her lips and took a long drag.

"I'm sorry."

"Sheree, I have to ask you some questions." Billy broke into a polite smile. Sheree Lynn beamed back at him. Billy read this gesture as one of panic. Here was a woman still in shock, he reminded himself, a woman who may be a suspect. Yet her fear, he saw, did not overcome her need to show off her beauty.

"I really want out of all this, Inspector. You don't know what it's been like here." Sheree breathed in. "You're Japanese. At least your last name is."

"Yes."

"Your family from here?"

"Yes. My father lived here most of his life."

"What about your mom?"

"She died when I was an infant. I never knew her."

"Seems like I keep meeting a lot of abandoned boys. I'm sorry. You don't find me rude, do you?" Sheree Lynn moved her eyes over Billy's face.

"No, Sheree. Not at all."

"Good," she said. She shifted her upper body, glancing briefly at Butch.

"Tell me about yourself, Sheree," Billy said. "How did you meet Cody and Darren?"

Sheree Lynn's face looked pale, and as she began again, her voice lost its coquettish tone.

"I was a youth care worker at family services. Chief Bochansky probably told you that already. Two years. I got the job right out of community college. I met Darren and Cody on referral, and mainly did their paperwork. It hurts to talk about those boys. I can't believe this has happened. I always hated the name Cody gave to this house. And the way those reporters made it sound so evil. It's like a curse on me." Sheree Lynn took a breath and waited. She looked up at Billy and brushed back her hair from her face.

"Go on."

Sheree smiled. She relaxed her shoulders and butted out her cigarette.

"Marilyn, our psychologist, did the interviews for the boys. I filed the reports, but I got to talk to them about their parents. I got to help them fill out the forms and take their pictures. Marilyn let me escort them home — that's where I met Sharon Riegert and Cody's mom. I tried to be understanding. Marilyn told me not to say anything, but I felt I, well, never mind. The boys and I got along."

"How do you mean?"

"We talked. They liked me. Everything was fine until I got downsized."

"When was that?"

She looked at Bochansky. "You didn't tell him?"

Butch blinked and sat forward.

Billy said, "I'd like to hear it from you, Sheree."

"Last October."

"Budget cuts? Reduced caseloads?"

"That's what they told me." She broke into a nervous laugh. "Sure!"

"You didn't believe them?"

"I had no choice, did I, Billy? May I call you that?"

"Yes. Go on."

"Look at me. People like me. I do a good job."

Sheree shook her head and rubbed her hands together.

"I was hurt. Very hurt, believe me."

"You've been unemployed for over six months by now. How do you pay the rent for this place? And buy groceries?"

"Randy, my boyfriend, helps out, and I have some savings."

"Butch told me you took in these two boys, is that right?"

"They stayed here once in a while. Yes." Her voice began to quiver. "I gave them meals. Why?"

"You did this all for free?"

"Yes. Is that against the law? I am a very giving person, Inspector. Cody and Darren begged me to help them. To let them come here and talk and hang out."

"Weren't you supposed to keep professional distance from clients?"

"But they weren't my clients anymore. Not after I left. I felt they needed me as a friend and not just a case worker who cross-examines them and then lets them go home to get beaten up."

"Cody was into drugs and Satan worship. Did your psychologist guide you in matters of counselling and giving advice?"

"I knew Cody had a problem. I helped him down once from a bad acid trip. They liked me, Inspector. That means a lot to a person, to share and feel comfort. I admit they were difficult, sometimes. I wanted to try soft love on them rather than tough love, which is the only thing

45

the service ever tries. Those boys needed me. I wanted to prove I could help them. I have the right to show people that I am not a useless person."

Sheree was almost in tears. She lit a cigarette and sat back in her chair.

"Did it ever occur to you," Billy continued after a pause, "these boys were using you? Taking advantage? Staying here so they could take drugs and not be disciplined?"

"I didn't allow drugs here. None."

"Did they ever steal from you?"

"No. Never."

Sheree refused to look at Billy or at Butch. She sat slumped down, and her mouth had formed into a pout.

"How was it both these boys ended up in your basement?"

"I don't know."

"Yet you said you were friends. You liked them, and they liked you. You didn't see any signs, any indication, that they might be depressed? Surely this was the first thing you should have noticed."

"I felt they needed a mother, Inspector, not a policeman." Sheree's voice was shaking with passion. "I had a lot of sympathy for Cody and Darren," she went on. "I latched on to them is the best way to put it. When they came to me and asked if I'd still see them, talk to them, I couldn't say no. I did what I could to help Cody. I never imagined he would hang himself. Maybe that's my fault."

She stopped suddenly. Billy looked at her in silence.

"You must think I'm irresponsible, Inspector," she said before Billy could frame another question. "I assure you I intended only the best for those boys."

Billy met her candour with his own: "But they both fooled you, didn't they, Sheree? You never suspected Cody would try suicide? But you knew he took drugs and had an abusive home life. And Darren? You sympathized with him, but why didn't you act? You knew about his mother and Woody."

Sheree's eyes flashed hot. "Are you accusing me of negligence? After all I did?"

"From what I've seen, adolescents often hide and distort the truth, very often the truth of how they feel. Isn't this a typical problem of boys in this age group?"

"It can be. I always probed them. Always tried to make them open up more. Do you know, Inspector, how hard it is to fight against a wall of fear and pain?"

"Sheree, you and I are in this to find out why Darren was murdered. Why don't we look at that right now?" Sheree's back straightened, and her breathing calmed down. Billy decided to take a different line. "You must have been really shocked this morning when you saw the body."

"Randy saw it. I didn't. I refused. I couldn't."

"You stayed at Randy's last night?"

"Yes, Inspector. Randy and I came back here at eight or so this morning. When we arrived, the back door was open. The light was on in the basement."

"You said earlier you got a call, Sheree," Butch said, interrupting.

"That's what really scared me."

"When did you get this call?" Billy asked.

"I guess it was around seven. Randy and I were still in bed. This crazy voice — a boy's, maybe fifteen or so — says to me 'Did they do it? Did Darren go?' Call display gave the number as unknown. Maybe it was from a phone booth. At first, I thought it was a prank from one of the kids I used to know at family services."

"Did they do it?"

"Yes, Inspector. That's what was said."

"What made you change your mind?"

"What do you mean?" Her chest rose; colour flushed her cheeks.

"That it wasn't a joke."

Sheree Lynn's voice broke. "A feeling . . . a hunch. Randy thought I was crazy. But I said something's wrong. I remembered finding Cody in . . . I prayed Darren hadn't done the same thing. I begged Randy to drive over here to check it out."

"Why didn't you call Darren's mother right away to check things out?"

"I never got a straight or caring answer from her. Why would I wake her up to have her abuse me over the phone?"

"But you did call her later. Once you and Randy got over here."

"Yes. I felt I had no choice then."

Sheree Lynn Bird retreated to silence, her head bent slightly down.

Butch shot Billy a quick glance. Billy wrote a few quick notes, then continued.

"Did you ever see any evidence of Satanic rituals or cult activities with either of these boys?"

"They read that damn book, *Thanatopsis*. It was like a bible to them, said it gave them a sense of power."

Billy examined her face more closely as she said the words, looking for any sign of remorse. He saw only fatigue, but discerned a defeat as palpable as the smell of her cigarettes. "In your opinion, Sheree, why are boys this age so fascinated with death and evil?"

"It thrills them. Gives them a sense of the mystery of the universe. At least, that's what Cody and Darren told me."

"You and Randy were here in this house with those boys quite frequently, were you not?"

"What are you getting at, Inspector?"

"I want to know about everyone who knew Darren or had contact with him."

"Randy didn't like Cody and Darren that much. Though he didn't say so. He was polite to them. When they'd appear at the door, or be here when we got home, Randy usually went up to our bedroom to work."

"The back door was always left unlocked, even after Cody's suicide?"

"Yes."

"How many people knew of this unlocked door?"

"Only Randy and me and the boys. They may have told their friends. I can't think right now of anyone they knew who might have come here."

Sheree's answers were short now, spoken in a flat voice.

"Can you think of anyone who wanted to hurt Darren?"

Sheree sighed. She rubbed her eyes. "Other than his horrible mother? Not at the moment. I know he didn't have many friends. Still, I feel sad for Sharon Riegert. She must be in a pretty bad state."

Sheree Lynn asked to go to the bathroom. When she returned, she had washed her face and brushed her hair and seemed to Billy much more relaxed. It was as if talking to him had removed a burden.

"I will need you to come down to the station this afternoon, Sheree."

"For the video camera?" She smiled.

"I have a personal question for you, Sheree. I don't know how it relates to the case right now. But why do you and Randy live in two places? You lease this old house, and he lives across the river."

"Randy loves me, Billy. He appreciates me. But he is possessive. He can be very demanding. I have to be myself and have a space I can call my own."

"Did Cody or Darren ever know when you'd be here or at Randy's?"

"I didn't leave them a schedule, if that's what you mean."

"The caller this morning knew where you were. Did you get a lot of home calls from your clients?"

"When I was with the service, yes. But that's common practice, Inspector. Surely you knew that." Sheree Lynn gave Billy a shallow smile.

"As far as you know, then, Cody and Darren and a whole bunch of kids could have come and gone through that unlocked back door at any time."

"Yes."

A man abruptly entered the room from the front hall. He took no notice of Billy or of Butch and ambled, matter-of-factly, to Sheree Lynn. He clasped both her hands and lifted her to a standing position, a gesture as smooth as a professional ballroom dancer's. Handsome, boyish-looking for middle age, with short brown hair. He wore khaki pants, a blue polo shirt, and a pair of Timberland loafers. Billy thought he seemed oddly militaristic in bearing, his shoulders held back and straight, his stomach flat, his chest shoved out. Early to mid-forties.

"You're all right, are you?" the man asked.

Sheree Lynn Bird fell into his open arms. "Oh, honey," she moaned.

Butch coughed. The man held Sheree Lynn tight to his chest, stroking her hair. After a moment, she tried to break out of his hold, but he held her a moment longer. "Stay, stay."

"My meeting was hell," the man whispered.

Sheree Lynn struggled loose. "Randy, this is Detective Inspector Billy Yamamoto." She looked flushed. Suddenly embarrassed.

"I beg your pardon. I'm Randy Mucklowe. Department of Archaeology."

"Professor."

"I'm sorry. I've been in a budget meeting."

Randy stuck out his hand. He shook Billy's quickly, dropped it, nodded to Butch, then turned back to Sheree Lynn and directed her to sit down. He surveyed the table and with a sweep of his right hand removed the ashtray to a nearby windowsill. Pulling up a chair beside Sheree, he grabbed hold of her hands.

"Can we continue, Inspector? I'm sure you have a busy day, as do Sheree and I."

"We'll need you and Sheree to come down to the station. To give a formal statement. But I want to ask both of you a few questions before I talk to you alone, Professor."

"You may call me Randy."

Sheree was gazing into Randy's face, her eyes soft and passive. Her glance told Billy she was now the adoring supplicant. "Let me sum up so far," said Billy. "You two got here around eight this morning after receiving an anonymous phone call. You, Randy, found the body, and then Sheree called in the police?"

"No," Randy interrupted.

In the time it took Randy to cross his legs, Billy decided to be cautious with him.

"Where have I gone wrong?"

"You haven't, Inspector. Your facts are just incomplete."

A gentle smirk flitted across Randy's face. Sheree was about to speak, but Randy squeezed her hand and raised his chin.

"We got this wretched call at seven," Randy said, his voice betraying a slight impatience. "Sheree picked up the phone and listened. I didn't hear the voice clearly, but it sounded like a male teenager's. I wasn't too perturbed, quite frankly. I've gotten used to being harassed at all hours by Sheree's two wards. In any case, she told me what the kid had said. She thought it was a joke. But in my opinion, the whole matter sounded grave. Sheree quite rightly felt upset, and I could see she needed my help. I thought first of calling the police, but after a moment I really doubted I would get much more than the usual shiftless sergeant who would have me come down and fill in a form and then do nothing. It seemed possible to me that this was a call for help. Sheree surmised it was Darren Riegert or one of his friends warning us, wanting us to pay attention to them yet again."

"Randy, please," Sheree said, her voice plaintive.

"Why did you decide then . . . ?"

"I didn't decide, Inspector. I guessed. I always had a feeling both Cody and Darren were bent on some kind of Satanic game. I didn't know for certain. But I figured Satan House — as they called this faded glory — would be somehow involved. Since the caller knew we were at my apartment, I felt we should try this house first. When we arrived here, the back door was ajar. I called out. Sheree was too frightened to investigate. Then I went down, switched on the lights, and found Darren."

"What did you see exactly?"

"Exactly? A body, bloodied, hanging, naked except for the boots, the chest cut with a pentacle shape, and the head in a noose."

"Sheree said the basement light was already on."

"Did she?" Randy looked quickly into her eyes.

She said, "Don't you remember?"

"Yes, of course, Inspector."

"And that was it?"

"No. That was not it." Randy made a point of sighing. "There were candles on the floor in a circle beneath the body. The boy's hands were tied. On the facing wall was a pentacle scrawled in some dark colour."

"What time was this?"

"As I said before, around eight, or minutes after."

"What did you do then?"

"Panicked, of course. Surely, Inspector, you've seen enough bodies yourself to know how shocking it can be."

"Were you shocked?"

"Don't be ridiculous. Of course I was."

"What was the first thing you did after you saw the body?"

"As I said before, Inspector, I panicked. I thought of calling the police right away, but then I thought I should go and comfort Sheree. I knew what this discovery might do. Once again, she would be hounded and blamed by those obnoxious parents. I came upstairs and told her. I suggested we calm ourselves. We then called the station."

Billy allowed silence to enter the conversation for a moment. He leaned back in his chair, jotted a few key details from Randy's description. When he looked up, Randy's face was close to Sheree's, and they were whispering very low. Randy then turned to Butch and addressed him directly. "Chief, if she may, can Sheree go upstairs for a quick shower?"

"You done for now, buddy?" Butch asked Billy.

Billy waited, then turned to Randy. "Please, Sheree, go ahead. Professor, I still have a few more questions for you."

"Go on, then," Randy said to Sheree, giving her a quick peck on the cheek. Sheree smiled sheepishly at Billy and Butch and left the room. Randy began brushing the front of his khakis as if dust from the ceiling had settled on them, spoiling the creases. When he spoke again, he did not look up at Billy.

"Tell me about the harassment Sheree has received."

"Briefly, Cody's suicide brought police. Social services heard of the business and wanted her to explain her actions, why the boy was coming to her, that sort of thing. The school called, wanting a full report. Sheree was questioned as to why she didn't intervene on behalf of the boy if he was in any way suicidal."

"Why didn't she?"

"Didn't you ask her?"

"I'm asking you."

"Boys lie, Inspector. You should know from your years of experience how certain psychopathic types can fool you."

"Are you saying Cody was a psychopath?"

"Let me take that back. He was disturbed. No, he was very unhappy. And on drugs. He saw Sheree frequently to discuss his hopeless home life."

"So she would have observed if he were depressed, even suicidal."

"Sheree tends to care too much, Inspector. She smothered those boys with attention, and in my view couldn't really see how secretive or desperate they were."

"Did you see it?"

"What are you implying?"

"You seem to have an answer to everything, Professor. You see things, you make educated guesses, and yet in the case of Cody, in spite of what you say, you did nothing."

"What could I do? I didn't want to meddle. Sheree needed to be on her own."

"Do you think Cody or Darren would have listened to you if you had got involved?"

"Oh, come now, Inspector. You know better than that. Speculation of that kind is nonsense."

"Hazard a guess anyway."

"No. I didn't care for them. Stayed away from them as much as I could."

"How often did the boys come here?"

"On and off, twice a week, perhaps. Some nights they ate us out of house and home."

"They slept here as well?"

"Sheree awarded them each a bedroom."

"You sound resentful, Professor. Did you resent them being here?"

"Since when did you become a psychologist, Inspector? I was not the least resentful, despite what you think you can interpret in my voice."

"Did Cody or Darren ever steal anything from you?"

"Money, you mean?"

"Anything. Money, pens, paper."

"No. I can't remember."

"Did you ever smell marijuana smoke in the house?"

"No, but Cody had dime bags sticking out of his pockets half the time. Sheree once brought him down from a bad acid trip and essentially saved his life."

"You were there?"

"I couldn't help but hear the noise the boys were making, yelling and carrying on."

"After Cody's body was found, did you notice any change in the way Sheree and Darren got along?"

Randy paused and gazed hard at Billy before answering. "Sheree tried to get Darren to go to another counsellor. He said no. I think she felt she was losing touch with him."

"Over what?"

"You'd have to ask her, Inspector."

"Can you think of anyone who wanted to hurt Darren?"

"No."

Billy stood up.

"Walk around with me, Randy. Show me the back door. Show me the basement stairs. I need to go down there for a short look around afterwards."

"Certainly. There's not much to see."

Randy led Billy into the kitchen. A large yellow room with a sink and fridge and a canister set with a yellow triangle pattern. On a rack, under the cupboards, hung a roll of paper towels, each towel with a border of little yellow flowers.

"Here."

Randy pointed to the closed kitchen door.

"Wide open this was. And the back entrance door, too. Kicked open, I figure. Both the doors slammed up against the wall."

"Any other signs of damage or vandalism in the house?"

"No."

"What's behind this door?"

Randy took hold of the kitchen door and pulled.

The cramped back porch was sunny. One wall held a large eight-paned window with glass shelves tacked up to hold pots of geraniums. On the bottom shelf was a neat row of empty plastic Coke bottles. A round green garbage can crowded a corner by the back door. Billy peeked inside. Nothing.

Butch joined them. Billy examined the floor. Small bits of dried mud led from the back steps, through the porch, and towards the kitchen. "Looks like they walked through the yard. Or through someone's yard."

A pair of rubber boots sat by the green garbage can, partly covered by a sheet of newspaper.

"These belong to Sheree?"

Randy frowned. "I think so. I think she owns a pair. For gardening."

Before he spoke again, Billy slipped a note card out of his suit pocket. He folded it over once, creased it, then slid it into his right hand, and with it covering his fingers fitted it onto the lip of the rubber boot and lifted the boot up. The sole was clean and dry. He put the boot down. The other one was dry and clean as well.

"What time did Sheree come over to your place yesterday?"

Randy pulled in a breath, then rolled his eyes; looking over the back garden, he rubbed his chin.

"I can't be sure. After dinner. Maybe nine or ten. She has a key and lets herself in. I was working on a budget for this morning's meeting." Randy tilted his head back and threw a glance at Butch. Billy sensed nervousness in the professor's voice.

"I don't have much interest in the garden, Billy, as you can see from the mess out there." It was Sheree. She had come up from behind and was drying her hair. She had changed into a pair of tight jeans and a pink blouse.

"Do you mind, Sheree, if I take a look around your basement and garden now?"

"Not at all, Inspector."

Randy frowned. "When do you want us down at the station?"

"The constable can take you in the cruiser," answered Billy. "He can call Dodd to get things set up."

Billy was taken aback when Sheree Lynn suddenly gave him a quick hug. "Thank you, Inspector, for caring."

Randy smiled woodenly. He steered Sheree Lynn outside through the front door. Turning away from them, Billy pulled out his notebook. He went into the living room, where he'd left his ballpoint, and sat down and began to write each separate piece of information he could remember — especially the description of the caller's voice "Did they do it? Did Darren go?" Then he stood and walked to the front hall, where Butch was checking over the see-through plastic Ziplocs. Each bag was tagged with neat handwriting. A book with a pentacle on its cover, a noose, a cloth bag with a blood stain, one wax candle, three matches, one paper set of four unlit matches, and a paint-coated stir stick, paint brush, both with black paint.

"Butch, what do you know about Professor Mucklowe?"

"Career wise? He's a big name at the university in Native sites. We did a background run on him during the Schow case. Divorced, tenure position, published articles, and a book on the Blackfoot Nation."

"On the level, then."

"Seems that way. What do you make of him and Sheree Lynn?"

"He likes to play boss. She likes it when he does."

"You think they're telling the truth?"

"For the most part. Neither one of them has an obvious motive for killing a young boy. Sheree Lynn shows remorse at least. I don't know, yet, what I think about Randy. He'd just as soon ignore the matter as he did the boys when they were alive. Still, it doesn't lie right. Sheree and Randy seem to be hiding something. At least holding back."

Billy opened Johnson's kit, pulled out a pair of rubber gloves, a set of tweezers, and a clutch of Ziplocs.

"Butch, I'm going to do a quick walk-around downstairs. How do you want to proceed?"

"You call it."

"Get Dodd to check the alibis of Sharon Riegert and her boyfriend, Woody. And have him record both Sheree's and Randy's formal statements separately. Then have him go through your reports and statements on the Schow case. Pull out names, numbers — teachers, friends, family — anyone associated with these two boys. Especially anyone who said anything about Darren. Did you say you'd met the counsellor at the school?"

"Yeah. Bill Barnes. I've got his number in another notebook, out in the cruiser."

"Call him. See if he can come up with any new names of boys around fourteen who might have known Darren. Or had mentioned being here." Billy hardly had time to catch his breath. "In a few days, the news of this kid's death will be all over the junior high school. They still have this extended semester system here? The kids go to school till mid-July or thereabouts?"

"There's summer school, too."

"We need to find out who phoned Randy and Sheree this morning. And we need to move fast. Somebody knew Darren was going into this."

The basement stairwell was darker than Billy expected. The stairs were steep and narrow, covered with chipped paint and dusty footprints. Billy examined the height of the overhang. Stairs leading to the second floor of the house were directly above. He regretted not having brought along his aluminum-cased flashlight. He would have to work in available light. The concrete at the foot of the steps was spotted with grime and what looked like burnt cork. Kneeling down in the dim glare of a forty-watt bulb, Billy touched the rotting rubber from carpet underlay.

The first room was empty. It felt lower because of a new drywall ceiling. Through a smaller passage, the second room was cordoned off by yellow-and-black police tape. Billy could already see the chalk line around the outer edge of the blood spill. He stood at attention, placed his hands behind his back. A legacy from police-training days: *Touch nothing. Observe all. Make no assumptions.* Entering the gloom of the murder scene, he felt the familiar uneasiness of being in a place where a terrible action had unfolded. There before him was the spattered pattern of Darren's dried blood. The conduit pipe overhead was at least seven feet above the floor. Out came the notebook. Had he measured the length of the body back in the morgue? *Damn!* He searched again, flipping back and forth. He'd have to guess. Maybe five feet, five-two? He'd have to wait and see Johnson's site photos before he could judge how the boy had been found, how far the noose had hung from the bottom curve of the pipe, and whether the rope had been looped once or twice.

Did he expect to find much? He wasn't sure. Billy walked slowly around the site. He looked closely at the walls. A black cross and two lopsided pentacles spread across the whitewashed concrete surface. A paint can with a closed lid had been left below the wall. There was black around the lid, the same colour as the scrawl on the wall above. Johnson had dusted. Billy could see the traces of white powder on the metal rim and sides. The floor was crunchy with dried mouse droppings. Billy lifted his left foot. Fresh faeces stuck to his heel like small black grapeshot. He wiped his shoe on the concrete and let his eyes roam over the room in case any of the creatures might be cowering in the corners. The smell of urine and tobacco soured the air. Along another wall, underneath a small square window, were a washer, a dryer, and a utility sink. Billy looked behind them. Dust and hoses and electrical connections to a metal plug box. Billy swivelled around and knelt. He swept his eyes across the floor.

"There," he whispered.

He moved back towards the wall with the painted pentacles. A small arrow-shaped piece of black broken plastic lay on its side. He shoved his hands into the rubber gloves. How had Johnson missed this?

Understandable: there was a dead body in front of her and a medic working around the site. He dropped the piece of plastic into a Ziploc. He clicked the tweezers together and stood up.

Billy looked at the one major pipe — the conduit — crossing the ceiling. "The *Roshi* offers the riddle — the *koan*," he said to himself. He let his mind float free for a moment. Gazing down at the floor, he studied the faint pattern of blood spatters inside the chalk line. Odd, as Butch had pointed out. There was nothing directly under the pipe, where the noose had hung. If the body was bleeding — cut up before it was hanged — the blood would have splattered onto the floor. There were some spots on the boots, Billy remembered. What was missing? Four burnt candles made a rough circle directly under the pipe. They were only partially burned. Billy presumed from the markings that a fifth had been removed by Johnson for the lab. Yet, here too, the candles were clean. Billy knelt down close to peer at the wicks and the melted sides. The light was too faint for him to see blood specks, but the candle in the lab would reveal if there were any. Billy remained still and stared.

Then he saw the smudge. It looked like dried blood. Square in shape, it had a distinct edge, a straight line, as if someone had pressed a bloody object — or dropped one — onto the basement floor. Billy thought for a moment, then moved to the utility sink, which was brown-stained. He leaned over and sniffed. Sewer and mould.

Butch called him upstairs

On his way into the kitchen, Billy Yamamoto took a quick glance around the pantry and the yellow breakfast room. Clean floors, a few boxes of newspapers stacked in a corner by the pantry's shelves. Cans of tomatoes, instant coffee, creamer, and instant macaroni dinners lined up on blue gingham shelf paper.

"I called the counsellor from the school. At his home," said Butch, leaning his lower back against the kitchen counter. "He said he'd contact any friends of Darren he knew about. Said there wouldn't be many, but that he might be able to round up at least a couple for interviews for later this afternoon. Or tomorrow."

"The sooner the better. Dodd find anything yet?"

"So far, he's logged on to the files of Cody and brought up a few names. Teachers mainly. All with phone numbers. Problem was these boys were loners or outsiders. They didn't have a lot of buddies. He also said Randy insisted on giving his formal statement first."

Billy slid open a drawer.

"What're you looking for?"

"This."

In his right hand, Billy held up a serrated bread knife. The wooden handle was smooth, the blade smudged with dishwasher spots. "This is pretty clean. Doesn't look like it's been washed too recently. Or used for cutting much bread." Billy pulled out the cutlery tray, a paring knife and butter knives, spoons and forks. All clean. Nothing under the tray.

"She's fond of yellow."

"Look under the sink, Butch."

Butch yanked open cupboards while Billy went through the towel drawers, lifting and sorting. Nothing.

"Did you or Dodd go through the yard this morning?"

"We didn't."

Billy felt a surge of impatience. Quickly, he reminded himself that he was in a small town. These police were not that familiar with homicide. "We'll need a thorough search, Butch."

"I figured it wasn't necessary since we did a close walk-around of all the upper rooms and the basement. Sheree Lynn let us go into the spare rooms and the closets. Mind you, we didn't go up into her attic."

Billy reached for his notebook and pen. "I'll tour the flower beds if you want to scout around that garage to the side."

The brown shaggy lawn, mostly crabgrass, folded thickly under Billy's shoes. Two days before, there was a heavy storm in the city. Clouds scudded over treetops like smoke from a grass fire, and the rains beat down. As Billy walked towards the old wooden fence, the elms and the weeping willows began to stir in the hot breeze now rising. The garden was square. A rock pile full of boulders filled one side beyond the lawn. A patch of mud and broken flower stalks — withered irises and overgrown hollyhocks — ran along the weathered wooden fence. In a sun-filled spot of stalks and mud next to a brick barbecue, one with a chimney and a tin covering, was a large speckled rock nestled into the stump of an extinct elm. Billy walked beside the fence, head down, scanning the mud. It was pocked with dirty puddles, dog prints, and bent, broken stalks covering the earth like a woven basket. Up above, a flicker hammered on the bark of an elm. Billy came upon trampled grass.

He knelt by the rock and stared, taking out his notebook and quickly sketching the layout of the garden. He put an X where the rock and the elm stump lay. The trampled grass bordered a line of half-distinct boot prints. Billy was about to step around the rock when he saw a bright spot of yellow. He took his notebook and with its long edge brushed away the flattened grass. A paper towel, like the ones on the roll in the kitchen. Thick paper stamped with yellow flowers.

"Hey, Billy!"

Billy turned; then he saw Butch waving from the side of the garage.

"What you got, Butch?"

Butch held up a shiny chrome-coloured boom box.

"Hang on. I've found something here, too."

Billy dug under the grass with his fingers. He found thick paper saturated with mud and water, buried under a handful of flower stalks and a fistful of packed dirt. The paper's edge tore. There was an object wrapped up inside. Billy pulled it into the light and peeled away the paper.

A serrated kitchen knife with its bloodstained handle and its bloodstained blade.

"Bingo!"

Billy got up, holding the knife, making sure his fingers touched only the torn paper in which the blade was wrapped. He took a Ziploc from his pocket and dropped the knife inside. *Why not clean the knife off?* He looked around the grass again. Then he moved on, around the yard, past the garage, and alongside the basement to the window that looked out from the room where Darren's body was found. Billy crouched. The earth was scored with a cat's paw prints. He studied the area. The window had not been tampered with. He walked to the back door and scanned the sidewalk and steps but saw only small pieces of dried mud. *Hard to tell where they came from. Could have been here for days, from the garden or the dirt front yard.*

Billy walked into the kitchen, then down to the front hallway. Butch held the boom box in his gloved hand: "This was shoved under a rotten tarp between the fence and the garage." The two men went down the basement stairs and into the second room, where Billy placed the boom box under the conduit pipe.

"You see," Billy said, "the box has blood spatters."

Butch knelt to look more closely, his knees cracking. "You figure Darren was standing on this when he was bleeding? Before he was hanged?"

Billy didn't answer immediately. He pulled out the Ziploc containing the broken piece of black plastic. With his gloved fingers, he lifted the piece out of the Ziploc, knelt beside Butch, and placed the broken knob onto the front of the boom box. "Fits," said Billy. "Can we assume the box tipped over at one point during the ritual? It seems to explain, at least, that the boy could've stood on this box. The blood pattern here leads me to assume this. When you lift the box up. . . ." Billy raised the boom box from the centre of the circle. "You can see the floor below has no blood pattern."

Butch coughed. "But the candles were clean. So was the book. Doesn't sit together. If you're cutting up a kid, lighting candles, and chanting with a Satanic bible, seems to me the blood would've spilled around on everything. We didn't find any rags in the garbage cans. I can't figure it."

Billy stood up. "I have to join you on that, Butch."

Butch handed the broken piece of plastic back to Billy and lifted up the boom box.

As the two men got upstairs, young Sergeant Royce was walking in the front door. "Good timing, Royce," Billy said. "I want you to seal the house and stay here until Butch and I can get an overnight arranged."

Butch's cell phone twittered. He unstrapped it from his belt and raised it to his ear. "Shoot. Yes, Dodd, I do." Butch listened impatiently before clicking off.

"Sheree Lynn and Mucklowe finished their interviews," he then said to Billy. "Johnson talked to Mucklowe's landlord. The man said he saw Randy and Sheree Lynn this morning on their way out."

Billy nodded.

"We need to keep this place off limits as much as we can. Butch, you've got to assign a night watch to relieve Royce. With a killer running loose, you never know if a site will be tampered with, especially if the press and the TV get a whiff of what's happened."

"Jesus." Butch wiped his mouth.

"And quirk number two, Butch. Darren's clothes."

"Yeah, I know."

"They are evidence. Royce, once we've gone and you've sealed doors and put up tape, go around the yards near here and look in garbage cans. Look under hedges. Keep your eyes peeled for pieces of clothing. Especially outer clothing. Killers sometimes steal underwear but toss away other bits they don't want."

Royce smiled. "I'll go as soon as I can, Inspector."

"Butch and I will be down at the station."

Butch and Billy left the sergeant standing in the front hall. They walked to the cruiser carrying the knife and the blood-spattered boom box in two Ziplocs. Billy opened the passenger door and placed the two objects on the floor behind his seat. As Butch spoke to Dodd a second time, Billy jotted down the location of the knife and the boom box and the impressions he'd had about the blood spatters on the box and the basement floor.

It was hot and bright, and the sun sharpened the shadows of the trees overhanging the sidewalks. A crest of white cloud was building in the west over the distant Porcupine Hills. Butch pressed open the glove compartment, found a package of gum, and handed a stick to Billy.

"No thanks."

"What are you thinking, buddy?"

"You and I have to keep close guard, Butch. That early morning phone call to Sheree Lynn is key. So are Darren's clothes. Keep everybody working hard on this. I hope you can find staff for what may come up."

"Hell, I hope so, too."

The white porcelain edge of the toilet bowl felt cool to his touch. Getting up, Justin Moore washed his mouth out and stared at his mussed hair in the wooden-framed mirror over his bathroom sink. He could hear the words of his ex-girlfriend Karen. "You've always been lucky, Justin. Good grades, good looks. But you're selfish. All you ever think about is what *you* want. Someday, you're going to hurt yourself bad." True, Justin thought. But lucky? Him? He wasn't so sure. She was no longer there when he needed her, and he wasn't certain which pain was sharpest — his yearning for Karen or his terror of Yianni Pappas.

With his stomach settling, Justin walked back into his bedroom. The room housed an oak dresser and a large computer table. Beside his bed was his backpack, ready for the dig Professor Mucklowe had arranged for the summer semester. Today would go down in the history of his life as Doomsday. He always thought of himself as a man in control. As a man of decision. But all that had risen in smoke as if he'd purposely torched his own life.

Justin's stomach heaved again. He hauled in breath to calm the spasms. His mind ran in a maze of questions and names. Who could he call for a loan? So far, every attempt had failed. On his way home, Justin had gone to the bank. The manager had welcomed him at first, but had pointed out that collateral was needed for a loan over five thousand. Justin then had driven to his former high school. He'd wondered if any of his old teachers might help him out. But who?

Now, with his pockets still empty, Justin found himself standing in his mother's room. He opened her closet and rummaged through the albums and boxes on the floor. Did she have any valuables he could pawn? He'd pay her back. She'd understand. The closet gave up nothing but the smell of leather and a faint hint of her perfume. To the left of her bed was his father's chest of drawers. Justin rifled through them. He pulled back the mirror over his mother's vanity table. Did she hide money behind there? All her jewels had been sold last Christmas. She hadn't gotten much for them.

Then he remembered. He dashed down the stairs into the den and tore open the cabinet where his father used to store his golf balls. A small box with a red tassel sat behind a pile of yellowing golf magazines.

Justin pulled it open.

"A ten. That's it?"

He tossed the box onto the floor and threw himself on the couch. The world conspired against him. The silver in the cabinets wouldn't fetch much. He couldn't sell the furniture. "Don't panic," he said to himself.

He went outside to the garage. It was an old wooden structure with a swinging door. At least in here, he thought, I can feel safe. Here was his father's old workbench. His gardening apron. Justin picked the apron up and hugged it, its earthy fragrance rising to his nose. He imagined Yianni in a bathing suit. Hairy, skinny legs, like a spider's. Justin started to laugh, but he stopped. Yianni hadn't been joking. *What am I going to do?* He prayed under his breath to his father, the apron like a security blanket. *What am I going to do?*

SUNDAY, JUNE 30

Crossing the border into the U.S. at Chief Mountain customs wasn't going as easy as Randy Mucklowe had hoped. At 8:10 on this warm morning, two U.S. officials wearing green short-sleeve shirts and brown flat-brimmed ranger hats were doing a thorough search of Mucklowe's old, cream-coloured Chevy van. Everything seemed normal when they began the standard interview, a procedure Randy knew well from frequent crossings and one that usually took no more than a few minutes. Chief Mountain customs was an outpost on the world's longest undefended border, in the middle of Waterton-Glacier International Peace Park. It was a summer crossing for tourist buses going from Waterton Lakes on the Canadian side to the U.S. parks of Glacier and East Glacier. Fir and pine forests lined the two-lane blacktop leading to the twin log cabin border stations that sat surrounded by the soaring peaks of the Rockies. The first U.S. border guard Randy spoke to, as he pulled his van in to the station, asked for his driver's licence. In an automatic and bored voice, he wanted to know the purpose of Randy's visit. Randy explained he was finalizing details for an archaeological dig on Indian land. The excavation was on shale scree below the northwest face of Chief Mountain. The guard immediately demanded to see Randy's permission papers.

"It was all arranged through the band council, officer," Randy explained.

But the guard hesitated. He broke into a nervous smile and signalled to another guard who was standing inside the border station office. The second guard strolled out, and the two of them spoke briefly in low voices, looking over Randy's documents. Then they insisted on a vehicle search. "We need to see your dig tools, Professor," one guard explained. "The Indian Act allows for certain kinds of shovels and picks but not others."

Randy sighed, then complied. Reluctantly he pulled out the spare tire in the back of the van and helped the guards unwrap the tarps around the steel spades and mesh sifting screens. Both men consulted a sheet with official numbers and diagrams. They looked closely at the mesh. They picked up and studied the blades of the shovels. Randy knew they were going through an act; neither could tell a shovel from a pick-axe. But federal U.S. law required them to cross-examine all Canadians coming into the States to do work on federal Indian land. Randy knew this, but sighed again. This would surely create complications later on, especially with his new plans. But he wouldn't let himself think about that right now.

"Thank you, sir," a guard said. "We'll need to run a check on the computer. It won't take a moment."

Randy started loading his gear.

"Morning, prof," a voice said from behind.

Randy turned to see a tall thin woman with blonde hair striding towards him. She wore a brown shirt and long pants. On her lapel glowed a red maple leaf pin. Her hat was the standard ranger model of the Canadian border guard. She came up to Randy from the station on the Canadian side, not twenty feet away.

"Margie!"

"The boys giving you a hard time?"

"You know. How are you?"

"Good. You on a new dig this summer?"

"Up at the Chief. Working a vision quest site. Just a week. I hope my comings and goings won't take this much time later on. I've got a crew of three students with me."

"What you looking for?"

"Skulls, burial items, prayer gifts. Site's been in use for over three hundred years. The Browning Museum is interested in the artifacts. *If we find any.* I've always wanted to do the Chief site, but for years the band in Browning wouldn't authorize it."

"You're looking fit, Randy. You and Connie still doing fine?"

Randy paused. He decided not to tell the truth. Margie didn't need to know about Connie and the divorce and. . . .

"Fine. Good. How come this border crossing's getting so sticky? Used to be so soft."

"Drugs, Randy. And some artifact smuggling. There was that Indian mask heist down at Missoula last fall. Looks like they may still be in the country. We've almost given up looking for them. Rumour was they might cross the border here or farther east. But lately, not much has been going through here but RVs and the gear jammer buses from Glacier."

"Well, you'll be seeing me on and off for the next few days. What shifts do you do, by the way?"

"Usually evenings. My supervisor put me on this morning as extra since they're expecting a lot of traffic, being the first big summer weekend."

"Do you need me to give you a list of the names of my students? I have the forms." Randy lifted his briefcase from the front seat of the van and snapped it open. He pulled out a sheet with the names of three students: Justin Moore, Cara Simonds, and David Home. Other papers included their passport numbers, student cards, and dig permit information.

"I can take it now if you want, prof. But there's no rush till we see you. You'll find it a lot easier coming back to Canada since we know who you are and the work you're doing."

"Thanks, Margie. I should be en route by now. I've got a meeting with Sam Heavy Hand from Browning in the next hour, and I also have to get back to the university to catch up on office duties."

Margie smiled, took the paper from Randy, and headed back towards the Canadian side of the border. Randy shut his briefcase and slid it onto the front seat just as the two U.S. border guards re-emerged.

They approached and handed him his permission papers and told him he was free to proceed.

"Thanks, officers," Randy said, knowing that a polite and obedient face gave you credit with men such as these.

Randy finished packing the van, folding the tarps over the shovels and mesh screens. He stood for a moment and ran over the words he would use to tell Sam about what happened. He wanted to make sure his partner understood the difficulty. He wanted to make sure Sam would trust him, especially since he now had plans that did not include Sam.

By 8:32, Randy was on the road again, driving south to Babb, Montana. He felt weary. His mind kept harping on the incident at the border and what Margie had said about the heist of the Indian masks. He and Sam had been right — lying low for a year had been a good idea. Still, Randy was worried. Would the Canadians search him every time he crossed back into Waterton Lakes after a day's digging? His plans were based on the crossing being hassle-free.

As he drove into the morning sun, Randy tried to encourage positive thoughts. He'd been a respected archaeologist for eighteen years. Digging up the earth of the Porcupine Hills and the foothills near the Rockies had been his principal joy. A year ago he published his fifteenth article on the prehistory of the Kootenay peoples. Before that, he had been well known for excavating Blackfoot campsites and buffalo corrals, and interpreting tipi rings. He owned rare amulets and obsidian arrowheads, and he was one of the few men in his field who could locate the legendary Flathead Pass, a trail walked for thousands of years by local tribes long before Columbus sailed west.

Yet the sight of the shimmering blacktop forced him to wonder if his reputation was worth anything now. Why was he staking his future on such a risky venture? Driving into Montana to cut a deal in a hole like Babb? It was nothing more than a cluster of rundown buildings huddling by highway 464 leading into the Logan Pass. Even thinking about Sheree Lynn and the good things they had together did not comfort him. At least she was loving enough to let him go his own way. Yet

Randy knew he must be cautious. *Never tell a woman everything.* Sheree didn't think his plan would work. Could she really be trusted? She'd done all right in the last twenty-four hours, but why had she hugged that supercilious detective? No way she could win him over. That bloody ethnic dick suspected her of criminal negligence. *Go easy, easy.* Randy hated it when his jealousy taunted him. It was true: Sheree could blow the plan if she got emotional. *If all goes smoothly, we can move out of that smelly Satan House.* Randy smirked. He was on the brink. Soon, he figured, his money worries would evaporate. And Darren Riegert? The image of his lifeless body in that dank basement rose in his mind, but he refused to look at it. "To hell with him," he said.

He drove on. Catbirds and brown thrashers arose from the warm fallow grass. They flitted into groves of diamond willow that grew in the hollows between the landscape's shallow rises. Randy had killed a couple of meadow mice, which had run faster than gunshot out from the deep scrub by the mountain highway. Sam Heavy Hand would've told him that killing them was a good thing. Sparrow hawks would feed the carcasses to their young.

Turning south, Randy had a cold feeling, a sudden premonition of doom. Then Babb appeared in the distance. Eventually Randy pulled into a parking lot, shut off the engine, and locked up. The air was warm and fragrant with pine as he walked into the smoky Horseshoe Bar. He looked at his watch: 8:55. He ordered a Coors Light, grabbed a stool, and took a deep haul on the cool liquid, debating whether he should bum a Marlboro from the bartender, a three-hundred-pound man called Babe. Sam Heavy Hand was late, as usual. Did he have them with him? Was there going to be an argument like last time? *On the brink.* And nowhere to go but on a student dig and maybe, if Randy played his cards right, well. . . . *Maybe* was all he would dare think. He remembered what his grandmother used to say: "Don't write your history 'til it's happened. Then change what you want to suit yourself." More than once he'd rewritten his history, and where had it got him? He'd lost his wife, his house. He'd been caught with "miscatalogued" artifacts from the dig on the Belly River two years back, screwing up forever his contacts with the prestigious Glenbow Museum in Calgary, a place where his reputation had been platinum-plated. He'd worked hard. He'd gambled hard. Life had made him some enemies. But he sure didn't want to spend the next twenty years paying loan interest and bickering with his ex-wife.

Leaning back from the bar, he recognized Sam Heavy Hand's huge frame coming towards him through the smoky air. Greed and anger were Sam's middle names. He'd been a good friend years ago. Randy had liked Sam's love of the outdoors, his belief in his people and their lost past. But ever since Sam had been in the Montana state pen for arson and robbery, ever since he'd started in on booze again and gone to work for his sister, Rita, he had turned against his old ways. All he wanted these days was cash. The only things Sam cared about now were new rifles, the half-ton he wanted to buy, and going to Las Vegas to win at blackjack.

"You ready?"

Sam's voice lay low in his throat. He was wearing a new Stetson, a jean jacket, and a pair of torn Levis. Randy paid for his Coors, nodded to Babe, then followed Sam out the side door of the bar and up a shale bank into a low grove of aspens. By the side road, he saw Sam's blue Ford half-ton. A tarp was thrown over the bed, and Sam's old hound, Crow, was sleeping on it. At the cab, Sam unlocked the door and hauled out a large canvas suitcase. He shut the door and signalled to Randy to follow. Randy waited a moment before going along behind, like they had arranged. Just in case anyone — a kid, Babe, a state police officer — might be watching from the distance.

Randy walked alone, scanning his mind for the words. His eyes squinted in the morning light as he followed Sam up the hill into a woodlot of cottonwoods and birches, then down into a gully cut by a creek running over blue-streaked boulders.

Sam sat under a birch. He pulled out a key from his jean pocket and unlocked the suitcase. Carefully and slowly he lifted the lid. Randy became nervous. He leaned in close.

Out of the suitcase's gloom shone the golden eyes, the thin pearl mouths. Each mask was no larger than a man's hand. They were flat, like plates, the features embossed and emblematic as if they had been made not to be worn but to be displayed in some kind of ritual. Randy picked one up. It was as light as a piece of paper. And as beautiful as he remembered from last October.

"You satisfied? I'll bring 'em up to Chief Mountain. To your dig. Just like we agreed. Meet you at the site after lunch. Then we'll take 'em over the border that same evening in your van. With you and your crew of students. It's such a perfect cover, right? Who'd suspect a famous professor? So clean and innocent. No one'll bother to check. I'll come behind, in the truck. You still agree?"

"I went through that crossing this morning. Your fed boys searched the van top to bottom. Made me unwrap all the tools."

"Good for them. Doing their job for once. So what?"

Randy sighed and gathered his patience.

"We should wait a couple of days so they can get to know us."

"Fuck, no. That won't make no difference. Chief Mountain's a soft crossing. Always has been. You keep puttin' this off. You keep wantin'. . . ."

"I want it to go right, that's all. We agreed we'd be careful. You're the one, Sam, who said we should lie low. We could've taken them over last fall."

"With every state trooper chasing our ass? You and your fuckin' dealer held us up. You went and talked to him, and he said we gotta wait till he gets the cash. What kind of dealer is that?"

"Sam, you don't know anything about that end, so shut up. Robert Lau is reliable, trust me."

"Trust is a big word, Randy." Sam stood up. He lit a cigarette.

Randy didn't like it when Sam stood to smoke. The last two times they got together, Sam always wanted to change things. At first, he wanted a bigger share of the money. Then he wanted to sell the masks to a local rancher for a third of the price Robert Lau was offering. Randy knew he had to change his own plan. Why trust Sam? Possession is nine-tenths of the law after all. Sam stubbed out his half-smoked cigarette and sat down again. Randy could tell Sam was ready to make an announcement. "I'm coming over with you. I decided I wanna come out to the coast with you, too. To make sure I get my share."

"What?"

"Forty, sixty. Sixty percent for me for stealin' 'em. Forty percent for you for settin' up the dealer."

"Yes, and I go to the dealer alone, as we agreed. Alone!"

"Old Sam not so slow, Randy. Me and you both want the cash. I gotta make sure I get my cut."

"No way, Sam." Randy walked into the grove of trees and stood alone, silent, with his hands on his hips. "Listen," he said, turning back. "I trusted you for six months to hold on to those masks. Now you have to let me sell them and carry back the cash. If you come, Lau will get spooked. He's a fussy man, doesn't like people breathing down his neck."

"Fuck what he likes. I'm comin'. I can sleep in my truck at your place in Waterton. I can pretend to guide you and your crew while you do the dig. I know the site. My people love the site, and I wanna protect it. We'll hide the masks in your cabin. On Saturday we fly out to the coast, get our cash, kiss Lau goodbye, and come home rich people."

"Either I go alone, or the whole deal's off."

Sam broke into a belly laugh. "Don't fuck with me, Randy. You're pantin' to get your hands on these little gold buggers. Look, we go, you meet him in the lobby of the hotel or somethin', say you need to feel out in the open. I watch you two, make sure no shit goes down, what's the big fuckin' deal?"

Randy was about to insist again when Sam slapped his thigh, stood, and closed the suitcase.

"I'll take these now. I stole 'em, I'm the one gets caught, I go to the state pen. You get to write your article on the dig. I gotta appreciate that. I gotta figure, too, that maybe you run off with my money."

Randy knew he was cornered. "Fine. Okay. So explain to me how we're going to get these over the border, when you've got them glued to your hip day and night?"

"Simple. I bring 'em to the site, here in Montana, just like we said."

"Okay. But for Christ's sake don't do what you did last time. Say you're coming, then you don't show up for a day or two. I am still responsible for three students, so this dig goes right to rule. I don't want any excuses about how you got drunk or how you're on Indian time."

"That's Native time, old friend. We're Natives now, Randy. And don't you fuckin' forget it."

Randy could see his partner's face flushing red with anger.

"Let's go over what we have to do one more time. Please."

"I come, like I said. To the site. You dig. Remember, we will be on sacred earth, so no shitting, no smoking. Understand? I drink some beer. I work on your van, but really what I do is hide the masks. I bring along some black garbage bags. I wrap up the masks in the plastic, see? I stuff 'em around the rim of your spare tire. Your students think, hey, what a nice guy. Good worker. He likes Randy. We drive to the border crossing. We shoot the shit with the guards. A guard takes a quick peek, what does he see? A spare tire, some plastic. Nothin' else. We cross the border into Canada, out of Montana, we get to your cabin, we got ourselves a fortune."

"I'm not happy, Sam."

"You will be."

Billy woke at 6:30 and took a walk. He heard the phone ringing as he crossed the yard through the wild spear grass, and he had to sprint to the porch, slapping open the screen door in front of him.

"It's me, buddy."

"Butch?"

"Yeah. I need to see you. How 'bout I take my Sunday drive out to your spread, and we can shoot the breeze?"

"Sounds fine. I get the feeling something's happened."

"Yeah. Something in the shape of an asshole with a need to smash up property."

"How long will you be? I can whip up some waffles."

"As fast as my cruiser can go at the speed limit."

Billy was setting coffee mugs on the porch table when Butch's cruiser turned into the yard. A meadowlark sang overhead as the dust settled. After breakfast, Butch told Billy the whole story as the sun played shadow tag on the butte beyond.

"We're not sure who it was. Snuck in through a back window. Smashed up Sheree's bedroom and stole some of her things. I think it was Mr. Ponytail, Woody. He's got a big chip on his shoulder, and he doesn't have a lot of polite things to say about Sheree Lynn."

"Sergeant Royce can't ID him?"

"The guy had pantyhose pulled down to his Adam's apple. Royce ended up with a black eye."

"How?"

"A plate got thrown at him during the chase."

"Any witnesses? Anyone see a man with pantyhose on his head running down the street?"

"Not so far."

Butch pulled a cell phone with a leather case out of his right pocket. "Here's a present for you, courtesy of city hall."

"Morning, Dodd," Billy said, trying out the new unit. He and Butch were now in the cruiser heading down the concession road towards Lethbridge. "I need you to get over to Randy Mucklowe's and pick up the professor and Miss Bird. Tell them about the break-in. Warn her there's a mess. I need to find out what's missing and maybe some lead as to who did it. Then I want you back on the files. Dig up anything on Keeler. Yes, Woody. Did he make a statement yesterday, by the way? Look up theft, any data on vagrancy, check arrest records going back ten years."

Out at the junction of Highway 3, Butch made the eastern turn into the fast lane and cruised the rim overlooking the Belly River valley. After twenty-five minutes, the two men reached the Lethbridge city limits. The cruiser crossed Oldman River, and Billy spotted two herons flying above the tops of the cottonwoods in Indian Battle Park. On Ashmead, Butch pulled up to Satan House. Dodd was on the front steps waiting with Sheree Lynn Bird.

"Morning, Miss Bird," Billy said. He reached out and shook her hand.

"Randy's in Montana this morning, Inspector. Working on his dig site plans." Sheree Lynn looked drawn.

"I'm sorry we had to bring you back here on Sunday," said Butch, climbing the front steps and opening the door. In the front hall was the chair where Sergeant Royce had spent part of the night on duty.

"Oh, God." Sheree Lynn raised her hands to her mouth when she saw the tumbled mess in her bedroom.

Billy fumbled for a second. "I am sorry. We had a night watch, and our sergeant had sealed the place, but. . . ."

"It doesn't matter."

"Take your time, Sheree," said Billy. "Go in slowly, look around, tell us what's gone."

Constable Gloria Johnson was at Sheree Lynn's dressing table dusting for prints. "Morning," she said.

The bed had been pulled apart. A candle lay broken on the floor by the window. All the brushes and perfumes on the dressing table had been thrown to the floor. There was broken red glass by the doorway.

"I can't really tell, Chief," Sheree Lynn whispered. She turned and came back to the doorway. "Maybe a book or a brush."

"Did any of the patients you counselled at social services ever do anything like this, Sheree?" asked Billy.

"No."

"You have any idea who might have done this?"

"Oh, I could guess. Some of the parents — like Cody's mom — have claimed I was trying to steal their kids from them. Who knows?"

"I've found no evidence of prints so far, sir," said Johnson.

"So all we have is guesswork here," Billy added.

Sheree shrugged. "No matter," she said. "At least the person didn't harm anyone." She started to cry and covered her face.

Billy handed her a tissue from his pocket.

"Thanks."

Downstairs, Billy inspected the back window, where the intruder had entered Satan House. He went out on the porch steps and gazed around, letting his eye fall on the area surrounding the window and the entrance to the house. He walked to the bottom of the steps and knelt.

A moment later, Sheree Lynn came and stood on the top step. "What is it?"

Billy raised his hand. "Call Butch to come here, will you, Sheree?"

Butch came with a Ziploc already open. "What'd you find?"

Reaching down, Billy folded the baggie over the thumb and pointer finger of his right hand and picked up a broken red elastic band. He folded the Ziploc so that the band fell down inside, then sealed the edge.

"Won't hurt to call on Woody this morning," grimaced Butch.

"You think this investigation will take a while?" Sheree sounded anxious.

"I'll tell you this," answered Billy, his voice betraying frustration. "The longer we take, the harder it is to piece together the puzzle. We're only one day into the investigation, and all we've got is a phone call and a caller who may know the person or persons responsible for hurting Darren. So far, we're still lacking firm leads. And witnesses."

As Billy knew only too well, the crime scene is the key to an investigation. Evidence leads to conviction; fitting clues together presents a logic of motive, opportunity, and means. It wasn't customary for him to give out details of the investigation to those who, for one reason or another, could be tagged as potential suspects. But then he'd often found that sharing selected information could prompt something of use, a hint, an attitude in the respondent, a revelation to be stored away for future consideration.

Billy noticed that Sheree Lynn blinked as if she'd felt a sudden pain.

"Inspector, I want out of this whole mess. I hope you can clear this up soon, and we can let Cody and Darren rest in peace."

"If we need you, we'll contact you at Randy's. Butch and I can give you a lift back now."

En route, Billy talked to Sheree Lynn, who sat beside him in the cruiser's back seat.

"There's got to be a motive for this killing," said Billy. "Somebody had a big need to hurt that boy. Is there anybody you know of who'd want to do that?"

"You asked me that already, Inspector," replied Sheree Lynn.

"What about Woody? What do you know about him?"

"He drank. He beat up Darren once. With a rope. He admitted it the time Children's Aid sent me over to the house to meet with Sharon. He was an angry man. Used to hitting people. The agency ran a check on him, but only in terms of complaints concerning family matters. We didn't find anything. Sharon told me Woody had been poor, brought up on a dryland farm near the Peigan reserve. I never saw him outside of the social services meetings I'd arranged with him."

"Can you think of any boys Darren's age, anyone who was jealous of him, or may have picked on him?"

"Jealous? There was Blayne Morton, I suppose."

"Was he part of a group with Cody Schow?"

"No. Just the opposite. Blayne was the outsider. I remember Darren told me about him a couple of times. I only saw Blayne once, standing out on the street in front of the house on Ashmead. He was a big kid. Darren was scared of him. He and Cody didn't like the boy much, and I think Cody once had a fight with him at school. Blayne often pestered Darren, always wanting to take his picture."

"You never spoke to Blayne?"

"No, Inspector."

"He never came into the house?"

"Not that I know of."

"Do you think he knew much about you? I mean, did he know where you went, what your phone number was? I'm fishing here. Could Blayne be the one who called you yesterday?"

"He may have gotten my — our numbers — from Darren. Who knows?"

They drove on in silence. Billy waited to see if Sheree might add more. In his experience, silence was a great motivator. Talkers abhor a vacuum.

But Sheree sat with her eyes down, fatigue turning her features pale.

The cruiser crossed the river and ended up in a housing development near the university grounds. Billy made a mental note of the apartment building where Randy lived. It was not impressive. He expected a professor to have a more fashionable address. "Randy rents here, Sheree?"

"Alimony, Inspector. Humbles a man's setting."

Butch dropped Sheree Lynn at Mucklowe's, then drove back across the river.

"Royce find any trace of Darren's clothes?"

"Nada. He was in pain after the plate-tossing incident and called in to dispatch for backup. I'll send him out later."

"The sooner the better, Butch."

"I'm running, buddy. As best as I can."

"We can't stop, not even for a breath. Killers who smash up houses, I figure, are on a roll. Darren's hanging and this incident are making me feel uneasy. I want you to get a team of sergeants on call for twenty-four hours. We need backup for Royce and Dodd."

Butch nodded and drove in silence up to Balham Street, where he parked the cruiser two hundred yards down from Dodd's unmarked car. He phoned Dodd, car to car, and told him that he and Billy would take over. Dodd waved, and Billy looked carefully at the small bungalow rented by Sharon Riegert. It needed paint, the yard was full of shaggy crabgrass. A broken fence sagged against both sides of the house.

"You figure Woody will be here? Not at his own place?"

"It's a hunch, Butch. I bet the two of them are lying low together, considering yesterday's events."

Butch called Dodd and handed the phone to Billy. "Dodd, go over to the Schow home now. Get the address from headquarters. Talk to Cody's mother, if she's sober. And to anyone around who might be nosy enough to keep tabs on the woman. Find out where she was last night. And push her, if you have to. Also call that junior high counsellor, Barnes, and see if he can locate a kid called Blayne Morton."

Billy hung up. He got out and walked behind as Butch sauntered up to the Riegert bungalow's front door. Chief Bochansky did not carry a weapon. But Billy insisted he phone the station to have a constable come by in case of trouble. Billy wasn't so sure they'd need backup. Yet, with a man like Woody, a gun was not out of the question. Woody could be sitting waiting for them, a rifle loaded to blast through a front window.

Butch knocked.

"Ya? It's open."

Butch pushed the door slowly and stepped to the side. Billy stood opposite him.

"Come in, boys." The voice was slurred. Butch peeked into a room darkened by a bedsheet pinned up over the front window. There was a smell of beer and fried food. Woody Keeler was standing in his shorts, holding a beer can, his shirt off, his feet bare. His hair was tied back. The doorway he stood in was lit from behind by a naked yellow bulb hanging from the ceiling of the kitchen. "Whad you after?"

Butch walked in, showed his badge, and told Woody why the two of them had driven over. Woody laughed. He turned and walked through the kitchen and went through a door leading to an open patch of unmowed lawn. He threw himself into a plastic lawn chair and raised his chin.

"You want to talk to me, Chief, you gotta come out here to do it."

Butch sighed. "Wait here, Billy. I'll handle this."

Sharon Riegert came through the doorway dressed in a long pink bathrobe. Her hair was matted and her face puffy. "What is this?" she said, her voice gravelly.

"We came here to talk to your boyfriend, Mrs. Riegert."

"About what?"

Sharon edged her way into the front room and lowered herself onto a couch covered with fake satin pillows and a giant pink dog. She grasped the dog to her chest, its plastic eyes the size of saucers. Billy thought the toy looked more frightening than cute.

"Where was Woody last night between ten and four in the morning?"

"How should I know?"

"Does he live here with you?"

"On and off. So what? What'd he do anyhow?"

"Were you here last night, Sharon?"

"Course. Where else would I be?"

She rubbed her hand across her nose.

"I wonder if you could help me, Sharon?"

"You sure are polite for a policeman. Whad you say your name was?"

"Yamamoto. Billy Yam. . . ."

"You a Chink or somethin'?"

"Japanese."

Billy watched her. She was half asleep. Hungover. Her eyes were glazed. On her hands were scratches as if she'd been mauled by a cat. He looked up. Through the far doorway, Butch was leaning down to talk to Keeler. Butch's face was contorted, his mouth moving fast. Woody was sitting stiff and still as if he'd been plastered to the chair.

"Woody went out," Sharon said. "He went out, then he came back in. I was tired. I don't know when. I don't know when."

"I am sorry about your son, Sharon. I want to find out who hurt him."

"You do?" Sharon Riegert looked up.

Billy had seen faces ravaged by grief before. They took on a softer look somehow. The eyes were always narrow as if too much light, or too much terrible truth, might blind them.

"She did it. That witch. Bird. She hurt my boy. He shoulda never been there in that house."

"Why would she hurt him, Sharon?"

"How do I know? She did, that's all. How come he was there in that basement?" She looked as if she wanted to cry but was too exhausted.

"Did you know Cody Schow?"

"Stupid boy. I didn't like him. Always sassing me. I told Darren, 'Don't ya go with him. He's shit,' I said. I told him not to go or he'd get a lickin'."

"What were your son's other friends like, Sharon?"

"What friends? I don't know. Just that fat kid with the camera."

"Do you remember his name?"

"Ya. You think I'm stupid? Blayne. He was hanging around here a lot. Always outside waitin' for Darren. I didn't know if he was pickin' on him or what. Darren sometimes went out with him somewhere."

"What kind of camera was it?"

"Black. Kinda old-fashioned. The front popped out. I think it was one of them where you get the picture quick, you know. . . ."

"Polaroid."

"I don't know, maybe. I didn't like him."

"Did he ever give any pictures to Darren? Did you ever see any?"

"Course."

Sharon struggled up from the satin pillows. "Come 'ere," she said. Billy followed her into a closet-like space off the living room. Dark cloth hung over the single window. A narrow bed had rumpled blue sheets. Posters of Marilyn Manson and Metallica were attached to the walls with staples. Sharon lifted a red notebook from a table beside the bed. She slapped it open, her hand smacking the paper. Two Polaroids were stuck in the back of the notebook. "I found these in the garbage a few days ago. Maybe a week or so. I thought Darren lost them, so I put 'em back in his schoolbook. You can have 'em. He don't need them." She dropped the notebook, covered her face with her left hand, and with the right thrust the two pictures at Billy.

"Can you remember what Darren was wearing on Friday?"

"No. Just his normal clothes."

"Did he wear jeans, a jacket, boots?"

"Sort of. I mean, he liked black. I guess it was a black shirt and jeans. Why?"

"We're still looking for his clothes, Mrs. Riegert. They may help us find the person who hurt Darren."

Sharon Riegert raised her hands. "I don't wanta hear." Quickly, she left the room.

Billy examined the photos; one showed a large red Valentine box of chocolates; the other was a picture of Darren, his eyes half closed, wearing a leather jacket. Billy looked in the closet and found only rumpled shirts and underwear. He bent down and scanned the floor under the bed, finding nothing. Where was the leather jacket? Billy returned to the living room. Sharon was wiping her eyes and holding the stuffed dog to her chest.

"May I keep these for a while, Sharon?"

"You can have them all you want."

"Do you know where Darren's jacket is?"

Sharon looked at the Polaroid and shrugged. Billy glanced towards the front door. A row of coat hooks held cloth jackets and a raincoat.

"Did Woody ever hurt Darren?"

"No. Okay, maybe he hit him once. I don't remember. It didn't mean nothing."

"Did Darren ever say Blayne hurt him? Or wanted to hurt him?"

"He never talked to me about the fat kid. I just saw them once in a while, that's all."

Butch came into the room. Woody was right behind him, wearing a drunken grin.

"You got nothing on me, Chief. Ask her. Ask her where I was!"

Sharon stood up. She began to shake.

"I didn't tell him nothin', Woody! I said ya went out for a little while. That's all. I was in bed. I was tired, I didn't. . . ."

"It's all right, Sharon," said Butch, toning his voice to sound calm.

"You men want a beer or somethin'?" Woody laughed.

"Come on, Billy. Good day, folks," said Butch.

"Mind you shut the door nice, now," cried Woody.

Back in the cruiser, Butch lit up.

"Nothing," said Butch. "Of course. We'd need a warrant to search the place. But who knows? He may have dumped anything he had, if he was there. But I got a bad itch in my armpit, and when I itch about someone I'm usually right."

"Was he wearing an elastic band in his hair?"

"Yeah. Bright red."

"She told me a little herself. Calls Sheree Lynn Bird a witch. But better, she said Blayne Morton had been around the house. That he had a camera. She gave me these."

Billy showed Butch the photos. "Look at the back of the one with the Valentine."

Butch read out loud: " 'Meet Me at Gym Later, or Else.' "

"Sound like a threat to you?"

"We got us a sweetheart. Can't wait to meet him."

"Sharon didn't know what went on between the two boys. She kept lashing out at Sheree Lynn Bird."

"That's guilt talking, buddy. She's a beater. Sheree was the only loving mother type the kid probably had."

"Perhaps," said Billy. Sheree Lynn Bird brought out a fear, an anger, in these people. Billy wasn't so sure the reactions of these parents could be so easily dismissed.

"Speaking of elastics," he then said, filling up the sudden silence between them. "Let's get the one we found today over to the lab. We might get lucky and find one of Woody's hairs."

Butch stubbed out his cigarette. "I'm pissed off about that bastard."

"Blayne Morton may prove to be a better lead," Billy said. "Two people have given me the impression he was a bully and possessive. And going after Darren."

Butch grinned. "How 'bout on our way to old Hawkes we get a Colombian to go?"

"Mac's is open on Sundays?"

"Buddy, Mac's is always open."

"Hawkes. Reggie Hawkes."

"Billy Yamamoto."

The medical examiner lifted the plastic sheet lying over Darren Riegert's body. The morgue was the same as when Billy had first seen it, but with Hawkes working this Sunday morning, the place took on a more portentous atmosphere. The institutional green of the walls seemed gloomier; the flickering fluorescents lit up surfaces with a harder shine. Even the sickly punch of fresh ammonia was more acrid.

Hawkes pointed to Darren's neck, the skin and part of the muscle layer pulled back like the rind of a peeled orange. He flipped open his forensic report chart. Stapled to the top sheet was an eight-by-ten black-and-white photo of Darren's body hanging by a rope from the conduit pipe in the Satan House basement. In the upper corner of the sheet, Hawkes had circled the lab report number in red ink. He'd also under-lined his full title: Dr. Reginald D. Hawkes, M.D. Ph.D.

"As you can see, gentlemen, comparing the photo taken by the capa-ble Miss Johnson, the ligature bruise on the neck — here and here — is consistent with the angle at which the body was found hanged. See here, as well, the suppressed and crushed bone of what is commonly called the Adam's apple. No finger marks. No concussion, no contusion on the skull. We found a little treasure in the mouth cavity. Lying on the tongue with the boy's blood smeared on one side."

Hawkes picked up a Ziploc. Inside was a stained piece of paper with writing on one side.

"A quote from the book of Daniel: 'Mene Mene Tekel' meaning 'God hath finished it. Thou art found wanting.' A gruesome thought, I'd say." Hawkes sniffed. He spoke with a clipped, high-pitched British accent. Above his thin-lipped mouth he wore an elaborate moustache, waxed and combed, the ends trimmed to two twisted points that curled inward towards his nose. Dapper was the word that leapt into Billy's mind. Hawkes wore a bow tie and a small microphone clipped in a circle around his neck, its grey cord trailing out from under his white lab coat. The mike cord was attached to a long extension, which led to an older-model Sony two-reeler. "Careful," he said to Billy as he started to move around the top end of the gurney. "Don't disturb that cord. If you dis-connect me, I'll have to repeat myself!" He flashed a thin sharp smile.

"First off, now that you've seen the neck, there is not much else I can point out. Time of death was between midnight and 12:20 a.m. The penis, anus, and rectum have not been molested, nor are there signs of other bodily fluids. I can see no evidence of sexual shenanigans with this chap. I had the medic do a quick lab run on the blood sample he'd taken at the site yesterday morning. No drugs of any kind in the bloodstream. The rest of the hospital's toxicology report also confirms no food in the stomach — except a trace of chocolate. Not real chocolate, mind, but the edible oil stuff dressed up to look like the real Swiss. No poison. The back and chest show no marks of beating. The knife cuts were shallow, inflicted with a serrated edge. That knife you dug up in the garden would've done quite nicely. The cuts were made before the body was hanged. The blood spill and flow on the skin tells us that. The streakings here and here and in the palm match the blood sample from the lab. So we can assume the blood on this corpse came from this body."

"Could this be a case of torture?"

"Certainly. Though the cuts were so slight, and the way they were indented here on the chest area, then drawn towards the heart, might imply self-mutilation. Any cut would hurt, though, wouldn't it? I must admit, I am stumped about the twine. It seems somebody tied the boy up after he was cut. After he was dead."

Billy gazed at young Darren's body. "With rigor setting in three to four hours after death, Dr. Hawkes, would it be difficult to tie up a pair of hands in this fashion? From the photo you have there on your lab report, the arms are protruding and the hands oddly stiff. If Darren was tied before he lost consciousness, the hands would look more relaxed; they would hang down, not sit out as they do in the photo."

"And indeed as they do on this gurney, Inspector," answered Hawkes. "This is an odd situation. The tied hands vexed me as well. Which is why I think it occurred post-mortem. Also, I've seen hangings in which a body was hauled up by a rope. A lynching, actually. Many years ago. If this child was lynched, the bruises would've been much broader, the damage to the throat much more severe. The way the rope markings occurred on this cadaver, I'd say the hanging was gentle. The bruise is slighter than I expected when I first saw Johnson's photos. This music player — the boom box — was used as a platform for the hanging, was it?"

"Conjecture only," answered Butch.

"Guesswork," replied Hawkes. "This boy's neck was bruised in a similar fashion to the other case we had last winter. The Cody Schow suicide."

"Thanks, Hawkes," Butch said.

"You related to a chap in Coaldale named Arthur Yamamoto?" Hawkes asked Billy.

"He was my father," answered Billy.

"I read about him a while back in the obituary column. I offer you my condolences. Arthur sold me and my wife bulbs in the spring. He was a fine gardener."

"Thank you," said Billy.

"I don't remember ever meeting you before, Inspector. I assume you're also related to Tosh Yamamoto?"

"My half-brother."

Billy shook Hawkes's ungloved hand. Then he pulled out the Polaroid with the printing on the back and compared the lettering to what he could see of the bloodied note in the bag. The handwriting at a superficial glance did not seem to match. Billy decided to have the note examined and compared to the writing on the Valentine Polaroid. Taking the Ziploc with the found note, he and Butch went back to the office, where Butch pulled out the file photos on Cody Schow. Picking up copies of the recently developed pictures of the Darren Riegert crime site, Butch and Billy spread the two sets of photos on the metal table in the reception room.

"The boom box had blood dripped on its top and back. Maybe it had been under Darren and then, somehow, tipped forward before it was removed from the scene." Billy recalled now how much the boom box had been bothering him. Why had it been hidden in the garden? Its blood splatters — small random round drops — were similar to those found on Darren's boots and on his body. Billy also remembered there were no blood drops on the basement floor under the pipe where the noose had been tied. Had the boom box been used so that Darren could climb on it before he was cut and before the noose was placed around his neck? But he must have been bleeding when he climbed onto the box since there were drops on the top. And why else would the box be in the basement? There had been no tape inside. Had one been removed? The stereo must have been hidden some time after the body had stopped bleeding or there would've been blood spatters on the surface of the concrete.

"Good day." Constable Gloria Johnson was in the doorway of the reception room, hoisting a bag of golf clubs over her shoulder. She wore a red cloth baseball cap and a golf shirt with a silk-screened picture of a flamingo swinging a club. "I dropped in, sir, to tell you the lab is finishing the blood analysis on the boom box and the kitchen knife. I put your elastic band under the 'scope."

"Anything?"

"Dirt, mainly. No strands of hair. No dandruff, no follicles."

"It was a long shot." Billy smiled. "How about prints from last night?"

"Clean. The whole place, including the broken window. No prints on the banisters. I thought I'd take an hour break since it's goin' slow and hit some balls at the driving range. If that's all right? I'll be in my lab office when you need to go over the prints and data from yesterday."

"Thanks, Johnson," Billy said. "Oh, before you leave, do we have a handwriting expert we can call on here in town, or in the precinct?"

"Yes, sir. The horsemen have one at RCMP headquarters."

"On your way to the range, take this Polaroid and this note and see if the expert is there to check them for us. Do we need a request form for that, Butch?"

"Hell, no."

Johnson grinned, took the picture, and left the room. Billy could hear her golf cleats clicking down the hall.

"Chief in here?" It was the dispatch sergeant from the front desk.

"Yes, sergeant. What is it?"

"I've transferred a call, Inspector. A woman is on line 201. She has information on the Riegert case."

Billy picked it up. "Yes. Inspector Billy Yamamoto."

"Mrs. Irene Bourne."

"Yes?"

"Sharon Riegert called me just now and told me about Darren."

"Are you a friend of hers?"

"Heavens, no! I met her once at a teachers-parents night. My daughter knew Darren. I felt I should call you." The voice sounded imperious, nervous. Billy pictured her as tall with a pearl necklace. Irene Bourne's voice continued with a sense of purpose. "I knew about that boy, Cody, from last winter. My daughter told me. She knew him as well, I'm sorry to say. I believe my daughter may know something about Darren."

There was a pause on the line.

"Can you come to our house, Inspector? My husband is ill, recovering from a heart attack, and I can't really leave him."

Before she spoke again, Irene Bourne paused a second time. Billy could hear her cover the speaker end of the phone, muffling her voice as she spoke to someone in the background.

"Emily," she continued, "was calling somebody all day, yesterday, from her room. My husband overheard her on the phone again earlier this morning talking about some friends being together. She used the word *witness*. And now that Riegert woman phones and tells me about her poor son. I thought it was important for the police to know since my Emily knew Darren."

"Thank you, Mrs. Bourne. I can come over right away. I'd like to talk to your daughter."

"She's done nothing wrong, Inspector. She's not a bad girl."

"I understand."

"Please come by all means, but I can't guarantee anything. . . ." She stopped midsentence. "I have to go. We live at 62 Brighton Road."

It was just after noon when Billy drove out alone to Tudor Acres, a large subdivision built on the edge of the coulee looking west towards the Rockies. Surrounded by a low brick wall, the subdivision's entrance was an iron gate that led into a maze of streets, each named after a city in England. Billy found himself driving past two-storey stucco houses with fake timbered fronts and huge two-car garages. The front doors were made of dark oak, and beside each door hung an antique-looking lantern the size of a soccer ball. In the distance, Billy heard the nasal high-pitched motors of lawn mowers and the jubilant voices of children in a playground.

He found 62 Brighton Road with some difficulty. The Bourne house was on a crescent and seemed to exude a smug challenge to visitors. To Billy, it was as if its architecture dared you to enter the false-fronted world of suburban respectability. Much of the yard was concrete drive-way. Two plaster dogs arranged near the front steps looked as if they could be guardians to a castle's entrance.

"Come inside, Inspector. I'll make you a cup of coffee," Irene Bourne said, folded her hands in front of her as if she were in a receiving line, and walked ahead of Billy into a blue-walled family room at the rear of the house. Her icy formality made Billy think she had rehearsed every move — placing a cup on the coffee table, sitting down beside him, laying one hand over the other in her lap. The room smelled of pine air freshener, and on the walls were pictures of her and her husband, of a boat, and of a young girl with long black hair wearing a white floor-length gown.

Irene Bourne placed a plate of shortbread cookies on the table beside Billy's coffee.

"I was looking at your photos. Is that your daughter in the white dress?"

"At her confirmation."

"I keep it there to remind me of happier times," she went on. "It's the nicest picture I have of Emily. Since that picture was taken, we've had some hard luck. Jack suffered a heart attack last fall. And Emily, well, ever since she's been in junior high school, she's been a different girl."

"I am sorry, Mrs. Bourne."

"Thank you, Inspector. I don't think you should have to hear all my tragic tales. I apologize for bringing them up."

"Let's get to Emily. About the phone calls and a possible witness. Do you know what happened to Darren Riegert?"

"Yes, his mother said he was found hanging and cut up in that place downtown the press called Satan House. Knifed was the word she used. Her drinking and neglect did much harm to that boy. I met him once. He seemed very lost, very gentle. I can't picture anyone wanting to hurt him. He was like a pathetic stray cat. I'm sorry, that must sound so callous. These are troubled children, Inspector. My daughter, unfortunately, is one of them. She ran with them, if I can use that expression. What she means about a witness is a mystery to me. This morning was the first I've heard of it, believe me."

Billy sensed suppressed anger in Irene Bourne's voice. She lowered her eyes and unfolded her tense hands.

"Come with me," she said.

Billy followed her into the front hall and up a curving staircase. She stopped by a closed door, beckoned to Billy to sit on a small sofa, then sat on the corner of a polished side table and stared.

"When Darren's mother called, she sounded drunk. She said she was calling everyone who knew Darren. I didn't know she had our number. She said the oddest thing. She said I should see if my daughter was safe. If she was guarded. I thought the woman was raving, quite frankly. When I told Emily Darren had died, she went into a state. She started weeping and yelling. She ran up here, to this room, locked the door, and has been in there ever since. She refuses to come out."

"I can hear you out there, Mother."

Emily's voice seemed to pierce the placid air of the hallway. It was hard and angry. Billy was surprised at its maturity. It sounded more like a woman's voice or a young male's than that of a fourteen-year-old girl.

"I have a police Inspector here, Em. He would like to talk to you."

"You what?" The voice hurled against the closed door. "You called the police?" Emily's voice then broke into a sob.

Irene Bourne stood up. "I have to ask you, Inspector, to accept something. I don't know how much I can help you with Emily. I have tried to speak to her. She's been ill."

"Mother! I can hear you. Stop lying about me."

"She's been ill since last December. Tantrums. Failing at school. Locking herself in her room. She seemed to change right after that boy, Cody Schow, died. I took her to a therapist. But I'm at a loss. I can ask her to open her door, but I'm sure she won't let you in."

"Mother, go away. Leave me alone."

Billy went to the door.

"Emily? My name is Billy Yamamoto. May I come in and talk to you? I want to know about your friend Darren. I need your help."

"Tell my mother to go downstairs."

"Emily!"

"Go, Mother, or I won't open the door."

"I'm sorry, Mrs. Bourne."

Irene Bourne rose and walked down the curved staircase. Billy watched the handle on Emily's bedroom door turn as a key clicked in the lock. Emily stepped back as the door swung open. She was dressed in a white nightgown and looked much as she had in the picture downstairs except for a small black tattoo of a spider on her neck.

"Do you want me to stay out here in the hall, Emily? You can talk to me from there. I can sit here on the sofa if you like."

"I don't want my mother spying on us. Come in."

Billy followed her into a spacious room with a canopy bed and white furniture. The walls in front of him were bare except for a bulletin board covered with photos of kittens and whales and postcards of the Rockies. On a bureau was a photo of Emily and two other girls. When the door was closed, Emily crossed the room and sat on the edge of the bed with her legs up under her nightgown. Billy looked around and was startled by the walls opposite the bed. They were painted black and purple and were covered with posters. It was like seeing the dark side of the moon. The room had two faces, one pristine and girlish, the other Gothic and gloomy.

"You like it?" asked Emily.

"Why have you done it this way?" Billy turned to see Emily's reaction.

"It makes my mother mad. She hates it, but I think it's cool. It's me."

"Have you ever read the *Thanatopsis*?"

"I found it boring. Cody Schow loved it. He said it gave him power."

"You and Cody were friends?"

"I got along with him okay. He was cool and treated me with respect. I don't know what my mother told you or why she invited you here. There is nothing I have to say." Emily's voice had lost its belligerence. She spoke with a firm decisive tone.

"Emily, it's not right to hold back information if there's suspicion of a murder."

"Darren was murdered?"

Emily's manner changed. She covered her face and threw herself onto her pillow. She lay silent for a moment and gave Billy the feeling she was ready to weep and scream and lose control. He stepped forward.

"This morning I saw Darren's body at the morgue, Emily. Somebody had tied up his hands. Someone had been with him in the basement. . . ."

"Stop!" She began to sob.

Billy felt his throat tighten. It had been a while since he'd interviewed someone with such quicksilver emotional reactions. *Calm yourself.* He placed his hands behind his back and raised his eyes and looked hard at the colour of the ceiling. Centring his thoughts, he lowered his voice. "I want you, Emily, to tell me about your phone calls. And what you know about a witness. You can help me and Darren's case a lot if you try to remember."

"Emily?" Irene Bourne's voice flew up the stairs. "Emily, are you all right?"

Emily sprang up. She brushed her wet face with the palm of her right hand.

"Mother, do not butt in. Go away and shut up!"

Billy heard Irene Bourne retreat into the back part of the house.

"Have you got any idea how hard it is to live with my mother?"

Billy remained silent. He waited.

Emily began to shift on the bed. She took in a breath. She looked at Billy, and then she looked away at the window. Her eyes seemed to go blank for a second, and then they refocused.

"I was supposed to be there. That's all. To be *his* witness."

Billy took out his notebook.

"What's that for? What are you doing?"

"I need to write things down, Emily. I need to get things straight."

"Are you serious? Are you trying to show off or something?"

"I'm a police detective, Emily. This is what police detectives do."

"That's cool. I mean it. I mean I saw this stuff on TV. But I didn't know you really did this stuff."

"Why were you supposed to be there, Emily?"

Tears rolled down the girl's face. "Darren and I planned it. He said I could come and watch him. We had a secret. I promised him I'd never tell anyone. I promised. But now what's the use?"

"It's not your fault, Emily."

"Darren begged me not to tell."

"You liked him a lot, didn't you?"

"We were friends. We trusted each other."

"Take the tissue, Emily. Take your time."

"Was Darren shot? Did somebody stab him?"

"It was a hanging, Emily. Somebody cut him with a knife. Not badly. And, as I said, his arms were tied."

"You know, Cody and Darren had this pact. They told me never to tell, and I didn't. They made it at Christmas. The Satanic stuff guided them. They told no one."

"Were you a witness when Cody hanged himself?"

"Darren and I were stoned. We watched him. Darren was so happy for Cody."

"You promise me you're telling the truth, Emily?"

She shot a hard look at Billy.

He quickly reacted and said to her, his voice gentle, "I'm not your mother, Emily. Just tell me the truth."

"I am. I swear." She cried again for a moment, then wiped her eyes.

"Who were you calling on the phone earlier this morning?"

"Did my mother tell you?"

"Yes, Emily. I think she was concerned."

"Sure."

"Who was it, Emily? Please."

"Just Dr. Massenet."

"Who is he?"

"*She.* My therapist. She told me anytime I needed to talk she would listen. Her stupid answering machine was on last night. Most of the night. So I called her this morning, too."

"Did you know Darren had died when you called Dr. Massenet this morning?"

"No."

"Did you tell your therapist about your secret plan? That you were going to be Darren's witness?"

"Sort of. I phoned her. . . . Yes, I told her Darren and I had a secret. That I was going to be his witness."

"What else?"

"I couldn't tell her any more. I was so upset with Darren. He . . . he betrayed me. Dr. Massenet told me I should always share my feelings with her. So I did. I tried to share them."

"Darren betrayed you?"

Emily's mouth tightened. "I don't want to talk about it."

"Is it true you were on the phone all day yesterday?"

"Did my mother tell you that?"

"Yes."

Billy waited, expecting Emily would shut down completely.

"He was supposed to call *me*. He promised to send me the signal. I thought he was still alive and. . . . He didn't want me there." She picked up a pillow from her bed and flung it violently to the floor. "He promised. He said I was the only person he wanted there. I didn't want him to die. But he said it was okay because of the sacred book. He was going to go to Cody. He was going to be at peace."

Emily's eyes blinked furiously. Her breathing sped up, her face flushed. Billy reached out to help her sit forward. He believed she was having a severe anxiety attack, even if her behaviour seemed exaggerated.

"Let me get your mother."

Emily stopped so fast she choked for air, momentarily paralyzed, caught between her own tumultuous feelings and her deep distrust of her mother. Billy held her hand. Regaining composure, Emily lifted her face towards his. "I'm okay. I'm okay." Calmed by her own voice, she backed against the headboard to realign herself.

"You were trying to call Darren, then. Yesterday. All day."

"All day. There was no answer."

"Did you call anyone else?"

"You mean Dr. Massenet? No."

"So, help me, Emily. You knew Darren was planning to go to Satan House some time this weekend to perform a ritual. As Cody had done before him. A suicide ritual."

A look of pained memory crossed Emily's pale face. She seemed all too aware that Billy was speaking of death and loss, of a morbid but romantic game made up by two teenage boys.

"The *Thanatopsis* gave them the idea. Cody planned it." Emily inhaled as if she were suddenly beginning a terrible ascent into a dark forest. Her voice became quieter as she went on, set back into her throat to hide the very sounds she was making. "He undressed and chanted and did a dance, in circles, around one way, then back. Three times, chanting a song."

"Do you remember the words?"

"Funny words. Cody learned them in the book. *Mene Mene Tekel.* Darren made me learn them, too, though I told him I didn't want to be in their ritual. Darren said I could just be a witness. To honour him and Cody and to remember them forever."

Her voice trailed off.

"Do you think this was right, Emily? Do you think it was right to witness this and not tell anyone?"

"I guess."

"When Darren didn't give you the signal, what did you do?"

"I waited. I thought he was going to do it on Friday night, late. So I called his house a few times, but there was no answer. Then it was really late, and I got so scared I called her. Sheree Lynn. I tried to call her at Satan House, but no one picked up the phone. I had to find out if Darren was over there. If Sheree Lynn answered and told me where Darren was, then I'd know things were all right. By the time I phoned her at her stupid boyfriend's place, I was so tired I don't know what I said."

"Did they do it? Did Darren go?"

Emily blinked, and a vacant stare overcame her.

"Did Sheree say anything to you when you finally got hold of her?"

"I don't remember."

"Try, Emily."

"I don't. Honest."

"Did you try to call anyone else this morning?"

"Like who?"

"Any of your friends? Anyone who might have known Darren?"

"No."

"And you didn't know about Darren's death until your mother told you?"

"I didn't believe her at first. I thought she was lying. Till you got here. When you got here, I knew it was true." Emily lapsed again into her vacant stare. She held it for a second before she recovered. "I wish I had known. Really! I can't believe he was murdered."

"Do you know who took this Polaroid, Emily?"

Emily carefully took hold of the picture Billy pulled from his pocket. She stared at the one with Darren in a leather coat. "Can I please have this one? Please?" Emily pressed the picture to her chest.

"Not right now, Emily. I need it as evidence. Do you have any idea who took it?"

"Piggy Blayne Morton."

"Did you know him?"

"I hated him. He picked on Darren all the time. He once said to Darren — right in the hall by home room — he was going to really punish him if he hung out with Cody."

"Did you ever see Blayne hurt Darren? Did he ever say anything else about threatening him?"

"Oh, God. You don't think it was him, do you? Blayne?"

"We don't know, Emily. We have no proof as yet."

Emily seemed to brighten. The idea of Blayne Morton as a killer sharpened her resolve. "Cody told me Blayne was always following Darren. Wouldn't leave him alone. He took that stupid camera everywhere. He was always so mad at everybody. I thought he liked Darren, but Cody said Blayne was calling him names all the time."

"Can I ask you a big favour?"

"You mean like a friend?"

Billy smiled. "Well, no. Like a detective."

Emily's face became curious. She wrinkled her forehead and leaned forward. "Like what?"

"Is that blue book by your table your telephone book? Your private numbers?"

"I never let my mother near it."

"Here's my favour. You can say yes or no. You can choose."

Emily grabbed the book from the table and held it open. "What do you want?" she asked eagerly. Her mood had changed. She was like a child at a party ready to play musical chairs.

"Count out how many private numbers you have. The numbers of your friends."

Emily drew back. "Why?" she asked.

"Please, just count for me. Don't show me, you don't have to show me names."

Emily began flipping the pages. "Eighteen," she said finally.

"How many of those names do you think knew Darren Riegert? Just guess."

Emily looked again through the six pages of names written in small green letters, many printed with happy faces dotting the letter *i*. "None. They're all girlfriends, and most of them I don't see anymore. They're snobs and bitches. Darren didn't know them. He was afraid of most people, did you know that? He was scared they'd hurt his feelings."

"Thank you, Emily."

Billy wrote quickly and then shut his notebook.

"You going now?"

"Yes, Emily."

"Did Darren look okay? Was he okay?" Emily's voice trembled.

"He looked at peace, Emily."

As he went downstairs, Emily closed her bedroom door. Billy heard the click of the lock.

Irene Bourne was standing alone in the entrance to the blue family room.

"Well, Inspector?"

"Your daughter admitted she and Darren Riegert were present when Cody Schow committed suicide. She also knew that Darren had planned to do the same ritual and that she was to be a witness."

"She must be lying."

"I believe her, Mrs. Bourne. She seems sincere."

"Of course, there's no reason for her to lie to you. She isn't really one to make up stories. She is much more prone — at least around me and her father — to say nothing at all." Irene Bourne's face suddenly became thoughtful.

"Your daughter was calling Dr. Massenet this morning. She said. . . ."

"She's our therapist. A pleasant and helpful person. She must have a lot of patience dealing with. . . . Emily could've stopped him, Inspector!"

Irene Bourne sat down. The idea of her daughter witnessing a death struck her forcefully.

"She could've helped him. Oh, my God."

"Help is a difficult concept in this situation, Mrs. Bourne. Emily said Darren and Cody Schow had some kind of pact. I must insist you call Dr. Massenet this afternoon and have her come by. Your daughter is in a state right now where she could commit serious harm to herself. There should be some professional intervention, as soon as possible. I need your assurance that you will follow through on this as soon as you can."

"Sharon Riegert warned me to make sure my daughter was safe. It's all so sordid and ugly." Irene Bourne stood up. She was agitated; she rubbed her hands together. "I will call Dr. Massenet right now." Then she paused. "My daughter is responsible. Will she be charged, Inspector? For witnessing Cody's death and not acting? God, the news won't sit well with Jack."

"I'll need to get a formal statement, Mrs. Bourne. But it can wait until later this week. The Schow case has been closed for months, as you know, but with Darren's death we will have to re-open the files. There was no evidence of foul play, but Emily's presence is suspicious. We'll need corroboration from Dr. Massenet. To find out how much Emily has confessed to her. Or made up. Your daughter said she was stoned when she saw Cody hang himself."

"I knew there were drugs." Irene Bourne did not look into Billy's face as she spoke these last words.

"For the meantime, I'll report this conversation as part of my investigation of the Darren Riegert case. I can let you know when Chief Bochansky wants Emily to come in for more questioning."

Irene Bourne managed a thin smile.

"Call Dr. Massenet and tell her about what went on this morning. It'll help keep things clear if she knows you have met me."

"Absolutely, Inspector."

"I must make a call to headquarters."

As Billy punched in the number on his cell phone, Irene Bourne sat down at the kitchen table and put her head in her hands. The rush of running water in the pipes of the house from someone flushing a toilet upstairs reverberated through the thin walls like river rapids. Billy could hardly hear the dispatcher on the other end of the line.

"Inspector, we've got a counsellor here. A Mr. Barnes," the dispatcher explained.

"Speak up, sergeant, sorry."

"It's the counsellor, sir, Mr. Barnes. He's brought in a young student — the Darren Riegert case."

"Okay."

"Chief suggested you should come straight over when you're done."

"All right. Tell the chief I'm on my way."

Billy clicked off. Irene Bourne was already standing in the front hall. She opened the front door.

"Let me know, Inspector," she said in a quiet voice, "if I can do any more to help. I can cope for now, at least, knowing what Emily has seen. You see, it was right after Cody's death that she began acting up. She never told me what she saw or did. I wish I could . . . well, I can cope, as I say."

"Goodbye, Mrs. Bourne."

The sun burned the hard surface of the concrete driveway as Billy put the Pontiac into reverse. He drove slowly, trying to remember the street names that led out to the entrance to Tudor Acres. He turned at Windsor, ended up at Oxford, and finally found the exit. He shook his head. He stopped, pulling the Pontiac to the curb, and wrote down in his notebook as much as he could remember as cars swooshed by on the four-lane ring road leading into the city centre. Did he believe Emily? He had no reason not to. His knee began to ache. This was not a good sign. Pain like this always came with fatigue and was the first sign of mounting frustration. A killer was on the loose. Evidence was scarce. And all he could do was wait.

It had been a bitter night for Justin Moore. A toss-and-turn marathon granting him no more than a fitful hour or two of sleep. He'd spent the evening alone drinking too many rum and Cokes and had fallen fully dressed into his bed, half sick but wired. When sleep finally came, nightmares of Yianni hounded him. Now as the hot noon sun bombarded his bedroom, Justin had to get up and face whatever the new day would bring.

He struggled into the shower. Later, he put on his khaki army shorts and a plaid cotton shirt and went downstairs to the dining room, where his mother had laid out a freshly cut orange for him on one of her Spode plates. Aileen Moore believed in formal meals at all hours of the day. Mid-Sunday was no exception. Justin's head was splitting.

"Well, sleepy head. You still want breakfast? I've got bacon all ready warming in the oven." His mother had poked her head around the swinging door that led to the kitchen.

"Just coffee, Mom."

Justin lowered himself into his chair and scowled at the oozing cluster of orange triangles. He sighed. Maybe Yianni would cut a deal. Perhaps give him another week if he could show up with a few dollars on Saturday and maybe a gift. But what? A bottle of whiskey? He knew Yianni would want something more.

Aileen Moore came into the dining room carrying a cup of steaming coffee and the phone.

"It's for you."

Justin hesitated before speaking. His mother sat down opposite him and lit a cigarette.

"Go on, dear. I won't listen in."

The voice on the phone was quiet and hesitant.

"I really need to talk to you."

"What about?"

"Let's say it's very serious, Justin."

"Look, Karen, you agreed. You gave back the ring. *We* agreed. . . ."

"I know. But something's happened. It's important."

"Look, I've got a lot of. . . ."

"Can you pick me up for coffee? Please, Justin."

Justin sighed. Thinking over how his life was going, he figured

Karen's crisis, if that's what it was, could not add much more of an edge to his own problems.

"I'll pick you up in ten minutes."

When he finished his coffee, Justin listened to his mother try to persuade him to cut the back lawn, but he managed to put her off for a few hours. He took the Olds and drove along Baroness for twelve blocks, then went east onto a side avenue. Cars swooshed by him, their sound punctuating the litany of words echoing in his head: *cash, Yianni, cash, police.* Karen's house sat at the end of the street. Justin slowed the Oldsmobile as new words and accusations broke into his consciousness: *You deal to minors. What if the police ask about Darren and Cody?*

The front porch of Karen's bungalow needed paint, and the pillars holding up its arched roof were leaning. The Oldsmobile's engine whined as Justin pulled to a stop. Karen ran out the front door and down the crumbling concrete steps. She was wearing jeans and a pink T-shirt, and her hair was tied back in a scarf as bright as a school banner.

"Let's get out of here." Karen slid into the front seat of the car.

Justin jammed the Oldsmobile into drive.

Downtown, at McDonald's, Karen sat with her coffee and started to cry.

"I'm pregnant."

"What? You're not!"

"Is that all you can say?"

"God, fuck, Karen." Justin leaned in closer to her damp face. "You told me you were on the pill."

"I was. Sometimes my timing is off. It was an accident."

"Oh, great." Justin leaned back. He began tapping his fingers on the top of the booth table. "You told your father, didn't you?"

"I had to."

"You had to? What do you mean?"

Karen started weeping again. She reached for Justin's hand, but he pulled back across the table.

"What do you mean, Karen?"

"I told my mom, and she told him."

"Great. This is just great."

"What are we going to do?"

"We?"

"Poppa will kill us. He'll kill you for sure if you don't do something."

"Like what, for Christ's sake?"

"Please keep your voice down, Justin."

"Like what?" Justin whispered.

"Marry me."

"This is not the fifties, Karen. You ever heard of abortion?"

"I can't do that." She covered her face with her hands.

Justin unfolded a paper napkin and handed it to her. "Here. Go on."

Karen wiped her eyes. "I can't. I love you, Justin."

"You can't do this to me, Karen. Not right now. And besides, we agreed to break up, remember?"

"You love me, don't you?"

Justin shifted. He wanted to get up and walk out and let the air and the warm sun wash him clean. He liked Karen and had been dating her for a year. But he didn't love her. She was a pretty girl, and they'd had wonderful, hot sex, but it stopped there.

"Poppa will kill you, Justin." Karen's voice was low and ominous. She had straightened and was looking at Justin head on, her brown eyes staring directly into his face.

"Is that a threat? Are you trying to scare me? Let me tell you, here and now. We're going to do something about this, and I don't mean buying a wedding ring. You understand? It's your fault. You fucked up and got pregnant. You fucked up telling your parents. You're going to do what I want now, you hear me?"

"Don't be so sure, Justin." Karen's voice had deepened with feeling. "Don't be so sure my father won't bring the wrath of Jesus down on your head."

Justin leaned forward and placed his face in his hands. "You have to help *me*, Karen."

"How do you mean?"

"I need money."

"Not again. You run up debts faster than anyone in the world."

"Don't kick me when I'm down."

Karen lowered her voice. But her tone was cold and disbelieving. "How much this time?"

"Over five."

"God help you."

"It's from Yianni Pappas." Justin looked at Karen's face.

She lifted her chin in a gesture of disdain. "How could you?" she whispered.

"I've been selling dope, too. *And* I got a call from some fuck detective who wants to talk to me about that Sheree Lynn asshole who lives next door. He wants to question me about those two losers, Darren and Cody. The police found Darren's body in her basement on Saturday morning."

Karen's face had turned white.

"But you had nothing to do with them."

"I sold those two losers dime bags, Karen. They were underage."

"Okay, but you didn't know them at all, right? You are not responsible for what happens to them."

"Maybe, maybe not. Those kids paid me with stolen money. I'm sure of it. The police could arrest me for selling to minors. I'd have no way to pay off Yianni then. You never know with Yianni. He could go after my mom. He could torch our house."

"Justin, calm down. You know I don't have anything to give you. Have you tried the bank?"

"Fuck the bank."

"Please keep your voice down."

Justin shut his eyes and leaned back and felt like he was choking. He slammed his fists on the table and stood up so violently he knocked his coffee cup to the floor.

"Come on," he said, grabbing Karen by her wrist.

He drove Karen home. They did not speak. Justin was dizzy: *Now you're going to be a father.* He waited as she climbed from the Oldsmobile, and he watched her cross the street and go into the bungalow. Her gentle walk prompted an old feeling. One of love. He had always liked her sweetness, and now she was being forced to act in a cruel and angry manner. "Karen, I'm sorry," he whispered. He started the engine and drove and drove until he found himself, half in a trance, his body in a cold sweat, by the rushing waters of the Oldman River. He sat stock still, his hands on the steering wheel.

So this is the new day, he thought.

It would be a bitter weekend. He rolled down the window. If only he could rise into the warm air and be free. Justin knew he must think and plan. He realized that now, above anything else, he had to keep his wits clear, his whole self alert.

Billy led Mrs. Morton into a ten-by-twelve interview room, a dumpy short woman in a pair of purple slacks and a cotton jacket. She carried a straw purse and had a soft colourless face and an air of defeat about her as strong as the odour of her cheap perfume. She entered not in fear but with a wooden obedience, like a dog trained to heel. Through the glass window in the adjacent interview room, a space covered in white soundproofing tiles with a table, two chairs, and a camcorder, sat her son. At fourteen, Blayne Morton was huge, over two hundred pounds. His dough-like face had guarded slits for eyes, and his hair was the colour of lime Jell-o. The mother took her seat as if she had no choice.

"We'll tape you first, Mrs. Morton," said Billy. "That's the camera. You don't need to be afraid. You remember Mr. Barnes, the counsellor from the junior high? He has joined us and is here to help you, if you wish. I have a few questions. All I want is the truth, Mrs. Morton."

Counsellor Barnes was a thin man with a closely cropped beard, a bald head, and neat brown clothes. He told Billy he'd been pruning his garden. Billy saw at once the man was used to helping others; he had a placid voice and manner.

"You ready, Mrs. Morton?" Barnes asked. "The Inspector won't take up much of your time. I know how upset you must be."

She sat still and passive.

"Tell me," Billy said, sitting down across from Mrs. Morton, "about Blayne. What you found this morning."

"For two years, my Blayne's been like that. Two years I've seen him doin' those things. I don't know why he does them. He says he's told to by a power. Since his dad left, my Blayne likes to sing in that voice. Oh, he reads that book, too. I got it here, Inspector. See, it looks like the Bible. But it's like no Bible I ever seen. He sings, and he takes those matches and puts them on his skin. Says he wants pain, says he needs pain so he can hear the voices."

Billy took the book from Mrs. Morton. It had a red cover, a pentacle embossed in gold. Billy flipped open the first pages. There were spells and drawings. He checked the cover. It was another edition of Darren Riegert's book, *Thanatopsis*.

"Was Blayne up all last night, too?"

"Oh, yes! Singing and rocking. Been almost two days now. Friday, I guess, he started. No, it was early Saturday morning by the time I got home, real late, from work. I'm a cleaner at the government building on Burdett. I found him in the front room. I couldn't sleep. I was so tired, but I couldn't sleep. I was afraid to leave him. Afraid he might hurt himself bad."

"What time was that? When you got home and found your son?"

"About one. I get a cab home 'cause it's so late."

"Did you sit with Blayne?"

"Oh, yes. I tried. He needs protection, Inspector. He needs the hospital again."

"You said you tried. What happened, Mrs. Morton?"

"Yes, sir. I truly did. But I fell asleep. I wake up around seven, that's seven on Saturday — real late for me — and he's on the floor rocking, curled up in the corner. Like he was at the hospital."

"Did he say anything to you?"

"Say anything? He kept singing is all. No, maybe he said, 'He betrayed me.' That was it. I couldn't hardly hear him. 'He betrayed me.' I reckon he was talking about his dad."

"Did you notice anything unusual about him other than his cigarette wounds? Were there any different markings on his clothes or his hands?" Billy suddenly found himself picturing Blayne Morton as he sat in the next room, his face and hands speckled with blood and black paint, unaware of what damning evidence he was wearing in full view.

"No. My Blayne is a clean boy, sir. He was wearin' what he's got on. In there. He looked tired is all." She looked towards the window and saw Blayne in the next room. "Like I said, he was on the floor. I got him up. I fed him. He slept all day. All Saturday. He slept in the clothes he has on. Then last night, he started again. He went all night, like I said."

"Did you stay up with him, Mrs. Morton?"

"I tried. I couldn't sleep much 'cause he kept singin', so I asked him. I said, 'Blayne, who betrayed you, who?' And he wouldn't say. So I got up early this morning. I watched him a couple of hours, and after lunch I put him and me into a cab. I kept thinking about what Blayne was saying. Maybe somebody hurt him? Betrayed him, hurt him somehow? I was scared. I figured I should come here. So I brought him. That man — Sergeant Dodd — he said I could wait with him till you got back."

"One more thing, Mrs. Morton."

A brief sigh of relief came out of Mrs. Morton's mouth. Billy handed her a tissue so that she could wipe her nose. Out of his pocket he slipped the Polaroid of Darren in his leather jacket and placed it on the table in front of her.

"Have you ever seen this before, Mrs. Morton?"

She peered at the photo, and her mouth opened slightly. She flicked her eyes up to Billy's, then lowered them again, cutting his face from her view. Her hand clasped the side of the table. "You get this from Blayne?"

"From a friend of Blayne's. A boy called Darren Riegert."

"The dead boy?" Her face fell.

"From his mother. She said Blayne gave it to Darren. Do you recognize it?"

"All I know is Blayne has a camera takes these kinds of pictures. I've seen lots of them in his room. He likes Valentines, too. One time he bought a red box for himself. Kept it to himself in his room."

"All right, Mrs. Morton. That'll be fine for now." Billy helped her stand up. "I want to talk to Blayne now. I want. . . ."

"He's tired, Inspector. You want me to be with him?"

"Well, for now I think it's best if I talk to him on my own. I'll be careful, Mrs. Morton. I'll just ask him a few questions."

"Yes, all right." The woman walked towards the door as if she'd been commanded to start moving forward. Counsellor Barnes then led her from the room. When he came back in, Billy was writing notes. "She's in the lobby. What'll you do with him, Inspector?"

Blayne remained staring at the tiles in the adjacent room. He was so still that it was as if he'd been put under a spell. "Dodd, can you call an ambulance, please. I think it's best this boy be taken to the psych ward for observation. Can you get the chief to fill out a deposition? Just for one night. The mother can go with him."

"Happy to."

"I need to talk to him, Mr. Barnes. At least, I need to see what he can tell me. I want to thank you for helping us out. Giving us names and calling up people like you did."

"You're welcome, Inspector. What do you expect to get out of Blayne?"

"Hard to say."

Opening the door to the adjacent interview room, Billy noticed how suddenly Blayne Morton reacted. He started blinking quickly. He unfolded his hands and lay them flat, palms down, on the tabletop. He looked up at the ceiling.

"Blayne, my name is Billy. I want to talk to you for a minute. Can I come in?"

Blayne Morton began to sing softly, rocking his torso back and forth. Barnes stood at the door and signalled to an officer in the hall. "Can you wait just outside?" said Barnes. "We may need you."

"My name is Billy, Blayne." Billy slowly sat down across from the swaying boy. He nodded to Barnes to activate the camcorder. "Blayne Morton, aged fourteen, Sunday, June 30." Billy spoke in a low, firm, cautious voice as he slid his notebook out of his upper pocket. Blayne was wearing a rumpled white T-shirt. There were dirt smudges on the chest area. Billy leaned closer. There was no indication of black paint or blood. He next studied Blayne's hands. On them were old scabs, round brown spots the size of cigarette ends. His skin was sallow, ill-fed, but there were no splotches of black or red. Blayne's green hair was in knots. Again, no signs of blood or paint. Billy bent down and looked under the table to check the boy's shoes and black jeans. Dirty smudges on the toes, streaks of dust on the pants. Counsellor Barnes stood silent. Billy watched Blayne move back and forth in his chair. The boy's eyes were ringed with grey circles, and he did not seem to notice either Billy's or Barnes's presence.

And then the boy's eyes filled with tears. "Help me," he whispered. "Help me."

"How can I help you, Blayne?"

"Darren," Blayne replied. "Darren betrayed me."

Blayne rolled his eyes back. He raised his scab-spotted hands to his face and covered his forehead. He began rocking again, singing in a low voice: "Darren loves peace, Darren loves peace."

"Officer."

Blayne ceased his chanting. He shut his eyes, rolled off his chair with a pounding thud, and curled up on the floor.

Billy threw a glance at Barnes. "Let him be," Barnes whispered.

The officer stood in the doorway, staring at Blayne.

"Go and get the boy's mother," Billy said. "She's in the lobby."

Billy and Barnes waited in silence while Blayne remained in a foetal position, his arms clutching his knees. Soft moans rose from the boy's throat until Mrs. Morton entered. She crept into the room clutching her straw purse to her breasts. "Oh, Blayne!" She crouched down next to her son, and the two of them were as pale as corpses.

"I've called an ambulance for you, Mrs. Morton," Billy said.

"Thank you, sir. Thank you, Inspector."

"The officer here will accompany you and Blayne. Will you be all right?"

"Will they look after him?"

"We'll put him in the hospital for observation. You can stay with him if you like. If he seems better in the morning, I suggest you give a call to your doctor."

"Oh, I did that already, sir." Mrs. Morton attempted a smile. "He's out of town till Monday."

Billy then realized that a man in a white medic's uniform was standing in the entrance. The ambulance had arrived sooner than he'd expected. Blayne kept his face covered with his arms. Billy stood back as the officer and the medic lifted Blayne and led him and Mrs. Morton through the doorway.

"Come on, Barnes," Billy said. "Let me buy you a sandwich. I need to get some background from you."

The air was still as the two men walked across the shady green lawns of Galt Gardens. In its centre stood the cenotaph, a bronze soldier leaning on a rifle, the butt rooted in a mound of bronze poppies. The cottonwoods and blue spruce had been planted by the first British settlers to come into the west after the Riel Rebellion. Beds of impatiens and petunias were thick with red and pink, and in the branches of the trees starlings and sparrows chattered in the afternoon heat. The two men entered the glass-domed mall, bought sandwiches and soft drinks, and walked back into the shade of the park. They sat down at a picnic table.

"What's your take on these boys?" Billy asked. "You had some acquaintance with Darren and Cody. And with this Morton."

"Outsiders. Loners. Kids from one-parent and broken homes."

"You met the parents of these boys at one time or another."

"I talked to them, yes." Barnes did not hesitate. He took a drink and went on. "The parents never said much about their boys. These kids were in trouble — missing classes, cheating, smoking in the washrooms. All of them were pretty quiet for the most part. Stayed by themselves. None of them was into sports. We never saw any one of them at the dances. Fourteen year olds are often shy, but these kids seemed too withdrawn. Now Blayne Morton, he's different. I didn't want to say anything inside. Not with his mother there. I didn't want to prejudice your judgement, but I'm not so sure what we saw today was real."

"How do you mean?"

"He lies. I've seen him go into that rocking act in a session in the counsellor's office when he was caught with some stolen textbooks in his backpack. An unstable kid. Putting him under observation may give you some better indication, Inspector. We've had him assessed and have intervened a couple of times over his semi-violent behaviour. That kid fits the A.S.D. profile. He can change moods as fast as the weather, and he also knows how to manipulate."

"I've heard he was pestering Darren and fighting with other boys."

"Cody didn't let Blayne into their little group. Blayne was only interested — as far as I could tell — in luring Darren away for himself. He was a bully who liked to punish people; he told me that in a session once, when I caught him hitting and threatening a young boy in the hall."

"Did Blayne know the boy in the hall? Was this an isolated incident?"

"Blayne had few friends. He's a big kid and was often made fun of because of his size."

"Do you think Darren Riegert's hanging was a suicide?"

Barnes stopped eating. He looked straight ahead, pulled off his sunglasses, and rubbed the fingers of his right hand.

"I hope so. That sounds odd, I know. Cody and Darren were friends. I know they both frequented Miss Bird's place. I fear that maybe the boys made some kind of pact. It's just a gut feeling. But knowing them as much as I could, I find it hard to believe each one would act entirely separate from the other. Now, from what you tell me about Darren, his being tied and cut by a knife, well, that's more difficult. Who knows? Maybe there's a revenge thing going on here. A jealousy thing. Blayne could certainly be a suspect, as I assume you are thinking. These teenagers have feuds and battles they don't tell us about."

"Let me toss this in. Two boys are found hanging in the basement of the same house. The last kid mutilated. Satanic books and Miss Bird are all part of the picture. We had a case a few years ago in Vancouver. Four girls — all fifteen — were found over a nine-week period in a number of different garages in the neighbourhood of Marine Drive. Every one of them dead from carbon monoxide poisoning. A suicide pact? No. A serial killer. A substitute teacher posted around the city. He'd lured the girls, subdued them with chloroform, then turned on the cars and watched them die. My late partner on the city squad, Harry Stone, found the chloroform and the gas mask the killer had worn hidden in the suspect's briefcase along with some of the students' schoolwork."

"So, Inspector, which one is more likely, do you think, in this case? The pact or the serial killer?"

"I don't know, Barnes. I need to see this from any and every angle. Do you know of any cult groups in the city? A link between that kind of activity and the boys' interest in Satanism might lead somewhere."

"I don't know, Inspector. I've not encountered cults here. That doesn't mean there aren't any. But as you know, they hide underground. And most of their younger members tend to leave school and disappear onto the streets."

"Right," agreed Billy. "Come on, Barnes."

Back in the office, Counsellor Barnes presented Billy with his card. Billy handed him a three-by-five lined note card with his cell phone number and the station's e-mail address. "Thanks, Barnes. I'll get a hold of you on Monday. Can we set up some more interviews?"

"You may not get many more, Inspector. I went through my files — I keep a copy of them at home on my laptop — and I couldn't find any more names associated with Darren Riegert. His one best friend is already dead."

"You ever counsel a young girl named Emily Bourne? Dark hair, spider tattoo on her neck."

"Not that I remember. How is she involved here?"

"She says she was friends with Cody and Darren. I'm looking into her connection to them."

Billy and Barnes shook hands. After he escorted the counsellor to the reception area, Billy walked down the corridor into Butch's office. He sat at the computer, entered the password Butch had given him, and began to skim the files on Cody Schow and Sheree Lynn Bird. He jotted in his notebook information from the constables' reports, the fingerprint data, the coroner's analyses. After reading for an hour, he logged off. He placed his notebook on the table in front of him. *Let impressions float for a time. How much was Sheree Lynn Bird involved?* Billy opened his eyes. *Now that's interesting. Why would that question come up first, above all others?* He shut his eyes again, leaned back in his chair. The hum of the office seeped into his meditation. *Is this a case of Blayne Morton behaving like a lunatic because he is trying to smoke-screen a feeling of guilt?* Billy placed his notebook into his suit pocket, next to his heart, walked into the coffee room, and found Dodd.

"Dodd, can you get me the Bird statement?"

"Yes, sir."

"And, listen, the junior high school will be closed, but get a hold of the principal and get this and last years' yearbooks from their archives. I need pictures of Darren and Blayne Morton."

Dodd was scribbling down the names on a piece of paper he'd grabbed from a pile by the mini-fridge.

"Also, get the principal to blow up a picture of Riegert and have it posted for when the students return for summer school. Print out a notice asking for anyone who might have known Darren or seen him in the past week. If you find a clear picture of Blayne Morton, get an identikit done and then take it to the city bus system today. Find out from their dispatch people who was driving the main routes up Ashmead and the street where the Mortons live."

"No problem."

"You got your notebook with you? Let's walk and talk."

Dodd fumbled in his pocket, pulled out his notebook, and followed Billy to the door. He flipped a few pages and read quickly.

"Okay, sir. I enquired of the neighbours of Woody Keeler and Sharon

Riegert, on Friday night. At both addresses, Keeler's and Riegert's. No one had seen them. I drove to the beer outlet near the Riegert bungalow. The manager said he knew the man's name — Woody — and that, yes, he had come in Friday night, as usual, and had purchased a two-four. The time was approximately six-thirty."

"Okay."

"The videotapes of Miss Bird and Professor Mucklowe were completed, as requested. Checked on Mucklowe and Miss Bird for whereabouts on Saturday night. No statements from landlord or neighbours since no one saw them. As requested today, went to the Schow household and asked of whereabouts for last night. Mrs. Schow was drunk and refused to allow questioning and shut the door."

By now, Billy and Dodd were standing by the entrance to the lab. They had come down a flight of stairs and gone through two sets of swinging doors, Dodd reciting from his notebook in a steady, low voice.

"Afternoon, Johnson."

The smell of disinfectant saturated the dry air. Billy and Dodd stepped into the brightly lit room, where Johnson was wearing an apron and gloves. A paper mask dangled from her neck.

"What's our wrap-up on Darren Riegert?"

"First, the handwriting man at the horsemen's headquarters took a quick look at the note from Riegert's mouth and the writing on the Blayne Morton Polaroid you gave me." Johnson handed back the picture of the Valentine box to Billy. "He said the printing was not similar, especially the formation of the capital letter *E*. The slant of the words was more pronounced in the message on the Polaroid."

"What else?"

"The basement at Satan House had no significant markings, no prints on the overhead pipe or on the utility sink. Prints in the stairwell, on the back doorknobs, and on the washer and dryer had been touched and smudged so often there were no distinct specimens to analyze." Finger-prints were only useful if they could be matched up with those from identifiable felons.

"The paper towel and the blood had obscured any skin oil or markings from the handlers. Same on the note found in the body's mouth."

"You get anything from the rope or the boom box?"

"All blood samples match. All are from the Riegert body."

Billy stood by the table. He let his eyes roam over the objects in front of him. Dodd had paused a few moments by the door, gulping in a few deep breaths, before he came up beside him. "The smell in here gives me the jitters, Inspector," Dodd said.

"I have a question for the two of you," Billy said, looking first at Dodd and then at Johnson. "How do we establish that this boom box is actually Darren's? For certain? These things don't have serial numbers. This one could belong to me, for instance. Boom boxes of this brand and year all look alike. It may have been brought to the scene by someone as a gift. As a bribe. As part of the ritual."

Dodd interrupted. "But only Darren's prints were on it."

"So we could suppose he carried it into the basement. Or that the murderer was wearing gloves since no other prints were found."

Johnson hesitated. "I tried something earlier before you came down, sir. I placed the boy's boots on top of the boom box. Hawkes removed them from the body after he was finished. Here, let me get them."

Johnson walked to a cabinet and pulled out a large Ziploc containing the blood-spattered boots of Darren Riegert. She brought the boots to the table and placed them on top of the machine, side by side. "See?" Johnson was pointing to the splatter pattern on the boots and the edges of the boom box. "When I lift up the two boots, you can see that there is a clean area along the top of the box where the boots were placed. When I put the boots back, the splatter pattern is continuous from the toe sections over to the edges of the box."

"The boy was standing on the box in his boots and was cut and bleeding."

"It looks that way."

"Which means what?" asked Dodd, who scratched his temple.

"Only this," ventured Billy. "The kid was cut just before or while he was standing on the box. The blood spatters I saw this morning in the site photos also suggest he was cut while standing under the pipe, in the location of the noose. So whoever was with Darren may have had him stand on the boom box around the time the cutting of the wrists and chest took place. We have the knife. And we have the smudge of blood in Darren's right hand. Was that smudge from holding the bloodied knife? Does the mark with the distinct line suggest the knife was dropped or placed by the boom box?"

Johnson tapped the boom box. "Sir, Darren could've cut himself, or the murderer could have forced him to stand and be cut, and then the knife was placed on the floor as. . . ."

Dodd shook his head. "The kid probably held the knife and then dropped it because he was in pain."

"Possible," said Billy. "Darren may have been forced to do so, but the palm smudge suggests he was holding the knife at some point while he was bleeding. But why was the box removed from the site? And why did the accomplice — we'll call the person or persons that for now — go and bury the knife? The burial looked haphazard to me. As if the accomplice wanted us to find it. The box was hidden more carefully. Was the hiding of these objects done in a moment of panic? Or did the perpetrator think that by hiding the objects any clues to his or her identity would be removed from the scene?"

When Billy was finished his hypothesis, Dodd and Johnson looked at each other. Dodd got out his notebook and flipped a few pages. He listed the questions Billy had asked, and as the silence of the bright room gathered, Billy gazed once more at the boom box, the knife, and the rope. Johnson had lain out the rope full length next to the box. Billy had been right about the rope burn but not about the material the rope was made from. It was nylon and shredded in places, like a hemp rope might be, but since the nylon was of cheap stock and worn from use, its rough edges had apparently bruised the skin in the same manner as hemp.

"You find anything on that rope, Johnson?"

"Yes. Dog hair. Some traces of skin from Darren's body."

"What about the bag with the blood stain?"

"The blood was Darren's. Nothing was in the bag — lint only, some nylon fibre from the rope."

Billy picked up Darren Riegert's book, the *Thanatopsis*. He wondered if Dodd or Johnson had flipped through it to examine the spells or if there might be something inside. The book was the one item left they had not analyzed. Billy shook and fluttered the pages. From its centre, a Polaroid dropped to the floor.

"Ah," Billy said, his voice gently teasing the other two.

The picture was of a red Valentine box. Billy slipped the other two Polaroids out of his pocket and laid the three of them in a row in front of Dodd and Johnson.

"Who took these, sir?" asked Johnson.

"Two of them for sure were taken by Blayne Morton. The third, from the book. . . ."

"Has to be his," chimed in Dodd. "It's the same red candy box."

"How did it get into the *Thanatopsis*? Is there writing on it?"

Johnson picked it up and turned it over. "Yes. In printing. 'Meet me tonight, please. Please.'"

Billy looked more closely. The handwriting here and on the other Polaroid was similar. "Try to get a print off that, Johnson. I suspect it'll be one of Blayne Morton's. Now we have three pictures from Blayne to Darren, and one of them was at the murder site. Was it carried there, or was it in the book to begin with?"

"It's still not conclusive enough, though, is it, sir?" asked Johnson.

"We need a hard piece of evidence that places Blayne at the site for certain."

"You get anything on Woody Keeler?" Billy then asked.

Both Dodd and Johnson grinned. "Yes, sir. We've been saving the best for last." Johnson removed her gloves and apron. Dodd reached the swinging doors first and shoved them open with a sigh of gratitude. He held the door for Billy.

The small computer room was two doors down the hall on the same floor. "This is our special-access computer, sir," explained Johnson. She unlocked the door with a set of keys and held it open. "As Dodd showed you yesterday, there are files here and on-line connections to other units in the province we can call up. Security, mainly. Chief said he didn't want his staff accessing what we've got here or they'd be playing all day at their desks." Johnson tossed a mischievous glance at Dodd.

"Wait a second," Dodd replied. He was about to go on, but Johnson sat down at the computer, keyed in her password, and took the mouse around the screen several times as Billy pulled up a chair and signalled to Dodd to do the same.

"Woody Keeler. Age thirty-four. Here's the welfare profile, Inspector."

Billy scanned the dates, the many changes of address, the file notations on jobs offered by the social agency, the one-line summaries of the job interviews given to Woody Keeler, and the reasons for rejections.

Johnson clicked the mouse; the screen reconfigured, and Woody Keeler's police record came up.

"Two counts of drunk driving. One count for driving a stolen vehicle was later dropped. See the date, September 1996. Keeler provided his ownership papers. Claimed he'd mislain them. Fined for driving without proper documentation."

"Go to the best part, Johnson," Dodd said eagerly.

"Woody was arrested back in 1990 for assault causing bodily harm."

Johnson led the cursor to Search, then Data File. A facsimile of a provincial RCMP report with Keeler's name on it filled the screen. "The horsemen require a handwritten and a typewritten version of every crime report so that the officers involved concentrate on accuracy."

"How'd you learn that, Johnson?" asked Dodd.

"They've been doing it since they came west, Dodd. It's an old military procedure. We can look up any felon in RCMP files from the past fifty years. Except top-secret files connected with the Ministry of Defence."

Billy read that Woody Keeler had been arraigned on suspicion of a beating that took place on the Peigan reserve, at Brocket. August 30,

1990. Keeler at the time was age twenty-six. On September 1, 1990, Keeler was charged with assaulting a juvenile, aged seventeen. The boy's name was Ervin Born With a Tooth, hospitalized at St. Michael's in Lethbridge with two broken teeth and a mild concussion. A witness to the beating testified that Keeler came out of a local Brocket hardware store carrying a bottle, bumped into the boy, and then started a fight. Later, members of the boy's family testified that Ervin's father, deceased, had been a school friend of Woody.

"The horsemen charged Keeler, and the court sentenced him to three months at the Lethbridge jail. But he was released on bail and signed up to do community work."

"Show Billy the last item, Johnson," said Dodd.

"I also found more on the boy, Ervin. On Saturday, September 16, 1990, two weeks after the assault, the horsemen filed another story. Classified under homicide. Unsolved. I thought you might like a hard-copy of this one."

Johnson took a key from her pocket, opened a filing cabinet, and lifted out a blue folder. She handed a glossy photocopy sheet to Billy. It was a printout of a short file entry with the same format as the one on Woody Keeler. With it was a newspaper article, also photocopied, from the Lethbridge *Herald* with the same date as the RCMP report.

Billy read the headline of the *Herald* article: NATIVE BOY FOUND HANGED IN GYM.

The hanged body of a seventeen-year-old Peigan boy was found Thursday morning in the Brocket High School gymnasium in Brocket. Local RCMP constable, Walter Schmidt, was called to the gym earlier that morning by the principal, Allan Houk. The body was found suspended from a basketball hoop. Foul play is suspected, according to Schmidt. The body was identified by family members. Ervin Born With a Tooth died from the results of asphyxiation. "We have no leads as yet," said Constable Schmidt. "We are concerned about the nature of the incident. The boy's feet and hands were tied with wire."

"What was the follow-up?" queried Billy.

"I did a search on six, eight, then twelve months of consecutive *Herald* pieces. Only two appeared saying the police had no leads and were calling for witnesses. I can show you the horsemen's files, here too, if you like. The police in Brocket and Fort Macleod found no leads or witnesses. The family was unable to give any help. Parole records on Woody Keeler's whereabouts at the time were in order. He reported to the community centre, did his work, called in when he got back home. He was required to serve only fifteen days in detention, in early November 1990. The case was declared cold in 1992."

Billy skimmed the article again.

"Tomorrow, Johnson, go to Brocket. You are in, I assume?"

"Yes, sir. I have a tee time at Henderson for 6:00 a.m., but I can be on the road by 9:00."

"Talk to the constable. I know the affair was a long time ago. And I know the Peigan may choose not to talk to you. This whole effort could turn into a big goose chase. But it's worth the chance."

Johnson nodded.

Billy went on. "Talk to anyone you can in the Born With a Tooth family about Keeler. Focus on him. Does he still go out to the reserve? Does he still have friends there? What about Ervin's mother? We need to see if there are any connections. Do we have a photo of Woody?"

"Don't think so," answered Dodd. "But I'll check."

"Brocket unit might have one, sir. On their arrest files," said Johnson.

"Refresh everyone's memory. We need to see if Woody Keeler has been leaving a trail. I'm not suggesting what we have now with Darren is related to the Ervin case. And Woody Keeler has no obvious motive for going after Darren. But we need to start somewhere."

Upstairs, Billy went to see Butch, but he was not in his office. The officer at the reception desk told Billy the chief had a last-minute meeting with the police board at the Lethbridge Lodge. He would be back later, after an hour or so. Billy stood still for a moment.

"I understand."

"I can give you the Lodge number, sir. If you wish."

"No thanks. That's fine."

The day was wearing on. Billy's stomach rumbled. His bum knee was beginning to ache, and he took a moment to return to Butch's office and find two Tylenols. A few minutes later, he entered interview room B, where a young man was waiting for him.

"Justin Moore?"

Justin thrust out his hand. Billy took in his clean-shaven face and nervous manner. He asked the young man to sit down; the camcorder was activated. Billy explained the context of the case and the problems he was having with finding hard evidence. Justin Moore listened attentively; Billy noted his polite demeanour.

"What I need from you, Justin, are facts as well as your memories."

"About those two boys?"

"We can start with them. Did you ever meet them?"

"I saw them in the yard, and sometimes I watched them waiting on the front steps of the house for Sheree Lynn."

"Did you ever speak to them?"

"No. I knew their names because Sheree Lynn told my mother who they were. My mother was very upset about those boys being there."

"Why?"

"She knew they were troubled kids on welfare. She was afraid they'd break into our house."

"Were there break-ins?"

"No." Justin sat up straighter in his chair. He took in a deep breath. Billy noticed Justin fidgeting with his hands. There was also the constant shuffling of his feet.

"How much do you know about Sheree Lynn Bird?"

"She rents my Aunt Marion's old house. I knew the two boys stayed there once in a while. We heard the boy, Cody, had drug problems. Sheree Lynn told my mother all this. I know Sheree Lynn lost her job. Her boyfriend is one of my professors at university. Is that enough? Sheree once asked my mother if she could have Aunt Marion's dump painted, but Mom said we couldn't afford it."

"How often did you talk face-to-face to Sheree Lynn?"

"I said hello to her. Not much, really. Though she was very friendly. She liked to flirt, Inspector. She's very hot. She came on to me once. Wanted me to come over to the yard and sunbathe with her. She wanted to go topless, she said. I was tempted, of course. But. . . . After that, she gave me the cold shoulder." Justin said these words looking up at Billy, trying to act the buddy, his manner relaxing as he sat back in the chair.

"Where were you Friday night last?"

"At home."

"With your mother?"

"We were watching TV. She went to bed early, and I stayed up and watched a video."

"Did you see anything unusual next door? Anyone coming or going?"

"Not that night. I don't really pay much attention to that place. I mean, I used to see those boys and Professor Mucklowe. Except that one time. About a year ago, maybe, or even earlier. They sometimes had parties. There was loud music at night."

"What kind of music?"

"Rock, heavy metal sometimes. My mother was threatening to call the police half the time. But the music usually stopped around eleven, so we let it go. Last November, I think. It was a warm night, unusual for that time. I remember looking out the kitchen window and seeing Cody dancing naked on the back lawn. Something heavy was playing. He was falling down and crying out like he was having a nightmare, but he was fully awake." Justin's eyes were focused on the tabletop. He was relaxed, his voice calmer than when he started.

"What did you assume was happening?"

"He was out of it. High."

"This was the only time you saw this type of behaviour?"

"Yes, but there was more."

"How do you mean?"

"Cody was acting wild. I was glad my mother was asleep on the other side of the house. I remember seeing Professor Mucklowe. He came out on the lawn. He was half naked himself. Wearing his undershorts only. He grabbed hold of Cody. Cody and he began to act like they were dancing or fighting. It was dark but light, too, because of the clear sky. It looked weird to me. Weird." Justin stopped for a second.

Billy waited. "Fighting or dancing?"

"I guess fighting. Randy held Cody in his arms and led him back into the house. That was it."

"You ever see anything like this again?"

"No, Inspector. But I always figured there was some weirdness in that place."

"In what way?"

Justin hesitated. "It's just a theory. Something between those boys and Sheree Lynn. I don't know. I never saw anything, but I always felt it was weird for those boys to sleep there."

"You think they were having sex?"

"I didn't say that."

"But what were you thinking, Justin?"

"Sex, maybe. Drugs and sex. I never saw anything, though."

"What video did you see?"

"On Friday night?"

"What was its title?"

"It was a classic. My mom had rented it. Black-and-white, about some people stranded in a lifeboat."

"Can you give me the name of the video store?"

"Not a problem, Inspector. Mom always rents from our neighbourhood place around the corner." Justin gave Billy the name and his mother's membership number.

"Can you remember what time you went to bed Friday?"

"Late. Two or two-thirty."

"What did you do Saturday morning?"

Justin sat up. He began to fidget again, his feet shuffling under the table.

"I went downtown, did some shopping."

"At what time?"

"I think around eleven or so."

"What did you buy?"

"Nothing. Nothing. I went to the mall, then I went to Boorman's to look at shirts. But I couldn't find anything I liked."

Billy thanked Justin. The other two neighbours from Ashmead had neither seen nor heard anything Friday night and knew little about Sheree Lynn or the boys. Going over his notes afterwards, Billy underlined Justin's statement about Cody's naked dance and Mucklowe's appearance in the garden. The idea of sexual misconduct was intriguing. He made a note to talk to Sheree Lynn and Randy the next time he saw them.

Walking out to the parking lot, Billy wondered momentarily if he'd made the right choice to come in from the ranch and join up with Butch on the case. After all, he had written off his former life as a homicide detective seven months ago, the day he'd signed his buyout and retirement forms at head office in Vancouver. Why not phone Butch tomorrow and tell him the weekend had been fun, but from now on it was Butch's show? The lines and demarcations had been drawn, the vector of the investigation had been charted. Johnson was bright. Dodd was thorough at least. What good was he, really, as Butch's "second pair of eyes"?

But Billy stopped. He looked at the light-filled sky, the open land of Arthur Yamamoto's country. Billy reminded himself of his promise to his father. A promise made when he was twenty, after the two of them had tearfully met for the first time and embraced each other as lost father and son. Billy remembered the very words he'd said later to his half-brother, Toshiro, words that had inspired him to forgo sleep, suffer long hours, work back-aching nights on stakeouts: "I became a policeman because of the injustice done to our father."

Billy found he had tears in his eyes.

"For Christ's sake," he whispered.

He unlocked the door of the Pontiac and rolled down the window to let the breeze cool the stifling interior. Waiting, he stared at the distant line where the earth met the sky. He found solace in the horizon, straight as a ruler's edge. He imagined the sky changing colour as the setting sun softly brought on the night. Five minutes later, Billy drove out of the police station parking lot and onto Dawson. He drove slowly through the city. Its streets were busy at the end of the afternoon, with half-tons and vans full of families finishing their Sunday shopping at the big malls. When he was a teenager, the city was deserted on Sundays, the streets empty of cars and people, the store windows with drawn drapes in accordance with the laws prohibiting the sale and the show of material goods. Then, the churches were full. Chimes played from steeples from ten in the morning until one in the afternoon.

Turning onto Dufferin, Billy passed a huge open pit of gravel and torn tree stumps where the old St. Michael's hospital once stood. He drove on and noticed the new paint job on the strip mall with its Mormon bookstore and the flower shop that bordered the parking lot of the regional hospital, a large new building with an enormous glass atrium filled with trees and a small pool. Hospitals look more like hotels these days, he thought. He rode up the elevator to the psychiatric ward, where Blayne Morton had been taken for observation. He arrayed the questions in his mind. *Who tied up Darren Riegert? Did you force Darren to stand on the boom box? Who placed the note in Darren's mouth?*

As Billy walked with the nurse into Blayne Morton's hospital room, he sensed he was getting further entangled in the net of supposition. Blayne Morton may have had a motive. It was the most prominent fact in the case so far. In front of him, the boy lay strapped into a bed behind half-drawn curtains. The nurse pointed to Blayne's immobile face, his thin shut lips.

"Today, Inspector. Whoa! Was this kid wild! Started yelling and hitting out at every wall in sight."

The nurse was short and thin with bright eyes and a sharp high voice. Peeking out of the upper pocket of her uniform was a pack of menthol cigarettes.

"He grabbed my smokes right out of my pocket. Nearly took off a layer of my skin to boot."

Billy asked the nurse what sedative the doctor had prescribed and about its short-term effect.

"This kid'll be out another ten hours, sir. Doctor said he must be kept under strict observation. I'd be glad to call you at headquarters if and when he wakes up. I'm sure he'll tell you his life story by then."

"Thanks," Billy said. He opened his notebook. "Mind if I write down a few things? I do this for my records. I won't take more than two minutes."

"Be my guest," said the nurse.

Billy described Blayne's state and the time of day and the type of sedation he'd been given. He noticed the chart report by the door of the room, the one with Blayne's vital information. "Has he been in before," Billy asked, "for similar treatment?"

The nurse led Billy into the hall and up to the nurse's station, where she punched in Blayne's first and last names and a code number. She waited a second, then ran her finger down the information glowing on the white computer screen. "Twice before. Once for an overdose of aspirin and Valium. Last December he was in and was sedated for three days. Violent behaviour. The attending doctor at first prescribed an anti-depressant." The nurse looked up. "I remember this kid, now. He was really upset that time in December. We couldn't get a straight answer out of him."

"Can you remember what kinds of things he was saying?"

"Stuff about the devil. He kept saying somebody was at peace. That death is the true life, nonsense like that. He lied about his own name and had crying tantrums. I recall he threw a bedpan at another patient, and we had to move him into a single room with a lock. After the three days, he came back to normal, right as rain."

"Did you ever think he was putting this on? That he was playacting?"

"No. And I've seen a lot of distraught people here, Inspector." The nurse interrupted herself by coughing and then clearing her throat. "Teenagers on drugs are frequent detainees."

"But Blayne was not on drugs the second time. Or was he?"

"No, you're right." The nurse checked the screen again. "No, he was clear."

Billy fished for one of the file cards Butch had given him, penned his cell phone number, and handed it to the nurse. She read it over, filed it on her desk on a steel spike, and then shook Billy's hand.

"Pleasure to meet you, Inspector," she said with a warm smile.

Billy counted the numbers as the elevator went down. *So Blayne had a similar reaction at the time of Cody Schow's death? The phrase "at peace" was uttered then as it was in the interview earlier today. At both times, Blayne was sober, too.* These facts would bear keeping in mind.

Randy Mucklowe sat perched on a stool in his kitchen drinking whiskey. Behind him, Sheree Lynn Bird was making herself a cup of herbal tea. He'd arrived home from Montana, and as soon as he'd got in the door Sheree had started whining and complaining about the break-in at Satan House. He had held her for a moment, pretending he cared. But Randy's mind was on Sam and the gold masks. And, above all, on the money they were worth, seven hundred thousand dollars. What did Satan House and Darren Riegert matter now? In a few days, he and Sheree Lynn would be in Vancouver. If they stuck to the plan, there'd be more cash than either one of them had ever seen.

Randy took a long sip. He reached for the bottle and refreshed his drink. Sheree Lynn pulled up a stool beside his and placed her hand on his arm. She drank her tea in silence. How the hell can I get rid of Sam? he wondered. Randy felt he'd gone as far as he dared in showing patience. Heavy Hand was going to ruin everything. Robert Lau had agreed to pay one hundred thousand for each mask, and he was not a man you'd want to surprise or mislead. Lau was ruthless, cautious. Randy believed once Lau had his hands on the precious gold, he'd pay up in full, though he would not welcome Sam's meddling.

Sheree Lynn remained quiet. By the time she'd finished her tea, she seemed ready to share Randy's concerns. He told her about what had happened earlier that day in Babb, Montana, and she said, "All right, so we can work around Sam."

But could they? Sam had stolen the masks from the lab in the university. He had hidden them and guarded them for almost a year. Randy felt a tinge of conscience as he thought about this. At the same time, he faced the yearning and fear he always had when he hatched a money plot. He fervently believed it was his God-given right to claim these masks for himself. After all, he had put his whole life into finding and preserving artifacts. He had found more of them and written more on their history than any other human being. What had he received in return? A bit of minor glory, maybe, but nothing tangible.

The phone rang. Randy didn't move. "Should I get it?" said Sheree Lynn.

"No. Let it ring."

"It might be the inspector."

"It can wait."

Randy sat still. His ex-wife had been pestering him again about alimony payments. Wasn't it enough he'd liquidated his RRSPs and moved to a cheap two-bedroom apartment? He drained his glass and reached for the bottle as the phone rang again.

"Goddamn it!"

He threw his glass into the sink. It thunked heavily before breaking against the stainless steel rim.

Sheree Lynn put her arms around him. "Honey," she said.

He pushed her away. "Let me alone." Randy walked down the hall to the room he used as his den. He shoved open the door. "What's the Goddamn use?" He went to the balcony and stepped outside. He needed air. When he turned to go back in a few seconds later, he saw Sheree Lynn at the far doorway. He paused, keeping his eyes on her nervous smile. It was like an order to him to gather his thoughts. He must not lose control of the situation. He knew he must control her as well and make sure she felt protected and wanted. Sheree Lynn must never be threatened by anyone to give away the secrets they now shared. Her beauty, as always, gave him much pleasure and in fact had a calming effect on him. It was true what his colleagues had said, even as they mocked him: she was a prize, a trophy, a woman worth suffering for.

"Come on," he now said, walking towards her. "If you have something to say, say it."

She stayed by the door, her arms folded. Her manner was hesitant, as if she were flirting. "Do you realize," she said, "that you hurt both of us with your anger? I know Sam is trying to trip you up. But be patient, honey."

Her voice soothed him. He came closer to her. "You're right, as always. We can work this through."

Even as he heard his own voice, Randy could see Sam Heavy Hand's arrogant grin.

Doubts brought on by the day's investigation had not blocked out Billy's mounting anxiety over his usual Sunday visit with his half-brother and sister-in-law. Since Arthur's funeral, Sundays had been set aside by the two men as times when they could both go through Arthur's estate. Billy dreaded the day, the silences that always fell between him and Toshiro as they cleaned up their father's rooms or read over documents for probate tax and the insurance money Arthur had left for the two of them.

The late-afternoon wind was blowing hard from the west as Billy pulled into Toshiro's front yard. The Pontiac clicked across the interlocking bricks of the driveway. Billy wanted to honk the horn but decided it would be better to park quietly in front of the white metal garage door and go and ring the back bell. Toshiro's house was on a new street in the town of Coaldale. It was a two-storey kit house built facing east with a Spanish-styled roof and coffee-coloured stucco covering its exterior. The backyard opened onto ploughed land. The yard grass stopped in a straight line between Toshiro's property and the flat farmland once used to grow sugarbeets.

"I'm here!"

Billy bent his head forward going down the narrow basement steps.

The concrete floor was painted a dull grey. The smell of dust and closed-in air made Billy think about the hanging of Darren Riegert. He looked up at the pipes and joists. This heating conduit was thick enough to bear the weight of a 130-pound teenager.

Toshiro poked his head through a small door by the furnace. "I've got the boxes in here."

Billy followed his older brother into a small neat windowless room.

Toshiro had placed four cardboard boxes and a leather suitcase on a paint-splattered wooden workbench.

"Here is your mother's stuff."

Toshiro handed Billy the small battered suitcase. The fasteners were made of brass. The corners were broken and dented.

"Dad kept this all these years?"

Toshiro didn't answer. He walked over to a stack of shirts and coats piled on top of a wicker basket.

Here were Arthur's clothes. Billy was thinking how worn they seemed with their frayed cuffs. How lonely they looked. Toshiro began sorting. He did not look back at Billy. At the funeral, Toshiro had acted in the same silent way. Billy knew the barrier between him and his *nii-san*, his older half-brother, would remain impenetrable. Toshiro lived in his own private country, a landscape of bitter regrets and petty jealousies. Billy moved beside Toshiro and began lifting and folding the old clothes. "Do you want to keep any of this?"

Toshiro nodded. "I can use the tweed coat." He picked it up and put it on the paint table nearby.

Nata came into the room. She and Billy got along well. Very often it was Nata who would speak to Billy on behalf of Toshiro. "I'm making tea," she said. There was a sweetness in her tone.

After an hour, the clothes were sorted. Billy told his brother he wanted nothing. Just his mother's suitcase. Toshiro offered him a few snapshots of Arthur taken when he was a young man. Billy shuffled through them. "I've never seen these before."

In one of the sepia-coloured snaps, Arthur looked tired. Despair seemed to hang in the air around him, and his forlorn face brought pain to Billy. How vulnerable and innocent had he been? For the first time, Billy felt an odd yet very real connection between his memory of Arthur and his feeling for Darren Riegert. He looked at another snap. It was a shot of the dirt road leading away from the farm where Arthur had worked. By the road stood a frail, dark-haired girl: Setsuko, Arthur's sister. Billy glanced through the snapshots once more before placing them carefully in his upper-right jacket pocket.

Then he and Toshiro closed the boxes, turned out the light, and went upstairs.

"Take care, brother," Billy whispered. He then turned without seeing his brother's reaction and walked quickly out the back door and towards his Pontiac. Billy opened the trunk, placed the battered suitcase in it, and slammed the lid shut. He drove away in silence.

Fields of barley to his right and left took on the pale mauve of the late-day sun. Passing into the city of Lethbridge, he drove off the ramp onto Burdett, took the turn past Galt Gardens and the old railway station, then continued north towards the central police station. As he drove into a parking spot, Billy could hear the rush of cars going down the old brewery hill towards the new subdivisions crowding the west bank of the Oldman River. He walked into the reception area and down the hallway of locked offices. The door to Butch's office was the only one open at this hour. Butch was leaning against his filing cabinet stuffing paper into a folder.

"I got a message from Professor Mucklowe," Butch said. "On the com system. Here." Butch walked to his desk, flipped on his com attachment, put the phone on speaker, and clicked a couple of code numbers on the touch-tone keyboard. Randy spoke: "I figured I should call you. I'll be in Montana for a week on a dig up at Chief Mountain. I'll be taking the student crew down with me to the site. Thought you should know my cell number — 456-7889 — just in case you needed to talk. Sheree Lynn is staying at my place at least for the next few days. I assume you wanted us to keep in touch. Sorry for this voice-mail message."

"That was nice of him, eh?"

"Seems eager to let us know where he is."

"You off home?"

"I plan to come in early tomorrow morning. To go over files."

"Finally got the police board to grant you a week-by-week honorarium. As a consultant. Dodd will have the numbers for you Tuesday. You see the Morton boy again?"

"Yes. He was heavily sedated. He'd been violent and disoriented when brought in. I found a third Polaroid."

"So I heard."

"The same subject, a red Valentine heart. It's actually a picture of a chocolate box. But it was stuck in the book from the crime site."

Butch gathered up papers from his desk, and the two of them walked to the parking lot. Gusting breezes lifted their hair and flattened their pants against their thighs. The wind was promising hotter weather for Monday morning. Butch climbed into his cruiser. "I'm helping out Lorraine at her store first thing tomorrow in Fort Macleod. Big tourist day. But I'll see you later in the morning, buddy," he said and drove off. Billy got into the Pontiac, fastened his seatbelt, and backed out of the parking space. He rolled down his window. The riddle, the *koan*, will turn and turn, he thought as he lowered the sun visor against the slanting rays in the west.

From the police station to the main highway was no more than a three-minute drive. Billy's Pontiac coasted down the brewery hill, passing under the huge iron High Level Bridge. Heading west on Highway 3, he drove over the Oldman, which cut between the greening coulee hills, its churning waters the colour of milky tea, then northwest through Kipp and Coalhurst, and onto the old Crowsnest Trail towards home. Pulling into the ranch, he shut off the engine. Still waiting for him by the front porch were the fir trees in burlap bags and the sacks of white stones. In the evening sun, the raked yard in front of the clapboard house and the gentle lift of the fields seemed to generate light on their own. Farther on, the butte of Head-Smashed-In Buffalo Jump shimmered in the dying heat.

After supper, Billy put on a light sweater and strolled out to the concession road. Evening was his favourite part of the day. To him, the changing sky had a mysterious order all its own. Clouds banked in the west, turning grey then gold, long soft-edged wind clouds hovering in the dying light over the cragged wall of the Rockies that ran up from the Montana border to the south. A white-tail buck sprinted across the gravel, its tail held up like a feather duster, then pranced over the gentle rise towards the butte. When he returned to the house, Billy walked around checking windows, locking the kitchen and the front doors.

He sat on the sofa in the parlour and closed his eyes. Quiet harmony: acting through not acting.

The *koan* floated like a petal on still water.

No fingerprints. The single link? His mind turned. He imagined Harry Stone sitting across from him, feet up on the edge of his desk as they used to do on night duty, the harbour of Vancouver twinkling outside the squad room windows. Harry liked to go over the day's business. "Let's add it up, Yam," Harry would say, cupping his hands behind his head. Billy would sit forward, flipping through his notebook.

"We got Blayne Morton."

"Possible nut case," Harry said. "He's hiding something with that playacting. A sad, mean bully. And bullies like to pick on losers — like Darren. Maybe Morton was into that Satan crap. Who knows? He may have been in love with Darren. Maybe taking his picture and cutting him up was a kinky kind of sex game they had going."

There was certainly a motive for Blayne's behaviour and witnesses to his treatment of Darren before the crime took place. "But watch yourself, Yam. Three Polaroids won't get you a conviction. You need hard evidence: an item that places Morton at the crime scene in the right time frame."

"And we have Woody Keeler."

"Well," said Harry, "don't push that issue yet. You figure he's a violent jerk? Of course he is. But a killer or torturer? Sure, the nicest old ladies poison their husbands. But what's his motive? Or is he a psychopath who needs no other motive than the pleasure of getting off on his victim's screams?"

Billy reflected on these ideas before glancing at the clock on the fireplace mantel. The close silence reminded him of the quiet in the basement rooms of Satan House. The quiet of a tomb. What about the cult connection? The candles on the floor? The markings on the walls? These were still worth investigation. He would review files on Monday, then on Tuesday find more on Blayne Morton and Woody Keeler. Perhaps a visit to Mrs. Morton with a search warrant.

Billy turned out the light. He stretched and, as he left the room, smiled.

"Night, Harry."

MONDAY, JULY 1

Billy bent over the sacks of white stones he'd brought home four days before from the Canadian Tire nursery. He hauled the sacks to the patch of dug-up earth for his father Arthur's honour garden. It was designed as a dry space, in the Zen tradition, and was kidney-shaped, the smaller end having a cairn of fieldstones arranged to represent mountains. Planted opposite the cairn was a dwarf pine. Billy ripped open the sacks and on a top layer of pressed sand raked the white stones first into separate mounds and then into long patterns of parallel lines. For an hour, he dug and arranged stones, standing back once in a while to make sure his patterns were even. By 7:15, his muscles were sore, but he decided to keep on working. He tore open the last sack. Like heavy snow, the white stones scattered, their polished sides catching the early light. He spread them, and with the handle end of the rake he drew swirls and eddies.

Stone imitating water. The perfect Zen paradox.

During breakfast, the phone rang. It was Lorraine Bochansky asking him if he could come to her store in Fort Macleod. She needed a favour. "Of course," Billy said. He rinsed the dishes, took a quick shower, and was on the road before nine o'clock.

Fort Macleod lay ten kilometres along the Crowsnest Trail due east of the Naughton ranch. The log stockade on the outskirts of the town was a replica of the first outpost of 1874 built by the Northwest Mounted Police. Main Street boasted gas lamps and renovated storefronts. Lorraine Bochansky's antique store was a narrow single-storey building wedged between the bank and the old-time livery stable. Its cramped quarters were stuffed with camel-backed sofas, roll-top desks, imitation Tiffany lamps, and the occasional four-poster.

"Hi, there," said Lorraine. She was pointing to a walnut cabinet on the back porch. The cabinet's smooth varnish and flawless grain were half hidden under a blue plastic tarp.

"Looks heavy enough," Billy said as he came up the steps.

Lorraine Bochansky had short brown hair and wore hoop earrings. She was just under six feet, and her face was a mass of freckles. When she talked, she stood with her hands on her hips. "Butch put his back out this morning, climbing into the tub." Lorraine clicked her tongue. "I warned him. 'Stress builds up,' I said. You bend the wrong way, and in a second you're flat on your back. You're a doll, Billy, helping like this. Tourists flock here on the holiday weekend, as you can imagine. I think this darling cabinet will be snapped up in no time."

Billy helped Lorraine fold the tarp, and then he placed a small dirty carpet under the rounded feet of the cabinet. Lorraine removed the bottom drawers, and Billy grasped the edge of the carpet. Only four feet to cover, but the porch was rough and slanted.

"Ready?" he asked.

The two of them slid the cabinet into the main area of the store.

"We did it," Lorraine cried happily. She hugged Billy, then went to her small office to turn on the automatic coffee machine.

Outside, Fort Macleod was waking up: boys flew by on bicycles, a dog pranced to the window and pressed its wet nose to the glass. Billy threw himself into a large wing chair, dust puffing from the sagging cushions. On a table, beside him, was a bunch of bills and papers that he carelessly picked up and began to peruse, his eyes glancing at prices and phone numbers and short descriptions of various pieces. The smell of coffee wafted into the brightening gloom of the store.

"I still like it," he said.

"What?" asked Lorraine, bringing Billy a mug of fresh coffee.

"'Keepsakes' . . . the name you gave the place."

"Why, thank you."

"What is this stuff, anyway?"

"Invoices, bills of lading, info sheets."

"No, I know that. But what is this stuff from the border?"

"Let me see. I got this at Chief Mountain. I had to show my licence when I declared a sofa, and customs handed me a whole raft of these descriptions. All to do with contraband, missing artifacts. As a member of the Antique Dealers Association of North America, I often get bulletins. I guess the border people are particularly sensitive this time of year with the high volume of traffic."

"To all dealers," Billy began. He read out loud one of the four yellow sheets with official government letterhead: "Found a year ago on the Cutbank Ranch, Montana, seven gold and shell masks. Decorative, religious objects believed to be ceremonial dating from late 18th century. Pueblo in origin. . . ." Billy took a sip of his coffee. "Shall I read on?" he asked.

"Please do, I rarely glance at those things since most of them don't really apply to the store." Lorraine was now preparing the cash register and lighting scented candles to place in the darker corners.

"Masks were sold by the Blackfoot community by order of the Montana Court of Appeals to the University of Montana. Subsequently stolen, they are believed to be in custody of the felons. Masks are five inches long by six inches wide, oval, flat not convex (see illustration), with incised mouth configuration of mother-of-pearl mounted under a two-inch strip of beaten Mexican gold with eye-shape cut outs. Valuable intact." Billy paused. "Sounds like a find."

"Well, I've never seen them. The woman I dealt with in Montana said the masks were dug up by her neighbour. He was charged with theft under the Antiquities Act in the States. That's why the matter went to court. Imagine finding such a treasure on your own land and then being labelled a thief."

"But then the goods were stolen by a real thief, so it says here. From the university. Why were they there?"

"Placed by the government as part of a new Native museum. I hear the masks are very lovely."

Billy finished his coffee, folded the bulletin, and put it back on the table. He rose from the wing chair. What mattered now was to get his day going.

"Thanks for your help."

Lorraine accompanied Billy to his car.

"How long has it been now, if you don't mind me prying, since you and Cynthia divorced?"

"Nine years."

"And you're still a lone wolf, aren't you?"

Billy didn't answer.

"I'm sorry," she said quickly. "Coffee's always on," she then said, cheerily, "if you ever want to stop by."

"Good to know. I'll call Butch when I get to town."

Thirty minutes later, Billy was at the station in Lethbridge, the halls quiet except for the dispatch sergeant answering a query on the telephone. He called Butch, but he was probably still sleeping. Billy found the Morton file. He copied down the address and phone number. Then he called the psychiatric ward at the regional hospital and spoke to a night nurse who was just going off duty. The boy had spent a quiet night, and he was still mildly sedated. His mother had not come by, nor had she appeared earlier that morning. She was expected soon.

Crossing reception, Billy went out to the station parking lot and searched for his city map in the tumbled mess he called his glove compartment. Mrs. Morton lived in a new subdivision in the southeast part of the city; Billy remembered it from his high school days as bordering the old stadium. The Pontiac sputtered a little as he drove down Dawson; by the time he turned onto Magrath Drive, the engine had settled. The new Loblaws signalled the street, and it took Billy only a minute before he found the small three-storey apartment building with the red front door. The superintendent, a tall Sikh woman with grey hair, accompanied Billy to Mrs. Morton's apartment and waited as he rang the doorbell. There was no answer. "She goes to her sister's once in a while, I believe," the superintendent said.

"Do you have an address for her?" Billy asked.

"No. The woman lives outside of the city on a farm, and Mrs. Morton goes by bus."

Billy drove back to the station. He went through the file on Mrs. Morton once more, phoned the company where she worked as a cleaner, and was greeted by a recorded message saying the company was closed for the holiday. Putting the file back, Billy went to dispatch and asked the sergeant to draft him a search warrant. Then he went to the canteen, found it closed too, and climbed back upstairs to Butch's office. He began reading through other files and reviewing the taped statements of Bird and Mucklowe. Rubbing his bum knee, he was starting to feel frustrated and fearful. Evidence was not turning up. There were petty delays. He sat back. At least he'd done good work on his father's honour garden. The other bother was yesterday's visit with Toshiro. But let that go, he thought. *Don't let anger get between you and him. Toshiro is the only connection you have left to Arthur.*

Billy stood and stretched his arms. He wondered if Butch would be back to work by tomorrow. Time was running out.

"Damn," he whispered. He sat down on the carpet, pulled his aching knee forward into the lotus position, and began to meditate. *Let it come, let it float. . . .*

Justin Moore paused in the open doorway. The brightness of noon sun shining into the hallway reminded him just how early he had awakened this morning. The wall facing the open door showed an Inuit print. A coloured bird dancing on a man's head.

Justin thought: Maybe Randy can help me. *It won't hurt to try.*

He heard laughter.

"Hello?"

"Is that you, Justin?"

Professor Mucklowe's voice came from somewhere down the hall. Justin walked towards it.

Maybe he can give me a loan.

The living room lay to Justin's left. It was a large empty square with one chair and beige wall-to-wall carpet. A glass cabinet stood by the window like a lonely monument in the echoing space. Its top shelves displayed Professor Mucklowe's collection of amulets and arrowheads. "The Plains Indians," Professor Mucklowe once said in a lecture, "have sown the prairie earth with their artifacts: spear tips, arrowheads, hatchets." The dining room was also empty. *Where's his furniture?*

"There you are, Justin. I was afraid you'd forgotten about our meeting."

Professor Mucklowe was standing beside a blonde student with shortly cropped hair. The kitchen smelled of freshly brewed coffee. The professor's cotton T-shirt and clean pressed Levis were part of his new image. Last winter he'd cut his ponytail. Justin thought he looked like a mediaeval warlord in a movie.

"How you doing, Justin? Get you a coffee?"

Professor Mucklowe reached out and slapped him on the shoulder.

"Thanks. Just black."

The blonde was wearing a red shirt and tight-fitting white Bermuda shorts. She smiled immediately at Justin when he came in. He smiled back and watched her lean against the kitchen counter, where she continued to sip from her mug. Justin knew Cara Simonds from Randy's class. Smart. Friendly. Sometimes too friendly, always trying to help Justin with his studying, offering her time, willing to drive him home some nights after a project in the university library. "Can't we be friends?" she'd say and smile in her shy way. At least she was good in archaeology, especially with details, and she didn't mind sharing ideas.

"Hi, Cara," Justin said.

"Have we met before?" Cara joked. "This'll be our first dig together, Justin. I'm looking forward to it, aren't you?"

"Sure. Of course."

A balding young man Justin's age sauntered into the kitchen. Justin knew him from history class. David Home was an A student who loved to talk about the Old West. He had asked Justin to go on the dig this summer. "You'll love it, Justin," David had said, his eagerness and enthusiasm lighting up his pale thin face.

"Dave!"

"Justin! Did you get that down sleeping bag?"

"Sure did."

"You guys will be bunking down in the back bedroom of my cabin," Randy interrupted. "You can bring along your bags if you want, but you won't really need them. We won't be staying up at the Chief Mountain site as we had originally planned. The band council at Browning didn't think it right to have camping on a sacred prayer site."

Randy clapped his hands. "Anyway, how 'bout we go down to the den?" He spread his arms to try to herd them out of the kitchen. "I've got the slides set up. We can get through this in no time. Help yourselves to more coffee. Oh, and please get out pens and paper. I need to have all your home addresses and medical health card numbers."

"Why?" asked Cara.

"For insurance. The university needs the data. Just your home addresses, where you currently live'll be fine."

"You mean my mother's address?" asked Justin.

"Is that where you are living, Justin? If so, I need just that. If you're in residence, you can add that address as well."

Randy and David left the kitchen. Cara Simonds poured herself another coffee. She turned towards Justin.

He realized she looked pretty with her new short hair, and he let himself stare at her brown eyes and at her full breasts. Then he stepped back. "You here for extra credits, Cara?" Justin asked, his voice catching a little in his throat.

Cara smiled. "Can I warm up your coffee?" She took hold of the mug, and her fingers lightly brushed against his. She poured the coffee and handed it back to him. "Careful. Don't burn yourself." She smiled again. She then answered Justin's question. "Not really. I actually wanted to go and work on a sacred site. Randy told me it was one of the hardest field digs he'd ever had to arrange. The Blackfoot band in Montana are very possessive of their history. Who can blame them?"

As she spoke, Justin looked at her mouth, her eyes, the way her hands moved. She was slimmer than Karen. Forget about Karen, he thought. Justin's stomach rumbled as he pushed the word *abortion* from his mind. There was something peaceful about Cara Simonds. *I wonder if she might have some money?*

"Come on, Cara. Randy'll get upset if we don't get started."

"Right."

The den was at the end of the hallway. A narrow room with a couch and two bookcases crammed with paperbacks. A sliding glass door led out onto a small balcony. Randy sat on the couch while David Home set up a roll screen to the left of the doorway. Cara and Justin came in with their coffees and sat down on the bare floor near Randy's feet. On a dented metal TV table, Randy had set up his old carousel slide projector. The carousel was half full of white cardboard slides. As the group got ready, Randy handed each a small booklet he'd prepared on his computer. Justin flipped his open. On page 1 was a table of contents explaining the nature of the site, the goal of the dig, the expectations of what they might find, and then a couple of Randy's published academic articles on vision quest sites and Blackfoot tribal history.

"We've got a week of hard digging and hot days together. But you'll find the place we're going to very nice. You won't have much free time, except back in Waterton Lakes, where my cabin is. On the way home from Chief, we can stop and swim in the Waterton river. And we can get pizzas and good burgers at Frank's Café on Main Street. Count on being tired, though. Digging is slow, fussy work. There's a lot of sifting. Don't expect a big find. Don't look forward to discovering a skull or any gold. Mainly think about how to use the dig skills and labelling techniques I taught you last winter. That's the point of the field trip. You get to work hard for me for little money, and I get to publish and receive the credit. And, yes, if we do find anything, all of you will be credited, and all of your names will appear on the article.

"Think of this as purely a search mission. We may get nothing. But the scenery will take your breath away."

Randy clicked on the slide projector. David Home adjusted the height of the screen. He pulled the curtain over the window and then bent over double and walked under the beam of light to sit down next to Cara and Justin. The screen lit up with a front view of Chief Mountain. A square-shaped shale peak, the mountain straddled the boundary of the Canadian plains and the rise of the Rockies. Its immensity belied its distance from Canada; however, as Randy explained. "Chief lies in the state of Montana. Though we like to claim it as one of our mountains."

Randy went on, "The Blackfoot of both countries do not recognize our political borders. Chief has been sacred to them and a part of their land and rituals for over two thousand years. The screefall base of the mountain remains a place of prayer and supplication. There a man of faith can traverse the invisible line between the human and spirit worlds and communicate with his spirit guide."

The next slide showed a vast sloping field of stone with open patches of earth and small wildflowers and the sharp edge of a pine forest. "Here's the screefall. Wear good boots for this. We walk over it; we dig under it; we haul stuff on it."

Randy clicked again, and the southwest side of Chief was shown — a commercial photo taken of the mountain at sunset to highlight its unique tower-like shape. To Justin, who'd seen Chief only from a distance, the mountain resembled a giant triangle of purple-grey stone. It almost looked as if it had been carved or built on a gravel foundation.

"The Blackfoot, or Blackfeet if you live in Montana, call this peak Nin Nase Tok Que. The King. We whites dubbed it Chief Mountain because it reminded us of a tribal leader in full eagle headdress. Our base camp, Site 125, is at the foot of the peak on the screefall."

Randy clicked. The vast field of stone was now shown photographed from another angle. "Looks like a giant football field someone broke up from a pit of boulders," said David.

"Pretty close," said Randy. "It's partially scree — rockfall from the mountain — and partly glacier rock and moraine earth left over from the ice age retreat. Our site is just above the tree line, the line of pines edging the scree. Chief is cracking apart. Last year a large stonefall occurred on the southeast face."

"Will we be safe up there?" Cara asked.

"Pretty well," answered Randy. "We'll be working farther west. We are calling the dig a vision quest for lack of a better word. A young Native would go to the mountain, alone, to fast and pray for a vision — a spirit animal, a sign in the clouds — which would bring him guidance and courage. The band council in Montana has given us a five-day time frame to do some exploratory digging in places where prayer and quests once took place. We're not sure if this was a burial ground, too. In the past, questors often left behind gifts for their spirit guides. I hope we can locate some amulets, some old beadwork belts — and I mean old. Maybe early nineteenth, late eighteenth century. The cold air and altitude and dry winters can preserve a lot. Luckily, the site was never plundered by ranchers or train track builders. It was too far out, and it's hard to get to by vehicle."

"But how are we going to get up there?" David Home's voice sounded anxious.

"Look."

The next slide showed a forest of pine and a narrow road. Through the trees, the huge base of the mountain could be seen glowing in the sun.

"A logging road?" asked Justin.

"Deer path. Used by Blackfoot who park down below — like we will — and walk up to the site."

"So," added Cara, "if we find artifacts, as you said, the museum in Browning, Montana, gets to keep them."

"Yes. There will be a Native guide with us at all times. A man named Sam Heavy Hand, from the Browning reserve."

"To make sure we don't pilfer?" Cara countered.

"Hey, Cara," Randy said. "Don't make us sound like a bunch of grave robbers. This is all above board."

"Sorry."

"You'll be billeted at my cabin in Waterton Lakes for the time we're on the dig. You won't need to worry about food or paying for gas since the university has given us a stipend. We can cook at home and take food up to the site, but we can't camp there. Bring your passports each time we cross into Montana. Bring spending money and take a look at the booklet I handed out. It lists all the stuff you'll need — boots, first aid, and the rest. Your honorariums of five hundred dollars will be paid out at the end of the dig, as I told you before. Cara, I know you asked if you could take your own car. And, yes, I got it cleared. You can drive over the border if you wish or come in the van."

"I'll only need the car in Waterton in case I have to come home fast. My mom is not well, and she may need me to come into town to help her. I told her I could do it after a day's dig, and she thought that would be all right. If it's cool with you."

"By all means."

"Will the border guards be checking the van every time we cross? For artifacts? Or looking in our pockets?" Justin was asking the question seriously.

"Most likely." Randy cleared his throat. "It'll be official only. Once they know us, they'll wave us through. But we do have to submit a site report every day. Sam will be helping us with that. Any more questions? Please do not forget to give me your addresses."

Randy gazed around the room. The sun now illuminated the balcony, and Randy stood up and pulled open the curtain.

"Come here, everyone."

David and Cara and Justin got up and walked over to Randy, who'd gone out on the balcony. Randy was pointing into the hazy light where far off, over the fields and the blue line of the Oldman River, the Rockies appeared. The dark square near the horizon was Chief Mountain.

"There it is. The King."

Randy went back inside and clicked the projector one more time. The screen filled with a picture of clouds and the cragged peak of Chief.

"The wind can cut you in half up there if you're not careful," Randy said, his voice suddenly becoming soft. "Spirits are everywhere. Some of them do not like to be disturbed."

Justin stared at Cara's face. She had stepped into the den and was lit by the glare from the projector. The hard light seemed to reveal the very bones under her skin. She fixed her eyes on the slide of the clouds and the mountain. Justin wondered what she was thinking. Every part of her body appeared taut, ready for action.

The crew of three were set to leave and go home to prepare for the trip. Randy reminded everyone about packing light but right. "On a mountain, the weather is unpredictable, so it's always wise to dress in layers to keep dry and warm." He also told Justin and the other two that departure time was 3:30. "We need an early start to get into the park and settle at the cabin." David Home left first. Cara Simonds dawdled in the kitchen and took extra time to wash the coffee cups while Justin dried. He then walked her to the front door and asked her if she was excited.

"I'll put it this way. It'll be good to get away from my mom for a while," Cara said, her expression darkening as she spoke. Justin wondered if she felt as lonely and isolated as he did.

After she left, Randy asked, "Justin, could you wait around?" Justin said yes. Randy grinned. "I'll just put away the slides. Have a seat. There's something I want to share with you." Randy left for the den.

Justin sat on the chair in the nearly empty living room. Restless, he felt the presence of Yianni in the panic growing in his chest. He wanted to call Karen, but he couldn't think of what he'd say. He got up and at the glass cabinet fingered one of the amulets Randy had collected. The blue flashes in the stone reminded him of sapphire. Justin looked over his shoulder. He held the amulet tight in his fist for a second.

"You got time for a beer?"

Justin jumped as Randy came back into the living room. "I could use one." Justin placed the amulet back on the glass shelf.

In the kitchen, Randy pulled open the fridge door. He took out two dark ales and twisted off their caps. Justin was about to take a drink when Sheree Lynn Bird appeared in the doorway.

"Randy?"

Her bare toes curled up from touching the cool tiles.

"Hi, Justin," she said, her voice barely audible.

"Hi," he answered. Justin found himself staring at Sheree Lynn's body. She was wearing a T-shirt, her nipples pressing against the cotton, and a filmy muslin skirt slit up the side. The familiar tension surfaced. Justin had always wanted to have sex with her, and she had never shown any interest in returning his glances or his tacit invitations. In the past, he had gone over to her back door and offered to mow her lawn, do any favours around the yard. He'd once asked her out for a beer, but Sheree Lynn had never gone beyond coy refusals. *She's a cock tease*, Justin reminded himself. *You're better off.*

Randy turned just then. Justin saw that he had been watching him and Sheree Lynn. "Come on, Sheree," Randy said, his voice irritable and impatient. "Justin and I have to talk business."

"Oh, do you?"

She sauntered farther into the kitchen and stood between Justin and Randy.

"You heard about Darren Riegert?" she said, addressing Justin directly.

"Let's not bring that up again," Randy complained.

Sheree Lynn turned and locked eyes with Randy. "What are you afraid of?"

Justin quickly looked away from them, towards the light in the dining room.

"You met Darren, didn't you, Justin?" Sheree began again, lowering her voice and ignoring Randy.

"Yeah. I saw him once or twice."

"Did you ever talk to him or Cody?"

How much does she know? Is she hinting . . . what if she goes to the police?

Justin shook his head. There was an uneasy silence in the kitchen.

"I see," sighed Sheree Lynn. "It's terrible what's happened. Really awful."

Randy reached out to her. He lifted her arms to his neck, surrounding her with his body as if she were a child. Whispering, he led her from the kitchen and down the hallway. Randy's voice disappeared when a door clicked shut.

Justin felt more confused than ever. He fixed his thoughts on Karen, but the memory of her weeping face stabbed at him. Fuck it, he thought, his mind now conjuring up the image of Aunt Marion's crumbling mansion. Satan House was always a place of sadness and bad luck. Justin had pitied his auntie, her bottle in her hand, her thin wraith-like body on the sofa in the living room, where she spent her drunken afternoons watching television.

"How did you hear about Darren?"

Justin was startled by Randy's sudden re-appearance in the kitchen.

"My mom told me," Justin said quickly. "She said the police were asking some questions."

"Can I show you something, Justin?"

"Sure."

Randy took a set of keys and walked out the main entrance of the apartment and down a set of stairs leading to the building's parking lot. The front part of the building was cantilevered over the slope of the coulee hill. Randy and Justin moved past the parked cars and onto the slope that faced the Oldman River valley.

"Watch your footing here. There's supposed to be some steps, but the landlord says the contractor has yet to show up to finish the job."

Randy slid down the grass and steadied his stance. He pointed to a long line of garage doors built under the arches of the ground floor.

"Those are our storage lockers. One day we may be able to park our cars in them. Come on."

In front of the locker where Randy stopped and searched for a key, Justin noticed tire tracks leading out from the locker's entrance. Randy inserted the key and slid up the wobbly metal door. Inside the narrow concrete space sat a huge black gleaming Harley Davidson. Spoked wheels. Double leather seat. Chrome tailpipes.

"My folly," beamed Randy.

Justin came up beside Randy and watched him run his hand along the polished handlebar. The air in the locker smelled of leather and motor oil.

"Impressive, eh?"

"Sure. You ride her much?"

Randy broke into a laugh.

"You want her, Justin?"

Justin blinked. It took him a moment to process Randy's question.

"How do you mean?"

"Your family has money. You must like to show off. I am in bad straits these days, to be honest. My ex-wife, Connie, is squeezing my balls dry, and I need cash. I can sell you this baby for nine grand. A great deal."

"But, Randy. . . ."

"You're young! This could be the machine for you, believe me."

Justin was surprised at the rush of his disappointment. This was not what he'd counted on. So that would explain the empty rooms, Randy's lack of furniture. He looked again at the Harley. Randy was staring at him, nervously wiping his mouth. Justin felt an ache rise in his stomach.

"I'm not sure, Randy."

"Look, Justin. Think it over. I know it's sudden. Don't tell anyone I showed you the hog. You're the first I've offered her to. Believe me. I can give you a deal, like I said."

"Thanks. Thanks a lot. But, sir, I have a confession. I wanted to ask you for money!"

"No kidding!" Randy forced a laugh. "You broke or what?"

"I owe some money, and I was wondering if I could maybe get an advance. On my stipend for the dig. Today, in fact, before we leave town."

Randy frowned and rubbed his right hand over his mouth. "Not at this short notice. Payroll is slow and sticky when it comes to that kind of arrangement, Justin. Believe me."

"Sir, you could loan the bike to me. I could maybe try to sell it for you. Maybe we could work out an arrangement. I pay off some of my debt, then I pay you back slowly, maybe pay you my stipend. . . ."

"Well, no, Justin. That'd take some time. You sound like you're in the same hole I am."

Justin walked into the open and gazed down the slope of the hill. How easy it would be, he thought, just shut the garage door, turn on the Harley's engine, breathe in the carbon monoxide. An easy crossing from life into death. He turned and watched Randy wiping the leather seat with a cloth. "You're right, Randy. It's a great machine. You could get a lot of money for it."

"Well, Justin. You like her, then?"

Justin's mind was running in circles. "Like you said. Nine thousand is a good deal."

"You bet it is."

"I should get going if you want us back by 3:30."

"I'll stay down here for a while. I may even take the bike out for a spin. You sure you don't want to try her out?"

Justin hesitated. There was no way he could bargain with Randy now. "I should move on."

"Okay. See you at 3:30."

Justin walked to the lot. It took him a minute to locate the Olds. He got in, started the engine, and drove towards the intersection. After speeding across the Oldman River valley, he headed up Ashmead and Dawson Streets, passed the post office and his old high school, and turned onto Parkside Drive. He parked and ran up a fieldstone walkway leading to the glistening oak door of a huge low-roofed house. "You've got nothing to lose by asking," he said under his breath. The garden was damp from a recent watering; the grass shone with hard green light. He desperately rang Patsy Hanson's door chime. He rang it again. Where was she? The chimes had a lilting sound, an expensive sound, as if they had been fashioned from a thin precious metal. "One more time." He pressed the chime. The last note was starting to fade when the door swung open.

Patsy Hanson stared into Justin's face. For an instant, it appeared she was looking into thin air. She did not focus on him but seemed dazed at finding a young man on her doorstep.

But then she smiled.

Her right hand moved from the doorframe to her hip, while her left hand held aloft an unlit cigarette. She smelled of gin.

"Well, Justin. Long time no see."

Justin first met Patsy six months earlier in his anthropology class. He was surprised when she asked him out for a drink; she was his professor, twenty years older than he was. Justin's instincts warned him not to get involved, even though Patsy was attractive and persuasive. And she was always so forgiving and generous. Justin shoved his hands into his pockets. Patsy's perfume and the gin on her breath gave him an erection.

"I need to see you," he said. The wet warm air from the lawn pressed against him.

"How nice for me," she said, throwing back her head. Her bikini was red and covered in black polka dots. Wiry pubic hair jutted out from the sides of the elastic along her upper thighs.

They made love first on the hallway floor. Justin kept his shirt and his hiking boots on. Patsy laughed when he grunted and came. She pulled him up and led him into her bedroom. Tossing her crumpled bikini onto her vanity table, she instructed Justin to peel off the rest of his clothes as she lay naked and waiting on top of the stretched starched white sheets. "I want to come back to you," he whispered in her ear. The lie came out so quickly that Justin had no time to think about what he'd said. After showering together, Patsy insisted he stay the rest of the afternoon.

"I can't. Honest. I've got Mucklowe's dig to go on at 3:00."

"I see."

She made him coffee and sat down next to him at the round glass table in the kitchen, kissing him and fondling his neck while he hurriedly drank the bitter espresso. He knew she would not like what he was going to ask next.

"I'm in trouble, Patsy. I need some help."

Patsy's face pinched.

Justin's next words came out choked, and his shoulders began to shake. "I'm really afraid. Yianni Pappas is after me."

"What?"

Patsy wrapped her arms around Justin's neck.

"How the hell did you get mixed up with him?"

"I borrowed money. A lot. I thought he was a friend."

"He's a crook, Justin. A mean one."

"Some guys at school said he played fair. I didn't know."

"How much do you owe?"

"Six grand. He wants full payment by Saturday. Or else."

Patsy Hanson let out a breath. She pulled her arms away. "I see," she said, staring at the kitchen cupboards. When she stood up a few seconds later, her naked body caught the mid-afternoon sun. She meandered to the large windows that opened onto the back garden. "You said you wanted to come back to me, am I right?"

"Yes."

"But you really came here to fuck for money."

Justin said nothing.

"Well, didn't you?"

"Patsy, I don't know what to do."

"I know." Her voice was hard-edged.

Justin thought he should wait it out. All he needed from her was a cheque. It'd be easy to cash it today. On the way out of town, he could pay off Yianni. Get off the hook for good. Patsy liked being with Justin, and Justin knew it. She would act hurt and angry, but he knew she desired him. Still, he waited.

Patsy stood at the window and did not move. She looked like a statue, posed with her arm against the glass.

Justin moved his legs. "You know, Patsy, Yianni burned a guy so bad with a blowtorch the guy almost died."

"I'm not sure that story is true, Justin."

"He did it. He burned half the man's body for a loan worth no more than. . . ."

"There are ways of getting money, I suppose, that don't involve sex. Like a blowtorch. Sometimes I think that might not be such a bad thing." Patsy's voice was flat and toneless.

Justin stood. She will tell me to stay or to go, he figured. Even so, he must try to get her to see his desperation. Moving closer, he put his arms around her.

"My problem is your problem, too, Patsy. If Yianni hurts me or even kills me, you'll have that on your conscience."

Patsy Hanson turned to face Justin. His heart was beating fast, as if he'd been running, as if he'd been with Yianni Pappas himself. He had done something he'd never done before. He'd used his fear to make another person fearful.

"You *are* right about that, Justin. You are so right."

Patsy walked to the door leading to her bedroom. "I don't want to lose you." She smiled, allowed her face to show a fleeting look of triumph. Justin moved back by the table, folded his arms across his chest, hoping his plea would work. If it did, all his problems would be solved, and he could go to the mountains feeling free. All his money problems, that is. "How long does your dig last?"

"Starts tomorrow. We get back in four days. Friday the fifth. Mucklowe is putting us up at his cabin in Waterton Lakes, and we'll be crossing the border every day to get to the Chief Mountain site in Montana."

"And Yianni? When does the bastard want his cash?"

"Saturday morning. And he means it. Saturday or else."

"Let me see what I can do." Patsy walked into her bedroom. She spoke to Justin from there. "I won't be a minute. Meet me in the front hall."

The hall had a long table and a view of the lawn. Justin waited by the front door, glancing at the ceiling, hearing Patsy humming to herself in her bedroom, opening drawers, closing closets. She came out in less than five minutes wearing a pair of jeans and a white long-sleeved shirt. She had pinned up her hair and put on lipstick. Is she going to take me to the bank? Justin wondered. She handed Justin a small box.

"Open it. It was a gift from my father many years ago. I want you to have it."

Justin lifted the blue paper lid of the box. A small rabbit's foot with a chain of brass lay on a bed of white tissue paper.

"It's for good luck. It's also a sign of trust between us, Justin. I know I've been angry with you. I know I can sometimes lose my temper. So I want to make things right. You have to promise one thing, though."

"Anything."

"You haven't heard me out yet."

"Okay."

She stepped closer, placing her hands around his neck. Gently, softly, but he could feel her strength.

"Promise me you will come to me Friday night. Right after the dig. As soon as you get home. Promise me you will stay with me for the whole night. If you do, we'll go to Yianni together. And I'll pay him off. Then the two of us can work something out. Start over."

Justin lifted his hands to hers. He held them and kept his eyes on hers.

"I promise, Patsy. On my life. But how do I know I can trust you?"

Patsy's face went blank. She stiffened, indignant.

"You have no choice. You want the money, you prove to me how badly you want it."

"If I come, will you have the cash?"

She said nothing, just smiled. Justin pulled away.

He turned the box in his hand. It was clear he had no choice. *Can I be sure?* Patsy liked to play games. She loved to tease and taunt, to say one thing but mean another. She opened the front door. And smiled again. Justin walked to the Olds without looking back at her, knowing he had come close. Very close. He started the engine. Patsy was draped against the open door. Justin raised his hand, and she waved back. Driving down Parkside, he did not feel anything but numb disappointment and fatigue. At the stoplight, he lifted up his hands from the wheel and looked at them. They were still empty.

He drove for a while, brooding, until he found himself by the banks of the Oldman River. He pulled the Olds into a stand of trees and got out and walked to the edge of the water. How easy it would be to fall in, *to let the current take me.* He pulled the rabbit's foot from his pocket and hurled it into the far rapids. *To hell with Patsy.* And yet she did say she'd pay Yianni off. She had money, she liked sex, she was risking a lot. So why wouldn't she come through?

Still, Justin needed a backup. Someone he could rely on if Patsy decided to slam the door in his face. But who? He crouched on the bank of pebbles and listened to the murmuring water.

Who?

The sun was still high in the west when Cara Simonds drove out towards the Rockies, her car following Mucklowe's Chevy van. Justin slumped in the front seat. He had not bothered to phone Karen, though he knew she'd be anxious to talk. He stared ahead at the black road, peering into the light as if his eyes were full of grit.

"You don't look too happy, Justin," Cara said, making her voice sound as soothing as she could. "Is there anything wrong?"

"Can I trust you, Cara?"

"You know you can, Justin."

"I need money. I need to borrow some money to pay off a debt to a loan shark named Yianni Pappas. He's threatened to kill me if I don't pay by this Saturday."

"Oh, Justin, I'm sorry. I wish I could help you."

"Do you?" Justin sat up.

"I don't mean money, Justin. My mom has been sick for a while, and my dad is unemployed. I'd rob a bank for you if it'd help." Cara smiled.

"I am serious, Cara," he said, his voice becoming gloomy.

"I believe you, Justin. But I really don't have any money. Have you tried going to the bank? Maybe the manager or your mother's banker could help."

"I'm afraid not. My dad left us with a lot of debt. My mother's job hardly pays for groceries."

Cara drove in silence. Justin slid down in his seat again. She meant well, he figured, but she didn't really believe him. He liked being with her, close beside her; the smell of her hair and perfume made the afternoon seem brighter. He looked up now at the broad stretch of Highway 5. Four lanes winding through farm- and ranchlands south to the small town of Cardston. Justin glanced at the passing fields of green and the shallow coulees trickling with small streams. Soon Cara was talking about school and the upcoming dig, trying to get his mind off things. Justin wanted to talk about her. He began asking about her mother, her family, if she was seeing anyone at the moment. She told him about her last affair, how it was over. Definitely over. As the light changed, clouds gathered slowly, their tufted undersides turning pink and gold. Cara pointed to the ditches alongside the road. The first blooms of July filled gullies and slopes with waving patches of yellow buttercups and wild lupine.

With cooler air rushing in the open windows, Justin recognized the region of foothills bordering the mountains. The sun was slowly descending, and he felt his dark mood returning. Randy stopped ahead at the entrance to Waterton Lakes Park. He bought two passes and walked back to Cara to hand one to her. "We've made good time, Cara," Randy said. He returned to his Chevy van and drove in through the park's entrance, with Cara following up a long curving hill to where the mountains came into full view. The vast spill-plain of the Blakiston River lay below them full of wildflowers. Justin did not feel elated. He saw only long afternoon shadows. Cara slowed to gaze at the purple hue of the shale peaks.

"Isn't that pretty?" she said as they drove on.

Justin looked up. A hotel painted brown and green and looking like a cross between a tipi and a Swiss chalet sat on a knoll facing an immense fiord. The mountains formed a corridor, each side a cragged line of immense stone shapes that rose from the edges of the emerald water. Cara said she wanted to take pictures when the dig was over. Justin couldn't understand her awe. The slopes of fir trees seemed to him desolate and lonely places where a man could lose his directions and starve to death. Waterton village buoyed his spirit a little. It looked cosy and clean, the stores with brightly lit windows. The village was spread over the sand delta of the Cameron River. Running parallel to the main street was the emerald lake's beach of smooth white stones.

When they finally reached Randy's cabin, the sun was turning the bushes of wild rose and fragrant kinnikinnick a cool evening blue.

"Your rooms are behind the kitchen," Randy announced.

The crew unpacked the Chevy van, hauling indoors the grocery bags and the luggage. Randy took out the tarps with the digging gear and locked them in a small wooden shed sitting in tall grass behind the cabin. The cabin itself had low beamed ceilings. The walls were of varnished plywood. The air inside smelled of cut firewood mixed with wild sage. Justin looked through the bedrooms. Old metal-frame beds were covered with red Hudson's Bay blankets. Back in the living room, he stood by the stone fireplace and examined an old buffalo skull over the mantel. Hanging in one corner of the room, above a wicker table, was a pair of beaded moccasins. "Those belonged to my grandmother," Randy explained. "She was a friend of a Blackfoot artist named Two Horse. He gave them to her as a birthday gift. Made by his wife."

Cara cooked dinner. She boiled corn and made a pie. While she was setting out plates, Justin went alone to his bedroom. It was the smallest room in the cabin, with a single bed, a sash window, and a wicker chair. He tapped in the number on his cell phone and sat on the bed, hunched over.

"What? Okay, okay. You'll be fine."

Justin rose. He turned so quickly Cara had no time to back out of the doorway, where she was standing in her apron. Justin covered the speaker part of the cell phone. "Cara! Please!"

Cara ran towards the kitchen. A moment later, Justin appeared in the doorway by the stove. Cara lowered her eyes. "I'm sorry," she said. "I didn't mean to. . . ."

"That was my mother," Justin said, lying. Karen had been crying. She'd said she was afraid to be left alone. All she thought about was Justin and the baby. "She panics," he went on, "when I go away. Ever since my dad died, she. . . ."

Cara rushed to Justin and held him. He let himself be calmed by the warmth of her circling arms. "I'm okay," he said to her, whispering in her ear. "She'll be okay, too." Cara pulled back. Her eyes and lips are beautiful, Justin thought. He leaned close and kissed her. When he looked into her face again, she was blushing. "How about some supper?" he said. Cara smiled and let go of his arms. Stepping backwards in the direction of the kitchen counter, she kept her eyes on Justin's. She opened a cupboard, pulled out a brass bell, and rang it loudly.

"Dinner, everyone."

She and Justin carried the platter of corn to the dining area. Randy had moved a table outside to a covered stone patio, where he and David Home were sitting in a couple of plastic lawn chairs, their bare feet up on stumps of wood, their right arms lifting bottles of pale ale.

After supper, Randy suggested the crew get settled and prepare for the next day. By eleven, the cabin was quiet. Justin undressed and took a bath. He leaned back into the warm water. Through the wall, he could hear Randy's voice rising and falling. He was on his cell phone, and he sounded angry. Justin leaned his head closer to the thin wooden partition. "Tomorrow. Yes, like we said, Sam. Don't fuck with me." Then a pause. Randy seemed to be punching in another number. His voice was softer now. All Justin heard were scattered words as if Randy were calming someone who was upset.

Later, in the hallway, his waist wrapped in a towel, Justin bumped into Cara. She was in her bathrobe. The upper folds slipped open, and Justin saw the full shape of her white breasts. Cara blushed and pulled her robe closed. In the dim light, Justin felt a sudden urge to hold Cara again, to untie her robe and slip his hands over her warm body. But he hesitated, and a shiver ran through him.

"Are you all right?"

"I'm just tired." Justin walked by her, his eyes looking down at the floor as if he were in a trance. He stopped and without turning back said "Thanks for dinner."

"You're welcome. Anytime."

TUESDAY, JULY 2

Billy Yamamoto had been awake most of the night mulling over memories of his father. Back and forth between the kitchen and the bedroom, he was still pacing when the sun rose. He dressed, made coffee, and went to sit on the back porch. The raked stones in his honour garden sparkled with dew. After breakfast, as he drove east along Highway 3, his mood lightened. He stopped for a second coffee in Monarch. The chittering of black-winged swallows in a Russian olive tree held his attention longer than he'd planned. Ten miles later, passing by the turnoff to old Fort Kipp, Billy went over the details in the Satan House case. Darren Riegert's tied-up hands, the rocking of Blayne Morton, the Polaroids, the boy's possible motive. And the problem of Woody Keeler.

It took Billy fifteen minutes to find the turnoff to the west side of Lethbridge. He was not familiar with the new highway and its conduits. He carried in his mind the old two-lane, the old single bridge across the Oldman River. It took him another five minutes to drive through the parking lots of the University of Lethbridge to find the building he wanted. The campus was once prime farmland made arable by Mormon settlers who'd built irrigation canals fed by the river.

Inside the low sandstone structure that housed the psychology department, Billy walked down hallways past locked classrooms. Would offices be closed as well? He felt relieved when he saw an open door and a sunny reception area in the office of the cult expert he'd made an appointment to meet. He was only a few minutes late: 9:03 by his watch. Professor Madelaine Van Meer turned out to be a pretty, pert woman in her mid-forties. She had red hair and a small mouth. An expensive silk scarf lay carelessly about her neck. She gave Billy a firm handshake.

"You want to know if this dead boy was a member or a victim of a cult," she said. "Am I right?"

Professor Van Meer ushered Billy into her inner office, its windows facing east towards the city's skyline. She asked him to sit down in a chair surrounded by bookcases.

"Yes," Billy answered. "I need to know if there is any connection between cult activities and this latest hanging."

Billy took from his briefcase the crime site photos showing Darren Riegert's body and handed them to Van Meer. He noted how the professor's small mouth twisted as she looked deep into the details of each photo. When she sat down opposite Billy, he said to her, "As you can see, there seems to have been foul play."

"And pentacles on the walls. And candles," she added, handing back the site photos. Professor Van Meer folded her elegant hands. "Anything else?"

"There was a note found in the boy's mouth. It had three words on it: *Mene Mene Tekel.*"

"Belshazzar's feast. Book of Daniel. A warning phrase. One often found, oddly enough, in the lyrics of heavy metal bands."

"The boy had a book with him."

"Yes, I saw it in the photos. What was it?"

"*Thanatopsis.* A book on Satanic ritual and spells."

"You can find it in all those awful head shops."

"We found a knife on the property, too. In the garden. Our coroner thinks it could be the one used to score the boy's body. Also, there was a large tape player found in the bushes near the house. Darren Riegert had been strung up. But we have doubts. The blood splatters on the tape player lead us to think the boy was standing on it, cut, and then. . . . *Strung up.* What a horrible way to describe a hanging. But I suppose lynching is an uglier word."

"I'm afraid all I'll be able to give you is a wild guess," Madelaine Van Meer said forcefully.

"Anything you tell me will be helpful."

"Well, first off, I'd say the hanging of the Riegert child was too showy for a cult. Somebody was trying awfully hard to make you take notice."

"How so?" Listening to her explanation, Billy noticed for the first time the woman's accent. It fell somewhere between South African and Australian.

"The pentacles on the walls. Not typical of cult rituals. Most of the time, in organized cults, the signs and symbols are on clothing or in tapestries or tablecloths. Things that can be quickly stored. Locked into a drawer, you see, so there's no trace. Most cults are secret societies. It's not like the cinema, Inspector. Cult groups in small towns usually want to remain anonymous."

"Same for the candles, too?" Billy asked. "The circle on the floor, placed under the body?"

"There should be candles in holders. Easy cleanup, you see. Cultists may be odd, but they are also tidy. If it were a group of young teenagers on drugs, I could understand the candles and the painted walls, but that kind of activity is not occult. It belongs more to the realm of heavy metal and Satanic music nonsense. Same with bloodletting and wounding. A sacrifice is not uncommon, however, in several cults. Some poor cat, unfortunately. Or if an animal is not available, cultists will often use fake blood for effect. This boy's chest bears the mark of a vicious game."

Billy let her words sink in.

"Sometimes, but this is rare, Inspector, blood is let to glorify a leader, a tin-pot dictator. Usually a white male, middle-aged, invariably divorced. Followers are adolescents, for the most part, who obey his every whim. Many teenaged cult victims are passive, even willing, participants."

"Willing?"

"They want someone to make decisions for them. To lead them."

"Do leaders ever indulge in torture?"

"Hanging is uncommon. Flagellation occurs from time to time. But as I said, this boy's wounds seem more a part of a cruel game."

Professor Van Meer stood. Walking behind her desk, she opened a black leather purse, reached in, and pulled out a small spoon and a kiwi. With the edge of the spoon, she deftly cut off the top of the kiwi and started digging into the green flesh, as if it were a hard-boiled egg. "Please excuse me, Inspector. I missed breakfast. If I don't eat this, I'll faint away." She smiled, chewed a large scoop of dripping fruit, and sat down again. Professor Van Meer took a few moments to eat.

Billy looked around at her desk. A silver frame held a photo of a boy of sixteen with the same red hair and the same small mouth.

"Do you have children, Professor?"

"Two. My daughter married a stockbroker, of all people, and lives in Tokyo. Paul is studying history and archaeology here at the university. His prof last term was Randy Mucklowe, who I heard was living with the woman who rents the place where these boys were found. I'm not very fond of Randy."

"How well do you know him?"

"Not well, I confess. But he's slick. He's good at finding his pots and his spearheads, but I for one know he's untrustworthy when it comes to funds and stipends. Last year he was caught out. Claimed expenses for tools and other items he needed for his lab that he hadn't actually purchased. My son says I'm crazy to think the way I do. Paul adores the man."

Professor Van Meer dried her hands with a tissue. She began shoving back her chair.

Billy could see she was ready to dismiss him.

"If you wanted to punish someone, Professor, say a boy you were fond of, a boy you knew did not feel for you as you felt for him, how would you go about it? How would a tin-pot dictator think?"

"Good heavens, Inspector. I am not one to. . . ."

"Hypothesize for me. Given what we've seen in these photos. Could this mutilation, this showiness, be the work of a cult leader who has been betrayed? Jilted?"

Professor Van Meer settled into her chair. "Jealousy being the motive, perhaps?"

"Yes. Sexual rejection is a powerful motive for revenge."

"I might persuade the boy to go through a test of his loyalty to me," she said, her blue eyes intense.

"What might that entail?"

"An act of daring."

"Like what?"

"Like walking on the ledge of a high bridge. I did a study on a California group called the Cult of the Serendipity that regularly demanded acts of physical abuse. All self-inflicted. Burns, cuts. . . ."

"Like Darren's markings? Could that carved pentacle on his chest be a sign of such a test?"

"Hard to say, Inspector. The thought processes of cultists are unpredictable."

"But within the realm of possibility?"

"Within the realm, certainly."

Billy leaned forward, resting his elbows on his knees.

"I have a long shot for you. A crime never solved. Maybe a crime connected to the Darren Riegert case but one that I think might be associated with a ritual of some sort. A challenge sport perhaps."

Madelaine Van Meer crossed her arms and threw back her head. "Carry on," she said.

"Do you remember, about eight years ago, an incident on the Peigan reserve? A hanging of a young boy found with his legs and arms tied up. The body hanging. . . ."

"From a basketball hoop! Yes, who wouldn't remember such a thing? Especially a mother. My son, Paul, once played the Peigan Chiefs in that very gymnasium in a junior high school provincial tournament."

"What do you think motivated the showy nature of that hanging?"

"Hatred. Racial hatred. No doubt of it. Certainly not cult."

"But what if, as you said, this was part of a dictator's dare? What if Ervin Born With a Tooth had been challenged to show his strength? A macho male gesture. Or, like in the old Sun Dance rituals, when the Blackfoot braves would be pierced with sticks and cords tied to their chests."

"Really, Inspector. You have a morbid imagination. And you are jumping to enormous conclusions."

"Why not? I believe I have to jump, as you say, to stir things up."

Madelaine Van Meer smiled. She paused for a moment and reflected, allowing silence to come between her and Billy. Brightening, she looked at Billy straight in the eye.

"You know, Inspector, I just thought of something. It's a jump, as you'd put it. But there's someone here, right on campus, who could tell you a lot more about that particular hanging. He was, in fact, directly involved with the mother of that unfortunate Peigan boy. The man was her boyfriend at the time, so we were told. He works in the plant here on campus. I can call him over for you if you'd like."

"What is his name?"

"Hill. Perry Hill. He's our head janitor."

Madelaine Van Meer stood up and walked into the reception area of the office. She found a number and dialled. She asked to speak to Perry Hill and then waited. "Yes," she said and hung up. She came back into the office. "Perry must be ill. He hasn't shown up for work today. There's no answer at his home. I hope nothing untoward has happened."

"Can I get his current address and home telephone number?"

"They're listed in our department files." She marched back into the reception area and with her fountain pen copied down Perry Hill's address and home phone number on a file card. "He's a quiet sort," Madelaine Van Meer said, handing the file card to Billy. "A bachelor. In my opinion, he drinks too much. But he's always on the ball here."

"I appreciate your time, Professor," Billy said.

"You are very welcome," she said, smiling back. "I'm sorry I couldn't be of more help. Do you have any suspects? Am I allowed to ask you that question?"

Billy smiled politely. "Right now I am withholding judgement."

"Inspector, from what I saw in those pictures, this could be the work of a vicious bully. And a violent one."

"Like your tin-pot dictator?"

"Possibly worse."

The U.S. border guards took apart the back seat last. They unscrewed the floor bolts, lifted the seat forward. The guard with the handlebar moustache ran his hand around the seams of the leather. The other guard, a young Native woman wearing shell earrings, shone a flashlight over the floor and up the back of the seat.

"Sir?"

Reluctantly, Professor Randy Mucklowe uncovered and pulled out the spare tire. All the shovels, mesh sifting screens, stakes, and tarps lay in an ordered line beside the van. Chief Mountain customs was supposed to be smooth and quick, thought Justin, nothing more than a routine check of passports and a cursory inspection of the van's storage area. Now, this Tuesday morning, the dig schedule was being delayed. The clock on the wall inside the customs bureau read 10:08, and the atmosphere was tense.

"I have the permission papers here. Everything is above board, I assure you." Randy's voice rasped with impatience. "I explained the other morning to the guards on duty then."

"Regulations, Professor." The guard with the moustache spoke in a flat but polite manner. "Indian land is government-status land. We'll need to search you every time you come into the States and when you leave. And I'll need a photocopy of your site report, as you know. I'm sorry, but international peace park rules for your kind of work require us to take some extra time." The guard flashed a quick official smile.

Professor Randy Mucklowe nodded and sighed.

Justin was thinking about Cara Simonds and the way she'd been so kind last night before dinner. He promised himself he'd call Karen this evening and talk to her once again about the baby. I want to be free, he thought, gazing at the bright morning air and the green woods.

"Thanks, Professor," said the Native guard. "We'll see you again this evening. Remember, we're on summer hours and short-staffed. So we're closing this year at nine-thirty, not ten as in the past."

Randy signalled to everyone to repack the van. "We've got about half an hour before we hit the logging road and the site gate."

The van pulled out and began to pick up speed on the narrow two-lane. Justin and Cara sat in the back seat, their bare thighs touching, a large folded canvas umbrella lying beside them. The Montana country was as broad and breathtaking as the valleys the van had left behind in Waterton Lakes on the Canadian side of the border. The van tilted and leaned into the sharper curves of the narrow two-lane, and Justin felt his stomach lurch. On either side of the highway, he saw shadows. Deep rows of Douglas-fir resisted the shafts of sunlight breaking through the mid-morning mists. Without meaning to, he laid his hand on top of Cara's. She did not pull away, and as the van slowed for the next curve, Justin took hold of Cara's hand. He smiled as Cara pointed to a cleared sloping meadow where a pond sparkled and hundreds of cattails stood stiff in the shallow water.

"You feeling okay?" Cara asked.

"A little car sick," answered Justin.

Randy and David Home started to talk about Blackfoot history. The two-lane rose onto a broad promontory. Spreading east, the enormous plain lay calm, the grass flatlands shimmering green and yellow. David spoke of the spirit guides and the long rides of the Blackfoot warrior-hunters. "They called this the land of the shining mountains," he said.

Justin closed his eyes to the huge broken towers and spires of stone, like a wall rising from the flatlands. His stomach was worsening, and he didn't know how long he could hold on before being sick. At least having Cara beside him gave him some comfort.

The van drove past sun-dappled woods of trembling aspen. Looming above the road now was Chief Mountain. The shale front of the peak was deeply creviced with caves and crenellated outcroppings that cast black shadows. Scree of small stones and boulders sloped in a curve like a giant bowl from the base of the mountain to the bordering tree line. Randy honked the horn and slowed the van. "Hold on," he said and turned the steering wheel hard. The van pulled onto the shoulder and bumped up to a chain stretched between two whitewashed fence posts. Black letters on a wooden sign warned trespassers: NO ENTRANCE — SACRED LAND. To his surprise, Justin realized that the physical presence of the great mountain demanded respect. For the first time, Professor Mucklowe's lectures made sense. Here were the walking grounds of the gods, the vision quest woods of the ancients.

Justin worked himself forward in his seat to look through the windshield. A man wearing a grey Stetson, his black hair pulled into two tightly knit braids, leaned on the chain barrier. He was smoking a homemade cigarette, his sunglasses reflecting the rows of pines. Justin watched him stub out his cigarette in the small stones by the barrier. In the abrupt silence that arose as the van's engine was cut, the crew stayed still in their seats, fixated on the man's stance.

"That's Sam Heavy Hand," Randy whispered.

How odd, Justin thought. Randy had no reason to lower his voice. He had explained at one of the prep sessions that Sam was very influential among the Blackfoot. A man of few but important words. Sam, he'd said, was the youngest elder in the Blackfoot council in Browning, Montana.

As Sam moved towards them, his features reminded Justin of the distant face of Chief Mountain itself — weathered and darkened by the sun. His huge right hand rose to tip the rim of his Stetson in silent greeting. His equally thick left hand reached towards the handle of Randy's door and pulled it open. Randy scrambled out of the driver's seat. The two men walked a few steps, said something to each other, and then embraced.

Justin slowly opened the sliding door and helped Cara out. David Home followed. Like obedient children, their eyes were on Randy, who moved ahead with the Native guide. The wind began to blow. Sam Heavy Hand stopped, his right hand adjusting the lie of his Stetson. He unhooked the chain leading to the logging road, where beyond, through the shadows, Justin could see light and stone.

"No cars allowed up here," Sam said, his voice low and deep. "You guys, you'll have to haul your dig tools up. We'll store them on the rocks under the tarps."

As Sam spoke, the wind lifted. Turning towards Chief, his silver glasses caught a mote of morning sun that flashed into the darkness of the swaying trees.

The old logging road through the woods was full of ruts and exposed boulders. Pine and spruce trees tied with strips of coloured cloth lined the edge of the scree. Leading away from the trees, the meadows of boulders resembled a sea of grey troubled water.

Cara shook her head. "Have you ever seen so much rock?"

Justin grabbed hold of her hand, and they made their way with caution, their first hesitant steps crackling and rattling on the loose, shifting ground. Cara snapped a picture of the trees tied with the strips of coloured cloth.

"No pictures." Sam Heavy Hand's voice was like gentle thunder. "This is our holy place. We don't want to upset our spirit guides. Old Napi, he's not fond of cameras. Doesn't like getting his picture took. He says cameras trick his soul to believin' he's a man!" Sam's mouth opened in a tight grin.

Cara looked to Randy.

"Sorry, Sam," Randy said. "He's right, Cara. I should've told you. Cameras aren't allowed on sacred sites."

Cara blushed. The legend of the trickster god, Napi, had been a subject of one of Randy's lectures. Now, Justin thought, the old god is here in spirit and in flesh — in the human form of Sam Heavy Hand.

"Come on," Randy said. "Let's get a good look at the place."

Sam walked ahead. Cara and Justin grabbed each other's hand again to keep their balance on the shuffling stone. The wind through the pines hushed. Justin watched Sam clamber over the clacking shale, placing each foot in a deliberate fashion, as if he had choreographed his movement. Sam's voice was loud but gentle as he explained the strips of cloth tied to the trees: "My brothers and sisters come here for the vision. Sometimes they come to find peace. When they come, they leave a tag. The pieces of cloth. They tell their stories to the trees and the animals. The spirits listen. You get your spirit guide to help you. Solve a problem. Sorta like goin' to a shrink." Sam broke into a chuckle.

Magpies and crows flew overhead, scolding as the crew continued the arduous ascent of the stone slope. An osprey, wings held open to catch the wind, floated above the trees past the plateau where Sam Heavy Hand now stood, his Stetson held in his right hand. Justin was sweating from the climb. "God, this is so hard," Cara panted.

"Sam, I'd forgotten how steep this was," said Randy.

Near the summit of the plateau, small white anemone grew between clumps of red Indian paintbrush. The scant earth of the scree guarded life in delicate pockets. Randy was bent from the waist, trying to catch his breath. "Cara, look," said Justin, pointing to Sam Heavy Hand. "He's not even breathing hard. Not even sweating."

The crew spread out in a circle on the plateau, and Sam explained where they could place their stakes and string markers for the first phase of the dig. Here the ground was a mix of pebbles and shale and packed earth. Justin wondered how they could ever break through the surface. Then Sam bent down and scooped up a handful of the mix. "The earth here looks hard, but it is good and giving. It holds a lot of our secrets." The crew surveyed the site for shelter points, places where they could store the dig equipment overnight under the tarps away from the winds that rose in the late day and could, as Sam explained, blow a man off the scree with one gust.

"Okay, gang," said Randy. "We've got some hauling to do."

Surveying the scree, Justin found himself brooding about Yianni and Karen. *You're going to be a father.* This huge rock world, this landscape of sky and stone, felt like a graveyard. "Stop thinking about it," he whispered, shaking his head as if it were wet. He saw the rest of the crew — Cara Simonds in the lead — half walking, half sliding back down towards the tree line. He could hear their voices rise and fall with the wind. Passing through the woods a few moments later, Justin heard angry voices. He stepped over the ruts in the road and hurried towards the open space by the barrier where the van and Sam's truck were parked.

Sam was shoving Randy against the side of the van.

"For fuck sake!" Randy was shouting.

Then Sam pulled away, wiped his hands on his jeans, and walked towards his truck. Cara Simonds and David Home stood like statues, frozen with fear. Randy's hair was mussed; his shirt was pulled out and open at the neck. "I'm all right," he said, his breathing erratic. Justin came up beside Cara. Randy took a second to run his hand through his hair and tuck in his shirt. "It's okay, really. Get in there and start unloading."

"What happened?" whispered Justin.

Cara began cautiously edging towards the van. Justin joined her and stood close to her and David. They watched as Randy walked towards Sam, who was leaning on the side of his truck, his right fist clenched. Randy moved slowly, head down, his left hand scratching the back of his neck. When he got closer to Sam, he reached out his hand. Sam unclenched his fist. He pulled down the front of his Stetson, said something to Randy. Randy patted him on the shoulder, and then they started chuckling.

"What the hell was that?" Justin asked.

Cara shook her head.

David Home let out a breath and pulled the folded tarp from the back of the van. "We don't know. Randy was on his cell. Suddenly Sam came up to him."

"The two of them started arguing about time," Cara continued. She looked pale and frightened. "When you got here, Sam was about to hit Randy. I'm scared, Justin." Cara's voice had a yearning in it.

Justin held her arm. "It'll be fine," he said. "They're old buddies. Maybe they work out their tension like that. Who knows? Look at them now."

Sam and Randy stood side by side, resting their backs on the hood of Sam's truck. Sam pointed to the summit of Chief, and Randy shaded his eyes to look at the mountain's edge. The two men laughed again.

"Let's just get this crap out of here," said Justin, lowering his eyes to the shovels and screens lying on the floor of the van. "We've got a full day ahead." He started dragging out a bag of wooden stakes. His arm was stopped from moving.

It was Cara; she was so close he could feel her breath. "Please don't leave me. Stay close by today."

Billy Yamamoto spent the rest of Tuesday morning in the computer room searching for data on cults and cult activity in and around Lethbridge. He leaned back in his chair, finally, where he could see on the screen the sum total of the names of defunct groups, their dates of demise, the records of arrests for their leaders, and the lists of young people who had survived and been "deprogrammed." He stood, his head full of doubts and more questions, and went out into the hall. Billy had a feeling the rest of his day would be an obstacle course.

Finding Constable Johnson was the next problem. After looking in the lab, he asked for her at reception and then finally had her paged. Billy wanted to talk about Perry Hill. In the cafeteria, one of the waitresses knew Johnson but hadn't seen her yet. It was already 12:05. Billy ran up the stairs and went into Butch's office. Butch was not there. Billy sensed he was missing everyone by a moment or two when he saw Johnson coming towards him in the main hall.

"Good morning, sir."

"Morning, Johnson. Afternoon, really. How did Brocket go? Were you able to talk to anyone in the Born With a Tooth family about Ervin or Woody Keeler?"

"Big problems there."

"We need to talk about it, Johnson. We also need to talk to a university maintenance guy called Perry Hill. He didn't show up for work, and no one's been able to contact him. Can we get an unmarked cruiser?"

"Right away."

Johnson crossed to the reception desk, where she was handed a set of keys, and came back to Billy.

The unmarked cruiser was parked in the covered lot normally used in the winter. Johnson offered to drive.

"Johnson, I found out Perry Hill put up bail for Woody after he was charged with assaulting Ervin Born With a Tooth."

"Right. What else did you find out about him?"

"Hill lives at 2301 Burdett. The prof claims he was a boyfriend of Ervin Born With a Tooth's mother. Madelaine Van Meer has an idea Perry knows something about Ervin's death. Can you recall, Johnson, if his name came up in any of the follow-up articles in the paper or on any of the horsemen's files?"

"I can't say offhand, Inspector. The police reports from 1990 don't tag him as being involved with the family."

"What did you find in Brocket? You said you had big problems."

"Plenty. The Born With a Tooth family said they had not seen Woody for years. Ervin's mother passed away five months ago. Ervin's uncles no longer live in Brocket. Only a few cousins are left in town, and they said they know nothing. The investigating officer from 1990 has moved to Edmonton."

"All that is better than nothing, Johnson. We know where people are if we need them."

"Right. I saw Dodd earlier this morning. He told me he got the year-books for you, and the posters are up at the junior high."

The two of them rode in a relaxed silence. By 12:25, they were on Burdett. The block had old wooden houses with large pillared front porches. Cottonwoods and blue spruce shaded the sidewalks. Johnson eased the cruiser around the corner to where the street suddenly changed. It ran down a gentle slope towards a large park ringed with weeping birches. Here the houses became weatherworn. Paint peeled from eaves. Stumps of old elms scarred the patchy lawns of the boulevards separating the sidewalks from the curbs.

The Hill address was a single-storey square box with a flat roof and yellow stucco walls. Johnson parked the cruiser across the street from the house. She and Billy walked up the narrow cement path and rang the doorbell twice. Johnson went to one of the windows and peered in. The dusty Venetian blinds were down.

"Come on, Johnson, we'll go around back."

The back door was shut tight. The kitchen windows had no blinds, and Billy noted the interior was spotless, the counters clear and clean.

"You think he's out of town, sir?"

Billy went to the side of the house and knocked on a window. "Mr. Hill. Mr. Hill, sir, this is the police!" Billy saw a head reflected in the window. He turned. The wrinkled face of a woman in her sixties appeared over the top of the wooden fence that ran between the Hill house and the neighbour's.

"Who in hell are you two buggers?"

The woman's voice was harsh and loud; her hair was dyed a bright poppy red. She wore an apron and a pair of sunglasses with the right lens missing.

"Inspector Billy Yamamoto."

Johnson showed the woman the official city police force badge.

"Oh, Perry's in there, I guarantee. I saw him come out for smokes this morning around eight. He went back in about half an hour after that."

"You know Perry Hill?"

"Know the bugger? I'm his mother! Perry won't answer you. You can bet on that, I guarantee. Perry shuts up, he shuts up for a spell. Don't know how he keeps that cleaning job, but they seem to like him over there at the school."

"We need to ask him some questions, Mrs. Hill."

"It's Rae now. Bette Rae. Perry's father's long gone from this world. Thank Jesus for that."

"How long has your son been shut up, Mrs. Rae?"

"Maybe since Sunday. I let him have this house rent-free. Keeps him out of my hair." With that, she wiped her mouth with the tip of the apron.

Johnson stepped forward. "Mrs. Rae, was Perry in town on Friday and Saturday?"

"Hell if I know. There was lights on. I swear he burns out more light-bulbs keeping on the lights in there."

"Did you see him Friday night, at home?"

"Nah, I was down at Loblaws. Then I went to Irma's. I got home late. Perry's house was lit up like a Christmas tree."

"What time was that?"

"Golly, maybe around ten-thirty or eleven."

"Is that green half-ton your son's?"

Bette Rae squinted towards the back fence of Perry Hill's yard. A battered green vehicle with a long bed was parked by two rusting garbage pails.

"I guarantee it is, officer."

"Do you remember seeing it on Friday night when you came home from your friend's?"

"It was dark out. I don't recall."

"Was the truck here on Saturday night?"

"I don't know. Maybe. Where was I on Saturday? I was home, watching wrestling. I can't say for sure. Perry didn't come for his supper. He was shut up by then. Shut up tight."

Billy sighed and began rubbing his bum knee. Johnson went to the window and banged.

"You won't wake him. I guarantee, once Perry shuts up, he shuts up for good. He comes out when he's good and ready."

Billy pulled out his notebook as Bette Rae walked back across the lawn into her house. He made a quick note about Perry's movements and the green truck and its whereabouts on Friday and Saturday. He also made a mental note to go and knock on doors that opened onto the back alley to ask if anyone had seen the truck in the past four days.

In the meantime, Johnson had strolled to the back of Perry Hill's overgrown yard. She stopped and looked over the fence, the part facing the alley and the rows of crumbling A-frames.

"Inspector!"

Billy rushed over to her and followed her through the wooden gate that led into the narrow gravel alley.

"Look at this."

"How many you figure are in the box, Johnson?"

"Fifteen or sixteen. Twenty-sixers every one of them. That's a lot of vodka. You figure Perry's hauling these out here by himself? Or is his mom giving him a hand?"

"If Perry is in that house, 'shut up' as his mother says, and if these belong to him, we've got a man on a big bender."

"This half-ton's been out in the country, in some mud. Dents and scoring on the panel here. The driver's door is locked."

"And there are a couple of whiskey bottles on the floor of the cab. A red baseball cap. Looks like a crow feather pinned or sewn on the front."

"This door is locked, too."

"He doesn't keep his truck bed very clean. What do you make of the stains on the blanket there?"

Billy leapt over the side of the truck bed and picked up the crumpled blanket. "Old paint, maybe, or dried blood. Smeared and spotted. Like someone was bleeding and then wiped blood from his hands or mouth." Billy folded the blanket and hesitated. He knew he couldn't take it away without a warrant. But was this evidence that might be linked to the Riegert boy? Quickly, he placed it under the tarp that spread over the back end of the truck bed.

"You knock on some back doors, Johnson. I'll try to wake Hill up again. His neighbours can fill us in on how long this truck has been here. The mud on the back wheels tells me Perry was out near my part of the country. Same topsoil mixed with clay and blue stone. It's heavy on the axle as well. Remember that bad rain last Wednesday or Thursday? It's safe to assume Perry's been out joyriding in the past three or four days."

"A few things," said Sergeant Dodd, pulling up a chair to the desk. Billy glanced at his watch: 2:45. Both Dodd and Johnson had come to report on their findings. Johnson was leaning against the filing cabinet. Billy sat forward in his chair and put his elbows on his knees. He took one sip of his fresh coffee and put the cup back on the table. "No wonder our schools have problems these days. It's the parents not minding their kids. The schools should clamp down on them."

"You want bars on the windows, too, Ricky?" said Johnson.

"Hey, Johns. I was only. . . ."

"Dodd. Carry on, please."

"Yes, Inspector." Dodd threw a disgruntled glance at Johnson, who grinned back at him. Dodd flipped the page of his notebook. "Mrs. Childs gave permission to talk to her class at the junior high. Some of the girls started to cry when I told the story. I asked if anyone knew Darren. Did he have any enemies? No response. I waited after class, but no one came up to me. Mrs. Childs said if she heard anything in the halls, or if later a student came to her, she'd call here. Seems Darren had no girlfriend."

"Was anyone absent this morning, Dodd?"

"No, sir. I put up the posters of Darren. The writing on the note Hawkes found in the kid's mouth matched the handwriting on a couple of his essays. I asked Childs about Blayne Morton. She says she doesn't know him well. She did confirm, however, that he is a bully. She's seen him arguing with and hitting other students in the cafeteria. Once she caught him handing in another kid's assignment as his own." Dodd finished by flipping back through his notes, checking for anything he might have missed. "The school nurse told me she'd seen rope marks on Darren's back once and reported it to social services."

Dodd looked at Billy and then at Johnson. Johnson grinned and raised her thumb.

"So where does that leave us?" Billy sat up in his chair and massaged his knee.

Dodd and Johnson remained silent.

"These boys were loners," Billy went on. "Outsiders. No one seems to know them well. We've got marginally suspicious actions on the part of the boyfriend, Woody, and one other student, Blayne Morton, and that's all. What did Hill's neighbours tell you, Johnson?" Billy was now pacing.

"I talked to a Mr. Hamer. Said he saw the truck come in early Saturday morning around eight. He noticed fresh mud on the wheels. He and Perry didn't talk much, claims Perry is quiet, lives alone, except for his mother, who goes over to visit on occasion. The truck was there till about nine on Friday night, he said, then Perry drove off, wearing a pair of jeans and a straw cowboy hat."

"Anybody else notice what Hamer saw?"

"A Miss Rhodes. Two doors down. She was jogging early when she saw the truck turn into the alley about quarter to eight on Saturday. Later that same day, she spoke to him briefly. She said she asked him if he'd been out of town. She described him as tired looking and unwilling to say much. After lunch, he drove out and came back with a box. She couldn't tell what he was carrying. A similar box was lying by the garbage cans, sir. He may have used it to carry in his vodka."

"Get a warrant to search the truck. I want that blanket seized. As soon as we can. Also, Johnson, take backup, another house warrant, and get Hill out of bed. Break in the door and drag him out if you have to."

Dodd and Johnson nodded and seemed to Billy a little stunned by his sudden anger.

"Don't look at me, Johnson. We've got evidence, maybe, and a lead — albeit a chancy one — and we can't wait around."

"Yes, Billy."

"Dodd, you get Marilyn Black on the phone. She worked with Sheree Lynn Bird. Tell her I want to see her."

"You got it." Dodd rose.

"Remember, we have a mutilated body, no prints, no *firm* leads, only one possible motive."

"You really think this Hill will lead us anywhere?" Johnson's voice was full of concern.

"In circles. But sooner or later we'll bump into something worthwhile."

Billy watched the two officers leave, his mind returning to the image of Darren Riegert's body on the morgue's steel table, boots splattered with blood. He then picked up his empty coffee cup and neatly pressed the Styrofoam sides together before dropping it into the metal garbage can by the desk.

Mrs. Morton held the door open and in her obedient manner welcomed Billy into her apartment. When he asked her if he could look around, and when he presented her first with a consent-to-search form, she blushed with embarrassment and signed the sheet without reading it. The official search warrant, folded in Billy's pants pocket, would not be necessary unless she put up resistance. But Billy explained what he needed to search out, and Mrs. Morton kept agreeing. "Yes, Inspector. He's a good boy, my Blayne."

Once she'd left him alone, Billy looked around the living room. Not much was there. A couple of old chairs and a TV. There were no pictures on the walls, no evidence of a newspaper or a magazine. It reminded Billy of a storage space, a spare room where people put unwanted furniture.

In Blayne's bedroom, three of the walls were covered in posters of heavy metal bands. Taped on the wall above the single bed and printed on a banner made of newsprint were the words *Mene Mene Tekel.* Out came the notebook. Billy sat on a low stool by the door and scanned the room, first describing the cupboard full of Blayne's huge boots and jeans, then the unmade bed and the chest of drawers, open and spilling T-shirts and underwear. The carpet was stained with patches of what looked like tomato juice and coffee. The curtain on the window was the kind of orange plastic netting found on construction sites as a barrier fence. The air felt brown; it reeked of unwashed socks and stale cigarette smoke.

Billy pulled the stool closer to the unmade bed. The top sheet had been pulled up as if Blayne had wanted to make the bed and then had stopped. The pillow was plumped into a tight ball; the blankets were a creased roll and shoved to one end. Billy leaned closer and examined the crumpled, dirty sheet lying at the foot of the bed. Small pieces of dried mud lay like coarse powder. Billy noticed the mud was also on the blanket just above the soiled sheet. Blayne must have lain down with dirty shoes. Lifting the corner of the blanket, Billy found more chunks of dried mud. In amongst them were smaller, darker pieces. Taking a Ziploc from his pocket, Billy folded it over his right hand and picked up one of the darker pieces. It looked like grapeshot. In the light of the window, he confirmed it was a dried mouse turd. Billy gathered up more, along with the powdery dust, and folded the Ziploc back over his hand to capture the pieces inside the plastic. This was a break: if the mud matched the consistency and type of that found in Satan House and the garden, it could stand as circumstantial evidence in court, as would the mouse faeces. Neither was enough, though, for a conviction. What was needed was hard evidence placing Blayne at the murder site at the right time on Friday night.

Billy next rummaged through Blayne's jeans and dirty laundry. He was hoping to find a T-shirt or a pair of pants Darren's size, his hunch being that Blayne had gone to the site, either as a witness or as a perpetrator, and then taken the naked boy's clothes as souvenirs. All the drawers were searched; under the bed amongst huge dustballs, there was only a leftover film cartridge for the Polaroid. The camera itself sat perched on the bedside table. Billy felt let down. He stood alone, thinking, wondering if the room would reveal any other secret to him. *If you wanted to hide something in this room, where would it be safe?*

Billy lifted the mattress. The box spring had been cut open. Billy shoved the mattress off the bed and plunged his hand into the slit in the box spring. He pulled out a small square book with a white cover. THE CENTINAL was written in green letters. Below it the words HAMILTON JUNIOR HIGH. The date was May, the paper smelled new, recently printed. Billy flipped through the yearbook, its glossy pages full of one-inch-square colour portraits of the students. It was the same book Dodd had brought to the station, the school's year-end graduation book. In the back were black-and-white six-by-sixes of the basketball teams, the chess club, plus random shots of students cheering from bleachers or mugging over plates of food. On page 20 were the rows of individual student photos and captions. Here was Mrs. Childs's class, the names at least familiar to Billy from his interviews. In Blayne's copy, the face of Cody Schow had been crossed over with black lines in the shape of a pentacle. In the space under the portrait was a line of handwriting. The letters were small and precise: "Death is Life." Could the RCMP handwriting expert match this lettering to the crude printing on the Polaroids now kept in the station files? Darren Riegert's picture was not marked.

Billy flipped back to the portraits of the principal and the teaching staff. Each one of the photos had a red X through it, thick lines drawn diagonally from corner to corner and ending in a neatly drawn imitation of a drop of blood about to ooze down the page. Over the title of the page in thin red letters was written "Death to All." Billy stared at the book in the silence of the dim room; in his mind's eye, he saw Blayne Morton crouched on the bed, his huge frame bent over the yearbook, cursing his teachers, his thick hand methodically drawing out each simulated drop of blood. Billy slipped the yearbook into a large Ziploc.

He then pulled apart the cut in the box spring, the coils wrapped in grey muslin. He pressed down on the spring to see if any resistance or noise might reveal another hidden object. Crouching, Billy again looked under the bed. His eye caught a thin white edge of cardboard between the box spring and the support slats. Billy propped up the box spring momentarily and slid out a narrow, flattened tie box.

It had been taped at the corners. Billy pried off the cover. Inside on the bottom were pasted six faded Polaroid snapshots of Darren Riegert. In one, Darren was standing wearing a leather jacket similar to the one in the Polaroid filed at the station. In another, Darren was talking to two figures whose faces had turned away from the sudden glare of the Polaroid's flash. Two others showed Darren on the street, and the rest were snaps of him staring blankly at the lens as if he'd reluctantly agreed to pose. The inside of the lid had been stapled with a red cloth. A red magic marker outlined Darren's name. In the upper and lower corners were miniature Valentines. Billy noticed two staples were loose, as if they'd been pulled out and then pressed back onto the cardboard. Under the red cloth, Billy felt the outline of another Polaroid. He gently pulled the cloth away. The Polaroid was facedown. Turning it over, Billy saw first the naked body, then the book and the knife just at the edge of the frame. Darren's bony arms were held forward, his hands cupped over his exposed genitals as if he'd been suddenly surprised. His boots were still on. In the background stood the sink in the basement of Satan House.

Billy put in a call to the station and found Butch at his desk. The afternoon was still bright, and Billy was elated.

"Butch, I found evidence. I'm at the Morton apartment building."

"You old dog."

"I've bagged the items; I suggest we send a constable up to the hospital with an arraignment order. Keep Blayne under observation. His mother will go there soon and will probably tell him of my visit, if he's conscious. I'll bring the items down for Johnson to look at. One is a photo that places Blayne at the site near or before the time of the hanging. It's our best bit yet. Also, I found some . . . well, you'll see. What we need is a witness, anyone who might have seen Blayne out and about on Friday to establish some time frame."

"You think we've got enough for a conviction?"

"We have a start. Sheree Lynn Bird can testify to Blayne's history of behaviour with Darren. I know it's hearsay, but it can help dispel reasonable doubt. The picture I have is the clincher. If we can confirm the time, and get Blayne to confess to how and why he was there, we can begin proceedings."

Tuesday afternoon had become very warm and windless, and as Justin cleared surface stone and worked the shovel blade into softer layers of soil, he wondered about the spirits of long-dead shamans and Blackfoot warriors, if this despoiled holy ground might conjure up vengeful curses. Would he and the others find themselves suddenly paralyzed or struck blind by the disturbed anger of an animal god? Soon his hands would be sifting soil through a metal screen and perhaps recovering a long-buried arrowhead, a sacred piece of worked bone, or a skull. Even though the dry heat was burning Justin's skin, it felt comforting and oddly refreshing. He was sweating, and his back and arms felt revitalized by the digging and lifting. The morning's fatigue had dissipated. When he and the others had stopped for lunch at 2:00, their roast beef sandwiches and sliced carrots had tasted as never before.

Now the air around him gave him inspiration.

Why not simply run away?

He could take the Greyhound bus into Lethbridge at the end of the dig. Patsy Hanson, he believed, would let him down. He could try her one more time, but she wouldn't have the money. She would make him pull double duty — sexually and emotionally — and then refuse to give him the cash. At home, he could pack a suitcase, borrow his mother's VISA card, and tell her he needed a weekend away. She wouldn't mind. Once he reached Vancouver, he could get a job, then pay back his mother. He could wait on tables, lie low for a year. Yianni would have to write off his debt as a lost cause. Not even Yianni could track him to the coast.

And Karen? Why not persuade her to run away, too? There were lots of abortion clinics there. Maybe the two of them might keep the baby. No, Justin thought, don't go there. After all, Karen said she loved him. Would she try to trap him into marriage if they decided to keep the baby? *Oh, God.* He shook his head.

Justin grabbed the handle of his shovel and started digging in earnest once again. He was surprised at how easy his new plan seemed, even if the Karen part was still not resolved. Why hadn't he thought of it before? He looked down. He had reached the level of soil where Randy and Sam Heavy Hand had said most of the ancient material probably lay buried. Here was the important part. Justin lay down his shovel, reached for his steel-meshed sifting screen. Around his square digging plot, there were four stakes joined by pieces of white binder twine. Each crew member worked in a similar square plot. Every day, once the digging and sifting had been thoroughly completed, the squares would be moved in a set pattern until the entire site had been examined. As a plot was completed, the soil was replaced, the shale covering like an outer skin of stone spread back over the ground. The Blackfoot frequently buried the skulls of elders in circles facing the mountain. Justin hoped to find one wrapped with a beaded cloth or a necklace.

Cloud was forming in the west as the sun began to move downwards into early evening. Justin had worked hard all afternoon. He slowed down his sifting. His hands were coated in grey rock dust.

"Have you found anything at all?" asked David. These were his first words to Justin since lunch.

"Dust and more dust."

"Don't lose hope, boys." Cara's voice was falsely cheery. At least she's been working as hard as the rest of us, thought Justin. Her clothes were dust-covered. Her hands were encased in the thick cloth gloves she had brought along.

Randy had spent the afternoon pacing from plot to plot; Sam Heavy Hand had gone back to his half-ton and taken off for about an hour. He had returned to the site with a grey-haired woman in a long beaded dress. Sam and the woman had talked to Randy for a while, standing at the foot of the slope by the tree line. The woman was in her early sixties, Justin thought, her strict posture adding dignity to a face weathered by the sun. On her left arm, she wore a large silver bracelet. Later, she and Sam left, and Randy sat alone near the trees, talking on his cell phone.

"Come on, everyone."

Randy was standing now on the edge of the plateau. "Put your tarps over your plots and gather up your shovels."

"He sounds like an army sergeant," said Cara.

The crew unfolded the tarps and spread them over the areas they had been sifting. They secured the corners with large stones taken from the surrounding scree. Climbing back down the slope towards the parked van, Cara sidled up to Justin.

"What's got into Randy?" asked Cara.

"How do you mean?"

"Where have you been, Justin? Randy almost went ballistic when that old Indian woman appeared with Sam. Didn't you notice?"

"Hurry, you two!" Randy's voice rang out from the trees beyond.

"I thought Randy was here to help us with the dig," Cara went on. "But half the time he was down in the trees with Sam."

"So what?"

"Justin, you're not very observant. I was surprised you are such a good worker."

"Thanks."

There was a blast from the van's horn. David Home was running ahead, towards the open door of the van, and Randy was in the driver's seat. Sam Heavy Hand was climbing into the cab of his half-ton as Justin and Cara broke out of the trees.

"You two planning on spending the night up there?"

Justin felt Randy was angry, not joking. "Sorry," Justin answered.

He and Cara placed their tools on top of David's in the back of the van.

"Careful," Randy ordered, looking back over the seats at them. "Put the tools by the side. I don't want a long hassle at the border unloading this van. Let's make it easy on ourselves."

As they buckled up, Justin noticed Randy raising his hand to Sam Heavy Hand, who signalled back from the cab of his half-ton.

"Now, everyone," Randy said, his voice tired and edgy. "When we get to the border, please let me do the talking. We may be searched, and you'll have to follow orders quickly. As we drive along, fill in these dig forms, describing exactly what you found — if anything — and the extent of your sifting. Just write down how many square feet you esti-mate you dug up and passed through the screen. I have to file these damned things in duplicate at both the American and Canadian sides."

Cara looked at Justin. She was about to say something, but Randy started the engine and jerked the van forward. As he did, Sam Heavy Hand flashed his headlights twice and pulled his half-ton in close behind the van.

"Sam is coming over the border with us tonight, just to make sure everything's in order," Randy explained. They headed for the highway, the half-ton following closely.

Justin turned and looked back at Sam and noticed he was still wearing his sunglasses.

"Why does he have to come?" whispered Cara. "Who is he, anyway? Can't Randy do this on his own?" She took hold of Justin's hand. Her skin was cold and clammy.

The van moved under the low evening sun, the sky a gold suffused with pale blue. To the northeast, thunderheads formed over the plains, billowing pure white clouds with flat dark undersides promising hard rain. Randy drove in silence. Every once in a while, he'd look frantically into the rearview mirror and clear his throat. Justin noticed how Randy gripped the steering wheel. Cara and David filled out their dig forms, but Justin could hardly write on his. The van was speeding towards the border crossing, around the curves of the narrow road, and Justin feared his old bane, car sickness, might force him to ask Randy to slow down. A couple of times, Cara turned and looked out the back window. She nudged Justin.

"Look."

Sam was flashing his headlights, on and off. Each time he did, Randy accelerated. As the van pulled into the border crossing, the two flags — the American stars-and-stripes and the Canadian red maple leaf — were lifting in the cooling breeze of the coming night. Lights were on in both border shelters. The road was empty of cars and recreational vehicles. Through the firs, the dying sunlight made long and ominous shadows across the two-lane road.

"Quiet, everyone," Randy ordered, even though no one was speaking. David Home, who had dozed off, sat up suddenly. Randy steered the van to the guard's window on the American side and waited. The office was lit, but the desk was empty. Randy tapped his fingers on the steering wheel. No one appeared. Randy climbed out of the van. Sam Heavy Hand pulled up, though he did not get out of his half-ton. Randy ignored him, walked into the lit office, and called out. No guard seemed to be on duty. Cara moved closer to Justin, and they watched Randy leave the office and go around to the back of the building and call out into the darkening woods behind the fence. Randy then came back to the van and began honking the horn with short furious blasts. Justin turned and saw Sam Heavy Hand sitting still, his face like a mask and his sunglasses glinting gold in the failing light.

A woman in a brown uniform began walking towards them from the Canadian side of the border. Randy went out to meet her, and they shook hands. She smiled at Randy, spoke to him for a moment, turned, and walked back to the office on the Canadian side. Randy scampered back, climbed in, and headed slowly over the border and into the parking lot next to the Canadian customs house.

"Hand me your forms, please. Quick," Randy said. "That's Margie," he said. "She's an old friend." He sounded relieved and got out of the van as Sam Heavy Hand drew up into a parking space beside the customs house, leapt from the cab, and lit a cigarette. Margie shook hands with Sam, and then Randy handed her the forms the crew had filled out. She put them on a shelf inside the customs house, came out again, and walked with Randy to the back of the van. Justin could hear Randy and the woman talking and laughing. Sam climbed back into his half-ton. Justin thought the way he did this was odd, as if he were trying to be quiet, or as if he did not want people to notice him. All the while, his mask-like face watched Randy's every move and gesture.

The back door of the van was opened.

"It's all in order, Margie," Randy said.

The woman shone a flashlight over the tools and the metal lunch container. She walked around to the side of the van, slid open the door, bent down, and inspected the floor. "Looks good, prof," she said. "Can you lift up the back for me?"

"Justin, come and lend me a hand."

Justin opened the door and felt a rush of cool air. He went around beside Randy, and they lifted out the tools, then peeled up the rubber matting that lay over the metal floor of the van. In its centre was the spare tire. Margie leaned in with her flashlight. The beam illuminated the tire and what appeared to be packets of black plastic garbage bags. Justin couldn't recall seeing those earlier. He looked at Randy. Randy shoved his hands into his pockets in what seemed to Justin a forced gesture.

"I keep extra bags in there for earth samples and, if need be, extra storage if we get lucky finding larger artifacts. Good place to store the bags, out of the way."

"Okay, prof," Margie said and clicked off her flashlight.

Justin and Randy reached into the van and pulled the rubber matting back over the tire and the metal floor. Randy was breathing heavily, as if he'd just climbed up the plateau at Chief Mountain. He flashed a quick nervous smile at Justin. "Thanks, Justin. You get back to your seat. Cara and Dave, Margie and I'll be a few minutes going over your forms. Then we'll be on our way."

Back in his seat, Justin slid down and put his head against the window.

"You tired?" asked Cara.

"Beat."

When Randy returned to the van, he climbed in and gave a couple of quick honks of the horn as if he were signalling to Sam sitting in his half-ton. Both men started their engines. Margie waved from the porch of the customs house as Randy backed out, honked again, and veered onto the two-lane. Sam Heavy Hand turned his headlights to high beam and followed Randy down the highway, away from the border crossing and towards Waterton Lakes on the Canadian side. "No problems," Randy announced to the crew. "Margie told me our American friends signed off early because of the lack of traffic."

"Is that legal?" asked David Home.

"They make their own rules, it seems," said Randy.

Justin drifted into his own thoughts again, turning his mind away from the day and Randy's behaviour over the last half hour. Leaning against the window, he rarely took his eyes off the landscape. Traffic was light — only one car drove past on its way to Montana. Justin nodded off to sleep but awoke a minute later as the van pulled over to the shoulder of the road. He heard wild honking. He sat up. Cara Simonds was pointing to Sam Heavy Hand's half-ton screeching to a halt only inches away from the back door of the van. The sounds of doors slamming and feet crunching on gravel filled the van, and Justin pressed closer to the window. He was beginning to feel uneasy, a result of hunger and fatigue and a touch of car sickness. He watched Sam run towards Randy on the shoulder of the road. Sam was whooping and waving his arms. In the glare of the half-ton's high beams, Sam grabbed Randy and danced with him, arms held aloft. It was the first time on the trip that Sam smiled; he flung his reflecting sunglasses into the air. Randy tried to break free. He kept saying "Quiet down, Sam." After a while, the two men separated. Sam climbed into his half-ton, brought out a two-four of Coors Lights, and carried it in his left hand towards the van, swinging the box as if it were light as a pillow. He yanked the door of the van open.

"You sleepy heads want a beer?"

"Sure," said David Home meekly.

"No thanks," said Cara. "Shouldn't we be on our way? I need a shower, and I'm. . . ."

Sam broke into a laugh. He raised a foaming beer can to his mouth and drank heavily. Justin couldn't understand why Randy and Sam had changed so suddenly. It was as if the end of the day were a cause for celebration. Sam's elation, especially, showed the two men had somehow released the tension the crew had seen between them earlier. But Justin decided not to think about it further. He had his own fears and plans. Though he was puzzled by the black garbage bags in the back of the van, around the spare tire, he wanted only dinner and a bed.

When they began moving again, Justin fell into a short sleep. He awoke to find himself sailing past the sparkling waters of Waterton Lakes, the rising moon turning the emerald water a deep, secretive black. The crew unloaded at the cabin around eight o'clock. The cawing of crows filled the air. Busy clouds of gnats flurried over the damp brush of fragrant cow parsnip. Justin helped Randy put the tools in the small shed. His professor was drinking a Coors, and Sam Heavy Hand was inside the cabin knocking about the kitchen, clattering glasses, and singing. Cara looked upset.

Tired and with a headache coming on, Justin turned away from her and went into the kitchen, past the living room, and into his small bedroom. After he pulled off his dusty clothes, he wrapped himself in a towel and headed to the bathroom. He knew he'd have to be quick and conserve hot water, so he dampened a cloth, rubbed his face and underarms, slapped on aftershave, and went back to his room, all the while thinking about Karen and Cara and Yianni.

Later, Justin joined Cara and David, who were standing by the door watching Randy and Sam drink and talk loudly in the kitchen.

"You hungry?" asked Cara.

Justin came up beside her and was about to apologize for rushing away earlier. Then he saw Randy stumble to the doorway. He was drunk, his eyes narrow and watery. Sam Heavy Hand was smoking and whistling by the sink.

"Why don't you kids go on downtown for a while?" said Randy. "Go and get yourselves a burger at Frank's Café. No use having to cook tonight when you're tuckered out."

"Yeah, get the hell out," said Sam, his voice heavy with beer. "Go and have some fun."

Justin looked at Cara and David. He could see they were tired.

"You go ahead," Randy said. "Do what Sam says and have some fun. We've got some planning to do for tomorrow. We'll scratch up some dinner here."

Sam broke into a hoarse laugh. Randy said nothing else, and after a second he walked into the kitchen and started talking to Sam as if the three members of his crew had simply evaporated.

"What do you think?" asked Justin.

Cara shrugged. David's face turned grey. His whole body looked limp with fatigue, but he shrugged, too. The three of them picked up their wallets, left by the side door, and headed down to Main Street, crossing over a small bridge onto a road that led through tents and trailers parked under fir trees for the night.

Yellow light illuminated the main street. The evening also brought with it the noise of cars and tourists talking and strolling by the restaurants and gift shops. This was the first time Justin had been in the centre of town. Overhead lights like Christmas tree decorations sparkled in the aspens and birches planted along the sidewalks. Frank's Café was a spacious building with varnished plywood booths and formica tables. The menu advertised Chinese chow mein, buffalo and beef burgers, chicken wings, and smoked trout. Justin checked out the bar, a long wooden structure with chrome stools. It was past nine, and his stomach growled. David and Cara found a booth. They ordered buffalo burgers and beer and waited in silence. Justin reached for his glass of water and slowly drank.

When the food came, everyone ate without speaking. Justin paid his portion of the bill after dinner while Cara and David counted out change. "I'll wait for you outside," he said. He put his wallet back into his pocket and got up from the booth. On the street, he breathed in the warm summer air. Over the tops of the buildings rose the huge dark mountains. The lake beyond the main street, seen through rows of cottonwoods growing by the stony beach, was now black and as hard as polished glass. Justin checked to see if Cara and David were coming. As he did, he noticed a man walking down the opposite side of the street. He was headed towards a general store, its windows covered with posters advertising trail rides and nature walks with the town's naturalist. Justin quickly stepped back into Frank's. He grabbed Cara's arm.

"What's wrong?" she asked, her voice low with alarm.

"Do you see that man over there walking past the café?"

"Where?"

"Just across from us. He's headed into the general store."

Cara looked at the man with the open shirt and the black shiny dress pants.

"Don't point, Cara!"

"Do you know that man?" she asked, standing closer to Justin as if to shelter him.

"Yes. He's Yianni Pappas."

"Who?" asked David.

"David, do me a big favour? Yianni just went into the general store. Go over there and see if you can find out anything."

"Like what?" David said with a sleepy voice.

"Justin, you're shaking," said Cara, taking hold of his right hand.

"Please, David. Go on over and tell me what he's doing. Maybe listen to what he has to say. He's standing in line. See? I need to know why he's in town."

"You in some kind of trouble?" David asked.

"No," replied Justin. "But I really need you to go over there now to see what's up. Please."

"I'll go with you, David," said Cara. She let go of Justin and opened the door.

Justin watched David and Cara go into the general store. The huge windows showed couples walking around with items in small wire baskets. The store sold dry goods and fruit. Yianni was talking to the two women at the cash register. Justin watched it all like a TV show with the sound muted. Cara lined up behind Yianni, holding a couple of apples. David stood next to her. Yianni's mouth moved slowly; one woman at the cash nodded, spoke until Yianni grinned, and pointed to the cigarettes stacked on a shelf behind the counter. The woman pulled a pack down, and Yianni paid and walked out into the street. Justin then turned and as fast as he could went past the bar and into the hall leading to the men's room. He peeked around the corner. Cara crossed the street and stood by the front of Frank's until David caught up to her.

"There you are," Cara said as Justin came back to the front of the restaurant.

"Well?" asked Justin.

"Guys, I'm real tired." David Home leaned against the yellow-painted logs of the façade of Frank's Café. "I didn't hear anything, Justin," David added. "I'm sorry. I'm going back to the cabin. I'll see you there." David started down the street.

Cara took hold of Justin's arm and began leading him in the other direction, towards the small marina. The bay had rows of docks and small motorboats. Benches overlooked the docks and were placed facing out to the lake. "Come here," Cara said. They sat down on a bench. In front of them at one of the docks, a man in his late seventies was struggling to pull a green tarp over an old boat. On the side of the boat was a small inscription: "Fifty Years on Waterton Lakes." Cara checked the other benches. On one, a young couple sat talking. The rest were vacant. A small speedboat slowed and pulled in to the docks, causing the others to bob and sway. Cara leaned close.

"He asked where Professor Mucklowe was staying."

"What?"

"If it was Yianni."

"Oh, it was Yianni. No mistaking him."

"He said he needed to get a hold of Professor Mucklowe. He didn't use Randy's first name."

Justin felt a chill run through him. Yianni was here in town, looking for him.

"Why was he asking for Mucklowe? Does Yianni know him?" Cara asked. She pitched her voice low. She took hold of Justin's hand again.

"He's after me, Cara. I told you."

"Now wait a minute. It's possible he knows Randy. Maybe Randy owes him some. . . ."

"I'm going to kill myself!"

Justin bent forward, slipping his hand free from Cara's and resting his face in his palms. He felt tears coming.

"Listen, Justin," Cara said. "Let me help you. You said Patsy Hanson would lend you the money. I can drive you to her place. We can go tonight if you want. We can phone first."

"Oh, Cara, I wish. I don't know if I can trust her. I need time to think. How are we going to walk home now? What if he's waiting for me?"

"Look, I'll run to the cabin. You wait here. I'll check it out. If everything's okay, I'll bring my car down and pick you up. Why don't you sit and wait?"

Cara got up. She held Justin's face in her hands.

"Be calm. It may not be as bad as you think."

On the edge of the bench, Justin rubbed his hands while looking to make sure Yianni Pappas was not nearby. *Where is Cara?* It felt like she had been gone for an hour. Too much time in any case. Was he just going to sit here in the open? He had to move. Cara would spot him on Main Street. He might as well walk where there were lights and crowds. He got up, turned his back towards the docks, and headed out, his calves and thighs stiff from sitting. The day had been long, and he needed to stretch his muscles before sleep.

He crossed Main and strolled into an open field in the centre of the village. Around him, new cement foundations were brightly lit by huge arc lamps. Randy had said the village was putting in a new lodge. One building was completed, its roof high and pointed and covered with large cedar shingles. Past it, by a chain-link fence, a second building was going up, skeletal walls of pine studs resembling a wooden cage. Justin saw a figure standing in the door frame of the wall smoking a cigarette. It was Yianni. There was no way he could avoid him. Yianni's face appeared chalk white in the glare of the construction lamps.

"Nice night, Justin."

"Hello, Yianni."

"How's the dig going?"

"Fine. How did you know I was. . . ."

"Your mom is a nice lady, Justin."

"What do you mean?"

"She said you had left town for the week. A school project, she said. I told her I was a friend of yours from your university."

Justin didn't move. Yianni stepped from the door frame and sidled up to Justin. He stopped a few inches from his face, tossed away the cigarette, and smiled.

"How come you didn't tell me, Justin?"

"I . . . I'm sorry, Yianni. . . ."

"I thought I told you not to go on a holiday. Didn't I tell you that, Justin?"

"This is no holiday, believe me, Yianni. I had to do this project, it's part of. . . ."

Justin felt Yianni's warm damp hand brush his arm and rise to his shoulder. Before he could pull back, the hand smoothly slipped to the base of his neck. Yianni did not hold him hard. But his thumb gently stroked Justin's Adam's apple. Yianni pressed his groin tightly against Justin's.

"You are a nice kid. I've always thought so. Tell me. You making any money on this project? Your mom said something about you getting a stipend or some cash for helping out your professor. A student . . . what did she call it?"

"Hon . . . honorarium."

"That was it. That's good, Justin. How much?"

"Five hundred dollars." Justin was breathing in the foul sweetness of Yianni's breath.

Yianni leaned in close to his ear, moist lips lightly brushing his earlobe.

"That's a start."

Yianni tightened his grip on Justin's neck, spat to his left, wiped his free hand across his mouth, broke into a smile, and, with the pointer finger of his right hand, tapped Justin softly on the chin.

"I got to drive back to town, kid. It's getting dark. I like the sound of five hundred dollars, but I like the sound of six thousand even better. I look forward to seeing you Saturday. Promise me we can see each other on Saturday. You won't let me down?"

"No, Yianni."

"You promise?"

"Yes."

"You sure now?" Yianni held his hand firmly around Justin's neck.

"Yes, I promise."

Yianni let go. He smoothed his hair and brushed something from Justin's shoulder. He rubbed Justin on his lower back, just below his belt line.

"See you Saturday."

Yianni Pappas walked away, going around a pile of cedar shingles. Justin stood still. Over his head, he heard a bird calling into the darkness. Then he began to run. Stumbling in the dark, he didn't care where he was as long as it was away from Yianni. Justin headed up through the construction site, across a field full of birch trees, down the slope that led to the river. Ahead lay the campgrounds. He dodged through trees and shrubs, and finally he saw the rooftop of Randy's cabin.

Cara had not made it back yet. Justin was sweating. The aspens crowding the cabin rustled with the hot breeze, and crickets buzzed in the humid grass. Sam Heavy Hand's half-ton was parked by the stone patio. Sam was sleeping inside the cab, snoring loudly, his head propped up against the passenger window on a bunched-up denim jacket. Justin made his way to the cabin door and opened it. What a relief it was to be inside. The kitchen and living room were full of shadows as Justin struggled to the bathroom. He threw up. After rinsing his mouth, he heard Cara's car pull in. He walked to the back door and met her.

"Oh, Justin. Thank God! I thought you'd gotten into trouble."

"I saw him."

"You look awful."

"He came here to threaten me."

Cara put her arms around Justin's shoulders. She led him into the dark living room and sat down beside him on the couch, her arms embracing him. "You're shivering," she said, holding him tighter. Justin breathed in Cara's warmth, the smell of her perfume.

"Come on," she whispered. He stood up with Cara's help and walked to the bedroom. Cara had her right arm around his waist. When she kissed him lightly on the mouth, he didn't struggle. When she stroked his hair, he shut his eyes and allowed her touch to soothe him.

"Come here, Justin."

He lay down beside her. The bed springs creaked. "Oh, Justin," Cara whispered. She laid her hand on his neck and stroked him. Justin breathed out, his heart calming. He let Cara caress him, and in doing so he let go of his fear.

Billy's disappointment tasted bitter. Maybe he was tired; maybe he'd been expecting too much too soon. After all, Blayne Morton had a motive, and there was the Polaroid of the naked Darren Riegert to orchestrate a conviction. But now Billy was asking a man called Axel Preis to repeat what he'd told him not two seconds before. The light in the small green office was too bright and stung Billy's eyes. The smell of fuel from the buses in the garage next door seeped everywhere, a pungent sweet odour of motor oil and rubber.

"I know the kid well. He's always riding up and down my route — Number 43 — down Ashmead, out to the mall, Loblaws, and round to city hall. Can't mistake him with that head of his. He's big. I see him pretty near every night and after school. Looks lonely. Never asked him his name. Friday, he was walking up Ashmead around 10:45. I knew it was him 'cause of the green hair. I figured, he's out walking tonight. I honked a couple of times at him before he saw me and ran to Stop 17 on the route, right next to the soccer field off Ashmead and Baroness. He looked pale. That camera was with him. Seems to take it everywhere."

"Are you sure of the time, Mr. Preis? Please be as accurate as you can. This is very important."

"I can see that. My timetable says be at Stop 17 by 10:45. I checked the old town clock. It's pretty accurate since they replaced the innards. Read 10:42. I checked my watch, 10:43. Out a minute. Why the boy was out so late, I can't say. He got on at 10:45. We rode around together almost a couple of hours until he got off at his stop, by the mall. No one got on,

it was him and me. His stop is a good sixteen blocks or more from
Ashmead, where the house you told me about is situated. I checked in
to the bus barn by 1:00, on the dot."

"Sign-in sheet is here, Inspector," said a man whose name tag
announced he was a supervisor. The sheet read 1:01. Billy wrote down
the men's names and the times they gave him and asked that they contact him in the morning so that a formal statement could be made. Billy
then received a photocopy of the time sheet and the name of the bus
route and the bus driver's name. He remembered his own deduction of
the time of Darren's death from the appearance of the tied arms and the
advance of the rigor mortis: from 11:30 to midnight. And, too, Coroner
Hawkes had estimated a time frame of one hour, from 11:30 to half past
midnight. Tommy the medic's first thermometer readings, he recalled,
verified his own hunch. *So Morton was at the site but definitely before the
hanging. Why was he there with his camera? And who else, then, partici-
pated?* Billy realized even in his late-day fatigue that he must force a
confession from the boy once he was out of sedation. He had to engi-
neer it so Blayne could not escape in his rocking game.

As soon as he got home, Billy fried up eggs and sausage. Right after
he washed the dishes, he brought in the chairs from the porch, wary of
a thundercloud that was rolling in from the southwest. Soon rain was
pelting the roof, and gusts of wind were slapping and rattling the doors.
The storm swept by after a loud half hour of cracks and rumblings, and
then calm returned. The air was moist with the perfume of wet sage-
brush. At the kitchen window, Billy stared at the dripping firs still in
their burlap sacks. He hadn't unwrapped them and planted them in the
honour garden, and with the last two days of heat, they had begun to
yellow and die. He promised he'd go first thing tomorrow morning to
the nursery. He tried to centre himself. Feeling uneasy and upset about
Blayne Morton would not help him sleep tonight. The air and his dinner
had revived him a little, and he decided to follow a hunch he'd been
nursing ever since getting home.

He called dispatch. When the sergeant answered, Billy told him to get Butch to meet Billy at the regional hospital. "I'll call the hospital to double-check on the boy in the meantime," Billy explained. He hung up, found his notebook on the kitchen table, looked up the hospital number, and was about to dial when the phone started to ring.

"Sir, I just got a call from Chief Bochansky. He's already on his way to the hospital. Blayne Morton escaped from the ward. Chief wanted you to know. I told him you had just called. Dodd has gone to get Morton's mother. Seems the kid struck one of the night nurses and ran out of the hospital in his bed gown."

"All right."

"And he yanked out his IV. The nurse said he used it as a weapon."

"All right, sergeant."

"Chief said he'd meet you at the hospital."

He grabbed his raincoat. Moments later, the highway shone yellow under the median lights. When Billy pulled into the emergency entrance of the regional hospital, the driveway was partially blocked by two city police cruisers. A lone man directed traffic and told Billy to leave the lane clear for ambulances. Once inside, Billy searched for Butch. He asked the info desk people, even though he knew where Butch had gone. He rode up in the elevator to the ward where Blayne Morton had been kept. Nurses were trying to divert inquiring patients and curious visitors away from the police activity; Billy could hear Butch's voice bellowing orders from a room down the hall. Then he saw Mrs. Morton sitting on a chair by the doorway to Blayne's room, her head bent forward with the same obedience and exhaustion as the first time he met her. She raised her head to him as he approached.

"Inspector. Oh, sir, my Blayne. . . ."

She fell silent as Butch came to the hospital room's doorway.

"You break the speed limit getting here?"

"Anyone hurt?" asked Billy.

"The night nurse, a Miss Morgan, may have a broken nose. She's been taken to emergency."

"How did it happen?"

A woman in a nurse's uniform appeared in the doorway from behind Butch.

"Are you Inspector Yamamoto?" she asked. Her voice was gentle, and Billy was reminded of the nurse who'd tended his father.

"Yes, I am."

He followed her into a narrow room across the hall, where she closed the door behind them.

"I've told this to your chief already. It's best if we come in here out of earshot of Blayne's mother. As far as we can ascertain, Blayne pulled out his IV needle and somehow pinched off the flow line of fluid. When we did a cursory check on him an hour ago, he looked placid and sedated. He must've retaped the needle under the adhesive to make it look as if he were getting the liquid. His sedative had worn off by mid-afternoon, but he seemed so quiet. When Nurse Morgan went in to check him after nine-thirty, he was waiting for her."

"What happened?"

"We think he hit her first, to catch her off guard. And then he pulled out the IV needle, popped it from the rubber conduit, and waved it like a knife. He ran out past all of us at the station so fast I couldn't believe it. Morgan was yelling, but by then Blayne had taken the back stairs. Security reported they saw a young man in a patient's gown running through the west parking lot."

"Did he seem woozy, or was he staggering when he ran out?"

"Come to think of it, he moved very fast. I didn't see him in the room with Morgan, but when he burst into the main hall by our station, he was carrying the IV. I shouted at him, and he simply ran. He was a good runner, Inspector. I was frankly surprised at his strength given he'd not eaten for a day and had been on sedatives."

Billy thanked the nurse. He handed her a file card with his name and the police station's number on it.

"Here's my temporary business number. Call me there if you have any other information for me. Especially when Nurse Morgan is ready to talk."

The head nurse opened the door and followed Billy back into the hall. As he went to join Butch in Blayne's room, the woman sat down with Mrs. Morton and put her arm around the frightened mother's bent shoulders.

In the pale green institutional room, Blayne's bed was mussed, and there were spots of blood on the pillowcase. Butch explained the blood was from the nurse Blayne had struck. "Chief?" A young nurse wearing glasses hurried into the room. Butch rose from his chair. The nurse spoke quickly: "Blayne Morton was spotted running down the hill to the country club. The clubhouse was broken into no more than ten minutes ago, and the cash register was smashed. There's a man waiting for you down there. He says he saw our young man in a blue hospital gown heading for the river."

Dodd suddenly appeared in the doorway, panting. "Just got here, Chief."

"Yes, Dodd, I see. You and Billy come with me in my cruiser. Billy, leave the Pontiac here."

Five minutes later, Billy, Dodd, and Butch were in the cruiser driving down Cutbill, then turning onto South Drive past the Mountain View cemetery towards the hill leading to the country club. Butch had turned on the flashing cherry light but not the siren. At the hilltop entrance to the club, Butch cut the cherry and put the cruiser's headlights on high beam. The road was wet, the grass and scrub shiny from the rain. Billy remembered the Lethbridge country club as a small nine-hole course laid out beside the Oldman. By the time Butch had reached the bottom of the winding gravel road, Billy realized the course had changed. The old gateway made of wood was gone; in its place was a stone marker with copper letters announcing the name of the club. The low wooden clubhouse had been torn down. The fairways had been widened and were now lit for night golfing with floodlights that created short shadows over the grass. The cruiser wound its way on a freshly paved blacktop to a parking lot in front of a glass and copper-roofed building crowned with a metal balcony.

"Times are good for golf nowadays," joked Butch.

Billy got out of the cruiser and followed Dodd and Butch into a broad carpeted lobby. The walls of the new clubhouse were of polished pine panelling with a wainscot of fieldstone. Two trophy cases held shelves crammed with silver and brass figures swinging tiny golf clubs.

A man in blue dress slacks got up from a chair beside the broken cash register. He was in his early eighties, a trim strong-jawed man with a firm handshake. "Cy Rankin," the man said.

"Inspector Billy Yamamoto."

"Here's the till. The lad didn't get a penny. The float and the day's cash were locked in the safe downstairs."

"How are you, Mr. Rankin?"

The man broke into a laugh and raised his right hand in a dismissive gesture. "He missed me," he said. "Was that a syringe he was waving around?"

"A broken IV," answered Butch. "He was under observation at the regional hospital and somehow broke out of the ward."

"He sure cleared out of here fast," said Rankin.

"In which direction, Mr. Rankin?" asked Billy.

"Well, sir, I didn't see exactly," Rankin apologized. "I think he went towards the ninth hole, over that way, southwest. He made for that staircase, and by the time I got up from the floor, I saw him crossing our parking lot in that direction."

"Dodd, you head out towards the ninth hole. I'll go due west and take the flashlight from under the seat in the cruiser. Dodd, you've got yours with you?"

"Yes, sir, I do."

Butch added, "Mr. Rankin, I need only a few more moments of your time. Use caution, men. It's dark out there, and he's had a head start."

"He can't go far," Rankin added. "We've put up a big barrier fence now in the brush beyond the fairways. We needed to separate the club's land from the nature walks down by the river. I don't know where the lad can get to, frankly. He'll have to lie low or circle round and get over and back up the hill you fellows drove down."

"Butch," said Billy. "I'll go to the fence and then cut back towards the hill."

"Good, buddy."

"Dodd, you do the southwest and then trail back behind the clubhouse. The boy may be leading us on a goose chase by now."

"He's losing blood, though," said Rankin.

"How so?" asked Billy, stopping in mid-stride.

"Well, sir, he cut his hand pretty badly on that till. He was determined to smash it open with his bare fist. He took a mug, and the glass shattered and cut his palm. I wouldn't want to be running too far without tending to a wound that size."

Billy reached the parking lot and immediately looked at the silent trees and heard the rush of the nearby river. Taking a two-battery flashlight from the cruiser, he shut the door silently and stepped beyond the shadow of the trees running parallel to the eastern edge of the river. On the wet splashy grass under the outdoor lights, he walked with care until he was behind the bare foundation of the old clubhouse. His flashlight shone around the edges. Would he see evidence of Blayne's fresh footprints? Billy crouched. No prints, no drops of blood. Up the crumbling steps of the clubhouse, he aimed his light over the perimeter. Only broken cement and glass and tall uncut wild oats. Circling the low walls, Billy kept his eyes on the ground until he'd come back to the place where he'd started. Could the boy see him? Billy swivelled to the left. In the distance, Dodd was running along the chain-link fence that bordered the fairway.

The humid darkness, full of smells from the river, was unsettling. He pointed his flashlight and marched towards the western section of fence and low bush, and then he turned right. Across the fairways lay shimmering blue-white streaks from the floods. The bush border sat low, Caragana and dwarf willow. The false daylight of the floods could easily reveal the pale blue of a cotton nightgown. Up ahead, Billy heard rustling. He moved towards the sound. *Steady*, he warned himself. A ball of ruffled feathers exploded from the willows in the shape of a prairie hen. Billy watched the bird fly up into the dark. He moved on, almost jogging, keeping close to the fence and the border between the bush and the mown fairway. Panting, he slowed, clicked off his flashlight, and stood very still. He thought he heard footsteps at the bend ahead.

The fairway here dipped into a shallow dale. Tall elms and cotton-woods loomed over the caraganas. The light from the floods was muted, softer. Pools of darkness nestled beneath the tree trunks. Suddenly, there was a faint rush of pale blue, the shape of a figure. It stooped in a crouch and dashed due north from the fence. Billy quickly moved to his left, using the deeper shadows as camouflage. He trained his eyes on where the figure might run next. By a large broken stump, he caught his breath. It had been a while since he'd been involved in a chase on foot, and his knee was aching badly. He looked up. Blayne Morton made a break for it, scampering onto the fairway, guarding his wounded hand close to his chest.

"Blayne! Stop!"

Blayne veered off into the trees again. Billy almost twisted his left ankle turning to pursue the boy on the rain-slick fairway. His stomach tightened. Sweat beaded his forehead. *Won't be easy to grab him.* The ground slid with broken twigs and divots of soggy mud.

"Come on, Blayne! You've got nowhere to go."

"Fuck you!"

Billy clutched the flashlight and half-knelt, ready to leap. *But where was he?* Caragana swayed, leaves hissed.

Blayne sprang from the brush like a cougar attacking a fawn. A thin jagged stick clawed at Billy's head. Billy ducked, raised his arm to shield against the rushing of the makeshift club. Down it came. Billy's shoes slipped. Again and again the thin hard stick broke skin, brought a warm sudden flush of blood. Blayne trampled bare muddied feet on Billy's kicking legs.

"Hey, Blayne!"

It was Dodd's voice hurtling out of the dark.

"Blayne!"

Blayne drew back. Billy sat up, blood running down his right cheek.

The boy was limping, sliding, trying to dash away from the huge frame that barrelled down on him. Dodd tackled. Billy lay back and pulled in hot breath, and through his pain heard Dodd speaking to the crying Blayne, his words coming gentle and kind.

Half an hour later, the nurse in the emergency ward finished taping gauze to Billy's wounded forehead. Butch sat across from him, perched on an empty gurney. "You should have that cough looked after," the attending nurse said pointedly to Butch. She rolled her rs with a Glaswegian accent. The nurse yanked open the white plastic curtain, and Butch helped Billy get up from the bed. "Careful now," the nurse said as the two men shuffled into the small patient lounge, its green walls as ugly as its green leatherette couches. A TV blared at one end. Billy could see the lights of the hospital's parking lot through the window. He winced as he touched the gauze and felt the hot streak of pain on his temple.

"I think once he's quieter and been bandaged for that cut from the beer mug, we should go and interview him. He's backed himself into a corner and knows it."

Dodd appeared in the doorway.

"Morton's back in the ward, sir. Abrasions to his left foot from the ground at the course. The nurse says his cut is deep, so they've frozen his hand and put in stitches. Blayne says he's not willing to talk."

The TV caught Billy's eye. As if expecting what he saw, he sighed. On the screen were the faces of Sharon Riegert and her boyfriend, Woody Keeler. A reporter held a mic to Sharon's mouth. She stood defiant, in front of the police tape strung across the front steps of Satan House. Her blouse was bright red, and her hair was crinkled in a fresh perm. Woody was dressed in a white shirt and sparkly bolo tie.

"Those bastards." Butch coughed.

Woody Keeler whined, "The police have done nothin'. Our Darren was number two."

"Somebody's killin' our babies," Sharon announced directly to the camera.

The reporter walked around to the back door of Satan House, pointing to the basement windows, explaining where the Darren Riegert hanging had taken place.

"Did the station clear this with you, Chief?" asked Dodd.

"Do they ever?" answered Butch. "Goddamn it!"

"And here," the reporter intoned. "Here's where this boy spent his last frightened hours. Who is mutilating our young people? Is there a serial killer loose in our. . . ."

By the time the reporter had finished posing his questions, Billy was on his way down the hall and into the elevator. His head throbbed. Suddenly, he felt brutally tired. His shirt was dirty, and he smelled. And he wanted more than anything to meditate and clear the mounting frustration and impatience out of his system. Butch had followed him. They stood silently as the elevator door opened. A constable greeted them at the nurse's station.

"He's in here, Inspector. Chief."

Blayne Morton sat propped up on a freshly made bed in a room the size of a large closet. The hospital's counsellor was present and explaining to Blayne, cautioning him as a minor, the procedure about to take place. A constable in a city police uniform stood guard. Blayne's nightgown had been removed, and he was wearing a pair of jockey shorts and a T-shirt. His left foot was bandaged, and Billy saw the line of fresh red stitches stretching across the centre of his right palm.

"When can I get outta here?" Blayne shouted.

Billy calmly pulled up a chair and sat down. Butch placed himself by the door after dismissing the constable. As he had entered the room, Billy had proposed a strategy. Butch would observe yet say nothing. He was to move only if Blayne attempted to jump from the bed or hit out at Billy, who would do the interview.

Billy crossed his legs.

"So?" Blayne's voice was surly and bored. "So?"

Billy knew this particular interview would require a careful combination of tact and pointed questioning. Blayne was now an official suspect. The confession must bring out his true motive and reveal who else was in the basement that night. Billy sensed that Butch had doubts about the boy. He himself believed Blayne would talk. What he wasn't sure of yet was exactly how much Blayne knew. A cardinal rule for an interrogation: allow the interviewee enough room, but always play the game in a cool deliberate series of moves. Billy raised his head and stared at Blayne. Touching his own bandaged head, Billy let his eyes fall on Blayne's wounded palm. Blayne's eyes followed Billy's gestures. Billy then calmly folded his hands in his lap.

"You mad at me or somethin'? Say somethin'."

Blayne sat up straighter in the bed. He wasted a minute plumping his pillow. Billy watched his halting arm movement. Noticed the dark circles under the boy's eyes. Even though he was a juvenile, Blayne would be charged with break and entry, with brandishing a weapon, with assault of a police detective and hospital personnel.

"I'm not scared of you," Blayne said, his voice suddenly sounding timid.

Billy responded quickly. He answered Blayne in a flat official tone, told him of his charges, of the possibility of his going to prison. Or a psychiatric hospital. Billy spoke automatically, defining each crime the boy had committed and its possible legal consequence.

"Fuck you."

Billy again folded his hands in his lap.

"Don't fuck with me!" Blayne shouted. Billy recognized the false defiance in the boy's voice. Blayne sat back and started to pick his nose deliberately. He pulled up his knees and sniffed loudly.

Billy spoke again, but this time in a more conversational voice: "I can help you, Blayne, if you help me."

Blayne pretended he hadn't heard. "What?" He spat the word from a spoiled pout.

"I can arrange for you to go to a detention centre, to participate in a program there, if you cooperate. And tell me the truth."

"About what?" Blayne sat forward.

"About Darren."

"That asshole! I got nothing to tell."

"How well did you know him, Blayne?"

"I didn't. He was in my class. He and that other loser, Cody."

"Do you know Sheree Lynn Bird?"

"Where's my mother? I want my fucking mother!"

"Answer the question, Blayne," the counsellor said, entering the interview for the first time.

"Fuck you!"

Butch cleared his throat and made a signal to Billy. He got up and crossed to the door and joined Butch in the hallway.

"Buddy, I'm not happy."

"What's the problem?"

"That kid is a goddamned weirdo. You think we're going to get anything truthful out of him? We are wasting our time in there."

Billy stood quietly for a second before he answered Butch: "I want to try to set up a pattern of questions and answers. I want to head us in the direction of the time frame around Darren's hanging and mutilation. For all we know, Blayne may be innocent. He left the site a good half hour before Darren's estimated time of death. But he is hiding something, Butch. I may be wrong. He could have witnessed the whole thing and be too afraid to tell."

Butch did not react immediately. He shoved his hands into his pockets, then checked the late hour on his wristwatch.

"What we need," Billy continued, "are the yearbook and the tie box."

The two men walked to the central hall and crossed into the main nurse's station in the psychiatric ward. Billy didn't want to leave Blayne alone for too long. Butch picked up the Ziplocs Billy had brought with him to the hospital. They went back towards Blayne.

"I'll stand sentry again," Butch said. "You nod to me when you want the Ziplocs to appear."

Billy decided to be more direct with the boy when he went back in. He didn't like to disagree with Butch, but he needed to make this call.

"Butch, we are going to go in there and talk honestly to the kid about the contents of the bags. I don't see any use in playing hide and seek. The boy knows we've gone out to talk and plan, so let's just go in, play it straight, and see what he says."

Billy didn't expect Butch to agree so quickly, but he said he was fine with the plan. Not a man to pull rank or press his own way of doing things, Butch acquiesced if he thought there was a better, clearer way.

They walked in without saying a word. Billy sat down with the Ziplocs and began where he had left off, without making any apologies for leaving or any explanations for coming back with a bag full of Blayne's things. Blayne sat forward and watched as Billy produced the yearbook and the tie box. Butch stationed himself by the door again, leaning in to watch the boy's reactions. As Billy opened the tie box with the pictures of Darren Riegert, he turned the lid of the box over so that the Valentines were visible. Blayne was frozen and pale with surprise.

"My fucking mother give you those?"

"Were you with Darren Riegert on Friday night at Satan House?"

"No fucking way. Those are my things, you fucking shit. How did you get them?"

"Your mother gave us permission to search your room, Blayne. I found them. I thought we needed to get them to help us find out who hurt your friend Darren."

Blayne burst into tears and with his free hand snatched the tie box with Darren's pictures off the counterpane. He held the box close to his chest. After he sobbed for a second, he gulped in a few halting breaths and started to rock, to sing and chant in the same voice Billy had heard him use at the police station. This is his coping pattern, Billy thought. And his diversion tactic. Billy knew he must break through it.

"Blayne," Billy said, "if you want, I can take you to the funeral home where Darren is now. We can drive you there. Maybe seeing your friend can help your memory a little."

"He wasn't my friend," Blayne said, his voice now pushed down far into his throat as if he were afraid of his own words. "I loved him. He said he'd be my friend, but he always hung out with that asshole Cody. I would've treated him good. I stole that leather coat for him. He said he liked me. . . ."

"Do you remember when you took this picture, Blayne?"

Billy was holding up the Polaroid of Darren standing naked and surprised in the Satan House basement.

"When did you last see Darren, Blayne? Look at me, Blayne, and tell me the truth about Friday night."

"I saw him at school in the morning, and he said he was going out that night, and he said if I wanted maybe I could come, but then he said he'd changed his mind. He said I should stay away from him. I wanted to go and have a beer or something with him. He sometimes stole beer from his mother, and once we smoked up and drank behind his house. So I went to his house on Friday, and he was there, but I didn't go and ring the bell. I waited for him out back because Darren always left his house by the back door. He came out late in his black boots and had his book with him, and I wanted to talk to him, but he was looking so bad, like he was mad or something or real busy to get somewhere. I followed him up Ashmead for a while, and he kept running ahead like he was needing to get somewhere. I knew it was no good."

Blayne put down the Polaroids and covered them with a corner of the hospital bedsheet.

"Did you follow him all the way to Satan House?"

"No."

"Tell the truth, Blayne."

"I followed him up to the soccer field, and I saw him go into the backyard, you know by the garage there. And I thought he was just goin' there like always, like he said he did, to go there and sleep instead of stayin' home with his mom."

"And then? Blayne?"

"I can't tell."

"Who hurt Darren, Blayne? Who did you see there?"

"I didn't know who he was meeting. I thought he had another friend and they were going . . . so I waited and went around the other side of the house and went to the back door. I heard him down in the basement, chanting. I wanted to see who was there. I had my camera, but when I got down there it was dark, I musta scared him, he was naked in the little room. He was so mad when he saw it was me. He started telling me to fuck off. He said he hated me, and he never wanted to see me again. He picked up a knife. It was big. He said he'd cut me, but I didn't see nobody else there. I ran up the stairs. I went around by the window, by the backyard, and I looked in, and it was dark, and I couldn't tell what Darren was doing. He was naked, and he had his boom box, and I knew that asshole Cody'd taught him some spells, so he was getting stoned I guess. I thought that lady would come down, the one living there, so I ran. I went home. . . ."

"You said you thought Darren had another friend. Can you give me a name?"

"No."

"Was there anyone besides Cody who Darren hung out with?"

"No. He didn't have no girlfriend neither."

"Did Darren ever talk to you about his friends? Anyone he liked or didn't like?"

"No. . . . Yes. There was a man. An older man. Darren said he was scared of him."

"Can you describe this older man?"

"I seen him only once, maybe twice. He drove a big green half-ton. He waited for Darren after school."

"What did he look like? Can you remember what he was wearing?"

"No. I just remember his green half-ton. It's long, and he was always in the driver's seat. Darren said he was a friend of his mom's boyfriend."

"Why was Darren scared? Did Darren tell you anything about the man?"

"Yes. Darren said this guy was going to keep him in line. Like he was a teacher or something. Darren told me the asshole wanted to discipline him. Discipline, discipline, that asshole kept saying. Like Darren was his son or something."

"You never met the man, never talked to him?"

"No."

"Tell the truth, Blayne."

"I wanted to tell the guy to fuck off."

"You never met him, then?"

"No."

"How do you know he said 'discipline'? Were you by. . . ."

"I was walking on the street. Darren got in the truck, and the asshole started yelling at him . . . like he was real mad. And he burnt rubber. Darren said he had to do what the asshole said or else."

"Did Darren ever show you his bruises?"

"From the rope? Yeah. He said his mom did it, but. . . ."

"But what? You think someone else hurt him?"

"Maybe that guy in the truck, maybe once Darren had a bruise on his chin, and he said, once, the guy hit him by accident. I don't remember. Darren said it happened a couple of times. He never liked to say the guy's name."

"You're sure you don't remember his name?"

"Yes. No."

"Did you walk home on Friday night, Blayne?"

"I don't remember."

"Did you walk or take the bus?"

"I took the bus . . . Old Charlie, he's always on that route. I call him Old Charlie, he's a big guy with a funny way of talking, like he was a general in the army, he drives fast, too. Always making sure you sit in the right place. No assing around on the bus, he says."

"Is that when you went home and started singing and rocking?"

"No. Yes. I got home, and I got stoned. My stupid mother was home late from work, so I started in then."

Blayne broke down again. Billy handed him a tissue, but Blayne batted it away. He grabbed the box of Polaroids and slid down as best he could with his injured arm under the sheet. He began humming to himself, staring forward. His eyes lifted towards the ceiling of the room. Billy stopped the interview by standing up and gathering the yearbook and the Ziplocs into his arms. Outside the hospital room, Billy checked his reactions against those of Butch.

"Seems on the level," Butch replied. "We have nothing else to go on, mind you. So we might as well ride with this confession, if you want to call it that. That poor kid is a screwup for sure."

With his head aching, Billy walked into the lounge and wrote down the salient points of Blayne's story. *So Perry Hill was connected. Was there a circle of adults abusing this child? No wonder these boys were frightened.* Butch came in, sat down beside him, and yawned. He looked furtively at his wristwatch.

"You know, Butch, you'll have to keep Blayne on ice for at least another twenty-four hours."

"I'll call Dodd before we go."

"And now we've got another angle on Perry Hill," Billy said. "We'll have to get after him tomorrow no matter what."

WEDNESDAY, JULY 3

Billy slept until 9:30. His knee was aching badly, so he spent a few minutes on stretches and light massage. Following instructions brought
home from the hospital, he then changed his gauze and dabbed his head
wound with antiseptic. After coffee, he dressed in a dark suit and tie.
Butch arrived in the Pontiac, and the two drove to the Zabusky Brothers
Funeral Chapel in Lethbridge to join Dodd at Darren Riegert's memor-
ial service. It was a package deal — plastic flowers, a Unitarian minister,
a closed pine coffin on a rolling bier with large rubber wheels. Only
Sharon Riegert stood in the front row. Behind her was Mr. Barnes, the
counsellor from Darren's junior high school. Billy had asked Sheree
Lynn Bird not to attend. Sharon Riegert had made it clear she never
wanted to set eyes on the "witch woman" again. Butch and Billy stood in
the back row, the chief looking at the fake ceiling beams and the blood-
red aisle carpet. Billy kept thinking about Blayne Morton's confession,
particularly the part about the man in the green half-ton, the man Billy
believed was Perry Hill. Now they had to establish Hill's whereabouts
between Friday night and Saturday morning. Was it possible Woody's
friend was at Satan House? Was Hill what Madelaine Van Meer might
call a "tin-pot dictator"? And what about Woody Keeler? Why hadn't he
shown up for Darren's funeral? After the last words were spoken by the
minister, Billy went outside and phoned Johnson. He told her to drive
over first to the Riegert house to see if anything was amiss. Was Keeler
drunk? Was he even at home? She would then proceed to contact Perry
Hill, if the warrants had turned up anything related to Darren.

It was past one when Billy stood aside to watch Sharon Riegert follow

215

her only son's coffin out of the chapel. A blue velveteen cloth hung over the sides, and two attendants from the funeral home solemnly wheeled the bier into the acrid sunlight. Sharon stood shivering by the hearse, her eyes shaded by her right hand. She was wearing old jeans and a pink polyester jacket. Her hair was tightly curled from her recent perm. She avoided Billy's gaze as she passed, but he could see her eyes were half shut as if she were sleepwalking, the pall of despair a familiar one. The hearse drove away, and Billy followed Butch's cruiser to the station.

There Billy was told Johnson had called in. The Riegert house was closed, and Woody Keeler was out. The stained blanket from the bed of Perry Hill's truck had been seized and sent to the lab. Hill's house had been searched, but there was no evidence of Darren's clothes.

Butch brought in coffees. Billy's head throbbed.

"You think this Perry Hill is pulling something?" Butch asked.

"He's been on a bender, but his place is clean. Blayne's confession implicates him, although you and I know it could be circumstantial."

"Point taken. I don't know if you're up to this, but we've got a visitor here from Brocket, an old horseman. I've known Clive for twenty years. He doesn't often come to me for favours since he's strictly by-the-book RCMP. He arrived this morning as I was heading out to Darren's funeral. Clive said he'd wait until we got back."

"He got something on the Darren Riegert case?"

"I'm sure you noted boyfriend Woody's absence this morning?" Butch's face brightened with a grin that Billy read as one of vindication. "Well, Clive just told me Woody Keeler was arraigned by the horsemen as of ten this morning."

"Which explains the closed front door at the Riegert house."

"Pending charge is assault causing grievous bodily harm. A Peigan girl of sixteen had the unfortunate delight of meeting up with Keeler. Clive has the full tale. He wants us, here at the city force, to help him with a lineup since he's got a feeling his case may be tied to Riegert's. Clive's next door in the records and dead-file room. I'll check on our booking schedule. Why don't you go on in and introduce yourself."

Billy stood up, held his stance for a second while the pounding in his temple subsided, then removed his suit jacket and draped it over the back of his chair. He was already sweating from being out in the parking lot, and for some reason the usual cool air in Butch's office had not kicked in. Billy went out and through a door that led into a dimly lit, stifling room. He looked up at the ceiling where the air-conditioning vent had been pulled off by a repairman, then at a small round fan busily whirring back and forth on a metal table.

"Cooler in here, once you sit down."

The strained, heat-tired voice came from a man with small, washed-out green eyes, facial skin the colour of raw hamburger, and jowls pitted from adolescent acne. Blue veins crisscrossed the man's large nose and puffy chin. His girth seemed all the more enormous since he was perched on the edge of a large oak chair, huge arms folded over his chest, and pudgy hands, the colour of lard, resting on the swell of a firm but massively rounded belly. Looking into the flushed cheeks, Billy hoped the man would open things up, make the last few days' events come together in a way he was fearing they may never.

Clive Erdmann introduced himself. He spoke in a low drawl, and the pace of his speech was as leisurely as if he were sitting by a river casting for rainbow trout. He was a longtime RCMP constable stationed on the Peigan reserve, fifty minutes from the city. He'd been a constable for thirty-six years, and he figured he'd spent all of those years dealing with the Natives. Erdmann shook Billy's hand with a hard, callused grip, letting go only when he sat back down. He talked without pause, as if he were in a doctor's office explaining a symptom, telling Billy he was a man with two grown-up sons and a dead wife buried in the cemetery at Fort Macleod.

"They call me Straight Eyes at Brocket. That's a compliment, by the way. The Peigan think I'm fair-minded. I say with pride I'm not one for violence. I seen it, though, over the years. Family beatings and gun-crazy boys wild on liquor and dope spoilin' to shoot the nostrils off any white man within thirty yards of a Winchester barrel."

Butch came into the room.

"Clive, you still stewing in here? I've got. . . ."

"No matter, Eddy. I'm sittin' easy with your detective inspector. I still didn't catch your name."

"Billy. Billy Yamamoto."

"Your folks from Raymond area, the sugar beet people? Worked at that factory before the war? A lot of Orientals around there, Japanese people."

"My father was sent here in 1942. As a political prisoner."

"I am sorry to hear that. Good folks they were, all hard workers. Bad done by, some of them. Your mother was white?"

"Scottish. A Naughton. She was a nurse — a von — for the city's health unit back then."

"They both passed on?"

"Yes."

Clive lifted his right hand and wiped sweat from his upper lip.

"Billy, I don't mean to take your time this afternoon."

"Quite all right, Clive."

"My problem is simple. One of our sergeants plays golf with one of yours, a gal named Johnson. Johnson was tellin' Sergeant Blacker about her case. A boy hanged in a basement. She told Blacker about a lead — a long shot — a man named Hill. Drives a green Chevy half-ton with a long bed. I need to get a hold of Hill, and I come to you now to locate him. He is a man I want to question about Miss Mary Running Rabbit." Clive shook his head. "Poor gal got beat up pretty bad."

"How is he connected with Woody Keeler?"

"Monday, young Wilson Running Rabbit come to my door lookin' like he stepped on a nest of rattlers. He come with a bad story, the poor Christer. Friday night he's lyin' at home with his mom, Lil, and his sister, Mary, when two drunk white men come a'poundin' late on the front door. Wilson said it was real late, 'bout eleven, and these devils come in and slam old Lil and take Mary out for a joyride in a green Chevy half-ton. I get on over the next day to Steve Little Plume and find out from him about Woody Keeler and his buddy, Hill. Steve likes to drink with Keeler, and he was the one sent the two devils to Mary's house in the first place. I reckon this is the same Hill who was out gallivantin' and causing bodily harm with Mr. Keeler. Keeler wears a ponytail, and Wilson said he had on a red baseball cap with a crow feather stuck to it. Them two devils took Miss Mary and beat her up bad, raped her bad, too. She crawled home by herself. Mary ain't no nun, on my word, but she's no more deservin' of a rape and a beatin' like these two white scum give her."

"You have a warrant out on Hill?" asked Butch.

"Only an arraignment. I need Lil to look at him and Keeler in a line-up. If she and Wilson point the finger at 'em, I can persuade Miss Mary to testify in court. Steve Little Plume owes me a favour. Keeler, you may know, has left behind a bad smell in Brocket. From that case years back, the Born With a Tooth boy gettin' beat up. Somebody told me Hill and Ervin's mom were runnin' together for a time. So I'd appreciate some help, Eddy, if you can oblige."

"Johnson was with Hill earlier today. She claimed he was too sick to talk," Billy said. "He's in for a surprise."

The afternoon air was thick with the smell of damp foliage and rising heat as Billy and Butch agreed to follow Clive Erdmann over to the RCMP headquarters. Once Clive had picked up a deputy, a short man armed with a .45 and wearing a flat brown rimmed hat, the two cars headed south through streets shaded by willows and cottonwoods. Clive got out at the top of Perry Hill's street and told Butch he and the deputy would go in the front if Butch and Billy would drive down the alley behind the house and cover the back in case Hill made a run for it.

Billy drove slowly down the muddy alley, the puddles splashing up goo on the tires. Ahead, the green Chevy half-ton was still parked by Hill's back fence. Billy cut the engine. He took out a pair of handcuffs Dodd had given him at the station. Butch wiped sweat off his neck and forehead, and the two of them waited until Clive Erdmann made his way ponderously up the steps to Perry Hill's front door. Billy and Butch opened their doors, checked the fence in front of them, then got out of the Pontiac. They crouched down, moved quickly up the alley to the corner of Hill's back fence. From behind a large honeysuckle, they could see Clive ringing the Hill doorbell. Then he pounded his massive fist on the door. His deputy, his hand grasping his holster, went around to each of the windows knocking on them and calling out Perry Hill's name. The leaves on the honeysuckle hung motionless with the moist heat. Billy watched a white cat dash from under Hill's green half-ton. He felt Butch nudge him with his elbow.

Perry Hill's mother was hiding under a lilac, its boughs and brown-faded blossoms shading her frail figure and camouflaging her. The lilac tree straddled the back fence between her house and Perry Hill's. How the hell did she get out here? Billy wondered. Had she seen the cruiser pull up at the top of the street? But that would mean she had warned her son. Bette Rae waved her right arm in a gathering motion. A thin unshaven man grabbed hold of the top of the wooden fence beside her. He hauled himself up and slid over, his T-shirt catching on the wood splinters. His mouth formed an O as he toppled to the ground next to her. An ugly fresh scrape appeared on his exposed chest. He lay there, writhing, wanting to howl while Bette Rae slapped her hand over his mouth. Blood lay streaked in a jagged line along the length of his T-shirt.

"Meet Perry Hill," whispered Billy. "Come on."

Billy and Butch cleared the six yards from the honeysuckle to the back fence in a few quick steps and burst through the broken gate into the shade of the lilac and the astonished shock of Perry Hill and his now-shrieking mother. Hill's head looked up, his face haggard, and his thin right wrist was suddenly clamped with a ring of steel. Butch crossed Hill's left arm behind his back. "Got him here, Clive," Billy yelled, as Butch connected the cuffs with a loud metallic snap. Bette Rae started beating her fists against Butch's shoulders. Billy moved in and managed to pry her away. Just then the deputy and a huffing Clive Erdmann entered from the front yard. Clive held a notice of arraignment in his left hand.

It felt odd, witnessing an arrest again after seven months away from active service. Once routine, now the locking of an individual into wrist irons seemed suddenly bizarre and extreme. Billy knelt and scanned the area under the lilac tree, looking for coins or keys from Perry's pockets. Butch handed Perry over to Clive, who read the arraignment and at the same time apologized for the handcuffing. Perry was too hungover and hurt to speak.

"He's done nuthin'!" his mother screamed.

When Perry Hill walked off with the deputy, his mother covered her face with her hands. Clive Erdmann folded the arraignment paper and put it into his right pants pocket. "I'll need a statement from you, ma'am," he said. "I won't need to trouble you much." Bette Rae walked towards the front yard with Clive, her head hung low.

Billy went down the alley and walked to the green half-ton and pulled back the tarp to see if he and Johnson had missed anything. When he went over to the RCMP cruiser, Perry Hill was sitting slouched behind a steel mesh partition separating the prisoner zone from the front of the cruiser. His hands were cuffed behind him, making him sit up straight. Billy thanked the deputy, who glanced at Hill. With a sneer in his voice he said, "Nasty!" and tipped the rim of his brown hat.

Just after three, a sudden rain shower pelted the car as Butch and Billy drove back to the station. Clive had invited the two of them to the lineup tomorrow. He also finished telling them the details of the beating of Mary Running Rabbit and Woody Keeler's involvement.

In the station, Billy washed his face with cold water and asked Butch if the officer at the reception desk had any aspirin since his temple and his knee were aching. He also needed to get to a garden store before driving home. He went to the canteen, got a Coke, and swallowed the pills, hoping they would kick in.

Butch drove Billy to the garden store in the North Side Chinook mall. It was 3:30; the sky was clearing, and a soft wet breeze was lifting the plastic flags strung around the parking lot. Over the western horizon, bright sun cut through the black flat-bottomed rain clouds, and huge shafts of rain-soaked light swept southward towards the

Livingston range and the Montana border. Butch opened the gate to the compound where the trees and shrubs were on sale in the Wal-Mart warehouse garden centre.

"Anything wrong?" Butch asked.

"Yes. There is. I'm beginning to ache from head to toe. Wonder if I'm getting a fever?"

"I'll take you home if you like."

"I must be getting old, Butch. Letting a head wound get me down."

"Take heart, buddy."

"There's a beauty."

Billy stopped and pointed to a small fir tree in a stiff brown paper pot casing. He leaned down and inspected the needles, the size of the trunk, and the price tag. A store employee approached wearing a red Wal-Mart apron and a name tag with black letters spelling out the name of Slade.

"Afternoon, Uncle Butch."

Butch grinned, and Billy stood up slowly, holding his hand on his forehead before focusing on the six-foot young man. His hair had been cut into a buzz with a Samurai-styled ponytail tied back with a swatch of black cloth.

"Billy, meet Slade, Lorraine's kid brother."

"Pleasure." Slade shook Billy's hand with a sudden tight grip. "You got another blue spruce anywhere, Slade?" Billy asked.

"Over here," Slade replied. "Small this year. Not a lot of snowfall this past winter where they were harvested."

Billy looked over the specimen. It was shorter and narrower than the first one he'd seen, but its needles had that blue-green glow that made the tree stand out against the snow of a plains winter. "I need a flowering crabapple, too," Billy said.

Slade went into the storeroom at the end of the outdoor compound and returned a few minutes later carrying a spindly thing with roots wrapped in burlap sacking. "It'll be a year before this one takes hold, but she's a tough little plant," Slade said.

Billy paid for the two spruces and the crabapple, and then he watched Slade and Butch carefully lay them on their sides in the trunk of the Pontiac.

When he got back into the passenger seat, Billy knew he should get straight home to the ranch and go to bed. That would be the reasonable and wise thing to do. But he told Butch to take him to the regional hospital first, to the emergency ward, where he'd had his wound tended. The nurse recognized Billy immediately and took a quick look at the wound.

"It's fine," she said. "It's clean. Bathe it tonight and try not to sleep on that side."

Billy then took the elevator up to the psychiatric ward and asked the station nurse if Blayne Morton had been checked out and registered in the detention home attached to the hospital. Butch stood beside him, reading over his shoulder the computer screen in front of the nurse. "Yes, sir," she answered. "A Sergeant Dodd committed Mr. Morton this afternoon." Billy thanked the nurse and then enquired after the woman Blayne had attacked. "She's fine," the nurse smiled in response. "Her nose wasn't broken after all."

Twenty minutes later, Butch was driving the Pontiac west along Highway 3.

Billy laid his head back.

"You feeling sick, buddy?"

"No, just meditating. Cooling down the brain."

"When did you get into this Zen stuff?"

"About ten years ago. Found it's a great way to relax and settle the mind."

"You just hum and trouble goes away, eh?"

"Not quite. The *Rinzai* sect teaches us to think from different angles. There are always paradoxes — like 'acting through not acting.' Or like this Riegert case. We know much, yet we know nothing. I like *za-zen* — the meditation. The riddle or *koan*, as our teacher called it, is not an easy thing to analyze through reason."

"So how do you untie such a riddle?"

"Well, meditation encourages intuitive insight. Flashes, if you like. What you're after is a sudden illumination. Something your reason hadn't considered before."

Butch shook his head. He thought for a moment. "I'd have a hard time sitting still," he admitted. "Meditation makes me restless."

Billy closed his eyes. Butch drove down the concession road and over the Texas gate and parked by the side of the ranchhouse. Reaching into the back seat for his beat-up briefcase, he pulled from it a box of peanut brittle with his wife Lorraine's initials on the homemade cover.

"Here's a thank-you from Lorraine, for helping her out."

Billy took the box of candy.

"You always drive around with one of these in your briefcase?"

"It doesn't hurt to have a box with me," Butch said with a smile. "Like now, for instance. Or when a lawyer asks me to come to his office in an official duty, takes me for a pricey lunch at the Lodge. I thank him with candy. It's a touch no one expects from a gruff chief of police. I'm a small-town guy, Billy. I work with small-town people."

"Thanks, Butch. Tell Lorraine she's more than welcome. I haven't had her brittle in years."

"We got anything else on our agenda for tomorrow, other than the lineup with Clive and the horsemen?"

"Marilyn Black."

"You're not going to mess around with social services are you? They can be pretty territorial."

"How much do you think she can tell me?"

"Maybe lots. Maybe zero. Sheree Lynn Bird is straight. At least that's what I found out when I spoke to Miss Black last winter. Bird was downsized, the agency was cutting back. Zero."

"We're still left with a mutilated teenager who may or may not have been murdered. And we're still not sure what happened to Darren's clothes. I asked Johnson to go back to Satan House and do a thorough search of the basement and attic. She called and said she'd found nothing."

The two men had a quick supper before Butch called Dodd to come to the ranch and pick him up. By the time Dodd and Butch had reached the end of the concession road and were on their way home, Billy was undressed and ready to climb into bed. He lay back carefully on the pillow, the wind gently whispering through the open window. Billy wondered when he and Butch would find the answer to the Riegert case. Almost a week had passed. The station was already busy with new cases — assault, petty theft — and Butch was eager to assign new duties to both Dodd and Johnson. Key evidence was not forthcoming. Billy worried, too, that his nemesis — insomnia — would cut into his life and make his days long and more anxious. He reached down and massaged his knee. *Pull yourself together.* From his side table, he took out a bottle of Tylenol and gulped back a couple of pills.

"You'll find an answer," he said out loud. But he wasn't certain he believed himself.

THURSDAY, JULY 4

By the time Billy had reached the RCMP barracks in Lethbridge, the domed clock tower showed 10:00 a.m. Billy crossed the parking lot, then took the cracking wooden stairs to the second floor, where the lineup chamber was located. It was a small, stuffy room with a long glass window separating it from an adjacent narrow room with a platform and a series of overhead spots. The spots lit up a gleaming white wall, and each standee held a number in front of his chest. Woody Keeler was number six; Perry Hill, looking pale and weak, held up number four. Lilian Running Rabbit was leaning against the wall of the lineup chamber, opposite the viewing window, when Billy silently opened the door and stepped in. Beside her stood a muscular but thin Peigan teenager wearing traditional pigtails and blue rodeo show boots. A sweat-stained Stetson dangled from his left hand. His right grasped Lilian's small shoulders. Lilian was in her late forties, Billy guessed. She was wearing a buckskin vest with beadwork, a long plain grey skirt, and a red bandanna. Sunglasses, thick-rimmed and black, shaded her eyes.

"Inspector Yamamoto," said Butch to the assembled group. Neither Lilian nor the teenager acknowledged his sudden presence. Clive Erdmann sat on a low stool, large sweat patches darkening his khaki shirt. Another man with traditional pigtails and a large scar over his upper lip moved from the wall. Clive asked the man to identify Woody Keeler and Perry Hill. The man hesitated. Clive spoke slowly but with a firm, loud voice.

"Steve, I'm asking you as a favour. I don't hold you responsible for these two fellas' wrongdoings. But you can help Lilian and Wilson by telling us the truth."

The man pointed first to number six. "He's Keeler." Steve Little Plume straightened. Blackfoot words then came from his mouth in a half whisper. Lilian Running Rabbit nodded. Then Steve stepped back: "And number four, he's Hill."

"We are positive now, are we?" Clive said, his voice still firm yet betraying no annoyance or impatience.

Steve Little Plume wiped his mouth. Wilson Running Rabbit blurted, "It's them for sure. The guy with number four, he has the Chevy." A silence overtook the room.

Clive dismissed the group and asked for another man to come in. "What about you, Ned?" asked Clive.

Billy hadn't noticed this other man, who had been waiting in the hall. He wore a new black Stetson, a pair of clean pressed jeans, and a green plaid shirt with mother-of-pearl buttons. Ned Wolds cleared his throat. His words came out clipped and short: "That one with the ponytail. Same one hitchin' a ride I picked up on Number 3 Saturday morning."

Half an hour later, Clive Erdmann had booked Woody Keeler and Perry Hill on assault charges. Butch took Billy to the RCMP barracks canteen and bought him a coffee and a toasted butter horn pastry. Hot white icing dribbled down Butch's chin as he spoke: "Woody was talkative this morning. Yelling for legal counsel. Clive and I had a polite chat with him. He denied everything until Clive pulled the red baseball hat out of a paper bag and asked Keeler if he'd stuck the crow feather on it himself. Perry Hill admitted to the drunken fight, but he said he couldn't remember too much of what went on in the bed of the truck. Maybe he had sex with Miss Mary, but he said he had to sleep off the whiskey for a while before driving into town. All of it a haze. Woody Keeler wasn't too cooperative walking up to the lineup chamber. He's now looking at another assault charge, for hitting RCMP personnel, dumb bastard. I also asked him how he enjoyed his visit to Sheree Lynn's house last Saturday night. His break-and-enter spree. Woody denied it, of course, but he had on him, in his wallet, a credit card — defunct it turns out — belonging to Miss Bird. The night clerk itemizing Woody's possessions had put it on the list."

Billy drank his coffee and made some notes in his notebook. "So, for now, we in the city force can only hold Woody for break and enter. He and Perry Hill have solid alibis for Friday night. Which means we don't need the blood sample on the blanket, and we're back to square one. We don't have a firm lead as to who was in that room with Darren."

"Afraid so."

Billy remained silent for a long time. "Okay," he then said. "I'm going to take a ride over to the north side today and call on social services. We need to jump-start this case."

Butch nodded in agreement. He paid at the register and walked beside Billy through the narrow halls of the RCMP building. Outside, he said, "I've got paper pushing to do, so we'll check in with each other later." Billy watched Butch stroll to his cruiser. Was it his own fatigue and frustration that made him aware of Butch's stooped walk?

Driving east of city hall, Billy turned left onto Cutbill and headed north, passing under the railway shunt line that led to the loading docks of the giant grain elevator. It had been a long time since Billy had visited this section of town, once virgin prairie. In his childhood, he'd come here with Granpa Naughton and was shown the sacred burial tree of the last great Blood warrior, Red Crow. He noted now the strip malls and car lots.

The bright yellow social services building resembled a Lego construction. Marilyn Black, the assistant director of the Lethbridge family counselling unit, proved to be elusive and difficult to reach. Her secretary tried phoning her home number again. "It's the same, it's her answering machine. Let me try. . . ."

"Here's my card," Billy said. "Have her call me at headquarters. The sooner, the better."

Billy spent the next few hours driving around suburban crescents and past domed hockey rinks and new public schools. He sat for a while by the edge of town and meditated, his eyes gazing deep into the vast flatness of the primal land. The case was slipping away from him, and it was little comfort to admit that his ruminations had brought no new revelations.

By 6:30, he was parked at a strip mall finishing a Coke. He tossed the empty into the garbage. The sun was still bright enough to turn the shade of the cottonwoods an inky black. He was restless and couldn't concentrate any further, and he began to drive again, soon finding himself on Ashmead, pulling up in front of Satan House. Why? He suspected its very shape might reveal the truth. He locked his car door and walked over the dirt by the tumbled garage and into the backyard. The grass lay brown and uncut. The shingles on the sloping roof over the kitchen and the upper gables curled with age and decay.

Billy went to the back door and looked at the wooden steps, the door with its padlock, and the yellow police tape. *The boy entered here.* He stepped back. The garden was full of large stones. Wandering around the north side of the house, he watched the evening sun dapple the boughs of the fir with yellow. A light came on in a side room. A figure lifted and moved things. Sheree Lynn Bird. The light went out. Billy returned to the front yard. He ducked under the police tape, went up the steps to the screen door, rang the door chime, and waited. Sheree Lynn said, "Come in." He pulled open the screen and discovered the inner door slightly ajar.

Billy found Sheree Lynn in the kitchen, packing dishes into liquor store boxes. He noticed first her frayed Nikes, then the light cotton sweatshirt with its sleeves rolled up to her elbows. Cups and saucers and cutlery lay strewn on the counters. When she turned to say hello, she was holding aloft a Mason jar in each hand.

"Inspector. I was right. It was you out there prowling."

"Evening, Sheree."

"Is there news?"

"Woody Keeler was arrested by the RCMP this morning for assault and battery."

Sheree put down the Mason jars. "You mean you charged him in the Darren case?"

"No. He'd raped and beaten a young Peigan girl."

Sheree Lynn's face went still. She sighed, wanting the arrest to be for

Darren, to clear up the identity of his abuser. "I told you he was violent," she said, bending over to bring up two more Mason jars.

Billy went on. "The RCMP arrested his buddy, too. A man named Perry Hill."

"I don't know him."

"You realize, Sheree, I'm at a loss here. I have no witnesses. I don't have any new leads. What I have is your testimony, a body with markings on it, and some indication of hokey Satanic rituals. Other than that, I have a bloodied boom box that tells us maybe one version of the crime, maybe another. I believe you know better than anyone in this case what the problems were, maybe even what was going on with Cody and Darren."

"I've told you all I know. Believe me. I didn't like that sergeant of yours coming here and sticking her nose into my cupboards. Darren's clothes are not here, Inspector."

"You abandoned Darren after Cody's death, didn't you?"

Sheree Lynn blushed. "How dare you suggest such a thing?"

Billy shoved his hands in his pockets and stepped closer to her. "You lost interest. You wanted him out of your hair. That's why you tried to force him to go to another counsellor. It had nothing to do with playing mother or showing you cared. . . ."

"How dare you? He pulled away from me, he. . . ."

"You were the adult, Sheree. And you threw this kid away. And for what?"

Sheree Lynn stiffened. She turned her back to Billy and walked to the sink.

"Darren was depressed, remember?" Billy felt his voice rise. "The kid lost interest in everything, not just you and your sweet talk. He was really alone after Cody died. What was on your mind, Sheree? What was it, really?"

"Get out of here. You can't bully me."

"And what about Cody? He died in your basement while you were upstairs in bed with Randy. How does a lost kid start off dancing naked in your backyard and then two months later end up hanging by a rope in your basement? Just where were your priorities, Sheree Lynn? I'm beginning to think you might be an accessory to something. Somehow, you *are* mixed up in this. . . ."

Sheree turned and ran at Billy. She had tears streaming down her face. He caught her by the wrists, and she froze, suddenly, her breathing short and shallow like a frightened dog's. "Let me go." She ran to the back door and tried to yank it open but then lost control and sank against it, her face pale and her voice hoarse with spent rage.

"Cody took acid. He got it on the street. I couldn't control him."

Billy wiped his mouth.

"They were all in a dark world, Inspector. Most of the time I couldn't reach them. I wanted to. You have to believe me."

The phone rang, startling Billy and Sheree. "Let it ring," Billy ordered, but Sheree picked it up and started to talk right away.

"Yes. Yes. Not now. Oh, God. Is he still saying that? Yes. Of course. I gotta go now. Call me after your supper. Nothing's wrong. No, I have not. Are the students working out? Fine."

When she hung up, Sheree was still visibly shaken. She walked to the counter, picked up her cigarettes, and lit one. Billy kept watching her, waiting for her to speak again.

"Inspector?"

Billy held her gaze, tilting his head a little to the left to say he was ready to listen.

"That was Randy. He's tired from the dig this week. I think they're all done tomorrow."

"Do you have anything you need to tell me, Sheree?"

"I . . . I can't. No. I'm tired."

"Did you like your job at social services?" Billy watched her eyes look away as he spoke to her. There was something she was hiding, but he couldn't as yet find a way to make her open up.

"You mean, did I like working with clients? With the boys? Yes. Of course."

"Any problems with the staff? With any co-workers?"

"Not really. Well, there is always a person or two who likes to stake out territory, but other than that, no. I was okay." Sheree's voice broke, but she quickly recovered. "Come on, now, Inspector. You know I want to get out of here. Randy and I are planning a trip to the coast, just for a short time, to relax. I have to put this damn chaos in order before we go."

"You ever meet a young girl named Emily Bourne? She was a friend of Darren's."

"No."

"She claims she phoned you on Saturday morning last. She was asking about Darren. 'Did they do it?'"

"I don't know her, I'm sorry."

Billy decided to let things rest. He pulled in a breath. Sheree stubbed out her cigarette. "When you want to talk to me, Sheree, call. Here is my cell number."

Sheree walked him to the front door, saying nothing as he went down the front steps. Climbing into the Pontiac, Billy sat for a short time and watched the lights in Satan House, imagining Sheree Lynn Bird alone in the rooms. The contours of her world still remained unknown to him, its regions closed in by a border made of her own insecurities and fears.

Randy Mucklowe read over the fax he'd handwritten and addressed to Robert Lau, China Import Company, Vancouver.

Then he pressed the start button. The white paper glided slowly through the machine, and for the first time that day, Randy felt relief. It had been hot on the mountain; Sam Heavy Hand had been drinking beer and smoking homegrown and sometimes coming onto the dig site, walking over the turned earth, making desultory remarks to Justin and Cara about Native religious practices, his own home life on the Browning reserve, his need to be in the air once breathed by his mighty ancestors. At supper, Sam had dropped his plate of food. When Randy told him to go and sleep it off, Sam had shoved him against the fridge, then slammed the screen door and stomped to his truck, where he eventually fell asleep.

Randy stood in the back of the drugstore dressed in a T-shirt, khaki hiking shorts, heavy hiking boots, and wool socks — the gear he always wore on a mountain dig. The store was closed for the evening, its shelves and counter bathed in a pale blue light from the street lamps on the main street of Waterton village. Caitlin, the owner, had lent him a key and said he could use the fax machine whenever he needed. Sneaking past Sam's truck had been easy, with Sam drunk and asleep and the sky covered with low cloud, muting the summer moonlight. Tomorrow, the dig would be over. Friday night meant the students would be leaving for their summer vacations. Stipends paid, dig reports completed, the work from a long week in the sun on the side of Chief Mountain done. Only two small amulets and three arrowheads. The site had proven to be relatively barren. But the golden masks — all seven of them — were safe in the cabin, and Sam was under control for the moment. Randy had not enjoyed Sam's company, except for the nights when they drank and smoked together. *Admit it. You feel tired.* Randy was frustrated, eager to leave and get on with his plans. Get Sheree Lynn on the plane, fly to the coast to clinch the deal with Lau, and somehow, the means not yet worked out, somehow shake off Sam, take the money, and leave the north forever. . . .

The fax machine clicked off. Randy picked up the sheet and read it one more time to be sure he'd made himself perfectly clear.

Robert, the dig is done, and Sheree and I will be going to the coast this Sunday, arriving at noon. We can take a taxi to the hotel as you suggested and meet you there by two. We will be alone, as promised. I have the seven items. We agreed one hundred K for each, in American funds. These are bona fide, I can assure you. As agreed, all cards and correspondence, including this FAX, will be handed to you for your records once the billing transaction has taken place. Randy.

Shutting off the light in the small room behind the store counter, Randy found his way to the phone by the cash register. He dialled out, used his long-distance calling card, and waited for Sheree Lynn to answer.

"Hi, it's me."

Sheree's voice was tired. "Where are you?" she said. "You caught me coming in the door."

"I'm in the drugstore. Sent the fax to Lau and told him when we'd be in on Sunday morning."

"What time is it?"

"Around eleven-thirty."

"Yamamoto dropped in this afternoon. I was with him when you called earlier."

"What's up?"

"He says he's still at a loss about the case." Her voice sounded nervous.

"Nothing happened, did it? You are all right? Everything under control, I hope."

"Please don't start." Sheree Lynn paused. "The inspector says he isn't sure the case is going anywhere."

"That sounds positive, then. For us, at least. You all ready to go for Sunday? You been to the bank?"

"Yes, but I had to pay a penalty on the lease, like I told you. An extra three hundred."

"Let it go, honey. Lau will have seven hundred thousand American."

"You really think this'll go through, Randy?"

"Why not? Lau claims he can sell these babies for ten times our asking price. I don't care what he claims. Just as long as we get our cash."

"And Sam? What about him?"

"The goddamn fool insists on coming. I don't know yet what we'll do, but we'll figure something out by Sunday."

"You home tomorrow?"

"Late. Or, if I need to clean up here, Saturday by lunchtime. I miss you."

"I miss you, too. I hope you're safe."

"I'll see you soon."

Sheree hung up, and Randy held the receiver for a moment, wondering if this July might be a turning point in their life. Smiling, he hung up the phone, went out the back door, and folded the fax copy into his right pocket. The streets were quiet, only a few cars and pedestrians. The air had warmed, and the cloud cover had lifted. Birches and willows were still, their shapes haloed by the rising moon as clouds scudded leisurely southward over the enormous black curves of Mount Vimy and the pyramid-shaped crown of Mount Cleveland. Walking into the woods by the river, Randy saw two figures by the rushing water. They jumped, startled by his approach. The young man looked frightened.

"Christ, man, you scared the shit out of us."

Beside him was a young blonde. Her blouse was unbuttoned, and Randy could see the round white softness of her young breasts.

"I'm just passing through."

Randy thought the young man might strike him, but instead he stood back, helping his girlfriend to her feet, calming her reaction by placing an arm over her shoulder. Randy walked off quickly, his boots cutting through the damp grass. A few moments later, he relished the refreshing cold spray from Cameron Falls. Standing on the wooden foot bridge, he leaned to look into the silver foam that swirled under the curtains and tunnels of splashing water. He turned and saw the couple moving off in silhouette across the moon-bright meadow. A crow cawed in the distance, and he heard laughter from one of the houses on the hill bordering the falls. He wandered down the road to the cabin, taking his time.

By midnight, he was sneaking past Sam's truck, the snores from the cab underscored by a low warning growl from Sam's dog, Crow.

"Easy, boy," Randy whispered. "Easy now."

Once through the screen door, Randy tiptoed to his bedroom. He pulled a flashlight from his bedside table, walked gingerly back to the living room, bent down, and checked the black plastic bags under the couch. The shapes were smooth under the plastic. He imagined the golden eyes and the small pearl mouths. He smiled to himself, stood, and went back to the bedroom, where he undressed and lay on top of his blanket. He opened a small box and lifted out one of Sam's joints, lit it, inhaled its sweet smoke, and rolled back onto his pillow.

It felt good, lying naked in the moonlight, the heady effect of the smoke leading him into sleep and vivid dreams. Tomorrow, all would change. But then, he reminded himself, that was what he wanted. *Tomorrow, the future begins.*

FRIDAY, JULY 5

Marilyn Black was leaning forward on the edge of a swivel chair, flipping through pages on a green blotter, her hair pulled into a slick tight helmet, when Billy stepped into her office. She took Billy's card and examined it, then nodded for him to sit down.

"You want information about Sheree Lynn Bird?" she asked. She gathered her many papers into a squared pile as she spoke. When she looked up, her blue eyes appeared to look right through Billy.

"I know you've talked to Chief Bochansky about her before," Billy said. "I've read over the facts of her employment and her downsizing. So what I'm after is more a personality profile, if you like. And perhaps, if I may, your permission to look at her former caseloads to see if I can get a. . . ."

"Those are strictly confidential, sergeant."

"Inspector Yamamoto," Billy said.

"Excuse me, I was told you were a policeman."

"I am retired now. But I am a deputy inspector with the city force."

"With Chief Bochansky?"

"Yes."

"The Freedom of Information Act cannot override the Charter of Human Rights, Inspector. Before we could give you access to files, we would have to have permission from our clients, many of whom demand and deserve complete anonymity. But since you have told me little about your case, and are here for a profile of a former employee, there is no need for us to go through a long and difficult process of asking permission."

"A fourteen-year-old boy was hanged and mutilated in the basement of Sheree Lynn Bird's leased house on Ashmead Street last Saturday morning. We — the city police — believe Darren Riegert was murdered, but we have no firm leads and no witnesses. All we have is Miss Bird's testimony and an autopsy report."

"Darren Riegert. What a pity. Sheree did work with him and his mother. Unfortunately, unless I contact Ms. Riegert and get her permission to open the files, I cannot help you. You could, of course, ask the courts for access to our archives." Marilyn Black's voice remained steady, cool, aloof. Billy noted how her well-manicured hands sat folded as she spoke. She looked up as she went on, glancing towards the open door to her office, where she could see her secretary working at a computer. Her eye movements betrayed impatience, and Billy could feel her reluctance to spend more than three minutes in his company.

"My problem is justice, Ms. Black. Someone is running around this city who may know about this killing. We need all the help we can get at this point. All the delay and paperwork would hamper the investigation. As each day goes by, whoever did the deed has that much more time to leave the city."

"I'm fully aware, Inspector, of the seriousness of a crime investigation." Marilyn Black's expression was cold. "But I'm entrusted with people's lives and welfare as much as the police. And I cannot speed up due process based on flimsy evidence."

Marilyn Black pushed back her swivel chair, stood quickly, and brushed down the creases in her navy blue suit coat. "About the other matter," she began, her voice measurably tighter and sharper, "the business of Sheree Lynn Bird. What you called a personality profile. She was efficient and kept clear records. We hired her right out of community college, and I'm not so sure that was the best idea. She was probably too young. Most of the time she was respected by her clients and colleagues."

"Most of the time?" Billy leaned forward.

"There were minor complaints about her attitude."

Marilyn Black allowed her professional face to soften and relax. Here was the social services worker coming out, Billy thought. The woman trained to listen rather than act the bureaucrat. "I do know Sheree had a tough childhood herself. I won't go into details. Most of us in the office also knew she had some nervous problems while at college. A doctor prescribed tranquillizers. That's all I can say, really."

"She was downsized for a misdemeanour, wasn't she?"

"I cannot officially answer you on that, Inspector."

"It wasn't a matter of budget or cutbacks. In fact, it was more than a personnel matter, wasn't it?"

Marilyn Black rubbed her hands together. She glanced at the open door. She lowered her voice.

"I like Sheree. I trusted her even though at times she could be overly emotional. Sadly enough, she made snap judgements she later regretted. Worse, Inspector, she might have crossed the line of decency, went beyond professional lenience in a case that was, frankly, one she should never have been assigned. Because of this, she was let go."

Pulling back, Marilyn avoided looking into Billy's eyes.

"Were there ever complaints of a sexual nature about her? Any of the boys come to you. . . ."

"None. Absolutely not. I know she's a vain girl, but all Sheree Lynn wants is attention. Nothing more than that." Marilyn Black walked around the desk and put out her hand. "If you don't mind, Inspector, I must now insist we finish up here." She waited awkwardly by Billy's chair. "If I think of anything else that could help you and Chief Bochansky, I'll phone right away."

The bureaucrat resurfaced, Billy thought. He shook Marilyn Black's cool hand. The secretary glanced up at him as he entered the reception area, and she turned her head back towards Marilyn Black, who was shutting her door.

"Wait a second, Inspector. I heard you in there."

The secretary opened a filing cabinet drawer. She noted a number and replaced a file: a smooth, furtive act perpetrated with eyes fixed on Marilyn Black's office.

"Here's a woman who can tell you about Sheree's downsizing. I know it's not quite legal. But maybe she can help."

The name on the piece of paper read Debby Fast.

Billy took Burdett Avenue over to Magrath Drive, got to the Dairy Queen in ten minutes, waited for Debbie Fast to start her mid-afternoon shift, and spent the time eating a barbecued hot dog and a soft ice cream with chocolate dip. Ten minutes after she was supposed to arrive, Billy was still waiting and wondering if he'd been stood up. He was about to go to the manager's office when a tall woman with a broad smile came up to his booth. She was wearing an apron and a white uniform, and a hairnet was cupped under the long hair she had braided at the back of her head.

"Howdy," she smiled. "I'm Debby."

Debby Fast's voice was clear and rich. She was over thirty, and her heavy makeup could not cover the myriad tiny lines around her mouth and green eyes.

"Thanks, Debby. Can you spare some time to. . . ."

"We're slow right now. Mr.?"

"I'm a detective with the city force, Billy Yamamoto."

"Yes, sir."

Billy explained the Darren Riegert case, the problems with the investigation, his need to find leads, and his belief that, sometimes, it was necessary to talk to all sorts of people about those who were directly involved in the investigation — like Sheree Lynn Bird.

"I see," Debby smiled cheerfully.

She had practised her manner, Billy thought. He then asked her to tell him what she knew about Sheree.

At first, Debby hesitated, but she went on to tell the history of her own problems with an abusive husband and a small baby. And about Sheree's subsequent care in helping her out.

"I hated her at first, to tell the truth. I thought she was a young know-it-all and had a lot of cheek telling me how I should be thinking, telling me my husband was a jerk. I was the jerk!"

"So Sheree was able to help you?"

"She sure did."

"Are you aware, Debby, that she lost her job because of her dealings with you?"

"What?" Debby's face fell. Her practised smile shut into a flat, tightly held mouth. "You're lying," she said. Gone was the singer's voice. Her eyes narrowed. "I don't believe you."

"What happened, Debby? Why would Sheree Lynn lose her job over what she did?"

Debby Fast's eyes filled with tears. She grabbed the wet napkin and daubed her eyelashes.

"Oh, shit," she said. She composed herself. "I'm so sorry. I didn't know. She said it was her first real job, too."

"Was she unfair to you? Did she harm you in any way?"

"Just the opposite." Debby moved her eyes towards the window and gazed out at the light bouncing off the asphalt of the parking lot.

"Debby, I'm looking for the murderer of a fourteen-year-old boy," Billy said quietly. "I don't know where to go from here."

"No way Sheree would do something like that, believe me, Inspector. She made a big mistake with me. No way she'd harm a living soul. That's her problem really."

"Tell me."

"I was hitting Troy. He was only four at the time. I was hitting him to get back at my husband, who was kicking the shit out of me. Sheree noticed the bruises on Troy and had to report them. But we became friends, of a sort, over the few months I worked with her. She got me into a rehab program and a support group. She went out of her way for me. One night, I got drunk. I slapped Troy around a little too hard, and he had to go to the hospital for stitches. When I brought him home that night, I phoned Sheree. I told her I wanted to kill myself for what I'd done. She came right away, she comforted me and Troy. He's such a brave boy. I begged her not to tell. She and me kept it a secret. Troy turned out okay. But the hospital phoned the agency eventually, they have to, I guess, and that bitch Marilyn Black hauled Sheree on the carpet for covering up what I did. Troy was taken from me then for a whole year."

"That was the only time she lied about you?"

"Yes, sir. She was a good-hearted person. Too good sometimes. I always said to her, 'You know your heart's going to lead you into some bad scrapes if you're not careful.'"

With clouds forming a canopy of pure white tufts, Billy drove slowly through the city, stopping to admire the huge weeping willows along Courtland Street, the sweeping boughs reminding him of mountain waterfalls. Reluctantly, he parked in the station lot and sauntered into reception, leaving behind the late-afternoon verdant heat. His head wound was healing. His ability to reason, though, was still in turmoil. Even the trust he placed in his intuition flagged.

In Butch's office, he sat down at the computer and called up statements made by Sheree Lynn Bird during the past seven months. He printed the documents and relaxed to the buzz and swish of the machine as each page slid out onto a plastic holding tray. He then gathered up the papers, turned off the equipment, and on his way out told the desk he was planning to stay home the next morning and to tell Butch he could call him at the ranch after ten.

That evening, after supper, Billy watched coyotes by the buttes of Head-Smashed-In Buffalo Jump. He sat low in the prairie grass, hoppers jigging about him in crazy arcs as the light faded behind a wing of cloud. In two hours, he spotted seven singles, one a bitch heavy with a late litter. Back home, he sat up late with a cold McNally ale and read through the statements he'd printed. The silence eased his worries about the case, despite his wounds and aching joints. He was determined to cherish the good things he had. The pain of his father's death was mellowing, becoming a part of his inner life in the way that it should.

Reading Sheree's words again, he hoped to come across something he hadn't noticed before. A pattern of thought, perhaps. He worked slowly, finishing his beer in small sips. Pulling the papers together, he lay back. What words surfaced? One simple phrase. One that repeated itself in every statement. It always came at the beginning, as she spoke about each of the boys she'd tried to help. "I wanted to protect them, to shelter them."

As a mother might, Billy thought. As she had protected Debby Fast, by lying, even at the peril of trusting a battering mother not to hurt her little son. *Who is she protecting now? Or lying about in order to shelter?*

Billy placed the papers into a folder. He rose and walked around the creaking floors, the darkness of the plain outside the window lit only by starlight. The deep black of the prairie sky gave him a sense of safety. He locked the kitchen door. In the bedroom, he slipped off his robe and climbed under the sheet. For a second, he imagined Cynthia lying there, her arm over her eyes: a sudden sense of joy mixed with loss. The answer to his *koan* would come eventually. Harmony would be restored. At least for the living.

SATURDAY, JULY 6

The revolving red lights from the fire engine and the police cruiser flashed across the doilies and stripes of the elderly woman's living room. Outside, the air was warm with morning sun, and cedar waxwings flitted in and out of the cottonwoods. Billy sat across from the woman and listened patiently as she told him how she'd recognized the broad-shouldered man who'd appeared at her front door, a worn desperate quality in his voice. She had shaken Chief Bochansky's hand and asked him and Billy why they had come. "When I learned your names," she explained, "I realized there was trouble." A body had been found. Perhaps murdered. The woman sat up straight in her pleated skirt and wool sweater. She spoke slowly and clearly, in a gentle manner.

"Really, there's not much more to tell, Inspector. I heard Spencer barking. He's a dear doggie. Except Aileen lets him out at night, and he barks at any living thing. What did I see? It looked like two men coming through the back gate, the one that joins Marion Bartlett's old place with the Moores'. I couldn't see their faces clearly because my glasses were downstairs on the hall table. I could tell, though, that one of them seemed drunk. He was holding on to . . . no, his arm was draped over the other fellow's shoulder. They were moving in the direction of the back door. Poor Miss Sheree. I didn't know her well. I'd heard she was taking no-counts into that house. None of my business, certainly. After that, I got up. Actually, I fell to sleep, then I got up because of Spencer barking again. I took the situation in hand. I walked through my hedge to the back door of Marion's house. The drunks had broken down the door. I wondered if Miss Sheree was safe. Little Spencer came bounding up the stairs from the basement. That was when I really felt afraid. I thought I smelled smoke."

"You've been a great help to us."

"Oh, yes, Inspector. Something else struck me as odd."

"In what way?"

"Odd to me, at least. Even without my glasses, I could tell the men had bare legs. Now I know it's summer, but would you be wearing shorts at night?"

"Was either one of them wearing a hat or. . . ."

"No. I'm certain of that. And come to think of it, they were awfully quiet for a pair of drunks. Usually, men like that are howling away or singing, but they were so quiet, as if they didn't want to wake anyone."

"When you saw the little white dog, you said you knew whose it was right away."

"To be sure. There's only one white terrier like that in this neighbourhood."

"Who does Spencer belong to?"

"Justin Moore, Inspector. Aileen's son."

As Butch led the way down the basement steps in Satan House, Billy resisted a sudden *déjà vu*. It was about this time last Saturday he had come down these same dusty stairs, alone, into the dank small room where Darren Riegert had been found. Butch pointed to a small lump of dirt lying on the edge of the bottom step.

"Careful, buddy. Dodd, did you get any of these mud samples earlier on the walk-around?"

"Yes, Chief. They're upstairs, bagged, on the kitchen counter."

"Was the scene tampered with by the firemen?"

"Not that I know of. The captain who called dispatch was in shock. He just told it like he saw it. The fireboys did tramp in mud from the garden, but there was also this other-coloured stuff on the steps, like shale or red dust. I figured we should get a sample."

Butch moved aside and let Billy enter first. The window above the dryer framed sun from the garden and made a bright hazy square on the soiled floor.

"Morning, Billy."

"Morning, Johnson. Morning, Tommy."

"Good morning, Inspector."

"You found him like this, Johnson?"

"Yes, sir. Slumped over to the left. I've done the site photos already and most of the dusting. Here, on the sketch, you can see the layout as we found it at 7:30."

"We did a full walk-around on all floors, Billy. While you were on your way in."

"Thanks, Dodd. The noose was hanging down like that? Undone?"

"Yep. The knot worked loose somehow, we figure, and the body fell."

"A slow fall, though, sir. The knot was probably a basic 'granny.' A slipknot. Like the one here around the wrists. The way the body ended up like this, the torso bent forward and the knees buckled, it's possible the knot loosened gradually, allowing him a slow slide to the floor. But what we can't figure. . . ."

"It's this bruise on the temple, Inspector. The colouring, especially the nature of the lividity, and the texture of skin tell me it's post-mortem."

"And yet, Tommy, the body has fallen the other way. To the left, not the right. What's that on the lip?"

"A small hematoma and cut. Pre-mortem."

"Johnson, can you lift the head for me? Turn the face up. Lift up the left eyelid a little more. Fine. Justin Moore all right."

"Let me get a closer gander. Jesus!"

"So the neighbour didn't look at the body?"

"No. She thought she'd smelled fire and called the smoke-eaters."

"By the way, where's the dog? What happened to the terrier she said was barking all night?"

"There was no dog by the time we got here. The fireboys and their lights may have frightened it off."

"Any sign of a dog being here, Johnson?"

"As a matter of fact, sir, there was a small bit of urine over on the wall by the dryer. The dog must have been marking its territory."

"You sure it's dog piss?"

"No, sir. But it's just a few drops. I took a sample and bagged it so we can run a lab check."

"Well, it makes sense the animal got in here; it would probably stake a claim."

"Understandable that it might also bark at a dead body."

"You need to look around the room, Billy?"

"I'll wait until you are done, Tommy. Any temperature reading yet for time of death?"

"I'm getting there, sir. Can you figure this black paint on the genitals and the chest?"

"Is it paint for certain?"

"Yes, sir. Johnson found the can in the other room."

"It's the same black paint used last week, sir. On the pentacle on the wall there. Whoever daubed it on the genitals was careful. There are few spill spots on the floor here, beneath the noose, where this new pentacle was painted."

"No candles or books this time, Johnson?"

"No, sir."

"What do you make of the torn shirt? And the shorts and underwear pulled down to the ankles?"

"Seems the shirt was cut with a knife rather than torn. Not much left, by the looks of it."

"Two pieces were found to the left of the body, sir. I've tagged and bagged them already."

"Any blood on the shirt?"

"No, sir."

"There is hardly *any* blood, Inspector. Except for the lip cut, which had congealed, there is no cutting or bleeding evident on the body."

"And the neck bruise? The ligature mark?"

"Well, Inspector. If this cadaver was hanged and asphyxiated, then it wasn't by this binder twine. From what I can gather here, the bruising is minimal, and the spotting at the neck leads me to guess the body may have been dead *before* it was strung up."

"Jesus! What are we getting into here? This town's going crazy with. . . ."

"Don't jump ahead, Butch. Let's go up to the back porch and garden. Johnson, you come with me. You're done with the dusting?"

"Yes, sir. In one second."

"Dodd, get out to the neighbours."

"It's done. Bolling's knocking on doors already."

"Then I want you to do a slow thorough walk-through in the garden. Comb the grass, the back fence, and the bushes near that garage. Look up on the garage roof and inside it. No one here has mentioned a knife or a weapon, but last time we found a bread cutter shoved into the mud by the fence. Also, where is the paintbrush that made the pentacle and decorated the kid's genitals? We need to find it, if it's still on site."

Billy found a space in the room where there was no one dusting or putting up tape or chalking and leaned his back against the rough surface of the whitewashed concrete wall. A pen hung suspended in his right hand, and he looked through the small window at the grass and the hot light of the Satan House backyard. To his side lay the cadaver, paint-smeared, bruised, its clothes half on, half off. Tommy, the medic, was kneeling by the buttocks and inserting a thermometer into the anus to determine body temperature and a possible time of death. Billy had watched Tommy take swabs of this area, the penis, the mouth, and fingers for any signs of body fluids other than blood, the assumption being that perhaps the body might have been sexually molested given the state of the torn and pulled clothing. And, of course, the painted genitals. Billy was shocked at the state of the body and its odd slumped posture. Satan House had been invaded once again. A door kicked in. The padlock smashed. And now a second victim. How much of a connection did it have with the hanging of Darren Riegert seven days before?

Billy was wearing jeans, a white T-shirt, and brown loafers. He'd been in the garden early, digging holes for the new trees, stopping occasionally to glance at the changing sky patterns. Granpa Naughton had once said that clouds and light were the prairie man's scenery. When Butch had called telling Billy another young man had been found in Satan House, Billy had left his shovel on the porch, knowing immediately that this presaged a turn for the worse, a veering towards a greater evil.

Now he pondered the myriad facts of the case and the new questions the scene in front of him would raise. Butch had been right. They were similar crimes — the room, the pipe, the pentacles, and the nudity. But so much didn't add up. Why would a body be strung up after death, if what Tommy had said was true about the ligature bruising? And the painted genitals? Also, Justin Moore was older than the others. *How much does Sheree Lynn Bird know of this already?* If at first glance there were too many contradictions, Billy always knew he was in for some difficult work.

"We're lifting him now, sir. Bagging him for Hawkes."

Billy turned and watched Tommy and Johnson, their hands sheathed in grey skin-tight rubber gloves, place the body into a plastic body bag. The legs were first, and then the arms and head were manipulated until the plastic zipper could be closed to cover the contorted face. Just as the zipper slid over the upper portion of Justin Moore's face, Billy took a last glance at his pale skin.

When the body had been carried up the stairs, and Butch and Dodd had gone to scout the garden, Billy took a few minutes alone to examine the empty room. As he had done a week before, when inspecting the site of Darren Riegert's hanging, Billy stood at attention. He placed his hands behind his back and whispered under his breath: "Observe all, make no assumptions." Although his mind had been racing and forming all kinds of suppositions, Billy decided to let the room "speak" to him, to let himself stand immobile and silent to allow the space to enter into his mind.

Out came his notebook. He lifted up his right hand and the pen he had been holding. The floor had been painted with a crude pentacle in the same black paint found on the body's genitals. Mud and mouse droppings crunched under Billy's loafers. He went to the sink, bent down, and smelled the drain. He knelt and swept his eyes over the floor. The intense light of the morning brought out the white in the brick walls. Daubs of black paint ran in a thin necklace from the pentacle in the centre of the room to the edge, suggesting to Billy where the paint can had been placed by the perpetrator. A small shred of the cheap cotton binder twine that had been tied around the cadaver's wrists and neck lay on the floor like a wisp of grass. Billy wrote a few notes, pulled in a deep breath, and went upstairs into the kitchen.

Johnson was waiting for him. Billy looked out the window to the garden, where Butch and Dodd were slowly walking along the fence, their heads held down towards broken stalks, stone, and mud.

"Let's you and I walk over to that gate, Johnson. The woman next door claimed she saw two men come into the yard from there. You have your kit?"

"Yes, sir."

"Bolling hasn't come back from questioning the neighbours?"

"Not yet."

At the back door, Billy pulled on a pair of rubber gloves and took a handful of Ziplocs from Johnson's kit. The two of them stood for a moment on the threshold, with Billy bending close to the broken padlock. Splinters from the screws that once held the padlock and its metal arm were scattered by the door and on the top outside wooden step. "Looks as if the lock was struck by a rock. Maybe one of those greys from the garden there."

Johnson stepped down to the area beside the back wall of the house. Overgrown with weeds, the mound of stones was composed of flat field rocks, potato-shaped grey boulders, and large lichen-spotted slabs of granite brought in from the quarries in the Crowsnest Pass.

"The gate is straight ahead, twenty yards. The two men walked or strolled from there to here. It's been dry for the most part, Johnson, so I don't expect we'll find any footprints. But you never know."

Billy headed for the gate, walking a foot or so to the left of the path he assumed was taken by the men. He watched Johnson keeping her head down, examining the grass. At the gate separating the Moore property and that of Satan House, Billy saw that the garage in the Moore yard butted up flush to the fence. A small, rain-spattered window faced out from the Moore garage and gave onto the backyard of Satan House. The glass in the window was so smudged it looked as if it had been painted with a light beige undercoat.

Passing through the gate, Billy noted trampled grass leading into the Satan House yard. He bent down, looked closely, then stood up. The Moore yard was small; the house was large, with a square open-air back porch made of concrete. Stairs led up to the back door on both sides of the porch, giving access to the backyard as well as the street beyond. The garage was built of wood, covered with faded red paint. Its old swinging doors had glass panes as dirty as the one in the back wall. The roof sagged in the middle, and there was a smell of car oil and dust and rotting timber. The right swinging door was ajar. Billy gazed into the shadowy interior.

"Someone's left a light on in there," he said to Johnson.

An Oldsmobile was parked close to the left wall.

Billy also saw bags of soil, a workbench, clay garden pots, a row of garden tools neatly arranged on a phalanx of hooks that ran parallel to the right side of the car. "We'll have to get permission to search in here. I wonder why that light is on, though? Unless the Moores leave it on all night for security reasons."

Billy walked to the back porch steps.

"We'd better call on Mrs. Moore, now, Johnson. This will not be easy."

Grabbing the metal railing, Billy suddenly stopped. He looked at the small flower patch ranged at the foot of the steps. White sweet alyssum grew in precisely spaced mounds. The ones nearest the steps had been trampled flat. "Hold it, Johnson." Kneeling down, Billy examined the soil. He then let his eyes roam past the step and towards the cut grass bordering the cement foundation of the house. He got up, moved to the foundation, and knelt again. "What do you think this is, Johnson?" Johnson climbed on the step above Billy, opened her kit, and pulled out a pair of tweezers and a Ziploc. She leaned close to Billy's face. In the grass were tiny shards of a shiny white material. Broken glass from a lightbulb? Billy raised his head and looked at the light fixture over the door. A round clear cut-glass globe sheltered a standard opaque white lightbulb. Johnson lifted a number of the pieces and placed them into the Ziploc, then held the bag up to the sun.

"Beats me, sir. It could be glass or shale. . . ."

"There is a lot of it right here, around the step, small bits, as if some- one had broken a teacup or a lightbulb. And look, the pieces are light enough to sit atop the blades of grass. Get as many as you can, Johnson, and we'll run them through the lab."

From inside the house, a sharp-pitched barking erupted. Suddenly, through a small hinged square flap cut into the bottom quarter of the wooden back door, a white terrier burst out onto the concrete porch, barking and wagging its tail.

"Spencer?" Johnson slowly reached out her hand to the dog's face. The terrier barked and shook its body, then out of curiosity sidled up to Johnson and quickly sniffed. "Spencer?" Johnson said. "Good boy." The dog's tail began to wag furiously. Then it pricked up its two shaggy ears, froze, suddenly, as if hearing a distant whistle, and dashed back through the swinging flap into the house.

Billy climbed the steps, yanking off his rubber gloves and putting them into his pants pocket. He rang the doorbell. Footsteps gradually grew louder, and when the door opened, a tall woman in a white quilted housecoat stood in the doorway, glowering into the sunlight.

"Sorry to bother you, ma'am," Billy said, holding up a badge Butch had lent him. Johnson pulled out hers, too. "My name is Billy Yamamoto, detective inspector with the city police force. This is Constable Gloria Johnson."

The woman took a second to register what was being said. Billy thought she must have just climbed from bed. She spoke in a slow, sleepy manner.

"Is there something wrong, officers? I'm sorry. . . ."

"Are you Mrs. Aileen Moore?" asked Billy, placing the badge into his pocket.

"Yes. Ah, do you need to come in? Has something happened?" Aileen Moore rubbed her face quickly with her right hand and seemed at that moment to waken. Her demeanour changed to one of alert fear. "I'm afraid I was ill last night and took a sleeping pill, officers. I just woke up. Has something happened?"

Billy looked first at Johnson, then to Aileen Moore.

"I'm sorry, Mrs. Moore. I have some bad news."

Butch led a weeping Aileen Moore to his cruiser as Dodd was reporting to Billy that he had found no knife or paintbrush hidden in the Satan House backyard. Billy then instructed Dodd to do alibi checks on Blayne Morton and a young woman whose name he'd been given by Aileen Moore. "She's a girlfriend, name of Karen Kreutz."

Bolling was stretching yellow tape across the entrance to the Moore driveway as Billy came down the back porch steps. The young sergeant dropped the end of the tape, pulled out his notebook, and strode over to Billy.

"What did you find out, Bolling?"

"Seems the whole neighbourhood's on summer holidays, Inspector. I checked at all the houses bordering these yards and on Baroness Street. I looked in a few garages, too. No cars, no one answering either front or back doorbells. One woman said she saw at least four of the families on the street packing up their vans and station wagons on Friday evening with groceries and suitcases. A lot of people around here have cabins down at St. Mary's and in Waterton Park."

"Did she mention hearing a dog bark?"

"I asked. She said no."

"Did anyone see a van or a car or any unfamiliar vehicle on the street at any time?"

"I asked that, too. No again. Two of the neighbours on the south side were out late and came home about midnight, but neither one could remember seeing anything."

"How many taxi cab companies do we have in the city?"

"Pardon me, sir? How many?"

"Get the names of all the night drivers. Check their logs and receipts and ask them if they saw any activity on the street." Billy felt restless; time was forcing his hand. "See if a driver was in this vicinity around midnight or later. Surely a single old woman wasn't the only person to spot two drunks strolling into Satan House. Dodd, drive to Randy Mucklowe's and Sheree's. Tell them what's happened, and bring Randy to the station. We need names — and alibis — of all those on the dig."

"Right away, sir."

"Ask Sheree, too, if she received a phone call. Remember last time? Someone called her to alert her about Darren's death. There might be a pattern."

"I'll do my best."

Spencer was barking as Billy and Johnson said goodbye to Dodd. Bolling finished taping outside the doors of the Moore garage as Billy walked towards it and stood in the doorway. Something felt odd. He looked at the wall of garden tools arranged neatly in a row on a series of hooks. One of the tools was missing. He glanced at the wall and the floor beneath the row, then scanned the broader floor of the garage. Underneath the Oldsmobile, the tip of a wooden handle protruded. Billy went towards it and saw it was a hoe. "Johnson, dust this."

Johnson brought over her kit, pulled out a small brush, some tissue paper, and a canister of fine white powder. With gloves on, she slid the hoe out from under the Oldsmobile. She daubed the brush and began lightly dusting the handle.

"You may only find smudges, Johnson, but I wonder why the hoe was left like that under the car."

THE BOY MUST DIE

Billy left her to finish. Meanwhile, he clasped his hands behind his back and moved over to the workbench. A forty-watt bulb hung over an area strewn with clay pots, jars full of pencils, and seed packets. Beside the bench leaned a large metal garbage can. Billy pulled on his rubber gloves. He began sorting through the papers and broken twigs in the garbage.

"Come over here, Johnson. I think I've found something."

A few moments later, Johnson and Billy were examining three pairs of soiled cotton underpants, a soil-stained T-shirt, a pair of khaki climbing shorts, and a blue plastic shaving kit. "Now who do these belong to?"

Johnson fingered the T-shirt. "The colour of the soil stain is similar to the red shale mud we found on the stairs in the basement."

"Can we assume for the moment these are Justin Moore's?"

A small flake of white luminous material fell out of the fold of the T-shirt as Johnson was laying it down on the surface of the bench.

"You have a Sherlock with you in that kit, Johnson?"

"A what, sir?"

"Magnifying glass."

Johnson laughed. She rummaged around in a side pocket of her kit and pulled out a two-inch glass. When she handed it to Billy, the light from the forty-watt bulb caught on the convex surface and sent out a brief flash of white. Billy lay the flake on the bench top. He held up the glass and leaned close. "Looks to me like a fragment of polished bone or shell. Here, take a look, Johnson."

"Yes, sir, it does." Johnson then scanned the top of the bench. Pulling tweezers out of her upper right shirt pocket, she placed the tweezers' pointed tips into a small crack in the grained rough wood of the bench surface. "Here's another piece, sir."

Billy took the magnifying glass from Johnson and had her hold up the tweezers close to the lightbulb. "Well, light passes through this little shard. Bag these, and we'll see, maybe, if they match those we found on the grass outside."

The two of them spent five minutes bagging the clothes and the

shaving kit and the shards, and then they did one last walk-around of
the garage before strolling out into the mid-morning sun. Billy walked
past the tape barrier to the curb on Baroness. He wasn't sure what he
was looking for, but sometimes, when a person is in the heated state of
committing a crime, things get overlooked, objects get dropped or mis-
placed. He walked across the street and gazed at the front of the Moore
house and then came back and joined Johnson, who was closing the kit
and shutting the door of the garage, sealing it with a section of yellow
barrier tape. From inside the Moore house, Spencer barked again. Billy
saw the dog at the kitchen window, its shaggy head pressed against the
glass. Billy looked down at the square entrance flap of the back door.
Was it now bolted from the inside, so that Spencer couldn't get out? The
sky above was clear, and the cottonwoods fluttered in the gentle heat,
and Billy wondered how all these small pieces would ever fit into a
meaningful picture.

"Johnson, did you pick up that sheet on the table in Aileen Moore's
kitchen? The one with Cara Simonds's address on it?"

Johnson handed it to Billy.

"I'll go and pay her a visit. Call in Hawkes for the autopsy. Butch and
I need it ASAP."

"Of course. I'll run these fragments through the lab, too. And do
some prints on the shaving kit."

"When you see Butch, tell him I'll call from the Simonds place."

"It was. . . ." Cara Simonds's voice was harsh from crying, though not
loud.

Billy thought: *She never expected to be speaking the words she is now
painfully sharing with me.* Behind her in the quiet kitchen stood her
mother, who had a look of frozen astonishment on her face.

"Tell me, Cara," Billy said. "Try again to tell me."

"It was. . . ." Again her voice trailed off. It was as if the two words
themselves were forming a barrier to her story.

Billy waited patiently. Cara sat up, and her mother broke in: "He was her boyfriend, Inspector. I think they had just started going together on this dig."

"Is that true, Cara?"

She nodded and wiped her eyes.

"I'm sorry, Cara."

Cara spoke again. But now her voice had become wooden, disembodied. "It's all Yianni's fault. Yianni Pappas. He was after Justin. Justin was so afraid of him. He owed him money. A lot of money. Yianni came to Waterton and threatened Justin. Then Justin said, on the last night we were together, he said he wasn't sure he could trust anyone anymore. Even Professor Mucklowe. Randy has no cash. And half the time he was drunk or stoned with his Native friend. I didn't like Sam. He was always pushing Randy around. He once pushed Justin, too, on the last morning of the dig. Justin was unloading the van and dropped a shovel near Sam's foot, and Sam went ballistic. Swearing and shouting about how Justin showed him no respect. Randy had to come between them. I think . . . I know Justin was hoping Patsy Hanson — she was one of his profs — could lend him the cash. But he was never sure he could trust her either."

Cara stopped and stared at the floor. Billy jotted down names and details in his notebook. Again Cara began to speak, paused, then resumed her story in her lost distant voice.

"I knew . . . I knew he was desperate. I didn't think Patsy or anybody else would really help him. I don't know what happened next. But on Thursday night, we were up late, and I was coming back from the bathroom, and I noticed this black plastic bag sticking out from under a sofa. Justin and I found all these beautiful gold masks inside, all wrapped in plastic. Justin wondered where they'd come from. They were beautiful. Small and gold and made of shell or something, I don't know. He said to me, 'I bet these are worth a lot. A lot of money.' I said, 'But why has Randy hidden them? Why hasn't he got them up on the walls?' Randy's cabin had a lot of stuff like that. Old Indian beads, antlers hung everywhere. But then Justin said they were probably fakes. Plastic toys that Randy had bought and stored away. Why else would they be stuffed into those bags? Then on Friday, we went to the dig for the last day, and we worked, and I. . . ." Cara's voice softened. She was looking pale and very tired, despite the rosy tan she had from working in the mountains.

"When was the last time you saw Justin, Cara?"

Cara's mother stepped forward and placed her hands gently on Cara's shoulders.

"Friday night, late. About eleven, I think. I drove him and David Home to the city. We all wanted to get back quickly because Sam was getting drunk again, and Randy told us he didn't need us for cleanup, and we could get our stipends at the university office on Monday morning. I dropped David off first, then Justin asked me to drive him to Patsy's house on Parkside Drive. He said he'd try one last time. He'd been calling her on his cell but getting no answer. I last saw him walking up to her door, and he waved me off. He said he'd call me after he saw her. He never did, and I remember when I held him before he got out of the car his hands were so cold."

Cara bent over in the chair. Her mother moved in front of Billy. She helped her daughter stand and led her into the living room. There she lay Cara down on the sofa and pulled a wool blanket up to her chin. Billy stood as Mrs. Simonds re-entered the kitchen. He thanked her and told her that Cara would have to go to the station to make a formal statement. If she needed help, or care, Mrs. Simonds was to call Butch at the number Billy had written on one of his cards.

Half an hour later, Butch and Billy met on Parkside Drive, in front of Patsy Hanson's house. Butch had brought Billy a coffee from the police canteen. He was wearing a white shirt and blue tie and looking like he'd not slept for days.

"She taking it badly, the girl?"

"Deep shock. As far as I can tell, she's lucid. That often happens right after bad news. The memory is razor sharp."

The sun was heating the grass and the flagstones of Patsy's front walk as Billy and Butch made their way to the oak door and pressed the chime. Billy had called Butch from the Simondses' house to get the address and phone number and then called to see if the woman was at home. A neighbour had answered the call.

Now that neighbour, a well-groomed woman with lacquered brown hair and expensive makeup, stood in Patsy Hanson's open doorway.

"I'm Dodie. Come in, please, gentlemen."

Dodie explained that Patsy was ill but that she would see them shortly. In the living room, Dodie sat down, and Billy began asking her a few questions about the last twenty-four hours, what she had seen and done, why she was now tending to Patsy. Dodie told Billy about seeing a young man pounding on the door of Patsy's house late Friday, that there had been shouting. "I almost called the police. But, you know, to be frank, Patsy often has young men drop by late. I let it go. He didn't stay long. He left and went around the back, and then he came out front again and began walking west past my front door. I couldn't really recognize him. It was dark. But he looked like he was wearing hiking shorts and a T-shirt and was carrying a backpack. Young, he was, by the way he walked. Patsy likes her men young." Dodie wiped the edges of her perfectly red lips with the tips of her right thumb and forefinger.

Butch then asked what time she had come over to Hanson's this morning. Dodie said she'd had a call, around 1:00 or so in the morning. Patsy had been raving drunk and sounded like she could hardly walk and talk at the same time. Then, this morning, early, Patsy had called again. She'd sounded upset and said she needed to talk to someone right away. When Dodie did come over, it was around 8:30, maybe 8:45. The front door was unlocked, and Patsy was in bed, fully dressed in a pair of tight jeans and a sports bra. Surrounding her on her pillow, her sheets, and her bedspread was a huge number of crumpled hundred-dollar bills.

"It was about an hour or so later that you called, Chief. I made coffee and tried to get Patsy to have some, but she was not well."

A voice was heard from one of the inner rooms of the house. It sounded like a moan or a faint call for help. Dodie stood up and smoothed down the front of her navy jogging shorts. "Patsy will see you now." Dodie led Butch and Billy through a series of spacious rooms covered with white broadloom into a large bedroom. The curtains were drawn. Patsy Hanson lay in a silk housecoat on the top of her bed. She was holding a glass full of a brown liquid. Pulled close to the bed were two pink-cushioned chairs. Patsy gestured with her free hand for Butch and Billy to come and sit.

Billy began the questioning. Patsy told the story of her arrangement with Justin Moore, the bills she had brought home from the bank, the champagne she had chilled for their Friday-night get-together. "But then I got cold feet," she said. "I felt he wouldn't come at all, even though I figured he was desperate for the cash." So, she told them, she started drinking and passed out. The last thing she remembered was waking up early, the bed mussed, her hair in her eyes, and thousands of dollars scattered everywhere. "That's it; that's what happened. So why are you here? Has something happened to Justin?"

Billy told her of the body in Satan House.

Patsy Hanson dropped her glass onto the carpet and raised her hands over her eyes.

"Yianni Pappas!" she cried. Then she lowered her hands. Her eyes held steady on Billy's face, her mouth contorted into a thin, angry grin. "I hope you castrate that filthy shit."

Dodie cleared her throat and bent down to clean up the spilled drink with a cloth she had hurriedly brought in from the bathroom.

"Leave it, for Christ's sake, Dodie."

Dodie blushed.

Billy crossed his legs.

"What was the arrangement between Justin and Pappas?" he asked.

Patsy straightened. "Justin borrowed cash. Yianni collects huge interest. Justin hadn't paid. Yianni was calling in the loan. Payment in kind, even. Which can mean sex, or worse, in Yianni's case."

"How well do you know Yianni Pappas, Patsy?"

"What kind of question is that, Inspector?"

"Just answer him," Butch said in a low voice.

"I borrowed from him once. And, yes, I gave him a blowjob as part of the interest."

"Patsy!" exclaimed Dodie.

"Shut up, Dodie."

Dodie fell into a stunned silence.

"Dodie," asked Butch, "you are sure of the time of Patsy's first call to you earlier this morning? You said it was around. . . ."

"I was watching a video. It finished about 1:00, or maybe a bit earlier, because I remember turning on the romance channel from Seattle, the American late-night sex channel, really, and it wasn't on yet. They start their soft-porn program at 1:00."

"God, Dodie," Patsy snarled. "Get a life."

"Where can we find Yianni, Patsy?"

"Do you mean to tell me, Chief, you don't know about this jerk?"

Butch managed a light blush, which surprised Billy. "I'm afraid not," Butch said.

"I give him credit for staying clean on the surface at least. He owns the sports store down on Dowell. He's been dealing dope out of there for twenty years — private-stock marijuana, mostly — and bankrolling loans for quite a few desperate people about town. Including Justin Moore. I am surprised you boys have never run into him before."

"Sadly, Patsy. I am unaware of the man."

"Well, now, you're in for a delight. I saw Yianni on the street two days ago, so he's probably still around. If I were you, I'd head downtown for a chat as soon as you can. He's not known for being a nice guy. He burned a man once, so the rumour goes, with a blowtorch. The guy owed him something like five hundred dollars. So be careful."

Billy and Butch stood at the same time. They moved away from the bed, and Billy thanked Patsy. She watched as they walked from the room. Through the house, all was silent.

In the front hall, Dodie came running after them. "Thank you for coming," she said in a fumbling manner. "Patsy's taking the Justin thing a little hard right now."

"How do you mean?" asked Billy, who had been perplexed at Patsy's initial callous reaction.

"Oh, I think she was crazy about him. And afraid he'd reject her. She's in her bathroom right now crying her eyes out. I was amazed to see how long she held it in before you two decided to leave. . . ."

Billy fished a card from his pocket and handed it to Dodie. "If you can think of anything else that happened here in the last twenty-four hours, please don't hesitate to call me at this number." Billy and Butch walked out the front door and across the lawn to the cruiser.

"I need to call Dodd, Butch."

Billy pulled out the com and dialled dispatch, who immediately connected him to Dodd.

"What did you find out at Mucklowe's, Dodd?"

"He's still up in the mountains according to Sheree. She doesn't expect him back until later today. He has cleanup and some logs to write, she said."

"Get an APB out on him — local and RCMP. Explain we need him for preliminary questioning as a potential witness. What else did you find out from her?"

"I told her about the body. She looked like she was going to croak. I asked her about her whereabouts and if she had received any call during the night or morning, as she had with the Riegert boy. She said she'd been alone and that no one had phoned. She didn't really feel like talking much, Billy. Two of Mucklowe's neighbours verified they saw lights on in the place and heard music, and one saw her take garbage to the communal chute around midnight. He said Sheree Lynn was in her housecoat."

"And the other alibi checks?"

"I located the girlfriend, Karen Kreutz. She and her mother had been at the hospital. Karen's dad, Henry Kreutz, had a stroke early Friday morning and has been in intensive care. Karen said she hadn't seen Justin for a week. She and her mom were real upset to hear about Justin's death. Karen said she didn't have a clue about who would want to kill him, although she said Justin was afraid of a man called Pappas. He'd lent Justin money."

"You know Yianni Pappas?"

"He runs a sports store downtown. Why?"

"Run a check on him in the city files. See if there've been any traffic violations, speeding tickets, anything. Butch and I are heading over to his place now, so I'll call in later."

"You suspect him of being connected to this Justin Moore incident?"

"I won't know until I meet him."

At 1:30, Butch and Billy entered the sports store of Yianni Pappas. The cold brush of the air conditioning brought Billy a memory from earlier that day, an image of the body of Justin Moore, his head slumped forward and his genitals coated in black paint. His hiking boots had looked oddly heavy and out of place in that dark room of sordid death.

"He's out of town," answered the young clerk when Butch asked for Pappas. The clerk walked the two men to Yianni's office at the back of the store and flipped on the overhead light. "Yianni said he'd be at his brother Pete's. He stays with him when he's up in Calgary doing business. You can try him there if you want."

"What kind of business does he do in Calgary?" Billy asked.

"What kind?" The clerk seemed lost for a second. "I think he buys sports clothes, equipment, that kind of thing."

"You known Yianni for long?"

"Me?" He hesitated for a moment and looked out towards the front of the store. "Not long, I guess. Listen, I can't talk to you guys right now. I'm the only one here on sales on the weekend." The clerk was eighteen, had short spiky hair, two rings piercing his left nostril, and a thin flat boyish body.

"Get the number of his brother." The clerk hesitated. Billy moved to Yianni's desk and began rummaging through the papers, tossing pencils and ledgers onto the floor.

"It's in the top-right drawer," said the clerk.

The clerk left the office, and Billy lifted a leather-bound notebook from the drawer. He flipped through the pages to P, found a Peter Pappas and a Calgary phone number. He handed the book to Butch, who sat at the desk and dialled. He waited, then hung up. "Answering machine," he growled, snatching a piece of paper and jotting down the number.

Billy searched Yianni's piles of invoices and open shelves. He picked up a brass letter opener, and when he turned it around, he saw it was actually in the shape of a penis. A green ledger book sat open on the filing cabinet. Billy drew his eyes over the page. There were a few names, a few telephone numbers. One listing was for J. Moore. Beside the name was a word scrawled in pencil. "Butch, can you make this out?" Butch was holding the receiver in his hand again and dialling information for the city of Calgary. "See, J. Moore, here in the ledger book. Coincidence?"

"Maybe. Maybe it's a note to himself, buddy. I can't make out the pencil scrawl." Butch raised his hand. "You got a listing for a Peter Pappas? Yes, okay." Butch waited, and then he grabbed the pen, started to write, but stopped. "Thanks." He hung up. "Same number." Butch pushed himself up from the chair, hiked his pants, and walked to a door leading into a large back storeroom. Billy followed him, and they toured the area, the workbench with the tools, the boxes piled to the ceiling. "Seems legit," said Butch. By the door, a calendar hung on a tack. The picture above the month showed a naked young man staring provocatively at the camera. Butch stopped and looked at the calendar and sniffed.

"Must be a favourite," said Billy. The month under the picture was December of 1991.

Back in the office, Billy found the white pages and looked up Yianni Pappas's residence, Lakeside Estates. "Let's go for a drive, Butch. See if anyone is at home at number 15."

The superintendent of the five-storey building on Lakeside Estates was a short man who wore black-rimmed glasses.

"He pays on time. Leaves me a cheque first of the month. I don't reckon I've seen him more than twice in my life. He in trouble?"

"Routine check," mumbled Butch. "Mr. Pappas have a parking stall in the building?"

"Number six, first floor down."

The stairwell was dusty and brightly lit by sconces of wire mesh surrounding hundred-watt bulbs. In the parking garage, Butch's and Billy's footsteps echoed off the concrete walls and the low grime-covered concrete ceiling. Number six was empty.

"If you were Pappas," Butch said, "and were angry with Justin Moore and wanted to hurt him, would you go to the immense trouble of snuffing him out and then taking him all the way to Satan House to hang him in the basement and paint his dick? I can't see it."

"You're not a psychopath. Passion leads men down strange paths, believe me. Sounds like the work of a vicious person. Could be a statement of some kind. It's possible Yianni has nothing to do with this, but there's got to be a link."

In the steady green light of the autopsy suite, Hawkes appeared ghostly in his white coat. His hands were encased in beige rubber; the tape recorder's mic lead looped down from his right lapel. The body of Justin Moore lay prone beneath his hands, its limbs purple-spotted, cold, and naked. Hawkes flipped open his forensic report, adjusted the eight-by-ten photo stapled to the corner of the chart, then double-checked the tag tied to the right wrist of the cadaver. "Moore, Justin. Male, nineteen, Caucasian, one hundred and fifty-eight pounds, seventy-two kilos, no cuts or weapon wounds on body, post-mortem lividity, post-mortem, et cetera, et cetera." Hawkes signed his name at the top of the sheet and placed the report on the front end of the metal gurney close to the bowl where his cutting instruments were arranged. Dodd and Billy were in aprons and masks and rubber gloves. Dodd was sweating and looking pallid.

"Time of death was around one in the morning," Hawkes announced. "We've run blood tests, and I've checked for molestation. No drugs or sexual molestation, no other foreign body fluids, and no anal bruising. The hematoma and cut on the lower lip are pre-mortem, the result of a blow by a soft instrument. Most likely a fist."

Hawkes cleared his throat. He was wearing a butter yellow bow tie. His brogues were brightly polished, and his white hair had been oiled and combed into a close precise shape that hugged the top of his balding head. "Gentlemen, I have perused the crime scene photos. And I've listened to your description, particularly the bit about the loose noose. Your medic was on the ball. This chap did not die that way. His wrists were tied up like the last cadaver's, the Riegert boy's, at that odd angle. Post-mortem I'd venture to say." Turning back to the body, Hawkes lifted Justin's neck and bent his head at a slight right angle. He slid the upper lip open; the clenched teeth were faintly stained a maroon colour. "Blood was found in the mouth, and the tongue had been bitten and was protruding just here, see, between these upper molars. Lips were slightly swollen from the asphyxiation. But there is no external bruising or marks on the epidermis."

Dodd drew back. He was beginning to rub his forehead with the back of his hand. His face had grown paler.

"You need some air, Dodd?" Billy asked.

"No, sir. I think I can stick it out."

Through all his years on homicide, Billy rarely had gone through a post-mortem examination without at least one of his officers becoming squeamish and jelly-kneed. He recalled that even Harry Stone, his ex-partner, had once fainted during the autopsy of a raped child. It's the odour, thought Billy. One needs the mask not just for pathogens and occasional splatter but also for the dank stink of death. Billy reminded himself how he'd trained his own sensitive nose: stand with the stench for a minute or more and your nose goes numb. You can't smell death or decay anymore.

For the next eight minutes, Hawkes took up his cutting instruments. Beginning with the muscle and skin around the neck, he began explaining the various layers of dermis and epidermis he'd be dissecting.

"Dodd, if you need a break," scolded Hawkes, "go out now before I start."

Dodd was holding his hand over his nose and mouth.

"Listen, for God's sake, take your hand down, man! Let yourself get used to it for a minute. It won't bite for long."

Billy watched Dodd blush above his paper mask. He lowered his hand and stood at attention, mindful of Hawkes's sharp voice. The coroner went on to explain the lack of a distinct ligature trace on the neck. He held up his scalpel as he talked.

"So, sir," attempted Dodd, "can we dismiss this as a suicide?" Dodd's voice was brave but hurried, nervous.

"Perhaps," answered Hawkes. The scalpel cut into the white of Justin Moore's neck. Pulling the blade towards himself, Hawkes cut a perfect line under the cricoid, the cartilage of the larynx, and then began section-cutting the creases of the epidermis.

Billy always found the autopsy intriguing, the layering of the skin, the measuring of body organs, and the precise analysis of symptoms of murder found in the smallest of punctures or the most blasted areas of bone and skin. Looking up, however, Billy saw Dodd turn ashen. Just as he was about to keel over, Billy moved. Catching Dodd under the left arm, he held the man as his eyes rolled back. Billy laid him gently on the floor and heard Hawkes march to the door of the morgue. "Bolling!" Billy loosened Dodd's collar and took his pulse. Hawkes came back to Billy's side. "He hurt himself?"

"He'll be fine," Billy answered.

Flicking open his eyes, Dodd panted. The sweat on his forehead started to bead. Bolling entered the morgue. He was carrying a glass of water. He knelt down, lifted Dodd's head, gave him a sip, and then helped him stand and walk into the hall, where he placed him on a chair, his head between his knees. "When he's steadier," Billy said to Bolling, "bring him back in. This is routine stuff, and he needs to get used to it."

"Yes, sir."

Hawkes waited while Billy pulled up his mask and moved to within two feet from the edge of the metal gurney. Then he pulled back the creases of muscle and epidermis to reveal the dermis, the underlayer of skin on the neck.

"You see? A soft ligature made of that binder twine could not have done this kind of damage. Here."

Billy leaned in for a closer look.

"These deep purple spots are hand marks. Middle-finger impressions. This boy was strangled manually. The force of the hand was on the thyroid. Here."

Billy drew his pointer finger along the trachea, his rubber-covered nail rubbing against blue, Jell-o-like flesh.

"Press down," said Hawkes. "The hyoid bone and cricoid cartilage are crushed."

Billy felt it was like running his finger over a mass of broken pebbles.

"Here, look." With one quick movement, the coroner slipped his arm under the shoulders of Justin Moore's corpse and flipped the body up onto its left side. "Come round." Hawkes had already peeled the epidermis on the back of the neck to show similar handprint bruising on the underlayers. "These are thumbprints." The blue-purple markings were oblong, wider, singular, side-by-side. "This kid was strangled by hand from behind."

Hawkes let the body down slowly. He yanked off his gloves, tossed them into a metal can by the gurney, and lifted his mask. Then, out of a nearby box of fresh gloves, he pulled on another pair, the faint puff of antiseptic powder floating above his hands.

"How's Dodd?" he asked.

"Dodd?" shouted Billy. He heard coughing from the hall.

The door to the morgue swung open, and Bolling stuck his head in and grinned: "He's tossed his cookies, sir. I'll need to fetch a pail."

"We're almost done, Inspector. You don't need a smoke break, by the way?"

"No. Gave up five years ago."

"I did, too, much to my regret." Hawkes's eyes twinkled, and he raised his thin eyebrows in a kind of lurid flourish. He then moved to the end of the gurney, examining the soles of Justin Moore's feet, raising his legs to peruse the inner thighs and scrotum. Walking back, he pulled a spool of waxed white rope from a drawer underneath the catch trough of the gurney. He began by tying the wrists, finishing with a tight double knot. "You know limbs can wander in various stages of rigor mortis." After tying up the ankles, he cut the rope and replaced the spool and the stainless steel scissors in the drawer.

There was a knocking on the door to the morgue. A dispatch sergeant leaned in. "Dr. Hawkes, it's your wife on the phone."

"Good Christ, man, I am in surgery! What does she bloody want?"

"She wanted me to tell you tea would be spoiled if you were not home within the hour."

"Thank you, Briggs. Tell her I am aware of the time. I will call her back shortly with the usual apology."

The door closed. Hawkes looked up at Billy, his face reddened, and he pulled down his mask with an impatient breath.

"Don't get me wrong. I promised Greta years ago that I would not perform. . . . Well, you can see the best-laid plans of coroners aft go astray."

It had taken forty-five minutes in total, a relatively brief analysis, but Billy felt satisfied that Hawkes had completed a first-rate autopsy. While Hawkes described in detail the conclusions he had drawn from his observations, Billy took out his notebook and followed along. He jotted down and paraphrased the coroner's words in a series of short, one-line notes. Later, he'd combine these with his notes and observations from the crime scene.

Dodd was upstairs lying on a couch in the officers' small lounge next to reception. He groaned and opened his eyes. "I'm sorry."

"It happens, Dodd."

"I can't take the stink, Billy."

"I have a couple of questions. Can you sit?"

Dodd pushed himself forward and rolled up.

"What about the background check on Pappas?"

Dodd stood. "Follow me, sir." They walked into reception and over to the desk where there was an envelope. "It's a printout."

"Tell me, what's on it?"

"We couldn't find any data on Pappas in our city file, as you know. But Johnson said she'd heard Pappas was into loan sharking. No proof, only rumours. Pappas keeps his store clean. So Johnson says let's go into the horsemen's files just for fun. At first we found nothing. Except that there was a notation from the last three days. Sometimes it happens when a new name is entered in the RCMP roster. We called it up and got lucky. That's what's in your package there. Last night, Friday, Pappas was in Calgary. He was arrested at 11:30 for assault. He attacked a man in the cocktail lounge of the Palliser Hotel. The man's family is pressing charges. Pappas has a brother in Calgary, but he wasn't able to come up with bail. Pappas nearly beat the man to a pulp, the report indicated. His prelim hearing is set for Monday."

"There's his alibi. Jail."

"Seems so, sir."

Billy and Dodd walked back to the lounge. Dodd was looking better. He went out, came back with two coffees, and sat down opposite Billy, who was reading over his autopsy notes. "Justin Moore was strangled from behind," said Billy. "By a pair of very strong hands."

"Murder, then."

"Murder."

"So why the black paint and binder twine?"

"The perpetrator may want us to think there is more. That the hanging is to show something else. But how does it connect to the other hangings? Or should we even be thinking there is a connection?"

Billy's head was aching, and his knee throbbed with mild swelling. The familiar sensation of impatience and frustration rose in his gut. Another wall. Another twist in the *koan*. He walked into reception, where the clerk had a message for him. "You're to call that number, sir." Billy picked up the phone and dialled. It was Dodie, Patsy Hanson's neighbour.

"Oh, Inspector, I'm so glad you called," she said. "Patsy's gone to hospital."

"What happened?"

"She tried to slash her wrists. About an hour ago. I took her there myself. I've had second thoughts since you left."

"Go on." Billy didn't try to play down his rising impatience.

"Patsy told me a few nights ago, she was drunk again, that she was so angry with Justin she wanted to kill him."

"What night?"

"Wednesday, I think."

"Did she ever say anything like that before?"

"No. I think she was really hung up on Justin and was in shock. Patsy takes all her affairs too seriously. I am sorry I've bothered you. I've made a worse mess of things."

"Is Patsy in the regional or in emergency?"

"Emergency. To be honest, she didn't do a bad job on herself this time. I've seen much worse, believe me."

What to make of this? Billy wondered as he hung up the phone. Time, it seemed, had accelerated. So many connections were being formed, and yet vital questions were not being answered. The patterns of reason, the shapes of the *koan*, were still murky and unreadable. He walked back towards the computer room. Sitting down by the door, he noted Patsy's whereabouts, then thought about Sheree at home alone. *Damn. And Mucklowe? Where the hell is he? How were Moore and Riegert connected?*

Billy found Bolling, Dodd, and Johnson out in the reception area a few moments later. The dispatch constable had paged Billy.

"Chief Bochansky wants to take you all to the El Rancho for steaks and for a review of the day," said the constable.

It was six o'clock by the time Billy climbed into the Pontiac and followed Butch's cruiser down Galt Avenue and then over to Magrath Drive, where the El Rancho Motor Hotel stood out from the rows of strip malls and burger joints lining the four-lane that cut across the eastern edge of the city. The hotel had been built in 1952 and was a paragon of Fifties Moderne. Its lobby was paved in red fieldstone; the front-entrance canopy was an inverted dish studded with small light-bulbs in imitation of a Las Vegas casino drive-through. The huge El Rancho sign boasted a neon cowboy, another nod to Vegas, the hat in white lights, the jeans and shirt outlined in blue and red blinking lines of illuminated glass.

Settling into the red leather plush of the half-moon booth, Butch ordered whiskies for the table and then without glancing at the menu told the maitre d', a man dressed in a powder blue tuxedo, that it would be sirloins all 'round.

"Cheers," Butch said, raising his glass when the whiskies appeared. They ate their medium-rare steaks in silence as an electric guitar twanged Garth Brooks tunes in the background. Over coffee, Billy called the meeting to order, starting with Dodd. Sergeant Dodd pulled out his notebook and began, first clearing his throat and taking a sip of water as if he were about to deliver an after-dinner address.

"Mud sample from basement steps. Taken at. . . ."

"Cut to the chase, Dodd. Where did it go?" ordered Billy.

Dodd looked slightly hurt at the sudden interruption. Billy noticed they were all weary from the day, from the week's work. Butch was particularly flushed, partly from the whiskey. But Billy needed to edge all of them towards a greater awareness of the panic he felt growing in his own mind. An uncertain fear that the killer might never be caught.

"I called the lab at the research farm, the one at Coaldale. Dr. Gore said he'd be able to place the sample in the Alberta area by Monday morning."

"Where do you think it's from?" prompted Billy. He was tapping his fingers.

"I figure up near Pincher Creek or Waterton. A lot of red shale canyons and scree formed from that kind of stone."

"Move on," signalled Billy.

Dodd grabbed another sip of water before continuing.

"Blayne Morton is in the regional detention centre for juveniles. Since last Tuesday, he's been under observation. Friday night, he remained in the centre even though his mother had come and asked if he could come out on a weekend pass."

"He slept there, I presume," Billy said, his eyes now heavy from the big meal and whiskey.

"Yes, sir."

"Mucklowe?"

"I phoned the apartment. . . ."

"For Christ's sake, Dodd!" Billy slammed his fist onto the table and rose. "Why the hell isn't Mucklowe here?"

"Hey, buddy," Butch cut in.

"The professor is a key player. He's a suspect, for Christ's sake. We're running out of time. This is not a bar brawl we're talking about. Where the hell is the APB I asked for? That's a priority. I needed him three hours ago, and instead I get a bunch of guys sitting around in a lounge having a fucking dinner party." Billy's fatigue caught in his throat, and he took a quick gulp of water.

The others sat stone still. Butch was about to speak when Billy started again. "We have to speed this up. Key evidence like Riegert's clothes is still missing. Mucklowe's off counting stones or fled the country, for all we know. Johnson, I want you to get onto the horsemen *now* and have them call locals in Waterton and the other RCMP units in the area. Have them drive over to Mucklowe's cabin and hold him for questioning if they have to."

Johnson leaped to her feet, grabbed her cell phone, and moved away from the table.

"The rest of you are on twenty-four-hour call. No time off. All phones to be active, and everyone ready to go at a second's notice. You can get a few hours sleep, but expect to be up early."

Butch stood. He looked white with exhaustion. "Okay, buddy. I'll stay up the first shift. Dodd, you and Bolling get home and get a few hours."

"Bolling, what have you got?" asked Billy, his voice still strained.

"A cabby named Myron Monk, works for Prairie Cab, says he was in the area of Ashmead and Baroness around midnight, maybe later. Saw a van parked out in front of the Moore house. He remembered it because it was pretty battered around the fenders, and he thought it looked out of place in the neighbourhood. Didn't get a plate. Said only that the colour was light, maybe white. The lights on Baroness are shaded, he says, by overhanging leaves. Says he has a hard enough time finding houses with the dim streetlights."

Johnson returned. "The horsemen got Dodd's earlier call. They couldn't locate Mucklowe at his cabin. They've put another man on it and are out looking, asking neighbours if anybody has seen him. The unit in Cardston has also been put on alert." Billy nodded. Johnson flipped open her notebook and continued without taking a breath. "We found dog urine in the basement and one distinct thumbprint on the doorknob of the back porch. Hair and prints, and a small blood sample, were on the razor blade found in the shaving kit. The sample matches the blood type of the Moore cadaver. As for the fragments we found by the steps, they are a rare white shell found only in the southern United States. Other fragments were mother-of-pearl."

Billy paused, thinking.

"Keep in contact. Bolling, go to headquarters and draw up warrants for Mucklowe and Sheree and anyone connected with the dig. Find out where David Home is, and keep on the line with the horsemen. We need to locate a man called Sam Heavy Hand. Mucklowe may know where he is. Call on Sharon Riegert first thing in the morning. She may know more than she's letting on. And don't, for Christ sake, let Sheree leave town. Butch, call Royce now and have him do surveillance on the Mucklowe apartment. Send a night constable to Satan House, too."

All rose from the booth, threw down a few extra dollars for a tip, and moved through the smoky bar to the side parking lot.

"Listen, buddy," said Butch. "You look bushed. Get some sleep. I've got a guard on Satan House. I'll go by the Mucklowe apartment myself and see what's up before I put Royce on duty. I'll see you tomorrow."

"You remember what Cara Simonds said about the masks she and Justin found?" Billy said. His mind was racing. "How did Randy get a hold of them? I read about a robbery of a set of gold and shell masks taken from the university in Montana. And I suspect the mother-of-pearl we discovered in the fragments in the garage is from those masks." Butch blinked and strained to listen. "Justin needed money," Billy continued. "There's our motive. Justin's clothes were stuffed in a garbage can, and we find broken bits of mother-of-pearl in amongst the folds. Randy and Justin have been on a dig. Just how much is Randy mixed up in this? And Sam Heavy Hand?"

Butch rubbed his sleepy face. "Jesus." He slapped Billy on the shoulder and walked to the cruiser.

Billy hopped into the Pontiac. The western sky looked like a swath of shiny mauve cloth stretched against a deeper scarlet. A warm light breeze had come up, and the trees along Cutbill gently swayed, creating dappled shadows on the deserted sidewalks. Crossing over the Oldman River, Billy felt the advanced hour. He really was too tired to do anything but head home. But then an odd sensation, a hunch, made him turn off the highway at the university. He drove along the road south and west until his headlights lit up the huge campus map, its green bulk attached to a concrete foot by the main entrance. Billy got out of the car. The map shone in the headlights' glare, and he had to shade it with his right hand to find the "YOU ARE HERE" arrow. He traced his finger along two curving roads to the building marked Science Complex. Then farther down to the drawing of a small round one-storey building that housed archaeology.

Billy drove on, following the yellow signs. He couldn't help noting the banks of lights on in the study library as he headed down a narrow darkened slope leading to the Department of Archaeology. Parked in front of the entrance was a light-coloured van, its fenders battered, its back door splattered with old mud and streaked with gravel dust. He checked the time. When does security lock up, he wondered? If it was at eleven o'clock, as he remembered from his own college days, he had plenty of time.

The corridor ahead remained dark and quiet. Billy moved quickly past the locked office doors. At the corner, by a water fountain, he found a list of the professors' names. ROOM 43: MUCKLOWE. For the next five minutes, Billy wandered. Mucklowe's office was locked, and through the small glass pane in the door, Billy made out a table and two bookshelves stuffed with texts and papers and what seemed like stacks of flattened cardboard shoeboxes.

Billy kept wandering. He moved through a set of heavy doors and down another hall that led towards a bank of windows. Along the hall, the doors read LAB 4, LAB 5. . . . Out of the gloom at the far end, nearest the window, a faint thin line of light emanated from under the last lab door. Billy stepped close to the wall. He walked stealthily, then stopped. What if it was a student working late? Studying for a project? Billy shoved his hands into his pockets. He walked to the door, found it open, and with his elbow jarred it slightly. The space he strolled into was a classroom with rows of desks arranged on an incline.

Facing the incline was a long counter topped in stainless steel, with two large sinks at either end. A blue light, the length of the counter, illuminated the steel with an eerie metallic glow. A man with short hair, a very sunburned neck, and thick legs in soiled khaki shorts bent forward studying seven gold objects that lay arranged in rows. The man did not look up. The objects, Billy realized, were small delicate masks. On the man's hands were yellow rubber gloves. One hand held a pair of tweezers. He was lifting a piece of white translucent material from a Manila envelope. When he finally raised his head, the man did not seem to notice Billy, and his eyes still showed his deep concentration. Then his mouth quivered. He laid down the tweezers. Rising, his back becoming straight, Randy Mucklowe nodded to Billy, blinking and arching his eyebrows.

"You surprised me, Inspector Yamamoto."

"Good evening, Randy."

"Come and see what I have here."

Billy stepped closer. Randy looked very tired. His eyes were bloodshot, and his upper arms were tanned but covered in dust and specks of dirt. There was a dark mark on his left cheek, dirt or a smudge of something Billy couldn't make out. Randy waved his gloved hand over the small gold and white masks glimmering in the steely brightness. "Treasures," he said, his voice sounding almost hoarse.

"You find these on your recent dig, Professor?"

"Ah, well, yes and no. These are special. The objects we recently retrieved at Chief Mountain are still in my cabin, to be logged and studied. These are from another site. I was given them, so to speak, as a gift, and I want them to be clean and ready. I have a museum here in the province that has shown interest." Randy spoke in a halting manner.

Billy wondered when the man had slept last. These masks were clearly those described in the bulletin Billy had read at Lorraine's store. The theft from the lab in Missoula would have been big news in the academic world. Billy would bide his time before asking Randy about the masks themselves. One mask was broken, its golden eyes attached to a jagged strip of cracked and splintered white material.

"What happened here?" Billy asked, moving even closer and pointing to the damaged mask.

"Sadly, I received the mask this way from one of my former assistants. He had been careless. It had been dropped or broken in transit. It won't be easy to repair it since so much is shattered."

"How small are the pieces?"

"Do you like archaeology, Inspector?" Mucklowe evaded his question.

"It searches for the truth in its way. I admire that."

"Nicely put. Yes, the truth is often hard to determine in cases such as these masks. For instance, we're not sure if they were brought up from Mexico via the Pueblo and then the Apache and Blackfoot. Trading was a common activity up and down the North American continent amongst nations and tribes. Obsidian for shells, corn for copper. These masks, I believe, are very early eighteenth century — from the eye design — and made, I conjecture, by a craftsman in New Mexico."

"What kind of glue do you use?"

"A special adhesive for mother-of-pearl. You see this section here, part shell, part mother-of-pearl?" Randy's hand shook as he pointed to the mask.

"Are you feeling all right, Randy?" Billy asked.

"The glue gets to me."

"When did you get back into town?"

"When? Oh, a couple of hours ago. No, an hour ago. Sheree is up at the cabin right now. She's very upset. I came back to get these masks ready for the museum. I should have dropped by the station. I know you wanted to see me. The last time I saw Justin, Friday night, he left with the Simonds girl, after the dig. I said they could go early, their stipends would be ready, for sure, on Monday. You needed me for something?"

"Yes, I needed to talk to you about Justin. By the way, is that your van parked outside the building?"

Randy paused for a second. He rolled his eyes up to the ceiling and then coughed. "Which one?"

"Light coloured, white, back fender dented, looks like a Chevrolet."

"Not really mine, no. I use it once in a while. For these digs. But it belongs to. . . ."

"Randy, what time did you leave Waterton last night to come here?"

"Pardon? You mean tonight, what time did I get here tonight? An hour ago or so."

"The van, or one very much like it, was spotted outside the Moore house late last night, around one in the morning. A cabby taking a fare home on Baroness."

"No. Imposs . . . really? But I was at the cabin on Friday. Working."

"Can Sam verify that for me?"

"Why not? Sure."

"You the only one who drives that van, right Randy?"

"Me? Yes. Mostly."

"Mostly? Does someone else use it?"

"Sam."

"I see. How is Sam?"

"Good!" Randy broke into a wide, strained grin.

"You two getting on okay?"

"Inspector, Sam and I go way back. Best of friends."

"Cara Simonds told me you two were fighting and doing a lot of drinking up at the dig."

"Cara Simonds said that?"

"She also told me Sam was violent. That he had blown up a few times at you. Had even threatened Justin."

"Well, yes, he did. Sam's no good when he's drunk. He took a big dislike to Justin. You don't think Sam's involved in this, do you?"

"How do you mean?"

"That liar. He said he was going out last night to drink. I was in bed early. Bushed. He may have, it was old Sam who. . . . You said you saw the van here in town last night? It must have been Sam. He was always sneaking off with my keys, playing Indian brother. He said, 'What's yours is mine.' Yes, it was Sam. He didn't like Justin at all, Inspector. Hated him. Now, you don't think Sam would've hurt Justin in any way, do you?"

"I don't know, Randy. I don't know anything for certain right now. We have some prints from the crime scene. That's one reason I want to ask you to stay in town. To not go far tomorrow. I know you have your trip planned, but I'll need to contact you in the morning to come down to the station to give a statement. You can tell me then about last week, the problems with Sam."

"Be glad to."

"Where is Sam now, Randy?"

"Now?"

"Where can I find Sam? For questioning."

Randy sighed, picked up the tweezers, grinned, and thought for a moment. His eyes were watering from fatigue. "I don't know. He ran out last night, as I told you. Took the van, and I haven't seen him since."

"How did you get the van back, then?"

"What? Oh, to come in. . . . He dropped it off. . . . No, wait, he came back very late. He was drunk as usual, slept it off, and left this morning for Montana. He's from Browning. You could call him or his sister Rita at the Friendship Centre there. They don't operate on Sundays, but maybe. . . ."

"Did he take the Greyhound or get a lift?"

"I don't know for sure, Inspector, he just up and left and told us all to go to shit. Fed up with us academic buggers, he said. I don't know why he was so angry; you see, he was paid well to be our guide, but he grabbed his bag and left. I was frankly glad of it. He'd been getting on my nerves for some time." Randy yawned.

Billy stood still and examined Randy's face, its unshaven chin, the look of exhaustion in the eyes. "Call me in the morning, Randy."

"Promise. I will."

Billy didn't leave immediately. Randy went back to pasting together the small pieces of mother-of-pearl. Backing out of the light, Billy turned and left the classroom. He found his way out by a side door. He walked to the light-coloured van. A Chevy. He knelt down by the front wheel. He grabbed a small chunk of the dried reddish soil that stuck to the inner rim of the wheel, placed it in one of his tissues, and then put it into his pocket. The back of the van was in darkness. The driver's seat was covered with papers. Around the other side, the passenger seat was empty. The side window on the sliding door was opaque with dried dust.

"All right," Billy whispered to himself.

He knew he must work fast. He unsnapped his cell phone from his belt and called Butch, told him he'd found Randy with a set of masks, one of them broken, made with mother-of-pearl. Told him there was little time for delay and that he and Johnson and two constables should come immediately to the archaeology department at the university. The masks were evidence enough to convict him for possession of contraband. They could also be linked to the materials found in the Moore garage and Justin's clothes. Billy asked Butch to have Lorraine fax the description of the masks she had on a brochure from the border guards at Chief Mountain. Dodd could double-check the data on the Internet. Billy was breathless as he spoke. "I'll wait in my car by the van. In the lot.

If Randy comes out and decides to bolt, I'll try to tail him. Get Dodd over to the Mucklowe apartment. Sheree needs to be brought in, too. If she isn't home, have Dodd alert the horsemen up at Waterton Lakes. She might be there. If so, we can arrange through Clive Erdmann to have Sheree brought into town ASAP."

"We're on our way," said Butch.

SUNDAY, JULY 7

"She was at the apartment, sir," Dodd explained. "Came without any trouble."

Billy knew Randy had been lying. Sheree Lynn Bird had not gone to his cabin. She was now waiting in an interview room, saying she was ready to talk. Early morning sun crept across the open floor of the quiet reception area as Butch and Billy headed towards her. Neither man had slept. Billy brushed his hand through his hair and was limping. Butch was carrying two cups of coffee; Billy had a cup of tea for Sheree.

Professor Randy Mucklowe had been arrested at 2:05 a.m. on one count of possession of contraband. He was also being detained for questioning in a murder investigation. His lawyer, Paul Barnet, had been called at 2:45 a.m. and was now in the process of preparing a plea for bail. For the time being, Randy Mucklowe was in custody at the Lethbridge city police headquarters.

Sheree Lynn Bird said she was willing to make a full confession, even without a lawyer present. When Billy entered the interview room, she was sitting alone at the table wearing a pair of jeans and a loose blue sweater. Her hands rested in her lap, and her hair was tied back. She was without makeup, and her face was white and creased with the anxious lines of broken sleep. Billy handed her the tea. He sat down.

"You look tired," she said. "I guess it's all over now, isn't it?"

"Is it, Sheree?" Billy asked, his voice weary.

Sheree remained silent for a moment. Billy gathered his thoughts. He was curious as to why Sheree had consented so quickly to a police cross-examination. And so he began by asking her why she had come.

Why had she not demanded a lawyer?

"I can't hold on to any more secrets" was her cool, laconic answer.

"Care to explain yourself?" asked Billy. Butch was sitting down, and the tape recorder was on. Billy had requested that a police matron be in attendance as a witness. She stood by the door to the interview room.

"Well, I guess I better start with the morning Randy and I got that phone call, from the teenaged girl, the one you said confessed to calling us, to warn us."

"Emily Bourne."

"I always feared Darren Riegert might try something drastic, like his friend Cody. Self-mutilation, suicide. But you have to know how desperately Randy and I wanted to build new lives together." Sheree stopped for a second and glanced over her shoulder, as if she'd heard someone enter the room.

"What is it?" asked Billy.

Sheree shivered. "I was always so afraid to say these things out loud. Randy would always forbid me to share my feelings." She regained her composure. "You see, he had suffered a bad divorce and was in debt. Well, it doesn't matter now. Sure, it seems crazy, but it made sense at the time. Last Saturday, after we got that phone call, we went to Satan House and found Darren's body in the basement." Sheree paused. "I couldn't look at him." She shut her eyes, then opened them. "*He* made me look. 'Go on,' he said. 'This stupid kid has ruined us.' Darren was hanging, his feet must have kicked over the boom box he climbed on. His chest and wrists were cut, and the knife was on the floor next to the stereo." Sheree pulled in a deep breath. Billy thought she was on the verge of tears, but she held her voice steady. A calm had come over her, an air of resignation. "Randy was so angry. He said he thought about covering up the whole matter, of taking the body and burying it somewhere and destroying the evidence. Worst of all, I didn't want to stop him. But then he had a brilliant idea. Randy always had brilliant ideas, Inspector."

"What was that?"

"To make the hanging look like a murder or a torture killing. Randy said he'd do it. Randy tied up Darren's hands. He put candles at his feet. Randy told me he wanted it to look like a Satanic ritual, so he painted a pentacle on the wall, and then he hid the knife in the garden. And the boom box. He said he got rid of Darren's clothes in a garbage dumpster down by the bridge."

"Surely finding a murdered body in the house was as serious as coming upon a second suicide?"

"Maybe. Randy made it seem so right at the time. He made me believe it, too. We were in a panic. We were planning to move away with the money from the sale of the masks. Randy imagined no one would blame us. He thought the police would forget us, start a search, instead, for a vicious killer. He believed that sending the police on a wild goose chase would buy us time. And freedom."

"How long have you known about the masks?"

"Randy and Sam stole the masks from the lab in Montana last October. Randy told me they were worth a fortune. Then *we* decided to take them, to cheat Sam Heavy Hand out of his share. We both agreed. Well, Randy forced me to agree with him. Then he set up the student dig and used it as a cover to smuggle the masks over the border. He picked July because of the tourists and because the crossing would be soft. Randy had arranged to sell the masks to Robert Lau, a trader in Vancouver. We were going to move to Mexico. Who would ever find us there? But then those poor boys died. Cody and Darren. I was afraid we would never be free again."

Sheree lifted her right hand and leaned forward. She spoke without hesitation and without remorse. She began once more, her words and her voice coming together in a clear, strong manner. Billy watched her eyes. They seemed distant yet focused. Butch was taking notes as well as listening.

"I loved Randy. I wanted to protect him. I know he was a bully some-times. That he kind of hypnotized me so that I'd lie for him. I lied to myself. You want a motive for what I did, Inspector? I didn't do it to hurt Darren, the poor boy. I did it for me. I was tired of being blamed for everything. For the boys' lives and the ugly violence of their parents. Tired of being spat at by people like Sharon Riegert."

Sheree stopped talking. She leaned back. Billy waited. He was trying to gather some questions and was hoping Butch would jump into the interview for a time. Instead, there was silence.

"What did Randy tell you about Justin Moore, Sheree?" Billy said finally.

"He told me he hurt Justin. Out of anger. He didn't mean to. He told me never to tell anyone what he did. I thought about what he said to me, and I knew, then, that I had to stop the lies. I had to. They were killing us all."

Billy looked again into Sheree's eyes. They were still, vacant, not really looking at anything in the room.

"Do you know where Sam Heavy Hand is, Sheree?"

"Yes. You'll find him in Cardston."

"In Cardston? Why there?"

"You'll find Sam in the hospital there," she said. Now Sheree broke into a timid smile. For a second, she held it, and then her face once again became blank. "He's not in any ward, though."

"Where is he, Sheree?" Billy asked.

"In the morgue, Inspector."

By 1:15, Sunday afternoon, Butch, Billy, and Dodd were in the police canteen eating sandwiches. Billy had taken three Tylenols for the headache he'd had since early morning.

"We meet with Randy and his lawyer in ten minutes," said Butch.

For most of the past hour, the three men had talked about Sheree's confession, about Randy's involvement in the Riegert case, his tampering with the body, and the fact that Sheree had implicated him in the death of Justin Moore. "Will you officially book her for withholding evidence, obstructing an investigation?" asked Dodd.

Butch answered. "Yes, once we establish Randy's role."

"I'm still not sitting comfortably," Billy said, rubbing his forehead.

"We don't have a lot of hard evidence for a conviction in the Moore case. We have only Sheree's word, and Sheree cannot always be relied on to tell the truth. That goes for the Darren Riegert story as well. What bothers me most is I'm not sure if our witness, the elderly neighbour, could identify Randy in a lineup. The broken mask is a clue, but it's circumstantial. All we know is that Justin was strangled by a pair of strong hands. Yianni Pappas has an alibi, and with Sam Heavy Hand lying in a morgue, we're down to Randy."

"Sam Heavy Hand was identified by his sister Rita, this morning, at nine." Dodd was reading out from his notebook. "He'd been found by the road to Waterton Lakes early Saturday morning. His truck had rolled into a ditch, and it was his dog, an old Lab, that had alerted a farmer with its barking. Heavy Hand's alcohol reading was over the top; he rolled a couple of times and suffered fatal head injuries."

Billy reached into his pants pocket and pulled out the soil sample he'd taken from the wheel of Randy's van. He unwrapped the tissue and held up the clump of dried reddish clay-like soil. "What do you think, Dodd? This look like the same soil that was on the steps leading into the Satan House basement?"

"Sure does."

A flash went through Billy's mind. *The koan reveals.* He stood up so quickly he bumped the table and spilled Butch's coffee. "You remember the Bible story of Cain and Abel, Dodd?"

Dodd blinked. "Yes, I guess so, sir."

"How the guilty Cain was marked by God for the murder of his brother?"

Butch snorted and ran a napkin over his spilled coffee. "The mark of Cain, buddy?"

"Butch, where is the van? Where did we park it when we brought Randy into the station this morning?"

"In the compound."

Billy ran through the canteen. He stopped suddenly at the door and turned to Butch, who was staring in amazement at his friend's abrupt movements. "You got the key?"

Butch rose and followed Billy to the hallway. He picked up the key and then ran with Billy to the compound, a fenced-in area beside the main building. Billy grabbed the key from Butch's hand. "I remember thinking it odd at the time," Billy said.

"What?" growled Butch.

"The papers on the driver's seat. They had splotches on them. In the dark, they looked like someone had spilled black coffee. But. . . ."

Billy unlocked the van door. The papers had been untouched and lay on the seat. They were spotted with black paint.

"Same colour as the paint on the genitals. And on the floor and wall of Satan House."

"You sure, buddy?"

Billy pulled out a tissue from his pocket and bent over and started to pat with his hand below the seat. "He must have painted the body, then come back to the van with *this*, hoping to hide it or destroy it later." Billy held up a small brush, thick with dried black paint. "But he didn't have time. He knew he had to get the masks and repair the one that somehow he or Justin broke. He had to work against the clock because he and Sheree were meeting Robert Lau in Vancouver. If Randy didn't get the mask repaired, he'd lose money. A lot of money. He meant to destroy this brush, but he forgot."

Butch rubbed his chin.

Billy rummaged again under the seat. "Well, well," he said and held up a small jackknife. "Do you think this may be the knife he used to cut Justin's clothes?"

"Sounds plausible, buddy. But you're running on a bunch of guesses here."

"When we go into the room, Butch, I want you to look hard at Randy's left cheek. Really hard. And remember the Bible story. There's a mark. A smudge. You nod to me if you think it's the same paint that's on these papers and this brush. It's that mark, I wager, that will place Randy at the scene of the crime. All we have to do is to get him to confess to being there."

287

There were two men in the room when Butch and Billy entered. Randy Mucklowe sat at the interview table. He was still wearing the hiking shorts and T-shirt he'd worn when Billy had surprised him in the university lab. Unshaven and pale, Mucklowe looked strained. His eyes shone with a preternatural intensity, partly brought on by fatigue. The other man, the lawyer Barnet, shook hands with a controlled smile. Butch read out the charges. Barnet listened with his hands crossed behind his back. After ruminating for a moment, he went to Mucklowe, bent over him, and explained briefly the procedure to follow. Billy kept his eyes trained on Mucklowe the whole time. Be careful, stay ahead of him, he thought. Barnet then walked over to Billy and whispered, "You haven't got enough for a conviction. You know that, don't you? All you've got is circumstantial evidence. Worth shit, as far as I'm concerned. And a worthless confession — her word against his."

In full voice, Barnet then said, "Shall we begin, gentlemen?"

Randy Mucklowe remained silent. Billy feared the man might not be able to answer anything in a rational manner. He pulled up a chair to Mucklowe's left, while Butch stood near the door. When Billy looked to Butch, he saw Butch's eyes blink twice, the signal they had agreed on before entering the room. The smudge on Mucklowe's cheek was still there, although also visible was a red quality to the skin around it, as if Randy had tried to rub away the smudge. *Is Barnet aware of what it is? Surely he must be.* The pounding in Billy's head was intense. Interviews of this kind were always difficult. How long could Mucklowe resist revealing the truth? And what *was* the truth Billy was after? Was this the man who had strangled Justin Moore? Who had placed his hands around the young man's neck and crushed the last breath out of his throat?

"Randy," Billy started, "I heard about your buddy, Sam Heavy Hand."

"Did you?" responded Randy, raising his face towards Billy's. His tone had taken on the arrogance Billy had heard when he met Randy for the first time.

"How did he die, Randy?"

"He lied to me." Randy sat back in his chair. "He and I were old friends."

"What did he lie about?"

"He stole my van. He lied to me."

"Randy, are you sure?"

Mucklowe now focused on Billy's face. He answered, his eyes brightening, "What're you after, Inspector?"

"Randy, you told me last night that Sam had taken your van, or so you thought, and then brought it back to you."

"Yes, yes, that's it. He did, the liar."

"Well, Randy. Sam died early Saturday morning, four or five hours before you got to the university. He was driving his own truck according to the police in Cardston. If Sam had his own truck, why would he borrow your van?"

Randy cleared his throat. "I don't follow you, Inspector."

Barnet spoke up. "I think we can shut this down right now. You cannot prove what Randy did or did not know since he was not anywhere near the scene of this so-called accident. Mr. Heavy Hand was a heavy drinker. Seems he ran off the road in a stupor. My client had no connection to this or any prior knowledge of Heavy Hand's whereabouts." Barnet signalled to Randy to stand up, but Billy motioned to the lawyer.

"I'm not done, yet, Barnet. We agreed I could question your client on at least two matters. I'm not quite finished with this first one." Billy crossed his legs and tilted his head. "This matter must be settled, Randy. From what the local police told us, Sam took a hard fall, into the ditch, and died of a massive concussion. His truck was in the ditch on the very road you were travelling on when you were returning to Waterton after killing Justin Moore."

"That's it," cried Barnet.

Billy shouted over the lawyer's protest. "And the investigating constable who was called to the scene early Saturday said you stopped by the ditch, saw the truck, and spoke with him. You were checking it out, weren't you? You must have known Sam was dead."

"Randy," cried Barnet.

Randy flashed the lawyer a hard glance. "I can answer for myself, Barnet. Shut up. Inspector, I don't know what you're talking about."

"Did you leave your cabin on Friday, late, and come into Lethbridge? Was it around midnight that you parked your van on Baroness Street outside Justin Moore's house? You knew where he lived. Your girlfriend lived next door. You were there for a reason."

"Don't be ridiculous. Mr. Barnet, *now* this interview is over. I'm not saying another thing."

"There's more, Randy. Listen. We found a witness."

"What?" Barnet demanded.

It was risky, Billy knew, and this next move could blow up in his face, yet Billy realized it was time to gamble. He avoided Butch's eyes as he continued. "The witness claims she saw you and Justin Moore crossing the backyard of Satan House very early Saturday morning. You were both wearing shorts. Justin was leaning on your shoulder, or rather you were making it look like that. You were dragging him."

Randy's eyes grew large. "Where was she? She's lying! That's not true," he said, his voice shaking. "That's a bloody lie!"

Billy pulled his chair closer. He placed his hands on the table where Randy could see them. He held them together. "I'm sorry, Randy, but I don't think that's right. I think you know that, too. You've been doing a lot of lying. Let's start with Darren Riegert. You lied about finding him. Sheree told me you made up a story, and a pretty good one at that! You had me and Butch running around after a cult killer, or was it a group of sadists? Anyway, someone who tied up Darren and lit candles underneath his body."

"Come, come, Inspector. Sheree didn't tell you any such thing. She's not even in town, as I told you. She's at my cabin relaxing."

"You never liked Darren, did you, Randy?"

Randy sat forward.

"He was a nuisance. But, Inspector, most civilized people put up with nuisances, as I am doing this minute. Just because I don't like someone doesn't mean I'd kill."

"You really thought you'd get away with it, didn't you?"

"Sheree likes to tell stories. She likes the attention."

"She'd do anything for you, wouldn't she?"

Randy smirked.

"You're going in circles," Barnet said.

"You tied up Darren Riegert, just as Sheree said, to create a lie. You wanted to destroy his body, but that would've been too much of a bother. A nuisance. Much easier to try to fool the stupid cops. The shiftless provincials you think we are."

"Oh, my," Randy snarled. "It hurts when you're outsmarted, doesn't it, Inspector? Really, Barnet, I think this has gone far enough."

Barnet was about to speak when Billy deliberately leaned in closer to Randy's face.

"Then there's your lie about Sam. When I met you in the lab on Saturday night, Sam was already dead. He'd been found by the highway almost eleven hours before. So your story about him going back to Montana was not true. And you lied about the golden masks. No one gave them to you. You and Sam stole them last October. You planned to steal them away from Sam, you and Sheree, so that the two of you could go to Mexico and start a new life." Billy paused. Randy's breathing became louder. Billy counted to five and then sat back and spoke with a fast, aggressive delivery, keeping his eyes centred on Randy's face. "We've got a dead body in the morgue. Justin Moore. Your student. A young man who once trusted and admired you."

Randy appeared to fold over into himself. Butch stepped forward. He was about to say something but then stopped. They both sensed Randy was cornered.

"You can help yourself, Randy, if you want to," Billy said, leaning in close again and lowering his voice.

"How do you figure, Inspector?" Randy was shaking, his face ashen, his hands clasped together as if he were suddenly in a tight space. As if his wrists had already been clamped into cuffs.

"The truth. Tell me and Butch what really happened."

"You live in a dreamworld, Inspector. You have no proof. Especially on Darren. And, yes, I was with Justin on Friday. We were drinking. We were friends, and we'd come to town after the dig to celebrate. And your claim that I saw Sam dead. That is sheer nonsense."

Billy pulled out the brush filled with dried black paint. He laid it on the table in front of Randy.

Barnet rushed forward. "What's that?"

Randy pulled back. Without thinking, he raised his hand to his left cheek and touched the black smudge.

"This is the paintbrush used to paint the genitals of Justin Moore, Mr. Barnet," explained Billy. "I found it under the driver's seat in Randy's van not twenty minutes ago. It is the same brush that Randy accidentally smudged his face with. The same black paint."

"You are a filthy liar!" shouted Randy. "A filthy yellow liar."

Butch stepped up to the edge of the table. He lifted up the brush. "Barnet, this brush will stand as evidence in court, as will the broken mask Randy had in his possession. You can see there is a mark on Randy's cheek. We can have the lab run a test on the paint on the floor of Satan House. We can determine the colour, the dyes, the age of the paint. It won't be so hard to prove a match."

An hour later, Butch and Billy went over the confession they subsequently heard from the mouth of Randy Mucklowe. Butch read his version first from his quick notes, sitting at his desk across from Billy, who listened while rubbing his temples. Billy then corroborated. By 3:35, Randy Mucklowe was climbing, cuffed, into the back seat of a Lethbridge city police force cruiser. Formal charges would be laid the next morning.

With the evening coming on, Billy gave in to his exhaustion. He craved food and sleep. It was always like this. A confession, a wrap-up, coming-to-the-end brought a mood of letdown mixed with mild elation. To be sure, all was in place. Billy printed out Randy's confession, bought a coffee, and read through the words one last time, content to see the riddle finally unravelled.

"Late Friday night, Sam and I discovered one of the masks was missing. We'd both been drinking hard. The students had left after supper. I was in the kitchen when Sam came in yelling, 'Where the fuck is it?'

'What're you talking about?' I asked him as his fist swung out at my chin. 'Where the fuck you hide it?' he screamed. Sam yanked me into the living room. The black garbage bags were on the coffee table. Only six masks were there. I was woozy with rye, and the facts didn't hit me right away. I dove under the sofa, pulled back the chair beside it. Then I ran into Justin's room and looked under his bed, by that time fearing he'd stolen one of the golden faces. 'Sam! It's one of the students. Justin Moore must've taken it.' Sam stumbled into the bedroom. 'I'll kill him!' Sam yelled, throwing his beer bottle against the wall.

I ran after him. I tried to convince him to follow Justin into town. 'Fuck you,' laughed Sam. 'You go! I'm stayin'. I ain't lettin' those gold buggers outta my sight!' I yanked at Sam's sleeve. 'Come on, I've got his address in my van.' Finally, I persuaded him. I said to him we should go separately. Sam would go in his truck, me in my Chevy van. Cara was taking the boys home. We could head them off. Me at Justin's house. Sam, at Cara's. We were drunk. The plan sounded good. We wrapped up the masks. It took me another bit of convincing to make Sam leave them in the cabin. We'd both meet back there after, I argued. We could lock up the place. We both had keys. That way we'd know where the masks were.

After a few minutes of argument, he agreed. I left Waterton in my van. Sam drove right behind me in his truck, but he was so drunk he could hardly steer, and I lost him on the highway, and I didn't bother to wait since I couldn't stop thinking about the mask and where to find Justin.

I got to Justin's house near midnight and parked by the curb, across from the front door. I figured Cara would bring Justin home. I was hoping that. I didn't want Sam to find them first. When Justin came up the street a while later, walking, his backpack on, he was alone. I got out of the van and went up to him. I was not thinking straight. Justin could see I was mad and drunk. His eyes were full of fear. 'I just want to talk,' I told him.

'I want to get my mask. I'll pay you for it, Justin,' I bargained. 'I can help you pay your debt,' I told him. That should have been it, but he backed off. He started to run towards the porch. I couldn't let him escape. He ran up the steps. I thought he'd get away from me, but then this stupid dog came running out of the flap in the door. That yappy terrier.

I grabbed Justin. Tore his cell phone from him. Got hold of his back-pack and swung him around. We both heard the noise. The crunching sound. 'Oh, shit, I'm sorry, Randy,' he said. I tore off the backpack, opened it, the bits and pieces of that lovely golden mask falling onto the grass. The rye rose in my throat. Justin tried to run. The pack was on the ground, by the steps. We struggled, stepping on that goddamned bark-ing dog. I was afraid we'd wake the whole bloody street. Justin bolted. I caught him by the collar. He turned, and I hit him on his mouth. I could hardly see straight. Then he ran into the garage behind his house. A light was on. He was falling over bags and clay pots. He reached for a garden hoe, and I knew I had to stop him. My hands were quivering. I clasped his neck from behind. I didn't mean to hurt him! I wanted to slow him down, to talk to him. I held on hard. He kept trying to pull away, swing-ing the hoe, his voice hoarse and coughing. And then he fell to the floor, the hoe clanging down beside him, scraping the edge of the car.

Right then I knew I'd killed him. The dog ran into the garage and began barking again. I escaped and shut the garage door, trapping the dog and the body. By the steps, I spotted the backpack and the broken mask, and it was as if the golden eyes spoke to me, as if they were the only things that mattered in the world. I searched in the grass, picking up the larger pieces of the broken mother-of-pearl. 'You're all right,' I whispered, as if the golden eyes could hear me. I took the backpack into the garage. The damned dog was lying by the body, whimpering. I went to the dim light, opened the pack, pulled out all the broken pieces, and placed them on the bench. I then threw Justin's things into the garbage pail by the bench. I sat the pieces of the broken mask inside the pack and left the garage, closing the door. The dog was moaning inside.

I ran to the van and climbed in. No one would find the pack here, I thought, under the seat. But where was Sam? There was no time. I was running scared. I knew Sam would tell. I knew if he arrived and found the body in the garage, Sam would figure it was my fault, and he would betray me to get all the masks. I leapt from the van and ran back to the garage.

The dog ran out, wagging its tail. Lifting the still-warm body, I looped Justin's heavy arm over my shoulder and began dragging him from the garage. I'll take him to the river. I thought I'd drown him in. . . . But no, he would be found. The body would surface by the new dam. No, I'll pretend he's been murdered by the same sadist who. . . . That's it, I thought! I was running crazy now. Make Justin's death look like the death of Darren Riegert. Make it look like a sadist cult murder. Maybe, when they find him, I can tell the police it was Sam who did it. So I dragged Justin through the gate. Carried him on my shoulder down the basement steps. I went into the room where there was binder twine and the pipe. I wanted to tie back the hands, the same way I did with Darren Riegert's body. It was such a coincidence, you see. A perfect setup. No one would suspect me or Sheree. They'll think it's a murder, I kept saying, reassuring myself. I lifted the body and tied it to the pipe. But then the body slipped. It fell onto the hard concrete. The temple cracked against the floor. I picked it up again; I tied it with a double knot. I ran into the other room.

There I found a brush, a can of black paint. I dashed back to the body. I took my jackknife and cut the T-shirt away. Threw it on the floor. Pulled the rest of the torn pieces and shoved them into my pockets. Must look like a killing, must make the police run in circles. I painted the chest and the penis black, painted the floor with a pentacle. It was like I was in a dream. I put the paint can away and took the brush and the knife and ran up the stairs and out to the van.

It struck me then that Sam must have had an accident. Or, worse, that he might be back at the cabin. He might have taken the masks for himself, back to Montana. Frantic, I knew I must drive in the night straight to the cabin so Sam wouldn't steal my fortune. It took me an hour. Down Number 5, through Cardston. By the time I hit the foothills, I figured Sam had cheated me for good. But at the turn to Mountain View, I saw the red lights flashing, I heard Crow yelping. Sam's old truck was turned upside down in the deep ditch. . . ."

MONDAY, JULY 8

The minute Billy walked into reception on Monday morning, at nine o'clock sharp, he sensed the day would bring him no surprises. A cool grey lid of sky lay low over the plain. The Rockies no longer fringed the horizon, lost under a thick fuzz of rain-heavy cloud. Butch sat in his office. This morning he was dressed in a blue shirt with a red tie. "Well, buddy," he began. "A few choice items for you to take a gander at."

Butch handed Billy a green china mug full of steaming coffee. "First, you now have your own official mug. Green for Yamamoto. You keep it in here next to my own personal collection of mugs." Billy took a sip. The coffee was black and tasty and fragrant. "Come with me," Butch said. He led Billy down the hall, through a set of swinging glass doors, and into the records room crowded with filing cabinets. "Professor Mucklowe's deposition is here, in this file folder, in case you want to check facts."

Billy handed the file back to Butch. "I've checked it already, last night."

"Patsy Hanson called today. She is back home. She wanted to know when Justin's funeral was going to take place. I understand Mrs. Moore is with a sister and that the family wants to keep the affair strictly private."

"Understandable."

Butch grinned. The walk back to the office took five minutes because Butch stopped at reception to talk to the dispatch sergeant. Billy spent the time thinking about Randy's van and the items he had located under the seat. Randy had panicked. Yet his confession fell together into a whole. Finding the paintbrush and the knife had been the clincher. But

297

then, moving back in time, Billy wondered how the painted body of Justin Moore related to the wounds — the cut wrists and pentacle on the chest — on Darren Riegert. Billy knew Justin Moore's body was desecrated in Randy's alcoholic stupor, yet Darren Riegert's mutilation was still bothersome. Butch cut into his train of thought. "Billy, catch you thinking there? Come on, we've got some paper pushing to do."

It had been months since Billy Yamamoto had sat down at the computer and gone through the endless forms and depositions and report formats required by a city force to close a homicide case. Now the sense of closure and satisfaction this complicated process engendered rushed backed. He was glad of it. No reason to doubt his faculties and his thoroughness. Billy and Butch sat down in Butch's office with the door closed. The site photos from both the Riegert and the Moore cases were spread out on the table by the computer. All the dispatch time logs and sergeants' reports and their own personal handwritten notebooks were opened and sequentially checked and reread for consistency and pattern. Two hours were then spent reviewing the confession and statement tapes of the witnesses and suspects. Billy watched both Sheree Lynn's and Randy's tapes for key statements, hints of anything that might reveal a hidden truth the investigation team might have missed. It was not unheard of. Facts stared you in the face, and you didn't see them. But all was in order. Three mugs of fresh brew later, Billy and Butch had completed the forms and written up their joint report. Billy leaned back in his chair as Butch logged off.

"We'll never really know about Darren, will we, buddy?"

"How do you mean?"

"I mean, was there someone with him when the wrists were scored and the pentacle cut into his chest? Hawkes claimed the cuts were premortem, so Darren was bleeding and in pain before he was hanged. I don't know. From what we learned about him, he didn't impress me as the type to self-mutilate. Not like your rocker-and-roller with his cigarette scars."

"Who knows? Look at the kid's home life, Butch. The mother's abusive boyfriend. What level of pain did that kid put up with all his fourteen years? Maybe the cutting was part of his own personal ritual. Look at the photos again of Cody Schow. The noose tie is almost identical. And we know Cody was suicide. I mean, it was deemed that for lack of any contradictory proof."

The two men rose, stretched, opened the door of the office. Butch notified the dispatch sergeant that he and Billy were out for lunch for an indefinite period. Walking into the grey air of the day, the men shrugged their shoulders and shivered. Two days of stifling heat turning to spring-like weather was not untypical for July. A moment later, they were in Butch's cruiser, heading down Dawson and turning onto Bond, where Mac's coffeehouse stood on the corner, its red sign over the front door swinging lightly in the cool breeze.

Butch drew into a space beside the back entrance. "You want to stay on stipend for a time?" he asked, pressing the button so that all the windows rolled up.

"I'm on call. That's part of the deal, isn't it?"

Butch grinned. "You're the one in charge, Inspector. Let's get a couple of Colombians and a cinnamon roll, buddy."

Butch and Billy climbed out of the cruiser.

Funny, Billy thought, how things come full circle. And then he walked beside his old friend into the cool, coffee-laden air of Mac's.